MW00639852

THIS NEW COUNTRY

A Western Double

HARLAN HAGUE

WOLFPACK
PUBLISHING
— EST 2013 —

WOLFPACK
PUBLISHING
— EST 2013 —

This New Country: A Western Double

Paperback Edition
Copyright © 2021 (As Revised) Harlan Hague

Wolfpack Publishing
6032 Wheat Penny Avenue
Las Vegas, NV 89122

Paperback ISBN: 978-1-64734-266-1
Ebook ISBN:978-1-64734-254-8

THIS NEW COUNTRY

A Western Double

A PLACE FOR MEI LIN

There is no history, only fictions of varying degrees of plausibility.
—Voltaire

1 WHO DO YOU THINK YOU ARE?

The Rat Trap was the West. It was a place to drink and laugh and tell lies, a place to take your pleasure or drown your sorrows in alcohol or in bed. A substitute for a wife or a refuge from a wife. Or a place to take refuge for a brief moment from the painful memories of a blessed past.

It was distressingly similar to saloons all over the West. Walk in through the front door, and there are half a dozen round tables on the left where at any time of day a few regulars and fewer drifters stare at their cards, trying to read their fortunes. On the right, the long bar that supported two or three patrons, a piano in the center of the room that looked more like a stack of kindling than a musical instrument.

The dark stair at the back, which creaked at each step, led to the four bedrooms upstairs where the sporting women lived and worked.

The rooms upstairs were distressingly similar. An iron-framed bed with a sagging spring mattress, linens as clean as their occupant, a small chest of two drawers, a narrow wardrobe accommodating a dozen hangers that held all the occupant owned. A small round table and single, straight-back chair set before the single window, thin curtains wafting lazily in the whisper of a breeze.

When not occupied at their trade, the women could stand at the balcony rail and look below, each woman wondering who would be her next job, wondering whether, this time, she should kill him or herself, knowing that she would quietly perform her assigned task and dream.

Caleb leaned on the bar, staring into his glass. He swirled the amber liquid and raised the glass slowly to his lips, took a sip, and set it down gently on the countertop, making no sound on the polished surface.

He looked around at a room that was at the same time foreign and familiar. He had never seen more than six or eight men at the tables, drinking and playing cards, never heard the piano played. He rarely strayed from the long bar that was his post and his support.

Caleb Willis was not one that would stand out in a crowd. His handsome face was weathered and lightly creased with lines more common in men older than his thirty-six years. His clothes hung loosely on his trim body, as if they had been bought when he was heavier. They were clean, but faded and a bit frayed at the extremities. His face was shaved, and his light brown hair, halfway to his shoulders, was clean and not very carefully combed. At one time, a lifetime ago, he had cared about his appearance, but that was when he was around people he cared about.

Caleb raised his glass, swirled the liquid and sipped, lowered the glass to the countertop. He glanced down the bar toward the bartender who sat on a tall stool within hailing distance. The bartender wore a soiled light gray shirt, buttoned at the top, always the same shirt unless he had a dozen soiled gray shirts, and a long apron that once was white. He was always there, staring at the opposite wall, looking at nothing. Or deep into his past, for Caleb had not missed the tear that had rolled down his cheek more than once.

Behind the bartender, bottles were arrayed in front of a large mirror that was so clouded at one end that patrons often stood there, laughing at the ethereal image of themselves that showed in the damaged surface. Beside the mirror, there was a print of a naked reclining woman, a hand over her most private part, smiling and fat as a cherub.

Down the bar beyond the bartender, two men stood, each with a boot on the rail, sipping their whiskeys, talking softly, occasionally throwing back their heads and laughing loudly. Caleb recognized them. They had nodded to him when he came into the saloon, but he had not responded.

He did not intend to be rude. He had never been considered rude, at least not in his other life. He just did not see any point in befriending people. Not now. He spoke to people when speaking was necessary, and he said only what was necessary. He had not engaged in what might be described as a conversation for at least a year.

A shuffling and muffled voices at the other end of the long bar drew his attention. He turned his head without otherwise changing his position, his eyes adjusting gradually to the dark corner.

Two cowboys were groping an Asian woman. She was young, small, hardly coming to the shoulder of her tormentor. A pretty face, her braided black hair tied up in a swirl on top of her head. She wore a simple cotton dress, a subdued yellow color, longish for saloon wear at mid-shin.

She was pushed against the bar and leaned backward from the weight of the cowboy pressing against her. He rubbed her lower belly with one hand. The other hand was at her throat. His grinning partner squeezed a breast through her dress.

Caleb looked back at his glass, swirled the liquid, raised the glass, and sipped. He recalled the saloons he had known during his wanderings. Most employed women in some capacity. Some tended bar beside the male bartender. Others sang and danced with patrons, all male, men who were starved for female company. They respected these women and treated them kindly. Saloon owners demanded it.

Then there were the soiled doves, the ladies of the line, the sporting women. They might also mix with the patrons in the saloon, but their function was not to engage in song or polite conversation. Their function was to satisfy the patrons' physical needs in this male frontier. The brothels were upstairs or out back.

The women, whether servers, entertainers, or prostitutes, were often lured to the trade by offers of good pay, exciting work, and nice clothes. Others were widows or poor girls escaping from the drudgery and low pay of mills or farms. Whether they became entertainers or whores depended on their appearance, their employers' needs, and how desperate they were. Most of the women had not chosen their employment. Circumstances seemed to propel them to the life.

"Barkeep," Caleb called. He knew his name, Matt, but never used it. Caleb pointed at his glass. The bartender blinked, pulled abruptly from his reverie. He stood, picked up a bottle behind him, shuffled over, and refilled the glass.

Caleb pulled a coin from his pocket, laid it on the bar top, and pushed it to him. The bartender nodded and picked up the coin. With his other hand, he pulled a handful of coins and a card from his pocket and deposited the pile on the bar top. The barkeep picked a coin from the pile and slid it to Caleb, pulled the remaining coins across the bar top and into his hand cupped at the edge of the top. Dropping the coins into his pocket, he picked up the bottle and returned it to the rack, retreated to his post, sat on his stool, and stared at the wall.

Caleb took a sip from the glass. He picked up the card that the barkeep had left on the bar. It was a picture of a young man with his shirt collar turned up and a stylized letter "D" on the left side of his chest. At the bottom of the card, the words "COBB, DETROIT."

"What's this?" Caleb said to the barkeep.

The barkeep turned slowly toward Caleb and saw the card that he held. "Baseball card," he said. "Comes in cigarette packs. Jack down there drops 'em all over the place." The barkeep pointed toward the far end of the bar.

Caleb dropped the card on the bar and picked up his glass. The barkeep stepped over to Caleb, picked up the card, and tossed it into the trash bin behind the bar.

"Stop! You stop! No do that!" Caleb looked toward the end of the bar. It was the Asian woman. She was not enjoying the attention. She twisted her body and tried to push the cowboys' hands away. She swung at the man in front of her, but he brushed her arm aside. He and his partner laughed.

The saloon madam, also the owner of the Rat Trap due to the propitious death of her husband two years back, stood at the other end of the bar. She was short and chunky, late middle-aged. Her heavy makeup gave her the appearance of a large animated doll. She wore a red dress trimmed with white lace that ended at her knees, but appeared extended by multi-colored petticoats that peeked from under the hem of the skirt. The dress and petticoats were hung with little tassels, sequins, and lace. The low-cut bodice of the dress strained against the weight and bulk of her breasts. Net stockings ended in pointy, heeled shoes. She might have been pretty and stylish once.

She had been watching the commotion at the far end of the bar and had become increasingly agitated. She walked down toward the end of the bar, glancing at Caleb as she passed behind him, to stand behind the cowboys.

"Ease up, boys. You squeeze the fruit too much, you pay the damages."

The cowboy who held the Asian woman looked at the madam over his shoulder and grinned. "Aw, Polly, we're just squeezing a little before buying."

"Ease up, Jack, you got no special privileges with my girls."

Jack turned his attention back to the girl, ignoring the madam.

Polly frowned and walked around the cowboys to stand behind the bar. She bent and busied herself with something, or pretended to busy herself with something, looking occasionally toward the woman and her tormentors.

Caleb looked back at his glass, then glanced back at the trio. Jack tightened his grip on the girl's throat. She gagged and made a sucking sound, then a whimper like a tortured kitten.

Caleb swirled the whiskey, raised the glass, and emptied it. He set the glass on the bar deliberately, gently. Straightening, he flexed his back, stepped back, and walked slowly toward the end of the bar. He stopped behind the cowboy called Jack.

"Let her go," Caleb said softly, almost a whisper.

Jack turned slowly. An unlit cigarette dangled from his lips. The opened cigarette pack lay on the bar.

"What did you say? You talking to me?"

"I am," Caleb said softly. "Let her go."

The cowboy straightened and stepped toward Caleb. He still held the girl's throat.

"Now who the hell you think——"

Caleb punched him hard in the stomach. Jack lost his hold on the girl. He doubled over, gasping and eyes bulging. Caleb gripped his arms and helped him back up to a chair and eased him into it. Jack wheezed, rocked back and forth, trying to get his breath.

Caleb turned back toward the bar in time to see Jack's partner coiled for a swing at him. Caleb interrupted the swing with a hard right to the cowboy's head. He crumpled and collapsed, landing hard on the floor. Caleb looked down at him.

Caleb turned and looked at Jack who leaned forward in his chair, his mouth open and glaring at Caleb, his hand at his side. Caleb shook his head, a slow brief movement, a warning. The cowboy moved his hand away from the holster.

The bartender and patrons gaped. They had never seen Caleb in any position except leaning on the bar, never saw him do anything more physical than lift his glass. Five men at a table watched Caleb, their cards forgotten. A middle-aged woman standing behind the table, her hand on a patron's shoulder, looked on in shock.

Caleb looked at the Asian girl who had retreated to the end of the bar. He walked over to her. Her hands were on her cheeks, and tears flowed between her fingers.

She was a mess. Her braid had come loose, and her dress was wrinkled and torn at the neck. Two buttons at the top were undone. A bloodshot eye was encircled with a black ring, and a cheekbone bore an ugly purple bruise.

She rubbed her neck.

"You okay?"

"They kill me now." She wiped her eyes with the back of a hand.

Caleb looked for the two cowboys. They stood near the saloon door, glaring at Caleb and the girl.

She looked at them. "They kill me," hardly more than a whisper.

Caleb pondered a long moment, watching the two cowboys, staring at them without seeing them. He turned to look at the wall, distracted, then back at the girl.

"No, they won't." He took her arm and moved her toward the door. She stopped, pulled her arm from Caleb's grasp. Caleb turned back to her.

"I no understand," she said.

He grimaced, impatient. "Do you want to stay here, or do you want to go with me?"

She looked around the room, saw the two cowboys near the door, glaring at Caleb and her.

"I go with you." He took her arm again and walked toward the door.

Polly stepped from behind the end of the bar into their path.

"Where do you think you're going!" she said.

Caleb stopped, his hand still holding the girl's arm. On other visits to the Rat Trap, he had seen the woman and was repelled by her. Until now, he had avoided her. Undoubtedly, she had noticed his reticence, and they had never spoken.

"Well, ma'am. This little girl isn't safe here. So she's going somewhere she'll be safe."

"She ain't going nowhere. She works for me."

"She just stopped working for you. She can go as

she pleases."

"The hell she can. I own her."

Caleb glanced aside, as if he had not heard her, as if he would rather be someplace else. He looked back at the madam. "You don't own anybody. Slavery ended a while back."

"I got a hundred dollars wrapped up in that girl!"

Caleb looked blankly at the madam. He squeezed his eyes shut, looked down. Pondered. *What am I doing here? Am I really involved in this? Does this have anything to do with me?*

He opened his eyes and looked at the madam. He released his hold on the girl and pulled a roll of bills from his pocket. Counting out some bills, he offered them to the madam.

"Here's $50. You'll get the rest soon as I decide no harm's coming her way. We'll be back for her things. If anything's missing, I'll deduct the cost from the $50 coming to you."

The woman did not move. She ignored the proffered bills. "Just who the hell do you think you are, beating up on my customers and stealing my property?"

Caleb laid the bills on the bar. "We'll be back. Have her things ready. All of them."

The madam stood with hands on hips, her face reddening. "By god! You'll pay more than you counted on, mister!"

Caleb touched his hat to her. He took the girl's arm and guided her toward the outside door. Near the door, the two cowboys watched. They retreated a step at Caleb's approach. The girl looked at the men and pressed against Caleb. The cowboys watched them walk toward the door.

Caleb glanced at the middle-aged woman who had

backed away from the card table and now stood against the far wall. Her frilly dress, cut low in front, identified her as a prostitute, plain and drawn. Caleb had seen her on other visits to the saloon and had acknowledged her. She had always smiled at him, gratefully, it seemed. Now she looked at Caleb and the girl, and a hint of a smile played about her lips.

Caleb and the Asian girl walked through the doorway, and the door closed behind them. The madam glared at the door.

Caleb stepped off the plank sidewalk, still holding the girl's arm. They walked to his horse. He looked back at the saloon door. It was closed. He looked up and down the dusty street. Across the street and down a ways, two old men stood at the hitching rail in front of the general store. They talked with arms and hands, laughing and gesturing. One of them guffawed, bent over, and slapped a knee. There was no one else about.

Caleb turned to the girl. "Climb up behind the saddle," he said.

She looked at the horse, frowned, and looked up at him. "How I do?"

He grimaced. "You never rode a horse."

She shook her head.

Caleb frowned. "Here," he said. They stood on the left side of the horse. He clasped his hands and bent over. "Step in here with your foot, and swing up."

She lifted her right foot and started to step into his clasped hands. He batted the leg aside. "The other foot, the left foot."

She raised her left foot and stepped into the cradled hands. "Hang onto my shoulders, and swing your other leg over the horse." She swung her right leg and kicked the horse's hindquarter, causing him to shy sideways.

Caleb sighed. "God, how difficult can it be to get up on top of a horse," he mumbled. She finally settled behind the saddle. He untied the reins and mounted, with some difficulty since he was not accustomed to human baggage behind his saddle.

"Hold on," he said. She sat with arms dangling. He looked up, exasperated. He reached around, grabbed an arm and pulled it roughly around his waist.

"Hold on!" He almost shouted. She put her other arm around him. Caleb shook the reins, and they moved off at a lope.

2 MEI LIN

The horse's loping gait caused the girl to move gently against his back. Press and withdraw, press and withdraw, press and withdraw. The movement was strangely disturbing. He leaned forward, but she pressed against him still.

He had left the town fringes behind and now looked at the orange-tinted outline of the Sawtooth range ahead. Earlier than he usually left the saloon. The sun had just disappeared behind the crags, and the filmy cloud layers colored and glowed with its memory.

He frowned. *Now what? The old whore hit the nail on the head. Who do I think I am? I'm nobody. I was somebody once. Had a wife back in Virginia I loved more than life. Two sweet kids that I would die for. But the sickness took them. All of them.*

Nothing was left for me. I wanted to join them in death, but I couldn't even kill myself, though I tried twice. Second time, the doc said my body shut down, and he thought I was gone. When he brought me back, I asked him if I was dead, whether he was St. Peter in his white gown. He told me later that I said that I couldn't see his wings. He laughed when he said it, said I was joking in my delirium. When I told him that I wasn't joking, he sobered and shook his head, patted me on the shoulder.

God, how I wanted to be dead! I hadn't the courage to try again.

Sold my business, told my agent to give the money to poor people, but he was also a friend and would have nothing of it. Said I was not thinking clearly. Said that since I was not working, not looking for work, didn't seem be in a proper mind to do any meaningful work, I would need the money just to live on till I got my affairs and my head settled.

I drifted. In mind and body. Drifted westward, one seedy town after another. I learned to fight. Everybody wants to take advantage of drifters, think they're an easy hit. I got beat up a few times, but I soon could hold my own and didn't mind beating the other guy senseless and walk away with no regrets.

I bought sex a few times, when I was too drunk to know what was good for me. I always cried, and the whores didn't like that. One actually kicked me off the bed. Another held me and stroked my cheek and cried with me.

Did an odd job from time to time, for something to do. Worked long enough on a couple of ranches to decide that I preferred the company of cows and horses to cowmen and their uppity women. Met some cowboys I liked, good old boys you wouldn't mind spending a cold winter with in the bunkhouse. Others I wouldn't give a bent nickel for.

Drew some cash from my bank account occasionally when I could find a Western Union office, enough for cartridges and a meal. Became pretty good with a six-shooter. Had to use it occasionally on men who wouldn't let me go my own way.

I have killed. Two mean sons of bitches who thought they were bulletproof. I'm not happy about killing those men, but

I don't regret it. They needed killing. Yeah, I know how to use a gun, well enough that when I gather the courage to kill myself, I won't botch it again.

Heard about Idaho. Lonely place, mostly wilderness, small town called Stanley. My daddy's name. Decided maybe I should go there.

He felt the girl's arms tighten around his waist. Her head was on his back and slid gently side-to-side, and her body was on his back, press and withdraw, press and withdraw, with the gait of the horse. She slept.

I got myself into a pickle. What am I going to do with this girl? I can't keep her, and nobody's going to take in somebody that may be a magnet for trouble. Especially a whore and a Chink.

In the gloaming, the trail was barely visible. Here it was a faint parallel double track, a wagon road that was lightly traveled.

They rode over a rising and into his world. He rode slowly now, in no hurry, almost reluctantly, almost home.

Home.

A one-room log cabin, sturdy and tight, a shack nevertheless, but it was all he needed. So he told himself. The wagon was beside the cabin. The two sleek mules in the corral adjacent looked in his direction, like statues, shadows, ears erect. Days, when they were not working, the animals were loose on the meadow. He tried to remember to put them up when going away, but he sometimes forgot or couldn't be bothered.

Beyond the cabin and corral, down a gentle slope, the pond appeared as a dark mirror, reflecting the waning daylight and the rising moon. His claim encompassed four hundred eighty acres of pond, meadow, and woodlands, but he hadn't even seen some of it. Curiosity was not one of his attributes of late.

Caleb pulled up at the cabin. A wave of melancholy swept over him. It was always so, always when he returned home, when he remembered how his wife and his children had been there, at home, how they came out to welcome him, or upon entering, how they looked up and smiled, silently welcoming him.

He shook his head violently and felt the girl jerk upright behind him. She released her hold on his waist, pulling her arms back sharply as if she had touched a hot stove.

He dismounted and tied the reins to the short hitching rail. He wiped his hands on his shirt and reached up to help her down. She extended her arms to rest on his shoulders. He took her by the waist and lifted her from the horse. She felt as light as his saddle.

She fell against him as she touched the ground. Her arms were still on his shoulders, and he felt her breasts press against his chest. He experienced a sudden sensation, a fleeting memory. He withdrew from her and stepped back. She dropped her arms, rubbed her eyes with the back of a hand, and looked around.

He walked to the door and opened it, stepped up through the doorway into the cabin, disappearing into the dark interior.

The girl looked inside and saw nothing. She heard a match strike and saw the flame light the wick on a kerosene lamp. Caleb blew out the match and dropped it into a small bowl on the table.

He motioned for her to come in. She stepped in hesitantly, looked around. The glow from the lantern softly illuminated the interior. Caleb closed the door and dropped the latch.

"Hungry?" he said.

"No. I eat before."

She stood near the door, trying to be invisible. She saw the wooden bedstead against the wall on the left. The edges of two blankets were tucked neatly under the thin mattress. The only other furniture was a small square table with one chair in the center of the room. There was a dark window beyond the table and the shadow of something on the floor under the window.

Against the wall on the right-hand side of the window, there was a sheepherder stove that was both cook stove and space heater. On the facing wall to the right of the stove, there was a counter with shelves underneath and a cupboard. On the wall opposite the stove, a pantry with a door on hinges and an opening to the outside for ventilation and cooling. The outside opening was partially covered with slats to prevent varmints and birds from raiding the contents. All of these units were constructed of hand-hewn planks and nicely finished.

On the counter, one tin plate, a ceramic cup, one knife, and one fork lay in good order, as if ready for service.

"Are you sure?" he said.

"Yes. I like. I hungry."

He glanced back at her, pointed to the chair beside the table. She sat. He went to the pantry where he took out a dish of butter and a slab of ham. From the cupboard, he got a half loaf of bread and cut four thin slices. She watched him spread butter on the bread and cut slices of ham.

"Where you get meat?" she said.

"Farmer on the Stanley road. He keeps pigs." This without looking at her.

"Where you get bread?"

He tapped the stove with his knife.

"You make bread?" she said.

He turned and looked at her. "You're just full of questions, aren't you?"

"Sorry." She sank in her chair and watched him. She straightened. "I help?" she said. He shook his head without looking at her.

He set two thick ceramic plates of sandwiches on the table. She jumped up from the chair and stepped away.

"Sit down," he said. His tone invited no discussion, and she sat. He pulled a small keg from the wall under the window and sat on it.

They ate in silence. For Caleb, it was as it always was. It's time to eat, and so you eat. For the girl, it was a wonderful new experience. She had always had to eat what was left, whenever it was convenient for her owner or her customers, and wherever she could find a place where she could be invisible.

When they had finished, Caleb took the two empty plates to the counter. He returned to wipe the table carefully with a wet rag.

"I help?" she said.

"You sit." Walking to the cupboard, he rustled around, found a small tin container from a shelf under the counter. He wet a cloth in a pan of water at the cupboard and brought it and the tin container to the table.

He cleaned her face with the cloth, dabbing the bruises slowly and gently. She did not take her eyes off his, though he looked only at her lacerations. When he had finished cleaning the injured areas, he applied a salve from the tin.

"Try not to let this stuff get on the blanket," he said. "It makes a mess."

He walked to the far end of the cabin at the head of the bed, picked up two hides from the floor, a thick buffalo robe and a bearskin, both with the hair on, and arranged them on the floor at the wall opposite the bed. He carefully pulled a blanket off the bed and spread it on the hides.

"Hope you'll be able to sleep," he said.

She walked to the pallet and sat down, pushed gently on the blanket with an open hand, feeling the thickness of the robe, smoothing the blanket. "It best bed I have ever."

He looked at her a long moment, frowned and shook his head, walked to the table, and lowered the flame on the lamp. He sat on the chair and pulled off his boots, tossed them under the bed. Facing the window, away from Mei Lin, he removed his pants and shirt, and draped them on the foot of the bedstead. His gray long Johns were a bit frayed at the extremities. Lifting the glass on the lamp, he blew out the flame.

The room was plunged into darkness, but for the soft shaft of light cast by the weak moon through the windowpanes.

He walked to the bed and pulled the blanket down, sat on the bed and looked at the dark outline of the girl, dimly illuminated by the moonlight. She still sat on her bed of skins, watching him.

"Lie down," he said. "Sleep." He swung his legs onto his bed and pulled up the cover with a grunt, rustling and moving about, coming to rest.

She sat on her bed of skins, waiting, until she heard his heavy rhythmic breathing. She lay down slowly, pulled the blanket to her chin, and stared into the darkness.

Caleb stood at the counter, washing last night's dishes in a pan of water on the countertop. He looked over at the stove, checking the progress of the coffee. The water in the percolator had just begun to bubble. He stacked the clean dishes neatly on the countertop to dry.

Carrying the wash water to the open door, he threw it out in a circular spray. He banged the empty tin container on the outside wall, squinting in the bright morning sun.

Turning back inside the cabin, he walked toward the stove. He stopped abruptly when he saw the girl. She was snuggled down in her blanket, and only the top of her head was visible. He had forgotten all about her. *How could I forget her? First time there's ever been a woman here.*

She stirred, turned on her side, and the blanket was pulled from her face. Caleb studied the face. In spite of the bruises, it was a soft face. He had not noticed when he treated her injuries. Yesterday, she had the look of a frightened, injured animal. Now she appeared at peace. *She has a sweet face, a pretty little thing.*

He shook his head, shifted his feet. At the sound, a hand appeared at the blanket edge and pulled it down. She looked up at him, blinking, midway between sleep and waking. Then she saw him, and she remembered what had happened and where she was. She vaulted upright to a sitting position, tensed, hands
pushing on the blanket, poised to jump from the bed.

He stepped over quickly and put a hand on her shoulder, pushing gently. "No need to get up. You sleep some more. It's early." *I don't want to deal with you just yet. You stay right there.*

She eased back and lay down, still watching him, pulled the blanket to her chin. She didn't know how to respond, or whether to respond. She was too accustomed to fear what she did not understand or had not experienced.

Caleb walked to the stove counter. She watched his every step, his every move, wide-eyed, wondering, fearful. Caleb picked up the percolator and poured coffee into a cup. He pushed the percolator to the back of the stovetop. She watched, every fiber of her body tensed, ready to leap from the bed and run.

He walked to the pallet and looked down at her. She

cringed and held the blanket to her chin. He hesitated, as if looking at a foreign object that he couldn't identify.

"There's coffee, if you want it." He motioned with his head toward the stove, reached over her bed to the wall pegs to fetch a broad-brimmed hat. He put it on as he walked through the door, closing it behind him.

She exhaled, stared at the ceiling. She was suddenly filled with an anxious yearning, hoping that something good was going to happen to her. But did she dare hope? It had been so long.

A shaft of sunlight shone directly on Mei Lin's face. She woke, squinted, and pushed the blanket to her waist. Pushing up on her elbows, she looked around. She was alone. She sat up and leaned against the wall, touched the lacerations on her face and winced. But she felt good, better than she had felt in a long time, a very long time.

She looked at the window and squinted in the sunlight, closed her eyes, and breathed deeply.

She was not afraid. It was the first time she could remember not being afraid. Ever. In her entire life. And she didn't hurt. The lacerations were nothing. She felt good, whole.

She looked around. The walls of the cabin were made of stacked logs, carefully fitted. Thin poles were nailed in the gaps between the logs. A mixture of animal manure and mud further sealed the spaces between the logs.

There was only the single window of glass panes opposite the door. A chest and the small barrel that had served as Caleb's chair were pushed against the wall under the window. On the wall above her bed, Caleb's shirts, pants, hats, and a coat hung from half a dozen pegs.

She had long been accustomed to the chaos and clutter and terror that was her life at the Rat Trap. Here was peace and order.

3 THEY SOLD YOU FOR MONEY?

Caleb sat on the bank of the small pond. He looked at the strange craft that was tied to the shore with two thick ropes, the bow nudging the bank. A boat of sorts, a barge actually, that rested on pontoons for flotation.

The bare uprights of what appeared to be the beginnings of a cabin, about thirty feet fore and aft and fifteen feet wide, thrust upward. A small pile of lumber was loosely stacked on the shore near the vessel.

He looked beyond the pond down the gentle slope to the valley. The slope was covered in lush two-foot tall bluestem. The waving green blades were just beginning to show the reddish hue of late summer. Scattered about the slope were silver-colored sagebrush and shrubby cinque-foil covered with delicate yellow flowers.

Across the wide basin of grassland and meandering streams, the Sawtooth range thrust upward. Caleb stared at the jagged crags and vowed, as he had vowed many times, to climb them. This view had almost brought him to tears more than once. He would climb the Sawtooths someday and see whether the experience would have more meaning for him than mere exertion.

He looked back at the dredge. The hull was in relatively

good condition. He had bought it from a couple of partners who had tried to make a go of dredging for gold on Stanley Creek a few years ago in the late nineties, but they had lacked knowledge, imagination, ambition, and capital, a sure collective deficit that spelled disaster.

Placer gold had been discovered in the creek thirty years before, but it had never been worked extensively due to the hostility of Indians. The Bannocks did not welcome the intruders and made life precarious for them. The Sheepeater Indians were mostly peaceful, but the crafty Bannocks were able to shift the blame for violent encounters on the Sheepeaters.

The most notorious incident was the massacre of a small party of Chinese placer miners. The Sheepeaters were blamed and punished by the whites. It was later found that the Bannocks had killed the Chinese and circulated a false report about a Sheepeater attack.

As the population of miners and ranchers increased in the Stanley Basin, the Indians gradually lost their lands, and game withdrew. The Indians became paupers, living on the edges.

Caleb had no use for the antiquated and abused dredge hardware, and the partners sold it in bits and pieces to hopeful entrepreneurs up and down Stanley Basin. The partners removed the planking of the superstructure to use in building a cabin on a placer claim downstream on the Salmon.

That was fine with Caleb since he decided that he could build a better craft, even though he had no experience with gold dredges or gold dredging. He would take his time and learn as he built.

He occasionally joined the old timers' gossip circle that wasted time sitting around the general store stove, smoking and trading stories and lies. Some had tried their hand at gold dredging and were happy to tell about their experiences. Most of their stories were about why they gave up gold dredging. That was okay with Caleb. At least, they told him what he should not do.

Perhaps he would find two or three men with experience on dredges to help. But he would not worry if he could find no one. He was not overly interested in success. He wanted only occupation.

He walked to the lumber pile, picked up a plank and dropped it, picked up another, discarded it, picked up another. He shrugged, carried the plank up the board gangway that ran from the shore to the gunwale. He stepped down from the gunwale to the deck and walked over to stand beside the wall of the structure. He stared at the wall, as if studying it. His mind wandered. He saw no wall, no dredge, no prospect.

"What you do?"

He turned to see the girl on the shore near the bow. "Nothing at the moment."

"Why you build cabin on boat?"

Leaning the plank against the wall, he stepped up from the deck to the gunwale. He walked down the gangway and across the grassy bank to the girl.

"It's not a cabin, and it's not a boat."

"I no understand."

He stepped off up the slope toward the cabin. "Let's get some lunch."

They sat in the shade of a tall aspen near the cabin. The small, almost circular leaves shimmered in the light breeze. A few leaves showed a hint of the golden tint of autumn.

They ate sandwiches silently. He watched her. She

stared at the Sawtooths. She appeared deep in thought, her mind elsewhere.

"You okay?" he said.

She turned to him. "Okay," she said. She looked down the slope to the valley. Her face betrayed no emotion.

Caleb watched her. *What can she be thinking about? Do I want to know what she's thinking about? Haven't I enough problems of my own?* He looked toward the pond, up at the aspen leaves whipping and twirling in the breeze.

"You okay?" she said.

This girl already knows me.

"What's your name?" he said.

"Mei Lin."

"Your name is 'Leen'?"

"No. Mei Lin. Two word. Mei, like April, May, and Leen,"

"Mei Lin," he said.

"Yes! That good." She smiled.

They ate in silence, looked at the valley and the Sawtooth range beyond.

"What your name?" she said.

"Caleb."

"Cay-leb."

"Caleb."

"Cay-leb." She frowned. "Why you choose hard name?"

"I didn't choose it. My daddy chose it. It was his father's name." He bent over his plate. "Cay-leb's okay."

They looked at each other, an uneasy silence, then turned back to their plates. He stopped eating, watching her as she ate. She glanced at him occasionally, solemn, with a blank face, then returned to eating, head down.

"What are we going to do about you?" he said.

"I help. You need help on boat."

He picked up the sandwich fragment, raised it to his mouth, lowered it to the plate. "Out of the question... Do you have any people here?"

"No."

"How old are you?"

"I not know. Maybe eighteen. Maybe twenty."

"How did you come to be in Stanley? You're the only Oriental here."

"I not Oriental! I Chinese."

He glanced aside, annoyed. "All right, Chinese."

She continued eating, looked up at him, took another bite.

"Tell me."

"I shame."

"I don't understand."

"My mother father poor. They say no can feed me. They sell me to man who say he need somebody help him."

Caleb frowned. "They sold you? Just like that? They sold you for money?"

"Yes. Mother father say they love me, but they no want see me die." She looked away, looked at the distant mountains.

"Is that done? Do other parents do this?"

"Many mother father do. They say they do so children can have something eat, so they not die. It called mai zhu zai. It mean 'sell little pigs'."

"I'm sorry," he said. "I had no idea."

They sat in silence, looking at the mountains and the pond and the forest, each waiting for the other.

"How did you get to Idaho?" he said.

"Man who own me, he name Fuhua, he hear about gold in Washington. He come to Seattle on ship, bring me to help. I scare of ocean. I sick most of time. I think I die. I want to die, I so sick.

"We go Rogersburg, place on river. Many people try get gold. We work hard. Very hard. Very hot, very cold."

"How did you come to Idaho?"

"He not find much gold Rogersburg. He hear about gold Idaho. So we go Idaho. Stanley. We find little bit gold. Bad men find out about his gold. They try take from him, and he fight. They kill him. Bad men take me Stanley, sell me madam. That end of story."

"That's all very sad, Mei Lin. I'm sorry. But Mei Lin, it's not the end of your story. It's the beginning. Your life has been filled with sadness. It will be better now. I will help you find a place."

She looked at her hands in her lap. "I no want find place. I here. I want stay here. This my place." She looked up into his eyes. "Please."

"Out of the question!" he snapped. He looked aside. *Why am I edgy? Why can't I just be nice to her? She's fragile. Why can't I be kind?* He lowered his head, stuffed the last wedge of sandwich in his mouth. She looked at him, questioning.

He could say no more. He didn't know how to respond. He could not care for her. He could not provide a home for her. He was an emotional wreck, he knew that, subjected to extended periods of deep depression. He was not often drunk, but when he was, he was neither rational nor gentle. He could harm her and not even be aware that he was harming her. *He . . . he . . . me . . . me. This is not about me! It's about her. This . . . has . . . nothing . . . to do . . . with me. I'm simply not able to handle this. What am I going to do?*

She looked over at him, waited. "You okay?" It was the second time she had asked him the question.

He nodded. "Yeah, okay." He turned to her. "Uh, your

owner. Did he ever . . . did you and he ever . . . ?" He paused. *What right have I?*

"Did we sex?"

He nodded.

"Yes, but not lots. He old man. He gentle, almost like he sorry he do."

"You're okay now?"

"Okay now. With you. Men at saloon not good. They hurt me." She put her hands to her face, and the tears came, like a dam bursting. She sobbed.

"Not just body. Hurt me inside, in head, in heart." She sobbed, and her body heaved, shaking, bobbing forward and backward.

Caleb was shaken. This whole affair was outside anything he had experienced. He had no idea how to respond. What would he want if he were in her place?

He moved over beside her. He put his arm around her shoulders and pulled her gently to him. He looked down at her, bewildered. She buried her head in his chest and wiped her face with a hand. She wrung her hands in her lap.

"Please let me stay," she said between sobs, her voice muffled in the folds of his shirt. "Please. I no trouble. I help. I do anything you want. Please."

They looked up suddenly at the sound of hooves on hard ground. Three horsemen rode at a lope down the wagon road toward the cabin.

Mei Lin jerked upright and looked anxiously at Caleb. "Who they? You know? They come get me?"

He frowned, stared at the approaching horsemen. "We'll see." He set his plate aside, stood, and walked toward the riders.

4 I NOT DO
SOMETHING WRONG

The three riders reined up before the cabin. They were roughly dressed, weathered faces, sweat-stained hats, working men. Each mount carried a loaded saddlebag.

"Mr. Willis?" one of the riders said. Caleb nodded.

"I'm Andrew Milner," the rider said. "Steve Adams in Stanley told us you were looking for help and told us where to find you. We're ready to go and would be much obliged for the work."

Caleb relaxed. He liked Andrew already. He was slight, about forty, with a face that showed he had endured hard work and cold winters.

"If Steve sent you," Caleb said, "you're hired. I do indeed need help. I asked Steve to hire men who had experience. You've worked on dredges?"

"Yes, sir. We've all worked on dredges, up north and down near Ketchum," said Andrew.

"Well done. Climb down." The men dismounted. "Glad to have you, Andrew." He shook Caleb's outstretched hand.

"This old rowdy here is Larry," said Andrew, gesturing to the tall, heavily whiskered, broad-shouldered black man. Larry smiled and waited.

"Larry," Caleb said and extended his hand. They shook, and Larry stepped back.

"That sprout there is Johnny," said Andrew, motioning with his head. Johnny lowered his head, avoiding eye contact with Caleb, and shook his outstretched hand.

All three men looked beyond Caleb at Mei Lin. She had followed him from their lunch tree. Now she looked blankly at the strangers.

Johnny, a young man of twenty, had a pleasant face and a tousled mop of blond hair. He had stepped behind the other men after shaking Caleb's hand. When Mei Lin made eye contact with him, he whipped his hat off and held it in both hands. A hint of an embarrassed smile played about his lips. Mei Lin glanced aside.

Caleb ignored Mei Lin and the glances of the men in her direction. He pointed beyond the corral. "There's your bunkhouse. It's pretty rough, but you can improve it any way you like. There's materials on the bank at the dredge, some tools at the dredge and others at the lean-to beside the corral." He pointed.

"There's a good sheepherder stove in the bunkhouse. Hope somebody in your lot can cook. We'll work out provisions. Somebody will drive the wagon to Stanley every week or so for supplies." The men smiled and nodded.

"Sounds good, we'll manage," Andrew said. "I'm a fair cook. Anybody complains has to take my place. That way, there's few complaints." The men laughed.

"You'll need to build a lean-to for your tack," Caleb said. "Use any materials and tools you can find around the place. You can use my corral if you want to, but it's pretty small. You can build your own behind the bunkhouse, if you like."

"Thanks for that, boss, we'll talk about it," Andrew

said. "Right now, we're ready to get busy on whatever you have in mind."

"What I have in mind is to finish building this animal," Caleb said, "then find some buckets of gold and make us all rich men. We'll begin tomorrow."

"Whoopee, I'm fer gittin' rich," said Larry. "That's fer sure!"

The others smiled and murmured their agreement. They mounted and set off toward the bunkhouse. Johnny looked back over his shoulder at Mei Lin.

Caleb watched them go, talking, laughing, eager to begin this new enterprise, for that's what it would be for this lot, a new beginning.

What nonsense. For me, at least. I sounded like I was talking to my employees at the plant back in Virginia, encouraging them to work hard, smile and be happy, onward and upward, success is in sight! Well, why not? I don't want to pass on my emptiness to other people, especially people who are dependent on me, people who still think the future has something good for them.

Caleb stood in front of the house, holding a dripping dishpan, watching the horseman riding down the wagon road toward the house. He didn't know him.

The horseman pulled up in front of Caleb and removed his hat. "Mr. Willis?"

"Yep. Get down." The rider dismounted.

"I'm Cal Morse. I heard in town that you was looking to hire men with dredging experience. I worked on dredges down south and sure would appreciate working for you."

Caleb frowned. "Well, I don't know. I just hired three men."

"I work good," Cal said. "I don't need a lot of pay, and I work real hard."

Caleb pondered. "Okay, Cal, let's give it a try. I'll pay you what you're worth." He extended his hand. Cal took the hand and shook vigorously.

"I sure 'preciate it."

"Ride down to the dredge," said Caleb, "and introduce yourself to Andrew. He'll get you set up. I'll be down in a bit."

• • • • •

Caleb and Andrew stood on the bank of the pond at the lumber pile. Caleb sorted through the pile, picked up a board and examined it, dropped it and picked up another.

"Did you get Cal situated?" said Caleb.

"Yeah, I had a good talk with him. You know, I knew I'd seen him somewhere, and then I remembered. He was at th' Trap when I was talking to Mr. Adams. He was real interested in our conversation. I wasn't surprised when he showed up today. He ain't the sharpest knife in the drawer, boss, but I think he'll do for a hand."

"Let's give him a chance."

The roof beams of the dredge housing were up, and the siding was almost finished. Sawing and hammering from inside the structure were evidence of progress on the housing.

Mei Lin held a plank in place on the outside wall while Caleb drove nails into it. That done, she selected another plank from the loose stack on the deck. She held it up to the wall next to the plank just attached. The edge was not straight and left an empty slot between the two planks.

"Ai ya, bu xing," she said. She tossed the plank to the deck and picked up another. She held it up for inspection. She frowned and ran her finger along the edge. She held it up against the attached plank. The join was straight and tight.

"Hao le," she said. "Xing le." She held the plank in place and turned to Caleb. "Ke yi le," she said.

Caleb had watched all this. He smiled. "Not bad," he said. "Couldn't have done better myself. But, Mei Lin, I can't understand a word you say."

"What? Oh, I forget. You no speak Chinese." He raised his hammer in mock anger. She laughed and jumped back.

Caleb smiled. She held the plank in place, waiting. When he simply stared, she cocked her head.

"Are you happy?" he said.

She sobered, frowned, serious. "What mean 'happy'?"

Caleb sighed heavily. "Mei Lin, Mei Lin."

"What? Never mind," she said. "You work. I go cabin make tea."

"Tea," he said. "How about coffee?" She frowned, put on a hard face. "Okay," he said, "tea."

Caleb and Mei Lin sat on a pile of planks on the bank near the gangway. They held ceramic mugs of tea. A metal tray holding a ceramic teapot lay on a plank beside Mei Lin. Caleb sipped his tea.

"Not bad. Not bad at all. I could get used to this. Had a hard time finding it. The Stanley clerk thought I was some kind of pervert, asking for tea. He said he would have to get it from the Chinese up north."

Mei Lin cocked her head. "What mean 'pervert'?"

Caleb frowned. "Um . . . somebody different. Some-body . . . never mind." He downed the last of his tea. He held out his cup to Mei Lin. "Any more in there?"

She smiled, picked up the pot, and poured into his mug, then her own. They sipped their tea in silence.

"Cay-leb?"

He looked up at her. "Yeah."

"Cay-leb, you have old clothes I can wear?"

He had taken no notice that she still wore the thin yellow dress that she had worn the day he took her from the Rat Trap. She had since worn an old jacket of his on cool days, but she owned nothing but the saloon dress.

"I think so," he said. "We'll have a look this evening."

"Thank you. I no like this dress. It remind me too much."

Caleb drained the last of his tea and handed the cup to Mei Lin. "To work." He stood, stretched, and headed for the dredge gangway. Mei Lin put their cups on the tray, stood, and walked up the slope toward the cabin.

She stopped on the path. A fresh breeze brought the sounds of sawing and chopping from the meadow where there was a long stack of logs. The logs were about four feet long and five or six inches in diameter. They would be cut later into shorter lengths to feed the firebox of the dredge steam engine. As soon as the dredge had a steam engine.

Caleb had hired a couple of drifters to cut the logs and stack them. They had a shifty look about them, and he restricted their access to the forest fringe where they cut the logs, the log pile where they trimmed and stacked the logs, and the bunkhouse.

Mei Lin strolled in the meadow, idly pulling at seeds from the tall rice grass, stopping to admire a particularly brilliant purple coneflower. She walked on and stopped at the long row of logs. At the sound of sawing on the other side of the logs, she walked around the pile.

Rounding the stack, she watched the woodcutter toss a log on the top of the six-foot high pile. He looked up at her, straightened, and flexed his back.

"That look like hard work," she said.

The cutter wiped his face with a hand. His long hair

dripped with sweat. His worn, wrinkled clothes seemed to be hung on his body rather than worn. He looked to be about thirty, but he might have been ten years younger.

"Yeah, it's hard work." He looked her over, grinned. She frowned, pushed a lock of hair from her forehead.

The cutter stared at her, still grinning. "Don't you remember me? I sure remember you."

She frowned again, glared at him. She tensed, stepped back. "Now I 'member. You come Rat Trap. You smell. Same now."

He grinned. "Yeah, I guess I smell like a man. But I think you enjoyed it."

She frowned and turned to leave. He dropped the saw and reached for her. He grabbed her arm and pushed her roughly against the stack of logs.

She struggled. "Stop that! Fang kai wo, asshole!" she shouted. She swung and struck him a hard blow to the side of his head. He winced. She swung again. He jerked his head backward to avoid the blow.

He laughed and tightened his hold around her shoulders while his other hand ripped her dress open and found her breasts. She tried to pull away, and his arm slipped up tightly around her neck.

She gagged, brought a knee up hard into his groin.

"Umph," he recoiled. He tightened his hold around her neck. "You bitch. I'll break your—"

The cutter was thrown violently sideways by a blow to the side of his head. Mei Lin pulled free and jumped away. Johnny threw the short limb aside. He grabbed the staggering man, whirled him around, and plunged his fist into his belly, a blow that lifted him off the ground. The cutter crumpled to the ground and lay still.

Johnny bent over him, gasping, his face contorted and

his legs spread, a coiled spring. Mei Lin cowered and stepped backward against the stacked wood.

Johnny straightened and jerked around to face her. He gasped, charged with the violence of the confrontation, but his face was soft.

"Are you okay?"

"Okay," she said, hardly audible. "Thank you."

"I'll take it from here." Mei Lin and Johnny whirled around and saw Caleb striding toward them. He had watched the incident from the beginning, running from the cabin upon hear

ing Mei Lin's first cry. Johnny was on the dredge, closer to the woodpile, and reached her first.

"Go on," Caleb motioned with his head toward the dredge, "I need to take care of this trash." He grasped the man by the collar and dragged him toward the bunkhouse, wondering whether he was unconscious or dead. He didn't care either way.

Mei Lin and Johnny walked slowly down the slope toward the pond. As she walked, she fumbled with her dress, all the while watching Caleb over her shoulder, striding up the slope with his inert burden. She almost stumbled as she watched Caleb disappear around the pile of logs.

Johnny looked straight ahead, only glancing occasionally at Mei Lin, looking back sharply to the front as she tried to repair the damage to her clothing. When she stopped at the embankment near the dredge, Johnny quickened his pace without a word and walked up the catwalk to the dredge deck. He disappeared inside the housing.

Caleb released the man, or the body, in front of the bunkhouse. He walked into the cabin and reappeared a moment later, dropped a canvas bag and an armful of clothes on top of the man. Staring at the debris a moment, he shook his head and walked down the slope toward the dredge.

Caleb saw Mei Lin who sat on the embankment beside the dredge, looking down at the valley. He stopped beside her, and she looked up. They exchanged a long silent look.

Mei Lin winced at Caleb's severe face. He turned away and walked toward the dredge.

"I not do something wrong," she called after him. He did not look back.

Mei Lin awoke early the next morning in her bed of skins and blanket. She watched Caleb pour coffee and walk silently through the door, carrying his cup. He did not look her way.

The door closed behind him.

And so it was for the day. He hardly noticed her. It was as if she weren't there. He prepared his own lunch. He ignored the tea she made in the afternoon and did not invite her to help on the barge. He ate his supper standing at the counter rather than at his usual place at the table.

Sitting in her chair, she looked up at him. Tears welled up in her eyes. "I not do something wrong."

He turned his back on her to wash his dishes.

Mei Lin woke the next morning at first light. Caleb, fully dressed, stood over her, waiting for her to wake up. He held a small packed saddlebag. She sat up and looked up at him. And waited.

"I'm going away a couple of days."

"Where you go? Why you go?"

"Stick close to the house. I told the men."

"Cay-leb?"

He shouldered the saddlebag and walked through the door. The door closed, and the latch dropped. Tears streamed down her cheeks.

Why? Why? Why? Why do I torment that girl? Why can't I be good to her? I don't want to hurt her. What do I want? Why am I holding back? I want what is best for her. Why do I think I know what is best for her? I'm going to come to no good end, I know that, and I don't want to pull her along with me. She has no future with me. She says she wants to stay with me. Of course, she does. She was a whore in a dangerous situation, every day a trial, death always a possibility. But am I her salvation? Me? I can hardly cope. How can I help her?

He rode on a game trail through a meadow of short buffalo grass. The long blue-gray blades showed a slight reddish hue, signaling the approach of autumn. Scattered maples along the narrow, meandering stream showed a hint of color. Hillsides on each side of the valley were dotted with dark pines and juniper.

Night. Caleb sat at a small fire, his saddle and blanket beside him. His hobbled horse nibbled grass at the edge of the firelight. Huge dark cottonwoods loomed over the site, the heavily leafed lower branches lightly illuminated by the fire, creating the illusion of a dwelling interior. He stared into the flames.

Mei Lin sat under the shade tree where she and Caleb often sat together, eating lunch or simply enjoying the view of the meadow and mountains. Tear tracks marked her face. She closed her eyes and wiped her cheek with a hand. She rocked back and forth, trying to hold back the tears.

She wore the pants and shirt that Caleb had given her. She had cut six inches off the pant legs and stitched a hem in them and narrowed the girth of the shirt with a vertical cut in the back, then stitched up the two sides. The sleeves were rolled up to her elbows.

"Miss?" Mei Lin jumped, and her eyes opened wide.

There stood Johnny with his hat in his hand. She remembered that he had taken off his hat to her that first day.

"I don't mean to bother you, miss, but I know the boss has been away these two days, and I saw you up here, and I wondered . . . uh, I wondered if there is anything I can do for you. Sorry to bother you."

She relaxed. "You no bother me." They looked at each other. He wrung his hat and looked aside in both directions. He looked down the slope to the dredge and back at her.

"You want sit down?" she said.

He fidgeted and looked back at the dredge. He turned back and sat down slowly in the shade of the tree five feet from her.

He held his hat in his lap. They looked at each other and at the mountains and the meadow and the dredge.

"What your name?" she said. "I forgot."

He jumped at her voice. "Johnny, ma'am."

She smiled thinly. "I not ma'm, Johnny, I Mei Lin."

"Hi, Mei Lin." He smiled. They looked at the valley and the mountain, glancing back at each other, smiling. A single bead of sweat rolled down his temple.

"Thank you, Johnny."

Johnny blushed a deep crimson. "It wasn't nothin'. You did right in yelling loud. I'm sorry you had to watch. I just lose my head when I see somebody hurting a horse or a dog or . . . oh, I don't mean—"

Mei Lin smiled. "I know what you mean, Johnny. You good man."

Johnny squirmed. He jumped up. "Well, I guess I'd best be gettin' back to work." He started to go, then turned back. "Uh, miss, uh, Mei Lin, if there's anything I can do for you, please give me a holler, and I'll come runnin'. Please do that." He turned and ran down the slope to the dredge.

Mei Lin watched him go. She lowered her head and wiped her moist eyes with the back of her hand.

The sun was low on the western horizon when Caleb rode into Stow. Or what was left of Stow. The Englishman who had founded the town, perhaps homesick, had named it Stow-in-the Valley, but the name had never caught on. A typical comment from newcomers was a variation of: "Stow-in-the-Valley? What the hell kinda name is that?" The name survived simply as Stow.

The town had been a thriving community of six hundred souls when the mine was flourishing, but declined when the mine played out. Now only twenty or so families called it home.

Caleb rode slowly down the single street, his horse's hooves raising little puffs of dust. A one-room schoolhouse on the left was shuttered, the white paint peeling on its sides. Beside the schoolhouse, the picket fence of a cemetery of two dozen graves sagged, some pickets loose and leaning, some missing.

On the right side of the road, a blacksmith in a soiled apron stood before his small shop that was set back from the road. He wiped his hands on his apron and watched Caleb. His stern look said what th' hell you doing here?

On each side of the smithy, buildings that once had been thriving shops of some sort now sagged, doors off their hinges, shingles missing, windows with broken glass panes, paint peeling, exposed decaying timbers.

On the slope behind the row of ruined buildings, the rusty bones of the mill thrust upward from the shroud of dark pines.

Caleb was seized with a deep melancholy. He shook his head and swallowed, choking back the tears. He rode on.

On each side of the street, thin smoke spirals from

chimneys of small ramshackle houses told of the precarious existence of their occupants. A woman dressed in a shapeless faded cotton dress stood on a front porch, leaning against a post, her arms folded, watching Caleb. Small gardens were laid out in front or beside some of the houses. No one worked the gardens.

Past the ghost of Stow, at the far edge, Caleb rode into a thriving community. The Chinese who had served the miners had stayed after the mine failed and the mining community had disappeared. As long as the mine flourished, the Chinese had washed the clothes of the miners and shopkeepers. They had cooked and cleaned for them, and they grew vegetables for them. Now they cooked, cleaned, and grew vegetables for themselves. They were not prosperous, but they were self-sufficient, and they were content.

Small neat houses lined the road, widely spaced with vegetable gardens in front and alongside. In some of the gardens, a man or a woman worked, clearing weeds or bending to gather vegetables. Two women walked on the road, chatting loudly, laughing.

Caleb reined in at a large garden fenced with short pickets where two men stood between rows of potato plants. They had stopped working when they saw him riding up and now watched him intently. Each man held a digging fork. Freshly unearthed potatoes lay loose on the ground before them, two partially filled buckets in grooves between the rows.

Caleb dismounted, tied the reins to the fence, and walked through the open gate. "Neat garden you've got here," he said. The men nodded. They had not taken their eyes off Caleb and held the forks with both hands.

"Bit late for potatoes, isn't it?" The men relaxed. They

smiled and lowered the forks.

"These late potatoes," one said. "We dig some in summer, some now. These late. We like potatoes. You know potatoes?"

"Used to grow some back east. Virginia," Caleb said.

The man sucked in his breath. "Ooh, that long way. I don't know 'bout Virginia. Idaho grow good potatoes. Better than my home China."

The other man stepped up and bowed slightly. "You want tea? Time for tea."

"That would be very nice. Thank you, I would. I like tea. A friend introduced me to tea recently, and I like it."

The man nodded and walked to the small house behind the garden, disappearing inside. The other man motioned toward an arbor and walked to it. Caleb followed him.

Under the arbor, Caleb looked up. The vine that covered the arbor was losing its leaves. Some of the tendrils were bare. Others held dry, crispy tan leaves and some that showed the subdued colors of early autumn. The man motioned toward the chairs at a table, and they sat down.

The man who had gone into the house returned with a tray bearing a ceramic teapot and four ceramic cups. He set the tray on the table, nodded, and walked through the garden gate to the road. He closed the gate and walked briskly down the road.

The man who sat with Caleb poured tea, and they sipped silently. Presently the other man who had made the tea returned with another Chinese. The man sitting with Caleb rose and bowed to the newcomer. Caleb also rose. The newcomer nodded and motioned for all to sit. They sat, and tea was poured for the two men.

5 I NEVER
HAVE PRESENT

The sun had just dropped behind the Sawtooth range, and the cloudless sky at the horizon was a brilliant orange yellow, blending upward to a light turquoise.

Caleb walked his horse down the wagon road toward the house. The mules in the pasture stood like statues, ears erect, watching him come. One of the mules sounded off, a whinny that became a bray and ended in what sounded like a rolling belly laugh.

The cabin door burst open, and Mei Lin ran from the cabin into the yard. She had long ago associated the mule's greeting with Caleb. Holding a stout piece of stove wood at her side, she watched him come.

Caleb pulled up before the hitching rail. He looked at Mei Lin who looked back at him, sternly, without blinking. Dismounting, he tied the reins to the rail and turned to Mei Lin.

"I hope everything—"

"No nothing talk! You tell me where you go! Why you go! Now! You tell me!" She waved the stove wood in his face.

Caleb retreated a step. He wanted to smile, laugh,

maybe grab her. "Okay. Let's get some supper. I'll tell you everything."

They sat at the table, Mei Lin in her chair and Caleb on the keg. Caleb's plate was empty. Mei Lin's had not been touched. Her hands were in her lap. She glared at him.

"They said they would be glad to welcome you. You would have to work, but you would be safe. They said that nobody bothers them. They get along well with the Americans who still live there, and that attitude seems to insulate them from outsiders."

"No! I happy here." She did not smile. Her look was one of resolution, neither submission nor timidity.

"It would be best for you. It's going to get nasty here. The sentiment against Chinese seems to be growing. Mei Lin, up north they have a tree they call the Chinese Hanging Tree. And they tell me in Stanley that the owner of the large dredge off the Salmon is raising hell with the owners of small dredges. He wants no competition. There could be trouble."

"No. I not go. I not afraid."

"You may not have a choice."

"I kill myself," she said.

He softened. "Don't talk like that."

"I kill myself!" She looked at Caleb as tears streamed down her cheeks. "I happy here," she said softly. "It first time ever I happy."

Caleb turned and looked at the dark window. "Mei Lin. Mei Lin."

The days passed, and there was no more talk of Stow. Caleb and his four workers finished the dredge housing, and Caleb sent word to the railhead office in Ketchum to inquire about the delivery of the dredge buckets, cylinder, steam engine, and other hardware.

The reply from Ketchum was encouraging. The delivery was on schedule. The shipment should arrive there in two weeks. It was getting late in the year to begin dredge operations, but Caleb was anxious to get in a few weeks of work before winter closed them down.

Mei Lin had watched Caleb as he carried out his usual household chores, and she gradually took over. She now did most of the cleaning and had taken to washing his clothes, though he had protested at first. Just do your own things, he had said, and I'll do mine. She had ignored him, and soon he was content to drop his dirty clothes on the floor and find them washed, dried, and hung on the wall pegs the following day before supper.

She washed her own clothes at the same time. Caleb had been surprised on his return from Stow to see her wearing the old clothes that he had given her, which she had altered. He had wanted to say something, but it didn't seem the right time. When they had reconciled and Stow had been put behind them, Caleb had commented and said that she looked like a clown.

"What mean 'clown?'" she had said. When he explained the meaning, she replied that she didn't care. She was glad to burn the saloon dress.

She also had watched his cooking and meal preparation and soon was doing most of the cooking and all of the cleanup after meals. He often stood in the center of the cabin, watching her. He had difficulty knowing what to do with his hands when he normally would have been cooking or cleaning up and putting away.

Her first attempt at baking bread was not successful. She had watched Caleb making bread, and she had welcomed his instruction at first, but when she interrupted him repeatedly with her "I can do!" he backed off.

Her first loaf looked like a large, fat, beige slug. Even the birds rejected it. Next time she made bread, she asked for help and was more attentive. Since then, she had become expert and had received high praise from the bunkhouse as well as Caleb's nod. He never made bread again.

A casual visitor would have concluded that Caleb and Mei Lin were husband and wife. But they were not, for there was no intimacy. They had hardly touched each other, just a brush or casual touching when passing a plate or tool. Each welcomed the other's company, sharing space and chores, but each withheld sharing their souls for their separate reasons.

Yet each occasionally watched the other when the watching could be done without notice. Questioning, wondering.

On a sunny afternoon, Caleb walked on the path from the cabin down the slope toward the dredge. He stopped. Mei Lin and Johnny stood together on the deck. She held a board up to the wall, and they cooperated in lining it up. Caleb heard their laughter.

He pondered. *Is Johnny the solution for Mei Lin? He is her age. He has proven that he cares for her and can protect her. He is a good worker and will make his way in this god-cursed world. He could make a place for Mei Lin.*

He watched them. Mei Lin held the board against the facing. Johnny positioned the nail on the board, raised the hammer, and struck the nail. After striking his thumb. He shouted and dropped the hammer that clattered on the deck. He shook his hand and sucked on a finger.

Mei Lin doubled over laughing. She took his hand and rubbed it. She giggled while Johnny stared at her, mesmerized. Caleb could almost feel his stare.

Yeah, Johnny. She can be distracting.

Caleb turned and strode back to the cabin, his head full.

The cabin interior was darkening with the waning day. A shaft of sunlight from the window described a patch of light on the floor. Caleb worked on the cabin wall, troweling daubing from a bucket to the spaces between the logs. Mei Lin sat at the table, watching him. Her elbows were on the table, and she rested her chin on her hands.

She pulled the lamp to her, struck a match, and lit it. Caleb looked around at the sudden brightness, then turned back to his work.

"Cay-leb." He ignored her.

"Cay-leb, you not speak for hours. You okay?"

He glanced over his shoulder at her. "Of course, I'm okay. It's all right if I work on the walls, isn't it?" She winced, and he noticed.

"Sorry, I'm just a little . . . out of sorts," he said.

She frowned. "What mean 'out of sorts'?"

He dropped his hands to his sides and stared at the wall. "Nothing. Let's get some supper."

He walked to the door, opened it, and set the daubing bucket outside on the ground. Standing in the doorway, he stared at the woods across the road, his mind racing.

He walked to the cabinets. Mei Lin closed the door, walked over to stand beside him. They made their meal together, silently, Mei Lin glancing at him while he studied the potatoes, squash, onions, and elk roast.

They sat at the table, Mei Lin in her chair and Caleb on his stool. Their plates were empty. The lantern on the countertop made a soft light on their faces. Mei Lin watched him and waited.

The meal was finished. He had to either get up or talk. He stared at his plate, picked up his fork absentmindedly, replaced it on the plate.

"Did you and Johnny get the wall finished this afternoon?" he said.

"No. He hit his hand and hurt it."

He looked at her. "Yeah, and you laughed at him. Don't get in his way, Mei Lin. He's a good worker, and you're distracting him."

"But I just try . . ." She stopped. Her eyes opened wide.

"That it! That it! You jealous!"

"Jealous? Nonsense!"

"You jealous! You jealous!" She jumped up and ran around the table to him. He stood quickly to fend her off. She grabbed his shirtfront, pulled his head down, and kissed him hard. She pulled back and released him, her hands on her cheeks, startled at what she had done.

He smiled thinly, pulled her hands from her cheeks, and held her hands. He leaned down and kissed her softly on her lips. He put his arms around her shoulders and pulled her to him, resting his head on hers, his face buried in her hair, breathing in her perfume.

"Mei Lin, Mei Lin," he said softly. "What am I going to do about you? I can't keep you. It's not fair to you. What are we going to do?"

Mei Lin held him tightly, her head pressed against his chest, and said nothing.

Mei Lin continued to help on the dredge, but as the construction neared completion, she had more time to simply enjoy her cloistered existence. Sometimes when her chores were finished, she sat alone under the tree where she and Caleb usually ate their lunch, staring for hours at the magnificent Sawtooths.

One pleasantly cool day, she strolled in the pasture, sweeping the grass tops with her hand, pulling seeds and chewing on them.

She stopped her walk in the meadow when she saw Caleb's horse ahead. The horse pricked up his ears and watched her. The horse was a buckskin gelding, the color of tanned deerskin, about sixteen hands. Sleek and muscled, with a dark mane and tail and lower legs, almost black.

She walked over to the horse and touched his muzzle. The horse raised his head, and she stroked his cheek. She talked softly to him, pulled at his mane, and rubbed his back and sides, talking all the while.

When she walked slowly away, the horse followed her. She stopped, stroked his back, walked again, looked back to see him following again.

Caleb stood on the bank near the dredge and watched all this.

That same evening, Caleb stood outside the cabin, drying his hands on a dishcloth, and watched Mei Lin in the corral. She stroked his horse's back and rubbed his muzzle, talking softly to him. She walked slowly away and turned to watch him follow her. She stopped and stepped over beside him, stroking him gently.

Mei Lin rubbed the horse's back with both hands. Then she dropped her hands to her side and took a deep breath. Facing the horse, she shuffled on her feet and braced herself.

"Uh oh," Caleb said softly to himself.

Mei Lin took another deep breath, grasped a handful of mane and swung herself up on the horse's back. The horse instantly shied, bucked, and she slid off, falling heavily to the ground on her stomach. The horse walked to her and nudged her shoulder with his muzzle.

She stood and flexed her back, hands on her hips. She put an arm over the horse's neck and spoke softly to him.

She stroked his back, grasped a handful of mane, and swung up on his back. The horse immediately bucked, spun, and she slid off, landing hard on her butt, rolled, and came to rest on her stomach.

She lay still a moment, then pushed up on her elbows. The horse walked to her and nudged her in the back.

She stood slowly, painfully it seemed, and grabbed a handful of mane. She shook a finger in the horse's face, talking softly to him. She walked toward the corral gate, rubbing her butt. The horse followed.

Caleb walked to the corral. He opened the gate, and she walked through. He closed the gate behind her. The horse walked over to Caleb. He reached over the corral pole to rub an ear. Mei Lin rubbed the other ear.

"Your horse not like me," she said.

"He's pretty particular."

"Your horse have name?" said Mei Lin. "You never say."

"Buck," he said.

"Why Buck?"

"Well, partly for his color, buckskin, and partly for the man I got him from. His name was 'Buck.' A stupid man who lost his poke at cards and finally bet the only thing of value he had left in the world. His horse."

"Pretty dumb," she said.

"Yeah. I paid him anyway. From the money I had just won from him."

"You good man."

Caleb shook his head, smiled.

Caleb sat on the wagon seat, holding the lines of the team. He swayed back and forth as the wagon rolled down the road toward the cabin. He pushed lightly on the brake with his foot to slow the wagon on the descent.

He had told Mei Lin when he left that morning that he

had business in Stanley and that he had to buy supplies. Yeah, he had lied, but now he smiled at the subterfuge. Behind the wagon, a pretty little mare was tied.

The very moment he saw the mare in the sale corral behind the livery, he knew this was Mei Lin's horse. She was sleek and muscled, about fifteen hands, three or four years old, a smoky gray color. She had a pretty neck and head, and her tail and mane were long and coal black. There was a distinctive black stripe down the middle of her back. He paid more than he should have, probably less than she was worth, and he was pleased.

Caleb's horse in the pasture nickered a greeting, and Mei Lin appeared in the cabin doorway. She saw the wagon approaching and walked toward it.

Caleb pulled the wagon up in front of the cabin. He wrapped the lines around the brake handle and jumped down. Mei Lin stared at the mare. Caleb followed her stare.

"I found her on the road. Pretty thing, isn't she? Friendly, too. Guess she's lost."

Mei Lin walked to the mare. She ran her hand lightly down the horse's back. The mare nipped at her hair. Mei Lin smiled.

"You pretty girl," she whispered. "You lost? Where you live?" She turned to Caleb. "Poor girl. I wonder who own her."

Caleb smiled. "You do."

Mei Lin frowned. She looked at the horse, then at Caleb. "What you mean?"

"I mean that she belongs to you. A present. She's your horse."

Mei Lin stepped back awkwardly. She held her cheeks in her hands, then covered her entire face. Tears flowed through her fingers. She lunged for Caleb. She fell against him, forcing him to step back to regain his balance. She reached around his waist and held him tightly, her head pressed into his chest.

She leaned back and looked into his eyes. She took his cheeks in her hands and pulled him down. She kissed him softly, pulled back, and patted his cheeks lightly with both hands, then again, this time almost a slap. Caleb winced, smiled, and glanced aside.

She bent over with her hands between her knees, straightened, tears marking her cheeks. "Cay-leb. I never have present." She ran around the wagon to the horse. She stopped beside the mare, looking her over, her hands on her cheeks.

"I can't believe." She turned to Caleb. "She really mine?"

"Yes."

Only then did she see the saddle in the wagon. She looked at Caleb. "That too?"

"Yes, that too."

She dropped to her knees, her head lowered and her hands folded on her chest.

Caleb walked to her. He looked down. "Are you okay?"

She spoke softly without looking up. "I so happy, I think I die."

"Don't do that," he said. "This little mare would miss you." He pulled her up. "She'll want to get to know you as much as you want to get to know her. She'll smell your hair, your shoulders, and around your neck. Fellow in the sale barn said to let her smell your hand. Don't know about that. She might think you're offering her a treat. Let her smell the back of your hand. Soon as you two feel comfortable around each other, untie the reins and lead her into the corral. Tell her that she's a lucky girl to have a new playmate."

Mei Lin extended the back of her hand to the mare's muzzle. The horse touched Mei Lin's hand, bobbed her head, smelled her hair, and nudged her shoulder. Mei Lin untied the reins and turned to go. She stopped and turned back to Caleb.

"What mean 'playmate'?"

"It means that you and she are going to have great fun together. Aren't you?"

"Yes. Thank you. It best present—it only present—I ever have."

Mei Lin led the mare to the corral. She opened the gate and closed it after the horse had passed through. She slipped the bridle off and hung it on a post.

She offered the back of her hand again. The horse touched it with her muzzle and nipped at her hair. Mei Lin rubbed the horse's neck and ran her hand down the black dorsal stripe, from the withers to the tail, all the time talking to the horse, telling the little mare what good friends they were going to be and what good times they were going to have.

Mei Lin looked up and saw Caleb outside the corral, watching her. She smiled. "Thank you," she said.

"Come here," he said. She opened the gate, passed through, and closed the gate. Caleb reached into the wagon bed for a package. "This is for you."

She took the package, looked up at him, uncomprehending, overwhelmed.

"It's not going to open itself, Mei Lin."

She unwrapped the package, and her eyes and mouth opened wide. She handed Caleb the wrapping and held up a pair of blue denim trousers, a calico shirt, and a denim jacket.

"Cay-leb! I so surprise!" She held the pants up at her

waist. She looked up at him and smiled. Pressing the shirt to her chest, she checked the sleeve length. "They my size! How you do that? Where you get them?"

"General store. They're boys' clothes. Uh, except this." He handed her a pair of knee-length flannel underpants. She took the underpants and held them up.

"Oooh, I never have before." She reached up and kissed Caleb. "Thank you for everything. Now I can help more."

Caleb and his four helpers worked long hours on the dredge, eager to complete the structure and housing by the time the hardware arrived.

However busy he was, Caleb found time each day to help Mei Lin with the mare. She groomed the horse so much that he didn't have to remind her to be sure there was no mud or other debris in the saddle area. He showed her how to place the saddle pad forward of the withers, how to put the saddle on her hip and rock it back and forth in order to gather momentum to swing it up on the mare's back, how to slide the blanket and pad back into place to keep the hairs aligned properly. He explained how to connect and adjust the cinch and latigo and the breastplate.

Mei Lin listened carefully and watched his every move. She asked intelligent questions. And hard questions. When he was teaching her how to mount, he began by telling her that she should always mount from the left side.

She frowned. "Why?" she said.

"Well, uh, that's just the way it's done."

"Why?"

"Dammit, Mei Lin, I don't know why. That's the way it's always been done. Maybe it began with a reason. I heard that it goes back hundreds of years, when knights wore swords on the left side, and if they mounted from the right side, the sword got in the way."

"I no wear sword. You no wear sword."

Caleb closed his eyes and tilted his head back. He didn't know whether to laugh at her or spank her.

"Okay, you mount from either side. Just be sure to be consistent. If you want to mount from the right side, mount from that side every time. Don't confuse your horse."

She smiled. "I mount from left side. Okay."

He managed to smile.

"Maybe I start wearing sword," she said.

He lunged for her, and she danced away.

Most of the time, she listened without interrupting, but she did not hesitate to ask him to repeat an instruction. Once he had demonstrated a task, she did not permit him to do it again. Her "I do!" was sufficient to cause him to back off.

She was a quick learner. After only a few days, rather than give instruction, he simply watched and occasionally pointed out an error or suggested a better way to perform a task.

One morning, he awoke to the staccato sound of hooves in the meadow. He looked out to see Mei Lin on the mare, galloping hard up the slope toward the line of trees, her hair and the mare's tail streaming behind. Later, he saw Mei Lin in the corral, rubbing the horse down, talking to her, the mare nuzzling her and following her, and he knew that his help was no longer needed.

On another day, he watched Mei Lin run in the meadow, laughing, the mare running alongside, bucking and prancing like a filly, galloping ahead, slowing to let Mei Lin catch up, running together.

Finally Mei Lin slowed and stopped, panting and laughing while the mare nuzzled her and prodded her back, eager for another run. The two playmates walked side by side to the cabin.

"Have you named her yet?" Caleb said.

Mei Lin rubbed the horse's muzzle. "Yes. She name 'Chica'."

"Chica? What kinda name is that?"

"It Mexican. I have friend at Rat Trap. She Mexican, sweet girl. She name 'Chica'."

"I never saw her at Rat Trap."

Mei Lin stroked the horse's back. "She stolen before you come. Just 'bout two month before you come. Polly very angry. Send two men find her. Same who hurt me. They not find them. Polly very, very angry. I hope he good man. I think he good man. He treat Chica good. Polly begin lock my door at night."

Mei Lin looked away as she stroked the horse. "I miss Chica. She my only friend at Rat Trap. My only friend almost two year." She looked up at Caleb. Her eyes glistened. She lowered her head and walked toward the corral. Chica followed, nipping her shoulder.

Caleb shook his head. *You've seen too much, little girl. Too much. How can you still smile?*

6 I THINK I
CALL YOU "HONEE"

Caleb stood in the road in the middle of Stanley beside the four-mule team hitched to a freight wagon. Three other wagons, each with a four-mule team, were lined out behind. Caleb had hired the wagons and teams for the sixty-mile trip to Ketchum to pick up the hardware for the dredge. Three saddle horses were tied to the tailgates of wagons for unforeseen circumstances.

Word had arrived a week ago that the buckets, steam engine, and other hardware had been delivered at the railhead. Now he was paying for storage and wanted to claim the materials as quickly as possible.

He had considered having the gear picked up and hauled by a transport group that made the run regularly between Ketchum and the Stanley Basin. The group transported everything from mining equipment to groceries.

Thus far, Caleb's experience with the transport people had been limited. Periodically he had entrusted Wally Custer, a transport worker and son of Abel, the general store owner who was a friend of Caleb's, with picking up money for him at the Ketchum Western Union office on his regular runs. With the other transport people, including the foreman, Caleb was singularly unimpressed.

Caleb had decided that he would handle the management himself. He was content to hire wagons, teams, and drivers from the transport group. They had the experience, and they knew the route and the wagons. But he made it clear that he was in charge.

The transport people weren't accustomed to a mere dredge operator questioning their expertise, but they wouldn't pass up the opportunity for the business. They even seemed to be quite satisfied to let somebody else bear the responsibility when things didn't go according to plan, which seemed to be common on the Ketchum run.

The caravan of four wagons from Stanley to Ketchum was a trial. At the start, the road was still wet from a light rain overnight, and wagons and mules slid about, especially on the grades. One of the drivers was nursing an aching head from a late night at the Rat Trap, and another complained to anyone who would listen of a throbbing toothache.

And there were delays. The right front wheel of the lead wagon, driven by Caleb, struck a rock protruding from the roadbed and broke the wheel and two spokes. Caleb tied the lines to the brake handle and got down. He looked at the broken wheel and shook his head. The transport foreman, who had been driving the second wagon, walked up to Caleb's wagon and looked down at the wheel.

Caleb frowned at the foreman. "Look at these spokes," Caleb said, pointing to the broken spokes. "Look how dry and brittle they are. They look a hundred years old."

The foreman raised an eyebrow. "No, boss, they've just wintered over a few years in Stanley. Cain't pull the wagons in the house, you know. Don't fret, boss. It happens. That's why we carry spares." He motioned with his head toward the two men who had just untied a wheel from underneath the second wagon. They pulled the wheel upright and rolled it toward Caleb's wagon.

Mei Lin sat Chica quietly beside the road, watching the wheel replacement. Caleb had invited her to ride on the wagon seat with him at the outset. He was not surprised when she said that she would prefer to ride Chica.

Not a few of the transport workers had glanced Mei Lin's way since the beginning of the journey. Doubtless some remembered her from the Rat Trap. Caleb put an end to their curiosity on the first day. He glowered at any who showed interest in her.

When one seedy character took a few steps toward her at a rest stop, Caleb strode over to stand between him and Mei Lin. "You got time on your hands?" Caleb said. "I'll ask your foreman if he still needs your employment." The man stopped, surprised, and withdrew. Caleb glanced at Mei Lin whose lips turned up at the corners ever so slightly. He frowned and strode away.

During the ascent of a difficult grade, Caleb noticed that a lead mule in his team was limping and ordered a halt. He questioned the foreman who admitted hesitantly that the mule had had a problem a few weeks ago, but that he had improved lately.

Caleb was so angry that he forced the foreman to dismount and add his horse to the team. Otherwise, said Caleb, he would reduce his payment by an amount determined by the loss of time due to the lame mule.

The disgruntled foreman walked beside the wagon a few miles before forcing one of his men to give up his own mount for him. The worker gave his boss a glare that suggested that he better watch his back.

Caleb emerged from the office of the Ketchum railroad

storage barns and stopped on the porch. He looked over the barns at the pastel shades of lacy cloud layers on the eastern horizon. The low morning sun cast gray shadows across the station courtyard. Caleb folded a paper and tucked it into a shirt pocket. He looked across the courtyard where his four wagons were lined up at loading docks. His goods were loaded, and transport workers were tying down the cargo. The workers had turned out at first light and had the wagons loaded before the sun ball had cleared the horizon. Not without a steady rumble of grousing.

He inhaled deeply, profoundly pleased that all was going well and on schedule. The transport foreman had succeeded in buying a replacement mule for the lame animal, so teams were at full strength.

Caleb had drawn some cash on arrival yesterday at the Western Union office, the same office where Wally had picked up cash occasionally. This was the first time he had visited the office personally.

The foreman, standing beside the loaded wagons, waved to Caleb, signaling that all was ready for a departure. The foreman smiled.

He had not been as jovial the previous evening. The caravan had arrived late, and the transport people had looked forward to their usual carousing at the Ketchum saloons. Caleb's announcement of a departure at first light was met with grumbling and not a few angry words, including those of a belligerent foreman.

Caleb had stood his ground and reminded the foreman that he, Caleb, was in charge and that payment of the contracted sum depended on his recognizing this. Caleb added, loud enough for the disgruntled workers to hear, that there would be a bonus if they reached Stanley at the scheduled time. The workers looked wide-eyed at each other, then raised a cheer and headed for their bunks. There would be time and the wherewithal for carousing in Stanley.

· · · · ·

It was not long before Caleb realized that the journey from Stanley to Ketchum had been a lark compared to the return. The wagons were so heavily loaded now that it was slow going, even on the level. The first day was reasonably easy on a mostly flat road, but the mountain range ahead was always in sight.

The first night was spent at Galena, a stopping place at the foot of the Boulder Mountains. There was a combination lodge, cafe, and livery where Caleb had arranged the stop. Mules were unhitched and turned into the corral. Caleb and Mei Lin took a room in the small lodge while the transport workers made their beds in the barn. Four-hour shifts of two transport workers guarded the loaded wagons during the night.

The next morning, the caravan pulled out at sunrise. Almost immediately, the road turned upward. On most grades, all four teams had to be hitched to a wagon to make any progress. Reaching a level place, the workers blocked the wagon wheels with rocks, unhitched the mules, and led them down below where the other wagons waited. They hitched the sixteen-mule team to the second wagon and moved up to the level behind the first wagon, then did the same for the third and fourth wagons. This time-consuming relay continued until they reached the summit.

At the pass, wagons were halted to give the teams a rest and to prepare them for the descent. The preparation for the descent was not a favorite chore for the transport workers. They had to find four large logs that would be tied with ropes to the rear of wagons to act as brakes on the downgrades.

The transport crew walked into the woods on each side of the road, looking at downed timber and living trees. One worker shouted that he found a downed tree that had fallen in last winter's storms. Other workers found three living trees with trunks the right size, about twelve inches in diameter. The crew set to work, cutting trees and sawing off limbs.

Caleb and Mei Lin strolled from the road to a point with an unobstructed view of the valley ahead. The forested slopes in the foreground gave way to the broad basin of grasslands and meandering streams. The mountain range beyond was lightly dusted with an early snowfall.

Stanley was visible as a small, dim patchwork in the distance. On the journey toward Ketchum, they had hardly glanced back at this view. Now they were silent at the magnificence of the wide basin and the Sawtooth range.

"Pretty," Mei Lin said.

Caleb looked at her, then back at the valley. "Yes, it is," he said. "We're blessed, Mei Lin. But there's no time for this. Too much work." He turned and walked toward the road.

Mei Lin walked beside him, her head down. "What mean 'blessed'?"

He picked up the pace, impatient to get moving. "That's a hard one. Let me think about it."

They reached the road where Caleb fidgeted as the workers pulled wagons to logs and tied them with ropes to the back of wagons. That done, the foreman waved to Caleb.

"Okay, boss. All set!"

"All right," Caleb said. "Let's go." The foreman waved,

and workers climbed aboard their wagons. Caleb took his seat, unwound the lines, and shook them. He moved off, and the other wagons followed. Mei Lin rode up alongside Caleb. He nodded to her.

As the wagons moved off, the ropes that bound logs to the rear of the wagons tightened, and the dragging logs prevented the heavy wagons from picking up speed on the descent. The tactic generally worked without a hitch. But the benefits were paired with risks.

Mei Lin usually rode near the lead wagon, watching Caleb. He glanced occasionally at her, then back at his team, than back at her. She still watched him. He shook his head, turned back to the front. She seemed to be always there, watching. He began to be annoyed by the constant attention.

But once when he looked, she was not there. He turned and looked behind, on both sides of the road, and she had disappeared. He looked ahead, and she was not there. His growing unease mounted.

Then he saw her, galloping in his direction on the back trail until she was beside the wagon. She pulled up, smiling.

"Where were you!" he said. "You need to stay in sight."

She cocked her head. "I had pee. You want me ask you next time?"

He sighed, looked back at the team. "No," he said.

"You want me in sight all time, you want watch next time?" She grinned.

He dropped his head, looked at her, and smiled. "No." He shook the lines, and the mules strained on the traces.

Mei Lin rode over next to the wagon and looked up at Caleb. "Cay-leb?"

He looked at her.

"I think I call you, 'honee'."

He frowned. "Honey? Where did you hear 'honey'?"

"Chica call her friend 'honee,' friend who steal her. She say you call someone you like 'honee.' That okay?"

He smiled thinly. "Yeah, that's okay." He turned back to the front and shook the lines. *Well, it's not okay. It's what Beth called me, honey. Honey, honee, I guess it's not the same.* He shook his head and shook the lines. *Let it go!*

"Cay-leb, honee, you okay?" She still rode beside the wagon and had watched him.

He looked a long moment at her, solemnly. She cocked her head.

"Yeah, okay," he said, "just ... a little headache."

"I sorry, Cay-leb, honee. Sorry, I do." She turned her horse and trotted on the back trail.

"Mei Lin, you . . . Mei Lin!" But she was gone. He faced forward and sagged, letting the mules find their pace with slack lines.

"Cay-leb, honee!" Mei Lin shouted. He turned sharply toward her and smiled. He had not seen her for a couple of hours and worried about where she was and what she was thinking.

He sobered when he saw that she pointed at the wagon tongue. In his dark mood, he had not noticed that the tongue was rattling and the team's traces were loose and flapping.

"The log!" She pointed at the log that was attached to the back of his wagon. It still slid behind the wagon, but the ropes were slack, and the log was moving faster than the wagon on the steep slick roadbed and was about to strike the rear of the wagon.

Caleb saw the log and the slack ropes. He shook the lines and shouted to the team. The mules tightened the traces, and the team moved ahead at a slow trot. The ropes holding the log stretched out, and the log was dragging again.

Caleb pulled the lines lightly, and the mules slowed to a fast walk. Caleb looked at Mei Lin. He smiled and nodded. She nodded in return, raising her chin ever so slightly.

Later that day, a light rain turned the road surface slippery. Riders on each side of Caleb's wagon tied ropes on the rear of the wagon and pulled them taut to prevent the wagon from sliding sideways. Caleb hoped the other wagons had no problems on the descent, for they had no outriders.

● ● ● ● ●

The transport workers cheered when the wagons left the descent and lined out on a flat road. Drivers pulled to a stop, wrapped lines around brake handles, and climbed down stiffly, stretching and stamping on the ground. One driver jumped up and down, urging legs and muscles to function.

Drivers walked around to the backs of wagons, untied logs, and rolled them aside. They coiled the ropes and tossed them into wagon beds.

"Now we roll free," the foreman said. The others nodded in agreement and climbed aboard their wagons.

The final night of the journey was spent at the Frank Shaw ranch on the Stanley road. Caleb had arranged the stop a couple of weeks ago. He had met Shaw in Stanley early in the summer and had had coffee and a whiskey with him occasionally since then. Shaw had said that he would welcome the visit.

This was unexpected luxury for the transport group. It was raining lightly when they arrived at the ranch.

They were accustomed to spending this night sleeping on the ground in a roadside camp. Now they were invited to put up in the comparative comfort of the hay barn, snug and dry.

Mrs. Shaw was happy enough to welcome the novelty of visitors to the isolated ranch, but she was uneasy about how to treat Mei Lin.

Her husband was not so conflicted. He was mesmerized by the pretty Celestial and had eyes and conversation only for her, virtually ignoring Caleb.

Mrs. Shaw was more amused than offended by her husband's attentions. She knew they would be gone in the morning. She was already curious about what sort of comment he would make about their visitors after their departure.

There was indeed little comment the next morning except for Caleb's thanks for their hosts' hospitality. But Mr. Shaw was quick to accept Caleb's invitation to meet in Stanley in two weeks time when Caleb would treat to lunch and drinks.

"Bring the Mrs.," Caleb said.

"Urn," Mr. Shaw said. "Bring Mei Lin."

7 OKAY, WE TALK CHINESE NOW

Caleb walked from the doorway of the dredge housing, wiping his hands on a cloth. He stopped. Above the meadow, he saw a dozen Indians at the edge of the forest. They were all afoot. They stood quietly, looking toward the dredge.

Caleb waved. The Indians did not respond. They stood a moment longer, then turned and disappeared into the woods.

"They friendly?" Mei Lin had emerged from the dredge housing and walked up silently behind him. He still looked at the woods where the Indians had vanished.

"Don't know. I've never seen any Indians about." He turned and walked toward the door to the housing.

"I'm going to cabin," Mei Lin said. Caleb waved over his shoulder as he disappeared through the housing door.

Caleb burst from the dredge housing door. The sound of terrified whinnying, almost a scream, sent shivers up his spine. At first, he could not pinpoint the source of the whinnying, but then he saw the horse's bobbing head behind the woodpile.

It was Chica and beyond her was the bear that was

causing the uproar. The huge bear had Chica boxed into a forty-five-degree angle of the woodpile. As the bear advanced slowly, Chica shied side to side, terrified. Her eyes were open wide, showing the whites, and her nostrils were flared. The bear also lunged side to side, blocking Chica's escape.

C'mon, Chica. You can get out of there. You've got space, and you're faster than that ol' bear. Break out.

Oh, god! There was Mei Lin running full bore across the meadow toward the woodpile. She screamed, waved, and yelled loudly in Chinese.

"Mei Lin! Stop! Mei Lin! Go back! Stay away!" She ignored him, if she heard him, and ran straight for the bear.

The bear heard her screams and turned toward her. She did not slow and still ran full out toward the bear. The bear moved his head side to side and took a step toward the oncoming two-legged beast.

Mei Lin! You're mad. What are you doing?

Caleb ran to the catwalk, danced down it, and ran toward the woodpile. His mind raced. *What am I doing? Am I as deranged as Mei Lin?*

"Mei Lin! Stop!"

The bear advanced another step toward the approaching apparition.

But the bear thought better of tangling with this strange creature. He whirled around and lumbered off toward the woods.

Mei Lin watched the retreating bear, then collapsed to the ground, gasping. Chica trotted over and nipped at her hair. Mei Lin stood with some difficulty and hugged the horse's neck.

Caleb was hardly halfway to the woodpile when the bear hightailed it for timber. He slowed and walked up to

Mei Lin. She looked over Chica's back at him, still gasping.

"Mei Lin," he said, "you're crazy! What would you have done if the bear had waited for you, then charged this screaming banshee?"

Mei Lin frowned. "I not know. I just so angry and frighten, I not think."

They walked toward the cabin. Chica followed, bumping Mei Lin's back repeatedly.

"You better think next time," he said. "That bear could have made a nice lunch outta you."

She looked up at him and smiled. "I don't think so. I taste Chinese sour."

They walked on. "What were you yelling in Chinese?" he said.

"You not want know. Not nice." She smiled impishly, stopped, and looked at him. "What mean 'banshee'?"

"Mmm." He looked up, pondering. "A banshee is a female spirit that yells a lot and tells people that somebody is going to die. I think. Maybe it's a female spirit that causes a lot of trouble. Anyway, it's a woman that is raising some kind of hell."

She smiled, satisfied, and they walked on.

First light. Caleb and Mei Lin stood on the bank at the dredge bow. Andrew and the others stood nearby, watching Caleb.

The dredge was finished. Interior hardware had been installed, and buckets were attached to the ladder. It was the culmination of weeks of construction and installation. All awaited Caleb's signal.

A heavy line ran from each side of the dredge, aft of the bow, to the bank where it was tied to a stout stake driven into the ground. The spud, an enormous circular iron shaft that was secured in a sliding mechanism on the stern, was dropped hard into the pond bottom to counter the digging pull of the bucket-line. The spud also served as a pivot when the dredge bow was swung to the side to begin a new cut. The bucketline ladder, hung from cables attached to the housing, extended about six feet over the bank.

The steam engine's boiler had been filled with water the previous evening. The firebox had been stoked and awaited the flame that would begin the process of getting up steam.

"Let's fire it up," Caleb said. The four workers raised a cheer.

"Okay, boss," said Andrew, "whatever you say."

Caleb walked up the plank to the dredge deck. Mei Lin and the others followed.

Inside, Caleb opened the firebox door, struck a match and ignited the tinder just inside the chamber. Workers raised another cheer. Caleb closed the firebox door.

"Now we wait," Caleb said. The four workers walked outside to stand on the deck or walk down the plank to the bank. A couple of men sat down on the bank and pulled out pipes and small tobacco sacks.

Caleb took Mei Lin by the arm, guiding her to the large room aft of the engine housing. Here was the apparatus for processing the soil dug by the bucketline. "You won't want to be in here once we begin operation," Caleb said. "It's going to be ear-splitting noisy."

"I see gold flakes before when we work in stream," Mei Lin said, "but I no understand how you take gold from buckets of dirt."

"Well, it's pretty hard to understand," he said. She frowned and cocked her head.

"Okay, I'll try to explain. The buckets dump the soil into this big round hopper. It rolls around as water is sprayed into it, and the fine stuff washes out through the holes in the hopper. The stones that are too large to go through the holes are sent to the big belt in the back where they are dumped behind the dredge. These are called tailings. Okay?"

"Okay."

"The small stuff that goes out through the holes of the hopper is called 'fines.' The fines are washed on sluice boxes, something like when you and your husband, uh, your owner, uh, your—"

"It okay, honee. Go on."

"Okay. The fines are washed on through these sluice boxes, and the gold is caught on plates—look over there—that are covered with mercury. The lighter stuff in the fines is washed overboard. We recover the gold from the plates. That's not all, but that's pretty much how the process works. I'll show you later when we get in operation. Sorry it's so complicated."

"It not complicate. I understand. You think I not understand? Why you think so?'

He smiled. "All right, get down off your high horse. I'll probably be turning over the operation to you."

"Sure. I can do," she said. She patted his cheek, then gave him a playful slap. He had winced after the pat, knowing the slap was next.

Caleb, Mei Lin, and Cal stood on the bank near the dredge bucketline, which extended a few feet over the edge of the bank. Andrew and Larry stood on the dredge deck. Steam issued from the stack above the engine house.

"Are we ready, Andrew?" Caleb called.

"Ready when you are, boss."

"Okay, do it."

Andrew and Larry went inside the engine housing. A moment later, a loud clanking rent the still air. The line of buckets attached to the ladder began moving on the belt, and the bucketline was lowered to the surface of the bank.

The buckets on the underside of the belt dug great chunks of soil from the bank. The full buckets revolved up to the top of the ladder and into the housing where they dumped their loads and, now empty, moved on the bottom side of the ladder back outside. As the buckets removed huge chunks of earth from the shoreline, the bucketline sank into the bank.

The sound of metal on metal and the slapping of bucketline hardware were deafening. Mei Lin put her hands over her ears. Caleb smiled and motioned to Mei Lin to back away. They retreated up the slope from the dredge.

When they had withdrawn far enough to be able to hear each other, they stopped and looked back at the dredge. Caleb pointed at the bucketline.

"See how the bucketline is sinking into the bank. When it has dug down about three feet, the dredge will be swung sideways by loosening the shoreline on one side and pulling on the shoreline on the other side. Then both shorelines are tightened, and the bucketline begins digging again, another three-foot slice. The dredge swings on the spud, the big spike at the back of the dredge. The spud also counters the pull of the buckets digging into the soil, pulling the dredge forward. Understand?"

"I understand. How deep buckets go?"

"Till they hit bedrock. Then the spud is raised, and we move the dredge forward to begin the process of digging and swinging back and forth all over again. It won't be long before the dredge begins moving upstream. We move our pond with us as the tailings pile up behind the dredge."

"I understand," she said.

They walked back down the slope and around the pond

bank where they had a view of the side of the dredge and the tailings that were already beginning to pile up behind the dredge. Mei Lin frowned.

"What's wrong?" Caleb said.

"It make mess. It look like dredge shit."

Caleb laughed out loud. "Gotta make a lot of shit to make a little sugar."

She stared at the steady stream of rocks issuing from the conveyor belt at the rear of the dredge. "I no like. It cover pretty pond and pretty land."

Caleb tensed. He looked hard at Mei Lin. "If you don't like it, maybe you'll be content to eat grass and wear rags instead of the groceries and nice clothes the gold is going to buy us!"

She looked hard back at him, turned, and walked away, fuming, up the slope toward the corral.

He watched her go, still upset at her comment, but also wondering at his sharp response. Had she struck a chord?

The single lantern on the table softly illuminated the cabin interior. Mei Lin stood at the cabinet counter, spooning biscuit dough onto a pan. She had been particularly anxious to learn how to make biscuits since Caleb liked them so much. He had taught her, and now she would not permit him to make them. She wrapped her hand in a cloth, opened the stove door, slid the pan inside, and closed the door.

She straightened, wiping her hands on the cloth. She watched him as he applied daubing compound to the log walls from a tin pail. She always knew when he was upset. He would methodically and silently mix the daubing compound outside. Then he would come inside without looking at her and work on the walls without a word.

"I sorry, honee."

He continued without pausing or looking at her. "Honee?"

He looked up, frowning. He softened and seemed to droop. He put the daubing stick inside the bucket and set it on the floor. He walked to her, touched her cheek.

"All right. I can't stay mad at you. Mei Lin, I don't like to eat up the land. But this is just a small piece of God's country, and we won't be here forever. The land will recover and go back to normal."

She put her arms around him and held him. "Okay, you say so." He put his hands on her cheeks and kissed her forehead.

"Now get those biscuits before they burn, or I'm going to have to get back to the daubing."

• • • • •

Mei Lin rode Chica down the slope of the meadow. The clanking and banging noise from the dredge grew louder as she rode closer. The steady stream of stones dropped from the conveyor at the back, building heaps of tailings above the level of the pond. She shook her head.

She pulled up near the side of the dredge and waved to Johnny who stood on the deck, watching the bucketline. He jerked off his cap and waved to her.

Both Mei Lin and Johnny started at a shout from the housing interior. Then another shout. Mei Lin recognized Caleb's voice. She slid off Chica and ran to the dredge, up the plank onto the deck, and inside the housing. Caleb and Johnny stared wide-eyed at the mercury-covered plates.

Caleb smiled at her and pointed to the gold flakes stuck to the plates. He opened his fist and showed her two nuggets. They were tiny, hardly bigger than raisins, but they were the first nuggets they had found.

They went out on deck where Caleb showed the other workers the nuggets. They raised a cheer amid hearty back-slapping all around.

Caleb and Andrew stood on the bank of Stanley Creek, about halfway up the hillside between the pond and the forest. The creek flow had dropped in the past few weeks and now was half its usual size.

"We're not in trouble yet," said Caleb, "but if we don't get rains soon up country, the dredge could bottom out, and then we're in trouble."

They looked at the dredge below. Steam issued from the exhaust pipe, and the clanking of the bucketline was faintly audible.

"Mary's Creek is spring-fed, so it will do for us if our creek goes dry. It flows in the next canyon east, and so far as I know, the water is not used. I don't know of any placers on the creek below, so there's nobody going to complain if we divert part of the flow to Stanley Creek."

Caleb studied the Stanley Creek flow, shook his head. "We need to get that sluice built now."

"Well, I've seen sluices, seen 'em gettin' built and operating, but I wouldn't feel confident to build it by myself," Andrew said.

"It's okay. Go to Stanley tomorrow. Find somebody who knows about sluices, and hire him for the job. He'll have to build a sluice gate on Mary's Creek that can be opened when we need the water and closed when we don't. He'll also have to supervise digging the channel from Mary's Creek to our meadow.

"We can spare two men to help him with the shovel work on the channel. Hire as many as half a dozen others as well if you can find any. Should be a few played-out placer miners around the saloons who would be willing to earn a little beer money."

"I'll git right on it," Andrew said. "You think we'll need the water any time soon? Gittin' near the end of the season."

"Yeah, it is. But I'm still hoping for a few more good weeks before the cold shuts us down. I wouldn't want to have an early shutdown from lack of water. We'll see. The sluice will be good insurance."

Caleb and Mei Lin sat at their usual shady picnic spot, bundled in jackets against the cool early autumn breeze. They ate from plates that lay on the ground beside them, chunks of bread and slices of pork that Caleb had cooked the previous evening. They looked down the slope at the dredge.

"Do you have any questions about the dredge operation?" Caleb said. "I don't expect you to understand everything, but ask me when something doesn't make sense."

Mei Lin bristled. "Why you think I no understand?"

"Well, you don't have a good understanding of English, so I thought that my explanation might not be clear."

"What! You think I no understand 'cause I no talk like you? Okay, I no talk good English, but I understand in head. You no like my English? Okay, we talk Chinese now."

"Xian zai wo men jian zhong wen. Zhe wo shun kou dou le yin wei zhong wen shi wo de moo yii. Er qie wo xi huan shuo zhong wen, ke shi wo mei fa shuo yin wei ni yi ge zhong wen zi dou bu dong."

She looked up at him, expectantly, as if to say, okay, it's your turn.

He smiled. "Okay," he said, "I get your point. Your Chinklish is just fine."

She bristled. "Chinklish!" She frowned, cocked her head. "Chinklish? Okay. Chinklish okay. You not even know one word Chinese." She leaned over in his face. "Say one word Chinese!"

He pondered, frowning. "Asshole," he said.

"That not nice word, and it not Chinese."

"Well, I thought it was Chinese. You say it often enough."

"I not say now. ... I don't say now. I don't say it now. It not nice ... it ... is not ... a nice word." She smiled.

"Hmm. Very good."

They returned to their lunch. They looked at the distant Sawtooths and listened to the muffled sounds of the dredge.

Caleb looked up. The cool breeze rippled the tall meadow grasses like ocean swells. The sun was brilliant overhead, but in the Northeast, a cloud on the horizon was darkening. The mass of the cloud boiled, and its edges rolled outward, expanding. The approach of the dark mass was accompanied by a low rumble of rolling thunder. A jagged bolt of lightning shot from the cloud to a distant wooded ridgeline.

Caleb stood. "Mei Lin, get the dishes up to the house. We're about to get some weather." She began collecting their dishes.

The sky darkened, and the breeze quickened. A few large drops of rain fell, a bolt of lightning struck in the forest above the meadow, followed by a loud crack of thunder.

And the sky opened. The rain fell in sheets, blowing in his face as he ran down the slope toward the dredge. Mei Lin ran toward the cabin, holding the dishes over her head.

"Shut it down!" Caleb shouted. "That's enough for the day!"

"Okay, boss, whatever you say!" Andrew shouted.

The bucketline ground to a halt, and the pulsing noise slowed and stopped. The steam engine was shut down.

Workers ran from the housing in the downpour and down the plank gangway, up the trail through the meadow toward the bunkhouse.

It would be a welcome evening respite around the stove in the bunkhouse, drinking coffee and exchanging stories and lies.

The hard staccato rain on the cabin roof was accompanied by thunder that rolled and cracked, rattling the windowpanes. Lightning flashed repeatedly, illuminating the cabin interior briefly, followed by absolute darkness.

Caleb jumped at a particularly loud crack of thunder. He settled back down in his bed and pulled the cover up. The room was suddenly illuminated by a lightning flash, and he saw Mei Lin.

She stood by his bed.

He rose on an elbow, spoke in the darkness. "Mei Lin? What are you doing up?"

"I scare, honee."

He looked for her and saw nothing but darkness. Then a flash of lightning showed her still standing there.

The lightning flashed again, and she saw that he had pushed the covers down. She crawled onto the bed and lay down. He pulled the blankets over her. She moved over beside him and snuggled against his chest, shivering. He reached around her and held her, stroking her hair.

Sunlight streamed through the window, casting a rectangle of light on the cabin floor. Mei Lin opened her eyes and sat up. She looked around, as if she were seeing the cabin for the first time. She looked over at the sleeping Caleb, leaned down, and kissed him lightly on the mouth.

He stirred and opened his eyes and saw her. He smiled and pulled her to him. She lay on his chest. His hand moved slowly over her naked body, caressing and fondling. She kissed him again and started to roll off him.

"Not yet, Mei Lin." He took her face in his hands and kissed her.

She pulled back and touched his cheek. "Honee, I love you. I never say before in my life."

He kissed her again, put his arms around her and pulled her close. He looked over her head to the skins on the floor, the skins that had been her bed.

Now what, Caleb Willis?

8 THE GATHERING STORM

Caleb buttoned his canvas jacket as he walked to the cabin door. He stopped and looked back at Mei Lin. Only the top of her head was visible under the blanket. Opening the door, he stepped outside and slowly closed the door, trying not to wake her.

He looked up at the sky, deep blue and crystal clear, not a cloud in sight. He walked around the corner of the cabin and looked toward the dredge.

But the dredge was not there. It was gone. He shouted toward the bunkhouse and ran down the slope toward the pond. The workers ran from the bunkhouse door, buttoning pants and pulling on shirts.

Caleb reached the pond edge. But it wasn't a pond now. It was a wide, swift-flowing stream that disappeared around a ridge in the distance. He walked over to an iron stake where a shoreline had secured the dredge to the bank.

He looked at the two-foot rope fragment that was still attached to the stake. He picked it up and examined it. Had it frayed and separated from the action of the current?

Not likely, he decided. The smooth edge of the fibers suggested that it had been cut. He looked at the other line a few yards away and reached the same conclusion. He cursed under his breath.

The four workers ran down the slope to Caleb, still buttoning and adjusting clothing.

"What th' hell's goin' on here?" Andrew said.

"We're gonna find out. Johnny, saddle your horse and mine, and come back here. Andrew, you and the boys saddle up. Johnny and I will ride down the left side of the stream. You and the boys ride back here and wait. I'll send word."

"Okay, boss, whatever you say," Andrew said. The four workers ran up the slope toward their bunkhouse tack room.

"Honee, what happen?" Caleb turned to see Mei Lin running toward him, tucking shirt into pants as she ran.

"Well, either the current carried the dredge away, or somebody doesn't want us working the creek and cut it loose. We'll see."

They waited, silent, staring at the tumbling stream.

Johnny rode up with Buck in tow. "Ready, boss. Hi, Mei Lin." She raised a hand in greeting. Caleb mounted, and the two rode at a lope on the left bank along the course of the stream. They disappeared where the torrent curved around a low ridge.

Mei Lin walked up the trail toward the cabin.

"We got us a problem here, Johnny."

They sat their horses on the bank, looking across the stream at the dredge. It was wedged hard up against a pile of logs and brush that had collected in the runoff. The stream at this point was about three times the width of the dredge.

"Seems to be intact," Caleb said. "Don't see any structural damage. But the problem is the creek flow. Runoffs gone down, and the water level is already dropping. The stream is usually just a trickle here. If the dredge bottoms here, we'll never get it back to the pond.

"We've got to hurry. Ride to the boys. Tell them to get the team in harness, and get here as quickly as possible. No wagon. Tell them to come on horseback. Bring all the rope they can find. Pull up on the other bank." He pointed across the stream. Johnny whirled his horse and rode away at a gallop.

Caleb paced on the bank. He tensed when the current momentarily surged. The barge rose slightly, and the bow began to move slowly away from the bank. He cursed under his breath. If the barge moved away from the debris that held it, it could move into the flow of the stream and be carried farther downstream where the creek was shallower. The dredge would never be recovered if that happened.

As he watched, the surge lessened, and the dredge settled back into the debris dam. He exhaled.

On the far bank, the four mounted workers approached at a trot, leading the mule team in harness. They pulled up, and Andrew shouted to Caleb.

"Ready when you are, boss!"

Following Caleb's shouted instruction, Andrew tied a long rope to the mule team's traces. Larry took the other end of the rope and climbed over debris to the deck of the dredge. He tied the rope to the shoreline coupling on the port side of the deck.

"Okay!" Caleb shouted, "take up the slack and keep it taut."

Still following Caleb's instruction, Andrew coiled the end of another rope and threw it to Larry who tied it to the shoreline coupling on the starboard side of the bow. That done, Larry stood and waved to Caleb.

"Good!" Caleb shouted. "Andrew, tie two rope pieces,

each about ten feet long, to the end of the starboard rope." Andrew fumbled among the ropes that had been brought from the lean-to's. He found two suitable pieces and tied them to the starboard rope. When he finished, he held the ropes up and waved to Caleb.

"Johnny, bring the starboard rope across! Cal, come with Johnny! Careful, the stream here is shallow, but it may be swimming in spots!"

Johnny took the end of the rope from Andrew and urged his horse into the stream. Halfway across, the horse stepped into a hole and was swimming. At the near bank, the horse found the bottom, and Johnny drummed his heels in the horse's side. The horse lurched up the bank.

Johnny looked back to the other side. Cal still sat his horse at the water's edge. He looked down at the stream, his face a mask of terror.

"C'mon, Cal!" Johnny called. "Just pretend it's your turn in the washtub." Larry, standing near Cal, guffawed.

"We don't have time for this, Cal!" Caleb called.

"I cain't swim!" Cal shouted.

Caleb grimaced, shook his head. *God help us.*

"You ain't swimmin', Cal!" Johnny said. "Your horse is swimmin'. He can swim better'n any of us. Point him into the water, and you'll be across in no time."

Cal gritted his teeth and touched heels gently to his horse. The horse entered the water and walked a few feet. Then he was swimming, and the water rose to his back. The horse was swept downstream with the current.

"I'm goin'! I'm goin'!" Cal yelled.

"The only place you're goin' is up the bank, Cal," said Johnny calmly in a clear, strong voice. At that moment, the horse found footing and lunged up the bank.

"Now, wasn't that fun?" Johnny said.

"Hell, no, it wasn't fun," said Cal, "and I ain't going back across. I'm gonna live here!" Everybody guffawed. Cal smiled.

"C'mon, playtime's over, boys," said Caleb. "We've got to move." Johnny and Cal took the two stout short ropes that were tied to the long line from the dredge and looped them around saddle horns.

"Okay, easy does it!" Caleb shouted. "The mules will do the pulling, and the boys on this side will pull the bow just a bit away from the bank."

Caleb turned to Cal and Johnny. "Easy does it. All you're doing is steadying, not heavy pulling. We don't want the dredge to pull you and your horses into the stream."

The mules strained in the harness, and the port line tightened. Johnny and Cal moved their horses ahead, and their ropes tightened. The dredge gradually pulled away from its debris wall. It was floating. The men raised a cheer.

Good progress was made as the dredge moved ahead in the slack current. The riders on the near side and the mule team on the far side had to slow or accelerate from time to time to keep the dredge at midstream.

A light breeze cooled Caleb's face, and he looked up. A dark cloud scudded overhead. The sun disappeared, and a few large drops fell, raising tiny eruptions on the stream surface.

The light rain increased and became a deluge. Runoff from the hard rain was immediate, and the current increased. The breeze quickened, and the dredge was soon dead in the water.

Caleb shouted to all to tie the lines to trees to wait out the rain. While Johnny and Cal tied their ropes to a streamside oak, Andrew and Larry on the other side untied the line from the team and tied it to the trunk of a large cottonwood.

The dredge, now in midstream, wavered side to side in the current. The ropes whipped and strained, and the rope on the port side snapped. The dredge, pulled by the starboard line, swung toward the near bank. It nudged the bank and wedged against the top branches of a downed tree that lay in the stream at the bank. Caleb and the others hastily loosened the line where it was tied, took up the slack, and retied it.

The men on both sides of the stream huddled under trees for a semblance of shelter and shivered in the cold rain.

The storm was over as quickly as it came. The dark cloud moved away, and the stream and banks were flooded with bright, warming sunshine. Everyone stepped from their dripping shelters and looked up. The breeze subsided, and birds sang from their perches on both banks.

"We'll wait a bit longer," Caleb said, "to let the current drop. Won't take long."

At the sound of hooves, all looked up the stream bank. Mei Lin rode Chica at a slow lope, balancing a bag in front of her. She pulled up beside the workers on the far shore.

"Hey, Mei Lin!" said Larry. "What're you doing out here?'

"I thought you like lunch," she said. She opened the bag and offered it to the men.

"You're some kinda angel, Mei Lin," said Andrew. The workers reached into the bag and pulled out sandwiches. They wandered about on the bank, munching on their sandwiches, steam rising from their wet clothes in the warm sunshine.

Mei Lin closed up the bag and walked her horse to the stream edge. Caleb, who had watched all this, shouted.

"No, Mei Lin! Stay there! Don't . . ."

But she was already in the water. Her horse walked on the bottom as the water level crept up her side. Mei Lin held the bag high with one hand, the other holding the reins.

She smiled at Caleb. Then her horse stepped into deep water and sank to her back. Mei Lin's eyes opened wide, and she almost dropped the sack.

"Honee!" she called.

"You're okay," Caleb called calmly. "She's swimming and has everything under control. Just stick with her. Everything's okay." He was not as calm as he pretended to be.

Chica found the bottom and lunged up the bank. Mei Lin rode to Caleb and handed him the sack. She smiled.

"I told you to stay there," he said.

"You did?" she cocked her head. "I not hear."

"Of course you heard. You . . ." He looked at Johnny and Cal. They looked on with silly grins on their faces. He dug into the sack.

Mei Lin stowed the clutter and remains of the lunch in her canvas bag. She and the others watched Cal kick his horse into the stream and swim for the near bank. He held the end of a rope. The other end of the rope was tied to the mule team. Once on the bank, Cal handed the rope end to Caleb. He grinned.

"Well done," said Caleb, remembering Cal's first crossing. Not long after that hair-raising event—for Cal, at least—he had kicked his horse into the stream and swam alone to the other bank just to show he could do it. Watchers on both sides of the stream cheered when he climbed out.

"Nothin' to it," Cal said.

Holding the rope end, Caleb went to the dredge, which

was hard against the shore and still lodged against the downed tree at the back. He climbed through the branches of the tree to the dredge deck where he tied the line to the port side shoreline coupling. He untied the fragment of the rope that had separated in the storm and dropped it into the stream.

Clambering again through the downed tree branches, he stepped up on the bank and walked to Mei Lin and the others. "Mei Lin, ride up this bank to the dredge site. You don't need to cross. We'll be along soon. I hope."

He shouted to the other side. "Move the team slowly to get the dredge to midstream. We'll take up the slack on this side. Let's go."

As Johnny and Cal attached their lines to their saddle horns, Caleb looked up the bank for Mei Lin. She wasn't there. He looked around. There she was, in the middle of the stream, swimming Chica toward the other side.

Cal grinned. "Want me to go get her, boss?"

Caleb sighed. "No, Cal, she might have to save your life."

Caleb looked across the stream. The water level was down, and the current had slowed. On Caleb's signal, the mules on the far side and riders on the near side moved off slowly. The ropes drew taut, and the dredge was eased away from the snag.

Mei Lin walked beside the team, leading Chica. She waved to Caleb. He frowned, pointed at her, then pointed at the ground. He hoped she understood his meaning: Stay on the bank! No swimming! Reluctantly, he waved.

The dredge was pulled steadily in the slack current and made slow progress upstream. They rounded a ridge and saw the house and outbuildings in the distance. The men raised a cheer.

The two lines on the dredge suddenly jerked taut, and

the horsemen and team were stopped in their tracks. All looked at the dredge. It was motionless in the stream.

"It's on the bottom!" Caleb shouted. "Let's put some pressure on the lines, but easy, to see if we can move her off. We don't want to break the ropes."

The riders and the team pulled gently on the lines, but the dredge did not move. As the runoff had decreased, the water level of the shallow creek had dropped just enough to settle the dredge on the bottom.

Caleb looked at the dredge. The slack current caused not the slightest motion on the pontoons. He looked around. Everyone stood motionless, watching him.

Now what? Is this where we winter?

"Cay-leb, honee," Mei Lin shouted, "how 'bout sluice?"

Caleb looked at Mei Lin sharply. *I'll be damned.*

"Andrew, Larry, ride to the sluice. Johnny, hustle across and help. Open the sluice, all the way. Mary's Creek will be full from the rain, and it just might do the trick. All we need is a few inches. Hurry, the water level here is still dropping. Cal, cross over and tend to the team."

I'll be damned.

Andrew and Larry mounted and galloped up the stream bank. Johnny and Cal kicked their horses into the stream. On the other side, Johnny galloped hard up the meadow to catch up. Cal dismounted and walked to the team.

The riders stopped at the cabin. Larry dismounted and collected three shovels from the lean-to. He handed one to each of the others and mounted. They galloped past the woodpile and up the sloping meadow toward the woods, holding their shovels out at arm's length to avoid hitting their mounts.

On a level just short of the edge of timber, they pulled up at the mouth of the sluice channel.

"Johnny," said Andrew, "you stay here. Clean the mouth. Watch for the flow, and don't let the mouth silt up. Larry, come with me." Andrew kicked his horse into a gallop along the sluice, and Larry followed. They disappeared into the woods.

Johnny dropped his shovel, dismounted, and tied his reins to a pine limb. He picked up the shovel and began cleaning the sides and bottom of the sluice at the mouth. The inside of the sluice was wet from runoff from the recent rains, but the channel held no water now since the mouth was open.

Fifteen minutes passed. Johnny looked up the channel. "C'mon, boys. C'mon, water," he muttered to himself.

Ten minutes passed. Johnny strained, searching, staring up the course of the sluice channel.

Then he saw it. A wall of water two feet high, filling the channel, coursed toward him.

"Yippee!" Johnny yelled.

The torrent shot from the sluice mouth, flattened, and flowed down the slope, finding its course until it merged with Stanley Creek.

Johnny grabbed his shovel and mounted hurriedly. He stared into the woods that bordered the sluice.

Andrew and Larry burst from the trees. Johnny waved his shovel at them. Larry waved his shovel in return. They came up to Johnny at a gallop and turned down the slope toward the pond. Johnny kicked his horse into a gallop behind them.

Caleb saw them coming. He waited, anxiously, pacing along the bank as they pulled up beside the mule team.

"Okay, boys, well done," he shouted. "Cal, come over here and help me with the lines. The rest of you, get the mules ready. Hurry now! The flow from the sluice should hit us full force in a minute. All we need is a few inches and a few minutes."

Cal kicked his horse right into the stream and up the bank on the near side, an experienced water rat now. He took a short rope that Caleb offered. Holding the second short rope, Caleb mounted.

"Okay, let's put a little tension on the lines now," he shouted. "Easy does it!"

Caleb watched the bow pontoons for movement. The creek was narrow at this point, and any increased flow should be more noticeable here than elsewhere.

Move, dammit, lift, move. The flow around the pontoons, hardly a ripple before, increased noticeably. "Be ready, boys. Keep the ropes taut. Be careful. Don't break 'em!"

Then he saw it. The bow rocked the slightest bit, an inch to each side. The pontoon unit amidships rocked almost imperceptibly, but it rocked, up and down, back and forth.

"Now! Everybody, move out, slowly, gently!" Caleb shouted. "Don't break anything. Easy ahead!"

The bow lifted slightly, then dropped gently as the stern lifted a few inches. The dredge was floating.

"Now, pull ahead! We're floating! Move ahead! Slow and steady. Don't break anything!"

Take it easy, Caleb. You're supposed to be in charge. Take it easy.

Caleb breathed a great sigh of relief when the dredge moved from the shallow creek into the deeper pond. The men raised a cheer, and Caleb joined in.

The dredge was towed back to its original mooring where workers tied the shorelines securely to the stakes.

Caleb and Mei Lin watched from the bank. She put her arms around his waist and held him.

"Okay I hug you when men can see, honee?"

He looked down at her and put his arm around her shoulders. "Yes, Mei Lin, it's okay."

He looked at the dredge and beyond to the Sawtooth range.

9 I KILL MYSELF

Two weeks had passed since the near disaster. The clanking and grinding and rattling evacuation of tailings now reverberated off the surrounding hills from dawn to dusk. The dredge moved slowly up the valley as it gnawed at the pond shore and dragged the pond with it.

The sluice had been closed at Mary's Creek and the sides of the channel raised a foot, more insurance in case it was needed again. It had proved its worth.

Gold flakes were found on most days, but in small quantities. They had taken no more nuggets. Caleb sold gold in Stanley often enough to realize that he was not making expenses. Always frugal in his expenditures, lately he had cut corners as never before. His eastern bank account, which he had long believed would be intact at his death, had been reduced severely with the cost of initially putting the dredge in operation, repairs, and daily expenses.

He had hoped that before winter cold and snow shut him down he would find enough gold to meet costs and finance the plan that was beginning to take shape. Now he was not so sure. In spite of the need for day-to-day expenses, he was careful not to touch the cash reserve that he was accumulating, hidden under the floorboards of the cabin.

Caleb and Johnny stood on the bank, Caleb at the stake for the starboard shoreline and Johnny at the port line. Caleb motioned to Andrew who stood at the engine room door. Andrew went inside. He shut down the bucketline and raised the ladder from the bank.

Caleb and Johnny untied and loosened the two shore-lines. Johnny walked over to Caleb. Together they pulled the dredge bow toward them about three feet. Caleb took a couple of loops over the starboard stake and tied the line securely. Johnny walked back to the other line and tied it to the port stake.

Caleb gave Andrew the high sign, and Andrew went back into the engine house. He lowered the ladder, and the bucket-line lurched into movement, chewing great chunks from the bank, beginning again the process for removing a three-foot wide layer of soil from bank surface to bedrock.

Johnny laid the plank that extended from the bank to the dredge gunwale and stepped back. Caleb stepped up on the plank.

"Boss," Johnny said. Caleb stopped and looked back. Johnny motioned with a nod of his head toward the timber above the meadow. A group of about a dozen Indians stood in the shade at the edge of the woods. A few held rifles.

"What do you make of that?" Johnny said.

"Dunno. I hope they're friendly." Caleb waved.

The Indians did not respond. They stood a moment longer, then withdrew into the dark forest.

"You got this animal working in fine order, boss, and it's time for us to move on. We been in one place far longer than any of us likes, so we're on our way." The speaker was Andrew, who always spoke for the others who were generally mute when Andrew was about.

Caleb and Andrew stood on the bank near the bow of the dredge. They had shut down for the day, and the only sound was birdsong and the rustle of dry leaves in the trees up the slope. The other workers stood at the foot of the plank catwalk, chatting and smoking, glancing occasionally toward Caleb and Andrew.

"Are you sure?" said Caleb. "You were in this at the start, and I wanted you to share in the benefits. I think we are about to hit a nice layer of pay dirt."

Andrew smiled. He had heard this hopeful prediction many times, from Caleb and from other bosses. He had been chasing the gold bug too long to put much faith in faith. Anyway, that's not why he and the boys were leaving.

"Well, that's mighty nice of yuh," Andrew said, "but we're beginning to grow moss, so we're headin' out. Cal says he's going to Montana, has a brother in Bozemen. We're bound for Coeur d'Alene. Hear the saloons there are worth lookin' at. And the silver mines there. And there's some nice placers at Warrens, now that they've chased the Chinese out."

Andrew winced. "Uh, sorry boss, but is Mei Lin going to be okay? There's lots of talk."

"You boys have been good workers," Caleb said, "and I hate to see you go. I'll have a little something extra for you before you leave." Caleb looked toward the cabin. "I heard in Stanley about the Warrens business. Don't worry about Mei Lin. She'll be okay."

"Take care of her, boss," Andrew said. "She's some woman. Uh, sorry." Andrew frowned at his own language. He brightened. "That's mighty nice of yuh, the something extra. Just enough to get us to Coeur d'Alene would be welcome.

"One thing I need to tell you," Andrew said. "You know

the big dredge that just began working the Pilgrim Fork?"

"I do. I rode over last week to have a look. Most impressive. I tried to talk with the owner—Bennett, is it?—but his workmen said he was too busy to talk."

"Figures. Point is, he don't want to get to know you. What he wants to do is see your backside. Watch out for him. He wants no competition in the gold-dredging business hereabout. He's a dangerous man."

"How do you know this?" Caleb said.

"I got friends who work for him. They don't like him, say he's a mean son of a bitch and plans to destroy anybody who tries to do any dredging in the country, but he pays well, so they stay. Until they find something better, I'll bet."

Andrew signaled to the workers, and they walked over. The men stepped up in order and shook hands with Caleb. Johnny held back.

"Johnny?" said Caleb.

"I'm staying, if that's okay," Johnny said.

"It sure is," said Caleb. "You can do all the work of these yahoos, can't you?"

Johnny grinned. "Yeah, maybe. I'll try."

"Work him hard, boss. He's got more muscles and brainpower than the bunch of us put together," Andrew said. "Sorry to leave you short-handed, but I figure you'll find good hands in Stanley. There's always men looking for work."

"Don't give it a thought. I'll do all right." The men walked away toward the bunkhouse, all smiles and back-slapping and happy to be unencumbered with steady work.

Short-handed indeed. Now Caleb had only Johnny and himself.

And Mei Lin. Always Mei Lin.

He had lost his workmen, and now this new worry. He already knew more about Roderick Bennett than he wanted to know. Andrew had just confirmed what he had heard from the gossip circle that wasted time sitting around the general store stove, smoking and trading stories.

Bennett was an ambitious man, they reported, not accustomed to sharing anything, whether it be occupation, reputation, or position. He had connections, acquired by persuasion, charm, and bribery, and he would entertain no competition to his ambitions or his reputation.

Mei Lin washed the breakfast dishes at the sink. She stopped and turned to watch Caleb. He stood before the pegs of clothing, seemingly deep in thought, staring at the pegs. He took a jacket from a peg and pulled it on. Lifting a hat from a peg, he started for the door.

"Are you okay, honee?" said Mei Lin. "You very quiet."

Caleb stopped, looked at her. "Yeah, okay, just a bit out of sorts. Stuff to do. Need to go to Stanley for supplies."

Mei Lin walked to him and put her arms around his neck. "I worry when you quiet."

He kissed the top of her head. "I'll be back for supper." He went to the door, opened it, and walked through. She walked to the door and watched him climb up on the wagon, shake the lines, and he was gone.

Mei Lin pushed the pot and skillet to the back of the stove. She went to the door and opened it. In the gloaming, she could hardly make out the road. But it was easy enough to see that it was empty. She stood a moment longer, then withdrew into the cabin.

An hour later, she heard a nickering from the meadow. She jumped up and ran to the door. She jerked it open and looked up the road. She saw nothing at first in the darkness, then heard the brushing sounds of harness and squeaking and soft rattling of wagon wheels. She watched as the gray apparition emerged from the darkness, became a shadow, then materialized as mules and wagon moving slowly down the road.

The mules stopped before the cabin. Caleb was slumped in the driver's seat, sleeping or unconscious. Mei Lin went to the wagon. She shook her head to clear it of the alcohol stench, stepped up on the tongue, and shook him. He roused and mumbled something she did not understand.

"Come down, honee. Careful."

Caleb half opened his eyes and mumbled. "Okay, honey . . . home." He leaned on Mei Lin as he climbed down from the wagon. Once on the ground, he stumbled and she caught him. She put his arm around his shoulders and struggled toward the cabin door, almost falling under his weight.

He stopped and leaned back, staring at Mei Lin from heavy-lidded eyes. "That you, Beth? I'm okay, just a little sleepy." Mei Lin looked up at him.

"I missed you so much, Beth," he mumbled. "Where've you been?" He slumped, reeled, and recovered. "Where's Bobby? Sissie? I . . ." His head drooped. Mei Lin shook him roughly. He raised his head and looked at her through glazed eyes.

"Thank you, ma'am."

Mei Lin tightened her grip on his waist and propelled him to the cabin and up the three steps. On the top step, he stumbled and fell heavily through the doorway to the floor. He sprawled on his stomach, arms outstretched.

Mei Lin helped him stand and guided him toward the bed. He fell headlong onto the blankets. Lifting his feet, she removed his boots, pushed him onto the bed, and covered him. She stood over him a moment, listening to his steady breathing. He was already asleep.

She walked to the open doorway and stood there, staring into the darkness. She sat down on the sill, rubbed her face with both hands, and rested her head on her knees.

The room was bathed in sunshine from the window. Caleb opened his eyes, blinked, and pushed the covers down. He squeezed his eyes shut and rubbed his temples, trying to ease the throbbing in his head. He looked down and saw that he still wore his day clothes.

He sat up slowly and looked about the room, disoriented, as if seeing it for the first time. The bed of hide and skins were on the floor against the opposite wall. The supplies he had bought in Stanley were stacked against the wall near the pantry. Then he saw Mei Lin, standing in the open doorway, leaning against the door facing, with her back to him. She was fully dressed.

"Mei Lin, what happened? I don't remember . . . the wagon . . . the team?"

"Everything done," she said without turning.

He swung his legs to the floor and stood. He wavered, reached back to the bed to steady himself, and walked slowly to the doorway. Mei Lin stepped aside. He walked a few steps into the yard and saw the empty wagon and beyond, the mules grazing in the meadow.

He walked back to the doorway and stepped up beside Mei Lin. He looked again at the hide and skins. "I was stupid. I don't remember. Why are the skins on the floor?"

Mei Lin looked out the door. "You not want me last night. You want . . . Beth."

"Beth," he whispered. He rubbed his face with his hands. "I'm sorry, Mei Lin. I was drunk out of my mind. I remember climbing into the wagon seat and nothing after that. The mules know that road better than I do... Thank you for taking care of me... I'm sorry." He put his arm around her shoulders.

"You must love her very much," Mei Lin said, looking at the forest across the road.

He removed his arm and looked through the open door into the treetops. "Yes, I loved her . . . and Bobby . . . and Sissie. Very much."

Mei Lin looked up at him. She thought that she could almost feel his pain. She put her arms around his waist and pulled him close. He wrapped his arms around her shoulders.

"They will always be part of me," he said. "I'm sorry."
"No, it okay. No sorry. I just want little place for me in your life."

He lifted her face with both hands and kissed her. "A little

place? It's your fault, you know."

She pulled back and frowned. "My fault? How my fault?"

"I need coffee. Can you make it while I try to do something?

about this roaring in my head?"

She forced a smile and kissed him. "Okay, you sit. I do anything you want." She walked to the counter and proceeded to make coffee. He went to the clothes pegs and changed his shirt. Picking up his boots, he sat on the barrel and watched her as he pulled on the boots.

Mei Lin carried two tin coffee cups to the table. She set a cup before Caleb and sat down on the chair.

"Okay," she said, "I listen."

Caleb took a long swallow, eyes closed. He set the cup down, rubbed both of his temples, opened his eyes and leaned back. "In the general store, that's the great rumor mill of Stanley, you know, I heard people talking about this federal agent who's making the rounds in central Idaho, checking papers of the Chinese. Every legal Chinese has to have a residence permit. If they don't, they can be deported."

He studied Mei Lin for a reaction. She looked blankly at him. "I thought about you, and I worried about you," he said, "and I started drinking so I would stop thinking."

Mei Lin studied her coffee cup.

"Do you have a permit?" he said.

She stared at the window, the door, the skins stacked in the corner. "I know you ask someday." She drank from her cup and set it down slowly on the table. She inhaled deeply and stared at her hands on the table.

"Every Chinese come here must have paper telling why come. My owner, he say he merchant. He say I his wife. He have papers. All false, how you say, forge."

"Forged," said Caleb.

"Yes, forge. Papers burn when bad men kill Fuhua and burn cabin. I have no paper. I not . . . legal." She looked up at Caleb. "They make me leave now? Deport me?"

"Rumor says the agent is coming to Stanley," he said. "The sheriff and some townspeople say they will help him find illegal Chinese. Rumor is that the illegal Chinese will be rounded up for deportation."

"I kill myself if they try take me."

Caleb and Johnny sat on the bench at the front of the bunkhouse. Johnny pulled on a pipe, raised his chin, and blew smoke straight up. Caleb watched, surprised. He had never seen Johnny with a pipe.

They sat in silence, looking down on the quiet dredge, the three horses and two mules bunched together in the meadow, the dark Sawtooth range across the valley.

"Everything okay?" said Caleb. "You must be rattling around in the bunkhouse."

"Little lonesome. I'm okay. Don't care much for my own cooking, but I'm getting better." Johnny knocked his pipe out against the bench.

Caleb looked up at the sky, cloudless, deep blue. "Warming up," he said. "Not likely to get hot, though. Autumn's coming."

They sat in silence a long moment. Finally, Johnny turned to Caleb. "What's on your mind, boss?"

Caleb spoke without looking at him. "Johnny, I want to ask a favor. I want you to watch what's going on at the house. I came home the other night from Stanley dead drunk. I don't get drunk often, usually just when something's going on that I can't deal with. Sometimes I just get quiet and mellow. Sometimes I'm violent and hurt people.

"This last time, I was just a stumbling drunk, and Mei Lin took care of me. But it could have been otherwise. And I would never get over it. Would you keep a watch on the house when I'm away and when I get home? If you see or hear anything happening down there, would you come down and check?"

Johnny stared at his shoes, pondered, pushed the cold pipe into a shirt pocket, turned to Caleb. "I'll tell you what. I'll come down, and if I see you abusing Mei Lin, drunk or no, I'll beat hell out of you, tie you up, and stick your feet in the hot stove. Will that do it?"

Caleb recoiled, surprised, looked at Johnny. Johnny's face was hard, and Caleb wasn't sure how to read his look. Then Johnny smiled.

Caleb relaxed, smiled. "Well, that sure would get my attention."

"Boss, you couldn't hurt Mei Lin if you was drunk as a skunk. I know that for a fact."

Caleb stood, put a hand on Johnny's shoulder, and patted it. He walked down the hill toward the dredge.

Caleb stood on the bank at the dredge bow, watching the buckets dig into the subsoil. He figured that the bucketline was near bedrock and almost ready for repositioning.

He started when he saw two Indians standing on the pond edge not twenty feet away. He had been so intent on watching the bucketline and listening for the telltale scraping on bedrock that he had not seen them come up. They were lean and dressed in a combination of soiled skins and white men's worn clothing.

The Indians watched Caleb. One made eating motions. "Hungry," he said.

Caleb pondered. He raised his arm in greeting or acknowledgment. He wasn't sure what he meant by the gesture. He assumed they spoke little English and motioned for them to sit. They sat down slowly without taking their eyes off him.

Caleb walked up the slope to the cabin and went inside. After a few minutes, he came out with two plates of food. A slice of pork, a chunk of bread, and boiled potatoes.

Mei Lin had walked out with him and stopped at the corner of the cabin. She watched him walk down the slope toward the dredge.

Caleb handed the plates to the Indians. They nodded to him and took the plates. They ate slowly. And with dignity, Caleb thought.

When they had finished, they stood, still holding the empty plates. Caleb reached for the plates, and they handed them to him. They nodded and, without another word, withdrew and walked up the hill toward the woods.

Caleb watched them go. He shook his head and walked up toward the cabin. Mei Lin still stood beside the cabin, watching the Indians disappear into the forest.

At first light, Caleb walked around the corner of the cabin and stopped. Three Indians stood on the bank near the dredge. They looked straight at him. The morning was still, and bird-song was the only sound. He walked down the slope.

When he reached the Indians, each raised an arm in greeting. Two of the men were those he had fed yesterday. They stood behind the third Indian.

"We work. Help," the third Indian said.

Caleb frowned, pondered. *Now what? Indians working a dredge?* "Well, I need help. I can't pay much."

"No need much. Food and little bit money."

"Okay," Caleb said. He smiled and extended his hand. Each Indian shook his hand in turn.

Caleb and the three Indians sat on the ground near the sluice. Four shovels lay on the ground nearby. Bare soil, some of it still wet, on the sides of the sluice revealed where they had been repairing the sides and cleaning the channel bottom.

Caleb pulled sandwiches from a canvas bag and handed them to the Indians. He offered the open bag, and they took out apples and grapes.

"You are Sheepeaters?" Caleb said to the spokesman of the group.

"That white man name for us. We call ourselves Tukudeka."

The Tukudeka were a branch of Eastern Shoshone. They had lived in peace in central Idaho for centuries, subsisting on game, notably mountain sheep, and gathering wild nuts and berries. They had not forcefully resisted the intrusion into their lands by miners and ranchers, but they had fallen on hard times when their neighbors, the Bannocks, skillfully shifted blame for killings and raids from themselves to the peaceful Tukudeka.

In the 1870s, the Sheepeaters were accused by whites of some scattered killings: settlers, ranchers, prospectors, and a party of Chinese miners. There was no evidence for any of the charges. The Bannocks probably killed the whites, and it was widely held at the time that white men dressed as Indians likely killed the Chinese.

Army leaders weren't too concerned with evidence. The result was the so-called Sheepeater War of 1879. In a campaign of six months in rough terrain against an enemy who knew their country, the army finally won with the surrender of a small band of combatants. The subdued Sheepeaters broke into small bands that thereafter lived in poverty.

"Where do you live?" Caleb said.

"Two canyon that way." He pointed to the west over the near ridge. "About three-hour walk. You come visit?"

The three Sheepeaters had returned to their village immediately on being hired, but they had not gone again during the following week. They had set up a small camp in the forest above the meadow. They had only a rude shelter that was fronted by a stone fire circle. Caleb had provided cooking utensils and food supplies. He had heard occasional shots deep in the forest as they supplemented his provisions with small game.

"Yes," Caleb said. "I would like that. I will come soon. What is your name?"

"Tindoor."

"Tindoor," Caleb repeated. The Indian nodded.

Caleb and Mei Lin rode behind Tindoor in the forest on

what appeared to be a game trail. The Indian apparently was a rider, but did not know what to make of the mule at first. He had seen army mules in harness pulling wagons, but he had never seen one saddled. But all went well, and he was content. When questioned by Caleb, he explained that his band had eaten most of their horses in recent years. Only a few remained for use in hunting.

The trail widened and opened to a clearing in the forest. The village was a cluster of half a dozen small cabins, shacks constructed of logs and castoff boards, and a dozen tipis of worn, frayed hides. Three of the cabins had round tin chimneys, but no smoke issued from them. Fire circles of stones fronted tipis. Thin spirals of smoke rose from a couple of the fire pits.

The ground of the village was swept clean, and firewood was stacked in small piles behind each dwelling. Caleb saw a deer carcass hung from a low limb behind one of the shacks. It was little more than a skeleton.

Tindoor followed Caleb's glance. "Deer go away," Tindoor said. "Too many people 'round Stanley. Now cold come." Caleb nodded. "Three men work Stanley, four men work on ranches, but not much money. We have garden there." He pointed at the garden at the back of the village.

In spring and summer, the garden might have borne good crops, but now it was mostly bare. Only some cabbages and squash remained, a few beets and onions. It looked a scant supply for a village of fifty people.

Caleb and Mei Lin wandered about the village, followed by Tindoor. The shy women smiled, withdrawing into their dwellings and into themselves. A few small children followed them, their eyes large and cheeks sunken. All were dressed in little more than rags, though they appeared clean.

Caleb and Mei Lin said their thanks to Tindoor and walked toward their horses. Mei Lin stopped and looked back at the village to see the people watching them leave. She turned back to Caleb.

"Honee, they hungry."

"Yes." He stopped, pondered. "Get the horses." He walked back to Tindoor while Mei Lin untied the reins of Buck and Chica and the mule. She watched Caleb talking with Tindoor and two more men in the center of the village.

Caleb sat on the seat of the wagon, holding the lines of the team. The wagon was loaded with boxes and bags and cooking gear. Behind the wagon, Tindoor, riding Buck, and Mei Lin on Chica drove ten cows and a young bull. Three of the cows were heavy with calves.

Caleb pulled up at the edge of the Sheepeater village. Men and women and children came out, shouting greetings. They wanted to help Caleb down from the wagon, but he smiled and waved them off. The women admired the nervous cows, exclaiming softly among themselves and gently rubbing the backs and sides of the cows. The men and children began carrying the supplies and utensils from the wagon to cabins and tipis.

Tindoor dismounted and tied the reins of the borrowed horse to the back of the wagon. He joined Caleb and Mei Lin in the village yard.

"You've got some grass here," said Caleb, "but you'll eventually want to put the cows on my land. I have plenty of meadow, and the woods above should keep pretty free of snow. They'll find protection there. You saw the spring at the edge of the woods. I don't think it will freeze. Be careful with the three mother cows. They will calve during winter, so keep them close.

"You can build a shelter at the edge of the woods above

the pond. I have boards. Build it big enough for the cows and a few of you, in case you have to stay with them any length of time." Tindoor nodded with each instruction.

Caleb shook Tindoor's hand and turned to walk toward Mei Lin. When they saw he was leaving, a dozen villagers followed close behind, saying their thanks in their own language and broken English.

A woman who had walked silently behind Caleb touched his hand. "Thank you, mister." She turned to Mei Lin and touched her hand. "Thank you, missy." She turned and, with arms outstretched, ushered the others back to the village.

"You good man, Cay-leb honee Willis," Mei Lin said.

Caleb and Mei Lin sat on the driver's seat of the wagon. The wagon tongue occasionally clattered as the mules walked easily down the narrow road on a slight downgrade.

"Keep the lines just a bit loose," Caleb said. "If you keep them too tight, you confuse the mules. They might think you want them to stop." Caleb reached over to adjust Mei Lin's hold on the lines.

She pulled her hands away. "Okay, you tell me. I know now. I can do." He smiled and pulled back. Then his face clouded as he remembered young Sissie's frequent response to his instructions: "I can do, I can do." He shook his head.

Mei Lin noticed. "Okay?"

"Yeah, okay."

They rode in silence. Caleb decided that he could hereafter trust Mei Lin with driving the team. Next he would teach her to put the team in harness. She should learn it in one lesson. He had gradually come to realize that she was exceptionally bright and a quick learner, traits that were hidden to him by her Chinklish.

"Honee, you mention winter to Indians. You never talk about winter before. What we do in winter?"

He looked at her and said nothing. He looked ahead at the road and the forest and the Sawtooths. He had said nothing about winter because he hadn't decided what they would do in winter. Not for sure.

Some miners who could afford it closed up operations and wintered in Boise. Some took up rough accommodations in Stanley. Some who had built cabins on their claims stayed and toughed it out.

Maybe he had said nothing because he was struggling with a prospect that could solve one quandary while casting him into darkness.

10 YOU JUST DESCRIBED ONE OF MY GIRLS!

Caleb stood in front of the cabin with Andrew, Cal, and Larry who had just ridden up and hallooed from the yard. They still held their horses' reins. There were handshakes and back-slapping all around. Mei Lin stood smiling in the cabin doorway.

"I'm glad to see you boys!" Caleb said. "But why? What happened to you up north?"

"Well," Andrew said. "No gold, no prospects. That's the whole story. You think you could use us again?"

"I can indeed. We're hitting some promising sign. Now we'll add a few hours to the day and see if we can make it pay."

Andrew smiled. Same old story, but he almost believed it. He wanted to believe it, coming from this boss that he liked above all he had worked for.

Caleb turned to Cal, frowning. "Cal, I thought you went to Montana. Bozeman, was it?"

Cal ducked his head, looked up. "Yeah, didn't work out. Uh, I don't much care for, uh, my, uh, brother's wife."

"Yeah, that was really a surprise," Andrew said. "Larry and I just rode into Stanley yesterday, and what do you know, we see Cal at th' Trap. How's that for a lucky chance? Anyway, we told him we're coming back to your place and asked him if he wanted to come with us. And here we are."

"And I'm glad to see the lot of you," said Caleb.

"We appreciate you taking us back on," said Andrew. "Now we'd best get that bunkhouse in order." The three men started to mount.

"Hang on, I need to tell you this," Caleb said. The men stopped, holding their reins. "The old boys at the general store gossip circle tell me that Bennett on the Pilgrim Fork is getting real feisty and is making plans to do exactly what you said before, to control dredging in the basin. They say he is going to get real nasty."

"Bring it on!" said Larry. "It was gettin' real boring up north. You got someplace we can do some target practice?"

With the addition of the three experienced men, the dredge operated from first light to dusk. They were finding gold, but not in large quantities. One more cut, Caleb said. One more cut. Again and again.

Caleb walked with Tindoor in the meadow. He counted the cows. Eleven. They had made the adjustment to the new pasture handily. The Sheepeaters had driven the cows back to Caleb's meadow just days after receiving them.

"Bull good," said Tindoor. "I think we have more calves in spring."

"That's good."

"Our people better now with more to eat. Everybody say thank you." Caleb nodded. "People want you come visit village. Can you come?"

"I would like that," Caleb said. "Tomorrow?"

Caleb rode over the wooded ridge and down the trail through the meadow. It had been a pleasant visit in the

Sheepeater village. He had been welcomed as a friend and benefactor. He was quite pleased with himself. He was also embarrassed that he was so puffed up.

Caleb hit the road and continued slowly down the slope toward the cabin. He looked toward the meadow when a mule whinnied a welcome. Caleb looked back at the cabin. He had become accustomed to Mei Lin's bursting from the doorway at the announcement of his coming by whatever animal saw his approach.

But she did not burst from the doorway. He rose in the saddle and looked around the cabin, to the corral, to the tree where they often sat, eating lunch or simply meditating, searching the valley and the Sawtooths. In the distance, he saw three workmen on the dredge, but no Mei Lin. That was fine. He had told her never to go to the dredge unless he was there.

He frowned and drooped. *Have I become that dependent on her? Of course not. Not dependent, just accustomed.*

He pulled up at the corral. He dismounted and removed the bag behind his saddle, tied the reins to a pole. He resisted the temptation to call her. That would be too much like calling his horse, or his dog, if he had a dog.

He walked to the cabin. The door was open. He had not noticed when he rode up. He was irritated, just for a moment. He had told her many times to close the door to keep the bugs out. He walked in and set the bag on the floor in front of the pantry.

He looked around. Nothing was out of place. *Where is she?* He admitted to himself that he missed her greeting. He wanted her here. Now he admitted that he was worried.

He strode down the hill, almost running, to the dredge. He walked along the bank to view the sides. Larry and Johnny saw him.

"What's up, boss?" Johnny said.

Caleb hesitated. "Nothing," he said, and turned to walk up the hill. He stopped, turned back, and shouted. "Have you seen Mei Lin?"

"Hadn't seen her since yesterday," Johnny said.

"Anybody been 'round the place?" Caleb said.

"Didn't see anybody. Heard horses, hooves anyway, 'bout noon, but it might've been the mules in the meadow. They been running around like a couple uh young 'uns. Didn't see any riders."

Mules? He walked around the cabin and looked up to the pasture. The mules and Chica grazed side by side.

Caleb frowned. *Where is she? Walking? Not likely. She never walks when she can ride Chica.* He walked back to the cabin. Inside, he looked at Mei Lin's things. It didn't take long. She had few things. He felt an uncharacteristic flood of guilt. He shrugged it off and decided that nothing was missing.

He stepped to the doorway and stared at the sky. *Mei Lin, where are you?* He looked down, pondering. *Where do I look?*

Wait a minute! He stepped off the doorjamb to the ground. He reached down and picked up a card. The picture on the baseball card showed a pink-cheeked young man wearing a gray shirt with a black, buttoned collar, the word "PITTSBURG" across the front of the shirt. At the bottom of the card, the words, "WAGNER, PITTSBURG." He flipped the card away, thought better of it, picked it up, and pushed it into a pocket.

He went back into the cabin, walked to the chest under the window, and opened it. Pushing a cloth aside, he looked at the pistol. It was the first time he had seen it since coming to Stanley early last spring.

He had hoped he was finished with guns. Oh, he knew that he would have to deal occasionally with rustics who would not let him go his own way. He figured he would likely have to resort to violence to protect himself and what was his. But he hoped he was finished with guns. He wrapped his hand around the grip and pulled the six-shooter from the holster.

He remembered the old stoved-up cowboy who had given it to him in a Deadwood saloon. The old man had looked a hundred years old, but he was probably not over sixty. Bent, bewhiskered, his cheeks more deeply creased than the clothes that hung loosely on his wasted frame, he had helped Caleb up after a couple of toughs had beaten him and left him gasping on the floor.

The old man had helped him to a chair, pulled the bandanna from his own neck, and wiped the blood from Caleb's mouth. He had sat down heavily in his own chair, as if his legs could no longer bear the weight of his body. Caleb thanked him and said he wished they had finished the job. The old cowboy had said that he didn't mean that. He said that Caleb had fought too hard to want to die.

You're a good man, the old cowboy said, I can tell a good man when I see one, and you need to live, for your own sake and to help rub out the bad sumbitches, like the ones that beat up on you.

But you need some help, he said. I see you got nothing on your belt but britches. The old man leaned back and unbuckled his gun belt. He folded the belt over the holster and pistol and handed it to Caleb. I don't need this anymore, he said. I try to use it, and it'll just get me killed. It's done me good service, when I was younger and fit, and I'm passing it to you. I'm happy to know that it's going to a good man who'll use it for good. You need to learn to use it.

Caleb looked at the belt. When he didn't take it, the old man reached over and laid it in his lap. He stood, patted Caleb on the shoulder, and walked toward the door, bent, wobbling, reaching for anything, chair backs, bar, ceiling post, to support him as he walked.

Caleb had learned to use the six-shooter, and it had become part of him. He had worn it like he wore his boots. He had even come to like it, this Colt Peacemaker forty-four. It had once had a shiny nickel finish, but now the barrel was scratched, and one of the ivory grips had lost a chunk from long, rough use. But the bore was still as bright as ever, and the single action smooth as silk.

Caleb spun the cylinder, confirmed that five chambers were loaded and that the hammer rested on the empty chamber. He pushed the six-shooter into the holster and strapped it on his waist. He picked up a sack of cartridges from the chest and emptied it into a pocket.

He reached into the chest again, pushed the fleece coat aside, the wool blanket, the spare long Johns, and pulled out the rifle in its scabbard. It was an old Winchester forty-four. He had bought it in Stanley just about a month after arriving. An old fellow at the general store gossip circle had been bragging about his new Winchester 30-30 and asked around if anybody could use his old gun. Comes with the scabbard, he said.

The oldster had reached around behind him, picked up the rifle in its scabbard, and showed them to the group. They passed them around, handling the rifle, their comments showing evidence that they knew guns. Caleb hefted the rifle, worked the lever action, smooth, ran his hand over the clean, worn leather scabbard.

They suited Caleb, and he bought them on the spot. He needed the rifle so he could hunt for the larder. He was glad to get a rifle that was the same caliber as his six-shooter so he would have to buy only one type of cartridge.

He shook his head, and he was back in his cabin. Laying the scabbard on the table, he went to the pantry. He took out jerky, a couple of apples, a chunk of bread, and a slice of ham. He wrapped the ham and bread in a clean cloth and stuffed everything into his saddlebags.

Carrying the filled saddlebags and rifle scabbard, he walked to the corral. Buck shook his reins in recognition. Caleb tied the saddlebags behind the saddle and attached the scabbard. He mounted, drummed the horse with his heels, and galloped up the road.

The Rat Trap was almost empty in midafternoon. Four men sat at a table near the wall opposite the bar. A middle-aged woman stood behind one of the men, fondling his ear. The man looked up, frowned, and brushed her hand away.

Across the room, at the back in a darkened corner, two men sat slouched over their drinks on the table, talking softly.

The saloon madam stood behind the bar, talking with the bartender who was bent over, washing glasses, displaying the bald spot on top of his head.

The outside door flew open, and Caleb stepped in. He looked around, his eyes adjusting to the darkened interior. The four card players looked up at Caleb. Two of the men laid their cards slowly on the table. The men spoke softly to each other, without taking their eyes off Caleb. They saw his six-shooter, the first time they had seen him armed.

The woman standing behind the card players stepped back. Caleb recognized her from his last visit to the Rat Trap when he had taken Mei Lin.

The two men at the table at the back stood slowly, hands

near pistols.

Caleb noted all this and turned to look at the bar. The bartender and madam stood side by side, watching him.

"You're not welcome here, mister," she said.

"Where is she?"

"Who?"

Caleb tensed. "Don't mess with me, you dried-up old whore! Where is she?"

"Walk out of here now, cowboy, or you ain't gonna walk out at all!"

Caleb drew his pistol, cocked it, and pointed it at her. "Talk to me, grandma!"

She was more nervous than her belligerent tone suggested. She cut her eyes toward the back of the room. Caleb turned to see the two men at the back table standing. One of the men held his pistol leveled on him. Caleb pointed and fired, dropping him. The other man at the table took a step backward and held his arms out, showing that he had no intention of drawing.

Caleb whirled around to see the madam raising a shotgun in his direction. He leveled his six-shooter at her before she could bring it up.

"Drop it, Polly, or you're dead," Caleb said. Wide-eyed and jaw agape, the madam dropped the shotgun to the floor with a clatter. She babbled incoherently, something about don't shoot, I'm not armed.

The bartender, wide-eyed and hands high over his head, cut his eyes at his proprietor. He turned back to Caleb and grinned.

The saloon was quiet as death. Smoke from the gunshot still drifted about the room, like fog in the shafts of sunlight from the windows. The four card players stood at their table, watching him, cards forgotten. The woman had disappeared. The man at the back table had not moved, except to lower his arms. He still watched Caleb.

Caleb looked around. He slowly pushed the six-shooter into the holster. He walked to the door and through it, closing it behind him.

Outside on the plank walk, he looked around, frowning, pondering, squinting in the bright sunshine. He saw the middle-aged prostitute standing on the walk near the side of the saloon. She beckoned urgently to him.

Caleb strode to her. She took his sleeve and pulled him into the alley between the saloon and the adjacent feed store. They hurried down the alley and stopped near the back of the saloon.

"Listen!" she said. "Mei Lin—"

At the shot, Caleb drew his pistol, pointed toward the shooter on the front walk, and fired in one rapid, continuous motion. The shooter was blown backward and collapsed. Caleb holstered the six-shooter and bent over the prostrate woman.

Caleb held her head. Her eyes blinked rapidly.

"Boise," she said.

"Boise? Where? Where in Boise?"

"Bo- . . . Boise." She gasped. "Ma-ma-datter." Her eyes fluttered, and she exhaled in a long sigh. He gently closed her eyes, still holding her head, and looked around. He wanted to do something for this good woman, this whore who had died well, but he knew that he could do nothing. He lowered her head to the ground.

He stood, walked to the saloon front, and looked down at her killer. His eyes misted, and he kicked the corpse violently. "Goddam son of a bitch," he mumbled. He kicked him hard again.

He looked up and glared at three men in front of the

saloon door, watching him. When they made eye contact, they rushed back inside, bumping and stumbling over each other. The door banged shut, echoing in the still air.

Caleb walked to his horse. He untied the reins and looked around. The street was empty. He grasped the saddle horn and stared at the seat.

"Ma-ma-datter?" he said aloud.

He swung up into the saddle and kicked Buck into a gallop.

Caleb rode at a steady lope on a lightly traveled wagon road on the valley floor. Hillsides on each side of the valley wore a patchwork of green conifers and deciduous trees in autumn color. Caleb saw nothing but the road ahead.

He sat on the ground, leaning against a tree trunk. Chewing on a biscuit, he watched Buck drinking from the shallow pool at the base of the small spring.

He looked up. The cloud layer had darkened and lowered in the past hour. Standing and stretching, he walked to Buck and pulled a yellow slicker from the pack behind the saddle.

Caleb rode at a lope, hunched over against the hard rain, his hat pulled down, slicker buttoned at the top and billowing behind.

The flames of the small fire cast a warm glow that described a circle of light that included Buck, hobbled and head hanging, and Caleb, lying beside the fire and covered with the slicker, his head resting on his saddle. His eyes were open, and he stared into the flames.

Caleb rode at a lope on a road that was little more than a wide trail in the forest, a sinuous narrow passage through the mountains. When the road turned upward, Buck wheezed and labored, and Caleb slowed the horse to a walk.

He rode into Boise at dusk. It wasn't a big town, as

towns go, but big for Idaho. He walked his horse through a residential district on the north side into the town center.

Riding down a street with shuttered shops on both sides, he turned into a cross street, up the next street lined with shops, a saloon here, another across the street, a grocer where the proprietor was moving crates of fruits and vegetables inside.

He rode aimlessly, not sure what he was looking for. Rounding a corner, he pulled Buck up so hard the horse backed.

"What th—" A dozen men and a few women stared at a strange vehicle that appeared to have dropped down on the Boise street from another planet.

Caleb looked at his first motorcar. The people walked around the car, wide-eyed, some talking softly, others laughing loudly. They wanted urgently to touch the gleaming black body, but every time a hand reached out toward the car, a burly middle-aged man in a severe black suit standing nearby smiled and raised a restraining hand. The hand belied the smile.

The seat of upholstered leather was worthy of a sitting room in a fine house. A gleaming gold-colored lantern was fixed to each side of the curved front dash. Four white pneumatic tires under narrow fenders complemented the black finish of the vehicle. The only other color on the chassis was a maroon panel on each side of the seat.

Caleb walked his horse around the apparition and continued down the street. The car, absurd or portent, forced him to think of the future. *What is coming for me?*

He shook his head and rode on. At the corner, he stopped and spoke to a man dressed in work clothes who appeared to be one who would know something about saloons and brothels. He asked him whether he had seen a young Chinese woman who didn't seem to belong. She would be scared, accompanied by one or two toughs. No, he hadn't seen such a woman.

Caleb rode on, stopping walkers and riders to ask the same questions. Most were not receptive to his queries. They were not friendly, not forthcoming, even suspicious of this stranger.

And why should he be looking for a particular young Chinese woman? There were ample brothels in Boise where surely he could find what he's looking for. Those who gave him any response at least affirmed that they had not seen the woman he described.

His crisscrossing pattern of riding the streets was taking him farther from genteel Boise toward a rougher district. On a dark street, he saw a staggering figure, a bit shabby, but dressed in clothes that at one time were high style. This man surely knows saloons. Caleb pulled Buck up beside the man and leaned over.

"My good man," Caleb said, "where would I find a first-rate saloon? One that has a stable of first-rate, pretty women?"

The man stopped, weaved, and looked up at Caleb. He furrowed his brow and pursed his lips, deep in thought. "Hmm. A first-rate saloon with first-rate whores." He looked down at his feet, staggered a bit. "Now, if I was looking for a first-rate saloon with first-rate whores, I would want to look at a goodly number of saloons that fit that description so I could do a comparison." Hic.

"You best ride two streets that way." He pointed. "That takes you to Main Street. There are . . ." He wrinkled his forehead, searching, counting on the fingers of both hands, "seven saloons of varying quality on one block. I would have a look there if I was looking for a first-rate saloon with first-rate whores." He weaved, grabbed a lamppost for support and looked at the gutter. "Or any kind uv saloon, akshooly."

Caleb leaned down and offered a coin. The man looked up, surprised, and took the coin. Caleb touched his hat and rode off in the direction indicated. The drunk watched him a moment, then looked again at the coin. He sauntered off, smiling, the evening having been salvaged.

Caleb rode two blocks on the dark street and turned onto Main Street. He rode slowly down the middle of the street, then pulled Buck up so abruptly, the horse backed down before Caleb got control.

There it was: The Mad Hatter.

He walked his horse to the hitching rail, dismounted, and tied the reins. He stepped up on the sidewalk, stopped and looked around, up and down the street, empty, and walked to the door.

Caleb stopped just inside the door and looked around as his eyes adjusted to the dimly lit room. The half-dozen card players at a round table glanced up at him, then returned to their cards and drinks and the two women that stood behind them. The women continued looking at him. One of the women smiled.

Caleb walked slowly to the bar. Two men at the far end leaned over their drinks, talking softly. The bartender, wearing a soiled apron over a bulging gut, waddled over and stood silently before Caleb.

The bartender's countenance said: I don't give a damn whether you order or not, so let's have it. Caleb smiled and ordered a whiskey.

The madam, standing behind the piano, had watched Caleb from his entrance. She strolled over and stopped beside him. She leaned her back against the bar. He looked idly at her, repelled by her painted face and blood-red lips. He turned back to his glass and sipped.

"New here, cowboy? First time I seen you."

"Yep, passing through," this while studying the amber liquid in his glass.

"You look a mite tired."

"Yep. I am that."

"I can fix that. Fancy a poke?"

He smiled thinly, sighed, turned the slightest toward her. "Now that would help, that's for sure."

"What strikes your fancy?"

Caleb replied, without enthusiasm, tired, looking into his glass. "Young, pretty, small tits, a little spirit. I like Orientals."

Madam perked up, wide-eyed. "Old son, you just described one of my girls! Oh, you will like her!"

"You're on," he said, looking into his glass, swirling the whiskey.

"C'mon," she said, "finish your drink. "Oh, you're going to love this girl!" He raised the glass and emptied it.

Madam took his glass, set it on the bar, then tucked her arm under his and propelled him toward the stairs. At the foot, she stopped and pointed up the stairway.

"Second door on the left. You wait there, and I'll send up your angel."

He nodded, looked up the stair, and climbed slowly, each step announced with a creaking protest. At the top, he passed the first door, ignoring the thumping cadence of the bedsprings. Stopping at the next door, he looked back toward the stairs, opened the door, stepped into the room. He closed the door behind him, listened for the closing click.

He looked around the room. Besides the bed, there were only a chest of drawers and a narrow wardrobe. The bed was rusted cast iron, supporting a thin, sagging mattress. The sheets surprisingly were clean and neatly tucked under the mattress. Lacy curtains, stained but clean, stirred before the open window.

He stood quietly, facing the hall door. Waiting.

A couple of minutes later, he heard a commotion in the hall, a shuffling and scraping. The knob turned, the door opened halfway, and he saw Mei Lin in the dark corridor. She wore a red dress, white lace at the knee-length hem and at the wrists of the long sleeves, all topped with a collar of pink lace and feathers. Surely it was somebody's castoff. If he weren't so tense, he would have laughed.

Mei Lin struggled against two men who held her tightly by her arms, pushing her toward the room's open door.

"You ni ma de, that hurts! Let me go, chou wang ba! You stink, wang ba dan asshole! Take your stinking hands off me!"

Caleb assumed that Mei Lin was pummeling her captors with Chinese expletives. The English expletives he understood only too well. He fought the impulse to smile.

One of the men released Mei Lin and stood grumbling in the hall. He rubbed his cheek that was marked with two long scratches. The other man pushed Mei Lin through the door, still holding her arms tightly. She turned around toward the room, her face full of anger, prepared to face her new tormentor.

She saw Caleb. Her eyes opened wide, and her jaw dropped. He frowned at her. She sobered, recognizing, comprehending.

She jerked an arm from her captor's grasp and took a swing at him. He ducked, laughing. He grabbed her again, pushed her into the room.

"Hao le, sumbitch, zho kal! Wang ba dan!"

The man released her. "Good luck, cowboy. Watch out for your pecker. She's a mean 'un." He grinned and withdrew, closing the door behind him.

Caleb and Mei Lin waited for the door to click shut. She lunged for him, and they embraced. Tears came and streamed down her face. She clung tightly to him.

"I know you come, honee," softly, almost a whisper. "I knew you come." Caleb kissed her and wiped her tears with the palm of his hand.

Caleb put a finger to his lips, drew his six-shooter, pulled back the hammer, and walked to the door. He opened it slowly, stepped into the dark hall. Mei Lin followed.

They walked slowly down the stairs, each creaking step announcing their progress. Caleb held the pistol behind him.

The madam, standing at the end of the bar, watched the pair as they descended the stairs. Two men standing in front of the bar near her turned to watch.

Caleb and Mei Lin reached the bottom of the stairs and stopped. Caleb glanced around the room.

The madam took a drag of her cigar and blew a stream of smoke over her head. "Well, you surprise me, cowboy. Bit quick on the trigger, huh?"

"You said it, Polly." He showed the pistol to her and the room. She and the two men beside her straightened and stepped back.

"Now you and all your lapdogs just step aside," Caleb said, "and we'll be on our way."

At a sound, Caleb looked toward the end of the bar and saw him, the man called Jack. He leaned on the bar, an unlighted cigarette dangling from his lips. Jack struck a match on the bar and lit the cigarette. He glanced up to the balcony above the stairs. A man stood at the balcony rail, pistol pointing at Caleb.

"You ain't going nowhere," Jack said.

Caleb flung Mei Lin aside, swung his pistol up, and fired. The shooter on the balcony fell backward as his shot went wild.

Caleb whirled to see Jack aiming at him. They fired simultaneously. Jack crashed back against the bar and slid to the floor.

Caleb turned back to the bar and saw the madam bringing up a shotgun in his direction. Caleb fired, and the woman was blown backward, the blast from the shotgun opening a hole in the ceiling.

Caleb surveyed the room, holding the six-shooter in front of him. Patrons stood and sat, tensed, all watching, jaws hanging. Caleb reached back for Mei Lin without taking his eyes off the room. She placed her hand in his, and they walked toward the saloon door, Caleb looking right and left at each step.

11 DON'T LET ME CATCH YOU ALONE

Mei Lin rode behind Caleb, holding him tightly around his waist. Her head rested on his back, and she rocked back and forth with the motion of the loping horse.

Hours passed. Caleb turned often to watch the back trail and listen for any sounds of being followed. He occasionally pulled Buck up, to listen and let the horse blow.

He set off again at a slow lope. Mei Lin adjusted her hold on Caleb's waist and felt a wetness. She looked at her hand. In the bright moonlight, she saw blood.

"You hurt."

"It's okay. You'll tend to it later. Everything's okay now."

They rode. After a half hour, Caleb weaved in the saddle, almost falling forward before catching himself.

"Stop."

"Later," he said, groggy, weaving.

"You goddam listen me! You stop now!"

He turned off the trail and pulled Buck to a stop. Mei Lin jumped off. She grasped his arms to help him down. He slid off, stumbled, almost fell. She helped him sit on the ground, then lowered him slowly to lie down.

She pulled his shirt from his trousers, revealing a

bloody gash in his left side at the waist. Ripping her dress at the hem, she folded the piece into a pad. She then ripped off both of her sleeves at the shoulder to make a tie, placed the pad on the gash and tied the joined sleeves around his waist.

She pressed the pad gently to stem the blood flow. He winced, then relaxed. His eyes closed, and his head turned slowly to the side.

"Honee? Honee? You still here? You hear me? Honee?"

"Yeah, I'm still here, my angel," he said softly.

"We stay here a while. Nobody come, I think."

They rode at a slow lope. Bright moonlight cast shadows of the towering pines across the trail. The shadow of horse and riders moved across the pattern of tree shadow. Mei Lin held Caleb with her arms around his body, her hands on his chest, more to support him than herself. He occasionally made a soft moaning sound. Mei Lin tightened her lips, knowing he was in pain.

When the road and the fields were just beginning to be described by the coming of day, Mei Lin reached up and took the reins, pulling Buck off the road and into the woods.

Caleb stirred. "What?" he said.

"We stop a while. Rest." She pulled Buck up, slid off, and helped him down. She supported him as he slowly kneeled and lay down on the ground.

He exhaled heavily. "Oh, this feels good," he said softly. "We may winter here."

She loosened the tie around his chest and checked the pad. It was completely soaked. She ripped another strip from her dress and made another pad. She applied the pad and replaced the tie. She lay beside him, holding his hand.

At midmorning, they were on the road again. They

alternately walked Buck and rode at a lope, saving the horse that was not accustomed to carrying two riders. They pulled off at secluded spots where they could rest in woods or behind outcroppings, unseen from the road. They nibbled on the remnants of the bread, apples, and jerky that Caleb had stowed in his saddlebag.

In the afternoon, the sun disappeared behind a gray overcast. A dark cloud appeared in the north and moved overhead. The breeze freshened and smelled of rain. Mei Lin pulled Buck off the trail and rode across a meadow to the edge of a birch copse.

She slid off the horse, steadied Caleb in the saddle, and walked into the wood. Here was an outcropping with a sharp overhang, almost a shallow cave, that should do.

She walked back to Caleb and led the horse to the overhang. Helping him to dismount, she supported him and guided him to the shelter. She held him as he kneeled, sat, and lay down. Kneeling beside him, she gently pushed him as far under the overhang as possible. Tying Buck's reins to a nearby limb, she removed the saddle and blanket, dragged the saddle to Caleb, and pushed it under his head.

She had hardly settled him when the rain began. Scattered, large drops, then a downpour. Mei Lin lay down beside him. She put the saddle blanket over him and scooted close against him, her arm over his chest. Rivulets of water dripped off the overhang, splashing on the ground a foot from where Mei Lin lay.

She was awakened by birdsong. The wet tops of tall grasses at the edge of their cave sanctuary sparkled in the bright sunshine. She reached for Caleb and touched his face. His eyes opened, blinked.

"You can ride, honee?"

He sighed. "Yeah, I can ride." She sat up. "If you'll help

me," he said. She placed her hand under his shoulder to help him rise. "With a kiss." She smiled and leaned over and kissed him.

"Okay," he said, "help me up, and we're off." She put a hand under his shoulders and lifted him. He squeezed his eyes shut and winced in pain.

"Sorry, honee. Almost home."

She stood and pulled him up slowly. She helped him walk to a sapling, which he held for support. "You stay here," she said. "I saddle Buck." Picking up the blanket and saddle, she carried them to the horse, saddled him, and came back for Caleb.

"Okay, ready," she said. "Almost home." She helped him mount, then swung up behind him.

They rode on a familiar trail now that branched off the Stanley road. Mei Lin had kept up a steady chatter with Caleb for the past couple of hours, fearing that he was drifting. She was unsure whether he was sleepy or failing. One more rise, and they would see their valley, the dredge and cabin, the corrals and meadow.

Before they topped the last rise, they saw a thin spiral of smoke ahead. Caleb kicked Buck ahead, and he galloped up the hill. At the top, Caleb pulled him to a sliding stop.

"Oh, god, Mei Lin. Oh, god." They looked down on the dredge, partially burned, still smoldering, the exposed frame of the equipment housing reaching up like bare ribs.

Mei Lin kicked Buck ahead. "You no worry 'bout god. You listen me. I get you to bed."

By the time they reached the cabin, Caleb was slumped in the saddle, weaving and in danger of falling. Mei Lin held him with one hand around his chest and the reins with the other.

She pulled Buck up in front of the cabin door, slid off

the horse, and helped Caleb down. He touched the ground and almost fell. Holding him around his chest, she almost dragged him to the door. She opened the door with some difficulty and supported him as he stumbled to the bed.

Mei Lin helped him sit on the side of the bed, then laid him down gently. He sighed heavily and closed his eyes. Pulling his boots off, she lifted his legs slowly onto the bed. She loosened his clothing and removed the pad from his wound.

She made a fire in the stove and heated water. After cleaning the wound with the warm water, she made a new pad from clean rags. First applying a salve to the wound, she applied the pad and tied the shirtsleeve band around his chest.

Pulling the chair from the table to the bedside, she sat, watching him.

Caleb opened his eyes. He turned his head and saw Mei Lin. She sat in her chair beside the bed, slumped over, her head on the bed, sleeping.

"Mei Lin," he said softly.

Her head jerked up, and her eyes opened wide. "Honee Cay-leb! You awake." She stood and leaned over him. "How you feel?"

"Hungry. What's for breakfast?"

"You need breakfast, dinner, supper. You sleep almost two day."

He struggled to rise. She pulled him up and helped him scoot back to a sitting position against the headboard. "Two days," he said. "What did I miss?"

"Honee. Somebody kill two Indian and two workmen. Tindoor and two workmen fight, then run away when bad men start shooting. They run to woods, come back when bad men leave. We bury two men. Everybody wait see if you want fix dredge."

Caleb had listened without comment, his face blank, staring at his blankets. "I will look at the dredge. First I want to see the graves. This afternoon."

"We see. You get up if I say you get up. First you eat, then I see."

He looked up at her and smiled. "Yes, ma'am."

She leaned over and kissed him, stroked his cheek. "We see."

• • • • •

Caleb and Mei Lin walked slowly toward the bunkhouse. Caleb held his left arm pressed against his bandaged side. He waved to Andrew who sat on a bench outside the bunkhouse. Andrew waved in return and watched Caleb and Mei Lin walk to the two graves beside the bunkhouse.

Cal stood at the graves, staring at the skyline above the forest. Caleb nodded to Cal who stepped back, head hanging.

A small wooden cross was pushed into the ground at the head of each grave. They were marked simply "Johnny" and "Larry."

"Those were the only names we ever knew, boss," Andrew said. He had walked behind Caleb and Mei Lin.

Caleb walked over to Cal who stood beside Larry's grave. Cal's face was screwed up, and he appeared to be on the verge of breaking down.

"Are you okay, Cal?" said Caleb.

Cal couldn't look at him. He stared at the grave. "I cain't get over it, boss. He got killed trying to save my life, and I told him he didn't have to do that. He just said git back, and he went for that guy. He pulled him off his horse, and he had him by the throat, and I told him he didn't have to do that, and he just said git away. Then they shot him. Why would Larry do that? I cain't get over it."

"There are still some good men around, Cal, and we're fortunate when we run across one. Larry was a good man."

Cal nodded, wiped his eyes with a sleeve, and walked to the bunkhouse where he sat down heavily on the bench at the front wall.

Mei Lin stood beside Johnny's grave. She looked down at the marker, glanced briefly at Andrew, then back at the grave. "How . . . how did he die?" she said.

Andrew looked at the grave. "He was like a madman. When this guy yelled to his pard that he was going to fire the dredge, Johnny just went for him, beating him with his fists, kicking at him, pulling at him. I thought he was going to kill him. Then this guy's pard shot him. Three times he had to shoot Johnny before he fell."

Mei Lin had not taken her eyes off the grave as she listened to Andrew. Tears rolled down her face. She turned to Caleb. "I will miss him, Johnny," she said. "That okay?"

Caleb pulled her to him with his good arm. "Yes, that okay. I will miss him too. He was a fine young man. They were all good men." They stood silent for a long moment.

"Tindoor took the Sheepeaters' bodies?" he said.

"Yes," she said. "He say he borrow mules, take them. I say we come village soon. When you can ride."

"Good." He put his arm around her shoulders, and they walked toward the bunkhouse. Cal stood and waited.

"Sorry, boss," said Andrew, "we tried—"

"Andrew, there's nothing you could have done except get yourself killed. I'm glad you did no more."

"They were white men," said Andrew. "They wore masks, but it didn't matter. I would've recognized the voice anywhere. They were Bennett's men. I told you I knew some men who worked for Bennett. We had drinks at the Rat Trap. I'd recognize the Irish accent anywhere. That's who burned us out. I know it."

Caleb pondered. "Hmm . . . let's have a look." All walked down the slope to the dredge. Caleb walked up the plank to the deck. He looked into the engine house and then into the sorting housing.

He walked back on deck. "You boys might have scared them off before they finished. The engine is okay, and the hardware is intact. They probably thought the fire would do more damage. But the damage appears to be just the housing. We can fix that. Are you with me?"

Andrew and Cal nodded. "Yeah," said Andrew, "let's get on it."

Bennett. Caleb knew he was going to have to face him sooner or later. It was well known that he intended to have no competition in dredging in the Stanley Basin. And that he would go to any lengths to get what he wanted. Now it seems he had proved it.

Caleb didn't have the men to confront Bennett by force, and he had no conclusive evidence that Bennett had been responsible for the arson. So he spread the word in Stanley that he was going to see Bennett.

He would count on the big man's ego. Bennett wanted control of dredging in the area, but he also craved respect. He wanted to be the great man behind the economic growth of the region. There were even rumors that he harbored political ambitions. Surely he could be dealt with.

Caleb tied Buck's reins to a bush near the dredge catwalk. He stood in awe. He had seen the huge dredge before, but he was still impressed with its size, its power. It was easily four times the size of his own dredge. The last time he was here, it had been in operation. The sound and energy pulsing from the dredge had been overpowering.

Now, it was quiet. The buckets hung from the still ladder. Water dripped from the lips of the buckets. The bucketline must have been shut down shortly before his arrival.

Three men stood at the open door of the dredge engine room, watching him. He stepped onto the catwalk and walked toward them. They waited.

Caleb walked on the catwalk to the deck of the barge. "Mr. Bennett, I believe," Caleb said when he came up to them. The other men stepped behind Bennett.

"Willis. What are you doing here? I thought I sent a message to you when you last were here."

"Yeah, you did. Actually, Mr. Bennett, I have come to ask your advice. You know better than anyone else in the basin what goes on around here, especially concerning dredging."

"Yeah," said Bennett, "that's so. What of it?"

"I suppose you know that I'm dredging on Stanley Creek. I got burned out last week. I was wondering whether you could give me any information on who might have been responsible."

Bennett looked hard at Caleb. "Willis, you're small fry. You'll never make a go of it. You're not making any gold, and you're just about out of cash."

"You know nothing of my cash position! How would—"

"Willis, you're a small fish swimming in deep waters. Get out while you can, while you still have a shirt on your back. And take your little Chinese whore with you."

"You bloated son of a bitch! I'll have you—"

"You'll have me nothing." Bennett smiled. "I might solve my Willis problem right now. You might slip and hit your head on the gunwale, fall into the pond, and never surface. Never seen again. A tragic ending."

Bennett motioned toward Caleb with a sharp movement of his head. The two men behind Bennett moved toward Caleb.

A shot sounded, and a lantern on the wall beside Bennett's head shattered. Everyone jerked away from the spray of glass. They looked toward the sound of the shot.

On the ledge above the pond, a dozen Indians were aligned at the edge of the woods. Rifles were leveled on the men on the dredge.

An Indian stepped from the woods, holding an arrow at his bow. He struck a match and applied the flame to the swabbed head. The head burst into flame. He held the arrow aloft in his bow, aimed at the sky above the dredge.

"All right! All right!" Bennett said. "Get outta here! Don't let me catch you alone, Willis."

"Watch your own back, Bennett." Caleb walked up the catwalk toward his horse. The Indians stepped from behind cover, their rifles still trained on Bennett and his men.

Caleb and six others worked from dawn to dusk on repairing the dredge housing. Besides himself, there were Andrew and Cal, and Tindoor and one other Sheepeater. Two men with some little experience on gold dredges were hired from Stanley. They were guaranteed two weeks' work. Caleb still had boards left over from the original construction, now well weathered, which would do nicely for the repairs.

The repairs finished, the steam engine was fired up, and the dredge was in operation again. Caleb still wanted to get in a few more weeks before winter shut them down.

Winter. He still was in a quandary about winter. He must decide soon. The deciduous trees had turned brilliant autumn color and now had lost most of their leaves. Cold and snow would not be far behind. What to do?

Caleb wanted one more look at the sluice before winter set in. They had not needed it since the incident of the loose dredge, nor would they likely need it early next year, but he wanted to be sure it was in good shape before shutting down the dredge operation.

Caleb and Mei Lin rode up the valley to the sluice. The mouth of the sluice was clean, and the sides recently had been smoothed. They rode along the channel through the pine forest to the point where the channel connected to Mary's Creek. The gate that closed the sluice here was in place and in good condition.

Caleb was satisfied. They rode at a walk back along the sluice through the heavy timber. At a clearing, Caleb pulled Buck up. He closed his eyes and sniffed.

"What?" Mei Lin said.

"Smoke."

Caleb kicked Buck into a lope. Mei Lin followed. They cleared the woods above their meadow and pulled up, looked at the northern sky, and saw above the distant ridgeline a wall of gray smoke.

12 I MISS YOU
TOO MUCH

"Forest fire. A big one."

Caleb turned Buck down the slope and galloped toward the dredge. Mei Lin kicked Chica into a gallop after him.

They arrived at the dredge where they saw the four workers standing on the deck, and the two Sheepeaters on the bank, all watching the smoke columns growing, spreading, turning an angry black.

"Andrew!" Caleb shouted, "lift the spud, and untie the shorelines. Pole the dredge away from the shore. Drop the spud hard in the middle of the pond. That should keep the dredge from drifting." Andrew waved and ran down the gangway to the near shoreline.

"Tindoor!" Caleb called, "drive the cows into the shallows. You'll have to keep them as quiet as possible. They'll spook if the fire reaches us."

Tindoor and the other Sheepeater ran toward the cows that were scattered about in the lower meadow near the pond.

Caleb turned to Mei Lin. "Mei Lin, we need to set a backfire."

"Backfire?"

"C'mon." He kicked Buck into a gallop toward the cabin. Mei Lin followed on Chica.

At the cabin, Caleb pulled up at the corral and dismounted, leaving Buck's reins hanging loose. Running to the lean-to, he picked up a can of kerosene and shook the can to verify that it contained a good supply. He looked around, picked up a box of matches from a workbench and shoved it into a pocket. On his way out, he stopped, picked up a handful of rags, and pushed them into another pocket.

Grabbing Buck's reins, he started to mount, stopped, dropped the reins, let loose a burst of profanity, and looked around frantically. He saw the stack of burlap bags under the workbench. He grabbed a couple and pushed them into his saddle's gullet. Collecting the reins in one hand and holding the kerosene can in the other, he mounted and kicked Buck into a gallop down the slope toward the dredge, Mei Lin following.

They pulled up at the dredge just as Andrew loosed the second shoreline from its stake. He had already tied the first shoreline to a heavy length of iron on the deck, which he would use as an anchor.

Caleb tied Buck's reins to a shoreline stake. Mei Lin dismounted and tied Chica's reins to the same stake.

"Now what we do?" she said.

"We're going to fire the meadow as soon as the cows are in the water. We have a slight breeze blowing up the meadow toward the woods. That's good. If we can burn the meadow and the woods above it, the big fire won't reach us. The grass is beat down on the bank, so the fire shouldn't be a problem here. I want to save the house. We'll probably lose the bunkhouse.

"I'm going to sprinkle the kerosene in the grass, starting right here. We'll work our way up the slope and around the house and corrals. Follow me, not too close, and fire the grass. If it doesn't light, we'll have to soak the rags and light them. That should do it."

"Okay, I take matches," she said.

"Here." He handed her the burlap bags. "Soak these bags in the pond. When we light the grass, we want it to burn up the hill, not down the slope. Use the wet bag to put any flame out that burns down the slope. Okay?"

"Okay." She took the bags and dropped to her knees at the edge of the pond, trailing the bags in the water.

He pulled the matches and rags from his pockets and dropped them on the ground. "Mei Lin!" he said. She looked over her shoulder and saw him point to the rags and matches.

"Okay," she said.

Caleb looked to the meadow and saw Tindoor and another Sheepeater walking the cows toward the pond. He counted. Ten.

"Damn!" Caleb mumbled. He untied Buck's reins, swung up into the saddle, and galloped toward Tindoor. He pulled up before reaching him so he would not interfere with the drive toward the pond.

He shouted. "Tindoor, where's the bull?"

"I not see!" Tindoor shouted. "Sometime he in woods, up there." He pointed up the hill toward a stand of tall pines. A wall of dark smoke rose from the forest beyond.

"Goddamned dumb animal," Caleb mumbled aloud and kicked Buck into a gallop up the meadow slope. He looked back down toward the pond to see the Indians pushing the cows slowly into the shallows.

Pulling Buck up at the edge of the woods, he looked into the dark interior and saw no bull. He rode slowly into the thick woods, looking right and left. The smell of smoke grew stronger.

Then he saw the bull. The animal stood rigidly, facing uphill, toward the approaching fire. Caleb rode slowly toward him.

"All right, you ornery cuss, let's go for a swim." He rode forward and turned the bull toward the meadow. Looking back into the dark forest, he saw a faint swirl of smoke in a sunny opening. He pushed Buck into a fast walk, nudging the bull's flanks with a boot, watching what was going on below.

The dredge lay still, well away from the bank. The spud had been lowered, and Andrew's makeshift anchor line was taut.

The cows milled about in the shallows, apparently content. The two Sheepeaters stood on the bank to prevent any from trying to return to the meadow.

Caleb pushed the bull to the edge of the pond where Tindoor urged him into the water with a switch. The bull obediently stepped into the frigid waters and moved into the midst of his harem. Caleb kicked Buck into a lope to Mei Lin. He dismounted and tied his reins to the stake.

"Okay?" she said.

"Okay. Let's get busy." He picked up the kerosene can.

"Honee. The mules."

Caleb winced. He dropped the can and ran to his horse. He jerked the reins off the stake, mounted hurriedly, and kicked Buck into a gallop toward the cabin.

Caleb rode past the cabin and pulled up near the corrals. The two mules stood on the slope near the road, ears erect, looking toward the wall of black smoke rising from the forest. Caleb rode around them and began pushing them toward the pond.

"Just move on, mules. You don't want any part of that

business. Just keep moving. Damn, you disappoint me. I thought you were smarter than this." He kicked Buck into a lope, moving right, then left, pushing the mules and keeping them heading toward the pond.

At the pond, Tindoor stood with outstretched arms to herd the two mules into the shallows. Arriving at the bank, the mules turned back on Caleb, but he shouted and pushed them into the water. When one started back toward the bank, Mei Lin waved her burlap bag at his head, and he turned back into the water.

Caleb slid off Buck and tied the reins to the stake beside Chica.

"Have I forgotten anything?" he said to Mei Lin. She shook her head. "Okay, let's get to it!" he said.

Mei Lin kneeled at the pond edge and soaked the burlap bags again. She gave one to Caleb. He removed the top of the can and sprinkled the kerosene on the dry grass. Mei Lin struck a match and dropped it on the wet grass. It ignited in a low flame and spread slowly along the line of Caleb's sprinkling.

The fire crept out in all directions as the dry grass caught fire, crackling and hissing. Caleb and Mei Lin smothered the flames that burned toward the pond. A slight breeze that blew off the pond and up the slope of the meadow caught the line of flames and pushed them up the slope.

Caleb stood, flexed his back. "That's what we need!" He looked past Mei Lin and saw the flames moving fast toward the slope below the cabin.

"Mei Lin! Take your sack and slow the fire below the cabin. We need to move up there and set the backfire be-hind the cabin." Mei Lin moved up the slope sideways, beating out the line of low flames.

Caleb looked toward the pond. The dredge was stationary, the anchor line still taut, holding the vessel still. Andrew and Cal stood on the deck, watching Caleb and Mei Lin.

Caleb saw the cows standing quiet in the shallows. Tindoor and the other Indian had waded into the pond and now stood in water up to their knees, watching the cows to prevent any attempt to regain the shore.

Caleb grabbed the kerosene can and ran up the slope toward Mei Lin. "C'mon," he said. "To the cabin." They ran to the back of the house.

The grass at the back of the cabin was beaten down, but it was dry and still flammable. Caleb walked around the perimeter of the cabin and corrals and outbuildings, sprinkling kerosene from the can. When he had reached the road above the cabin, he shouted to Mei Lin who stood where he had begun below the cabin.

"Light it! Be ready with the bag. Don't let it burn toward the house!"

Mei Lin struck a match and applied it to the grass. A low flame appeared and spread slowly. She fanned the flame with her sack. The flames licked at the dry grass and moved away from the cabin.

"Come up here with the matches!" Caleb shouted. She ran to him. "Light it here beside the road so it will move up from the corrals. The road will act as a firebreak. I hope."

Mei Lin lit the grass, wet with kerosene, in three places. That done, they watched the progress of the flames. The line of low flame, pushed by the gentle updraft from the pond, moved slowly up the sloping meadow toward the woods.

The wall of smoke rising from the forest darkened and lifted, churning, expanding, black arms thrusting from the mass. A tall pine that rose above the tops of the other trees suddenly burst into flame, showering sparks and burning limbs. Other trees ignited, and the treetops were aflame. The trees at the edge of the wood above the meadow were still strangely untouched, as if they were immune to the conflagration.

Then, suddenly, the line of trees at the edge exploded into flame. The fire spread along the edge, and the entire forest was engulfed in flames. Caleb and Mei Lin watched, entranced.

Flames from the forest undergrowth spread quickly to the grass of the meadow. The line of flame moved slowly down the slope. The backfire moved faster up the slope, pushed by the breeze.

Caleb and Mei Lin were snatched from their trance by flames that erupted almost at their feet. They swatted the fire with their damp bags until the flames were extinguished. Caleb took Mei Lin's bag and soaked both bags in a water trough beside the corral. He handed a dripping bag to Mei Lin.

They stood like statues, holding their bags, watching the two lines of flames approaching each other. They waited, helpless to do more than watch.

The two lines of flames merged. And disappeared. Smoke from the joined line appeared to increase and rise, then subside and smolder.

Mei Lin looked at Caleb. "Is it over, honee?"

He looked at the smoldering meadow and the forest above. The flames were gone. Smoke swirled and lifted to add to the heavy gray overcast. The bunkhouse had been spared. The ground around it had been so trod and trampled by horses every day that there was no tinder to burn.

"It's over," he said.

For days after the fire, thin spirals of smoke continued

to rise from the forest, swirled about above the treetops, and vanished. Then a light rain settled the smoke and ash, and the forest was shrouded in fog for a week. When it lifted, the trees were bare, black skeletons outlined against the deep blue of a clear sky.

The dredge was tied up again at the pond edge, and work resumed. The sounds of the buckets dumping their loads into the cylinder, the cylinder rotating and the stones falling to the belt for disposal fused into one pulsating, deafening roar.

Caleb stepped from the housing door to the deck and took a deep breath. He saw three men standing on the bank, holding the reins of their horses. One waved to him. Caleb walked around the deck and down the plank gangway.

"Mr. Willis?" said the man who had waved. He wore a white shirt and dark tie under his thick woolen suit. The other two men wore working clothes. Caleb recognized the two and waved to them. The dandy he did not know, but assumed he was in charge here.

"I'm Willis," Caleb said. He already did not like this.

"Mr. Willis," the man said, "I'm with federal immigration in Boise." He held up an identification card. Caleb stared at the agent, ignoring the card.

"I'm told you have a Chinese woman working for you," the man said. "I understand she may also be living here."

Caleb raised his eyebrows. He snickered. "Well, you're partly right. She was here. Little bitch ran off. Took my watch and a jar of cash. You looking for her? Maybe she heard somebody was looking for her. Maybe that's why she run off. If you're looking for her, you can't miss her. She's riding the horse I gave her. Pretty little paint gelding."

The agent frowned. "You're not helping her, are you? There's laws against aiding a fugitive."

"A fugitive? What's she done?"

"We think she may have entered the country illegally, using forged papers."

"Be damned. She never said anything about her past. Never thought about it. Hmm."

"And you never asked?"

"Nope. All I ever needed to know about her was whether she could cook and keep me warm at night." Caleb smiled, then turned serious. "A fugitive, you say?"

The agent frowned. His look said that he knew Caleb was lying. The two other men, Stanley men, smiled at Caleb behind the agent's back.

Caleb had learned about the federal agent with only an hour's advance notice. A grizzled member of the gossip circle at the general store, the same who had sold him the rifle, had overheard the agent talking at the saloon and had ridden hard for Caleb's claim. He had passed the agent and the two Stanley men on the road. The Stanley men had been willing to ride with the agent who offered them a half-day's wages just to show him the road.

The friend told Caleb that he would take a circuitous route back to Stanley to avoid being seen by the agent. He had hardly ridden from sight when Caleb told Mei Lin to get ready for the road. Caleb had saddled Chica while Mei Lin packed a saddlebag. She kissed him and hugged him, then mounted Chica and galloped up the slope. He watched until she disappeared into the forest. She would be safe with the Sheepeaters.

Caleb stood on the bank downstream from the dredge at a still backwater of the pond. He wore a fleece jacket and a scarf about his neck. His hat was pulled down to his ears.

He looked down at the pond edge. A thin film of ice extended from the shore about three feet into the pond. He prodded the ice with a stick. It broke up into tiny slivers that floated away from the bank.

He looked up at the sky, a snow sky. Small flakes swirled about in the breeze. A dusting of snow lay on the bank and slope.

Then he saw Mei Lin. She rode at a lope down the meadow, her heavy jacket buttoned at the top and collar raised, and around her neck a scarf that flew out behind her, bouncing with the gait of the horse. She wore no hat, and her hair flew in all directions. She waved to Caleb.

He waved and suddenly was warm. The three days had dragged, and he realized how much he had grown accustomed to having her at his side and in his bed.

She pulled up and slid off Chica. She ran to him and collided hard, forcing him to stumble backward to avoid falling. He never learned. They embraced and kissed.

"I miss you too much," she said.

"I missed you too. All okay in the village?"

"Yes, everything okay. They have enough food, not plenty, but enough, and they have firewood for winter. They okay. I take care of Chica, and I come back."

She kissed him again, mounted, and kicked Chica into a lope up the slope toward the cabin.

The cabin was dark, illuminated only by the faint shaft of moonlight from the window. Caleb lay on his side, the covers pulled up to his chin. His mind raced, remembering the night. Mei Lin's face was a foot from his own. He could feel her steady exhalations lightly caress his face and hear the faint sound, almost a whimper, with each breath.

They had made love earlier, and when it was over they had collapsed on their pillows. She had noticed his misty eyes and had risen on an elbow to look at him.

"What wrong, honee? You okay?" she had said. He had

stroked her cheek and kissed her softly on her lips and closed her eyes with a hand.

No, he was not okay. His thoughts were increasingly about Mei Lin. Was he putting her in danger by keeping her? The movement to rid Idaho of the Chinese was intensifying. Legal action was the norm, but on occasion, malcontents became violent. There had been deaths. The whole Chinese population of Warrens, a majority of the town's inhabitants, had been forced to leave with only what they could carry in saddlebags.

Caleb turned to lie on his back and stared at the ceiling.

Caleb walked to the dredge and went aboard. Inside the housing, he saw Andrew, Cal, and Tindoor standing near the boiler. They wore heavy jackets and thick scarves, but the cold and their obvious discomfort convinced Caleb that a decision had to be made. Now.

Caleb was not surprised by the snow. Winter was late this year, but the heavy cloud cover foretold the approaching storm. They had to secure the dredge before the cold and snow made work on the dredge impossible.

He gave the order to begin shutting down the dredge for winter. The others set about their tasks, whether from relief or foreboding, Caleb could not tell.

He had worried about winter for weeks. What to do with the dredge and with themselves? He knew that he should have decided and made plans long ago, but he was torn between options.

Caleb and the others stood on the pond edge. The quiet was almost complete, disconcerting, broken only by birdsong, wind in the pines, ringing in the ears of those who had worked inside the dredge housing. The ringing was only temporary, they said, they hoped.

They were quiet at first, reluctant to talk about uncertain tomorrows. Andrew finally said that he and Cal would go their separate ways, what they had done in previous winters. Maybe to Boise or Challis, maybe just tough it out in Stanley. People did live in Stanley over the winter. The Sheepeaters would return to their village and prepare for winter, exactly as they and their people had done from the beginning of memory.

"Andrew, Cal," Caleb said, "if you have no place definite to go, or people you want to spend winter with, why don't you stay here? You could winterize the bunkhouse, and we'll load it up with provisions. You could watch the stock and the dredge. I don't suppose the dredge will need much watching. It'll be froze solid."

"Sounds like it might be a fit, boss," said Andrew. "Much obliged. Sure would be cheaper than going someplace else. Let me and Cal talk it over and let you know."

Andrew and Cal glanced at each other, a knowing glance, which said that the boss had finally and surely, whether intended or not, announced that he and Mae Lin would not be spending their winter on the claim. Andrew and Cal had speculated at great length on that question.

Caleb nodded. "Take your time. Nothing's going to happen for a while."

And Caleb? He had finally decided. He said nothing to Mei Lin though he suspected that she knew he had plans for winter. Each time she asked about what they would do, where they would be, he had found ways to avoid answering. There would be time for that. Time for announcing, time for explaining, and time for reflection. Time for regretting.

13 I LOVE
YOU HONEE

Caleb and Mei Lin stood in front of the cabin with Andrew and Cal and Tindoor and two other Sheepeaters. All wore thick jackets and hats. Some wore heavy gloves. The sky was clear and still at the moment, but the low dark cloud promised snow and a further drop in the temperature.

Caleb and Mei Lin gave the Sheepeaters two sacks of provisions and thanked them for their hospitality when Mei Lin had ridden to their village ahead of the federal agent's arrival. Tindoor assured Caleb that they had winterized the rough dwelling at the edge of the forest above the meadow where they would stay occasionally when tending the cows.

Thanks and handshakes all around, and the Sheepeaters were gone. They walked through the meadow toward the forest above. A small flurry of snowflakes materialized and seemed to hover and swirl above their heads.

"Ready for the big freeze, boys?" said Caleb to Andrew and Cal.

"Gettin' there," Andrew said.

Andrew and Cal had decided to stick it out on the claim and had been busy winterizing the bunkhouse. They had spent hours at the edge of the forest above the meadow, shirtless in the freezing temperature, cutting burned trees, sawing and splitting the dry wood into lengths to feed the sheepherder stove. They hauled wagonloads of the firewood down to the bunkhouse and stacked it under a newly built lean-to. The roof of the lean-to connected with a roofed walk to the bunkhouse door. Now they would not have to trudge through snow to reach the woodpile.

"So far as I know, just one more chore. Just need to do a bit more caulking to keep the cold on the outside. C'mon, Cal. Let's get on it." Andrew and Cal waved and walked up the slope toward the bunkhouse. Their footsteps were clearly outlined in the light snowfall.

Caleb and Mei Lin silently watched the two men, small snowflakes drifting and swirling, until they went inside the bunkhouse. She turned to him.

"Now, Cay-leb honee. You will tell me." She did not smile.

How do I do this? He replied to her stern look with a blank face. Then he relaxed and smiled.

"I wanted it to be a surprise. We're going to Seattle."

Her jaw dropped, and her eyes opened wide. She cocked her head. "Seattle? Why we go Seattle? What we do in Seattle? How we go Seattle?"

He took her arm and took a step toward the cabin door. "Let's go inside. I need some coffee."

She stood her ground and pulled away from his hand. "Honee, every time you want talk 'bout something hard, you say 'C'mon, I need coffee'."

He laughed. "Do I? Let's go in. We'll talk." He stepped up on the stoop and opened the door. She looked after him, unsmiling. He motioned inside with a movement of his head. She stepped through the door, head down, grim.

They sat at the table, each holding the handle of a mug. He took a sip of coffee. "I thought you would enjoy the trip. We'll ride the train, and we'll stay in a hotel. We'll walk along the sea-front. Maybe we'll see the dock where you arrived from China." "I no want see that place... Why we go Seattle?" He looked through the window. "I need to see a shipper. I've been told that he can supply dredge hardware cheaper than having it shipped overland or around the Horn."

"What dredge hardware you need?"

He shifted on his keg. "Well, none just now. I just wanted to make this contact, in case I should need something in the future. And we need someplace to winter. And I want to show you a good time." He smiled thinly.

She relaxed, seeming to droop. "Okay, I just ... I get scared, anything new. Thing I no . . . don't . . . understand."

He scooted his keg over beside her. He took her in his arms and held her. "I just want you to be happy," he said softly, "this year and next year and the next year." He did not add what he really meant, what had tormented him for months. He wanted her to be safe.

She leaned back and looked at him. "I love you, honee. You know that."

Caleb pulled her to him again and rested his head on hers so she could not see his tears. He stared through the window. "Yes, I know that."

Caleb and Mei Lin stood beside the table, looking about the room. He touched the stove again, checking for the third time that the fire was out, and the stove was cold. The cabin was in good order. All that needed stowing was stowed. He slid the window curtain on its pole, darkening the room. Sunlight and cold air flowed through the open doorway.

Caleb picked up the two suitcases. He looked around the room again, wondering silently when and in what condition he would return.

Mei Lin grasped the handle of her suitcase. "I take my case." Caleb looked at her in surprise. "I never have case before," she said. "Always sack or box." He released his hold on the case.

They walked through the door to the yard. Andrew sat in the driver seat of the wagon. The two mules shifted in the harness. Andrew smiled. Cal sat his horse on the far side of the wagon. He removed the cigarette from his lips quickly, like the little boy caught smoking, and waved.

Caleb nodded. He pulled the door shut and dropped the latch. He stood on the step a moment, staring at the weathered planks of the door.

"Morning, boss, Mei Lin," Andrew said. "Beautiful day for a drive." Caleb turned around and walked to the wagon. He waved to the men.

The day had dawned clear and cold. Yesterday's snow had left but an inch or two on the ground.

"We're getting you on the road just in time," Andrew said. "Weather should hold till we get back. Might be a bit of a chore getting over the pass, but we should make it fine."

Caleb nodded. He tossed his bag into the wagon bed beside Andrew's and Cal's saddlebags. He reached for Mei Lin's bag. She ignored him and swung her bag back and forth, as Caleb had taught her to swing her saddle, and tossed the bag over the sideboards into the bed. She smiled smugly.

She let Caleb boost her up to the wagon seat, and he followed. Andrew shook the lines, and they moved up the road. Cal pulled his horse into line behind the wagon.

Caleb turned his coat collar up and buttoned the top button. He reached over and pulled Mei Lin's collar up. She turned to look at him, her face blank. He could usually read her expressions, but he had not seen this face before.

He stared into the forest beside the road. He was not looking forward to this trip. He had reached a decision just two weeks ago. He had retrieved the sack of cash hidden beneath the cabin floorboards and had gone to Stanley where he sold his small stash of flakes and booked the train tickets. He would have many daylight hours during the trip from Ketchum to Seattle.

He would have to talk with Mei Lin.

What am I going to talk about? When will I tell her? How am I going to tell her?

The first night on the drive was spent at the Shaw Ranch. Caleb had arranged the previous week for overnights at the ranch and the lodge at Galena.

Frank Shaw was delighted to welcome the visitors. He said his hellos to the three men, then ignored them. He insisted on carrying Mei Lin's suitcase as his wife showed their guests to their rooms.

In the sitting room after dinner, Mr. Shaw had eyes and conversation only for Mei Lin. He served her tea, sat opposite her, and talked only with her. Mei Lin was a bit embarrassed by the attention, but she accepted it graciously while trying unsuccessfully to draw the others into the conversation.

Mrs. Shaw smiled at Caleb behind her husband's back, a what-do-you-expect smile. She had known what to expect, remembering the last time Caleb and Mei Lin had stayed with them.

The next morning, Mrs. Shaw and Caleb stood on the front porch, watching Mr. Shaw help Mei Lin climb up to the wagon seat. After seeing her settled, he picked up her suitcase, which he had carried from the house, and deposited it in the wagon bed.

"The old goat likes kittens, puppies, and young women," Mrs. Shaw said to Caleb. "He's harmless."

They spent the second night at the Galena lodge. Andrew and Cal were pleased that they were given a room in the lodge rather than having to put up in the barn, though they were not at all pleased when they were told that they would have to share the room's only bed. Cal opted to sleep on the couch.

· · · · ·

Andrew pulled the mules up beside the standing train. They had reached Ketchum without mishap. The drive to Ketchum was easier than the regular freight runs since the wagon was almost empty, and the mules were frisky from little work. The weather had been tolerable, and the road was dry.

Andrew wrapped the lines around the brake handle and jumped down. He strode around the wagon as Caleb climbed down. Caleb took Mae Lin's hand and supported her as she leaned over and then jumped to the ground. Andrew took the two bags from the wagon bed and set them on the ground beside the wagon. Cal dismounted and tied his reins to the back of the wagon.

Caleb turned to the two men. "We've got a while before we have to board, but you boys better get something to eat in a hurry and move out. You may get some weather on the way home."

"Yeah, okay, boss," Andrew said, "whatever you say."

They looked up at the heavy cloud layer that had darkened and lowered since setting out that morning from the

Galena lodge. A few small snowflakes drifted to and fro in the light breeze that swirled about the train yard.

"We'll do fine," Andrew said. "If we get caught by snow, we may just stay at the Galena place and drink beer till thaw." Cal guffawed and sobered quickly, embarrassed. The others smiled.

Caleb shook their hands, patted each on the back. They said goodbye to Mei Lin, each with something between a nod and a bow. She smiled and said goodbye to them. They backed up a few steps, then turned and walked away, Andrew to the wagon and Cal to his horse.

Caleb and Mei Lin stood silently, their bags at their feet, and watched them set out. Caleb glanced at Mei Lin. She still watched, her face expressionless.

"C'mon, let's get coffee," he said, reaching for the bags.

"C'mon, let's get coffee," Mei Lin said, frowning. "Something goin' to happen." She looked up at him, her face a mask. Then she smiled, a smile without warmth. He picked up the bags and walked toward the cafe across the yard from the train.

They sat in the last seat against the rear wall of the coach, Mei Lin at the window and Caleb in the aisle seat. She leaned against the pane and watched the countryside flash by. Sagebrush, telegraph poles, a fence line, a few scattered cows, an occasional pine, a cedar.

Eyes opened wide and jaw hanging, she turned abruptly to look at him. He smiled, wondering at how little she knew of the world, wondering at her eagerness to discover and absorb new things while his mind had long ago closed. She turned back to look again through the window.

He looked her over and smiled. She was stylishly dressed in a straight gray hobble skirt that reached just above her shoe tops. Over the skirt, she wore a slim jacket of the same color.

He had been relieved to read in the Sears Roebuck catalog that corsets and bustles were no longer the rage. He knew that Mei Lin would have refused that nonsense.

With the help of the Stanley general store owner, Caleb had ordered the clothes two months ago from the Sears catalog. At the time, he had simply wanted her to have clothes fit to come to Stanley or any other Idaho town. Now she would wear her fine clothes in Seattle.

Caleb glanced around the coach. The seats were no more than half filled. Seats faced each other, so perfect strangers were forced to either befriend those sitting opposite or endure hours of silence. Or endure their private conversation.

Caleb studied the older couple facing them on the opposite seat. They were dressed as if they were prepared for church. Or a wake.

The man wore a black suit with cuffed trousers, a tall collar that was once white, and a wide gray tie. His jacket was flecked with breakfast crumbs. His wife wore a long, severe black dress that projected starched frills up to her chin and ears. She had a look of bewilderment, thought Caleb, or stupidity.

They stared at Mei Lin, without any attempt to mask their stares. The man frowned, his mouth turned down into an inverted bowl. Caleb wondered whether he had ever smiled.

Mei Lin turned from the window to Caleb with a contented look on her face. She sighed and took his arm, pulled him to her, and leaned against his shoulder.

The woman straightened. "Well, I never!" She leaned toward Caleb. "She certainly takes liberties. Does she speak English?"

Caleb put on a thoughtful face, forehead furrowed. He pulled back from Mei Lin, looked grimly at her, then turned and spoke to the woman. "Hmm. I don't know. I must ask." He leaned back, pursed his lips, and spoke to Mei Lin.

"Do you speak English?"

Mei Lin pondered, frowning. She leaned back and replied stiffly and slowly to Caleb, ignoring the man and woman. "Only if I speak to a person who understand proper English," she said. "You understand good English, I think, honee."

The woman's jaw dropped. "Well! Well! I never!" She stood stiffly and glared down at her husband. "Wilbur!"

Wilbur pulled a face that said either, "Sorry," or "I never!" Caleb couldn't decide which. Wilbur stood, and with a "Yes, dear," the pair shuffled up the aisle, bouncing against seats on each side with the rhythm of the train.

"Funny," said Mei Lin, smiling.

"Prigs," said Caleb.

She laughed, sobered, turned to Caleb. "What mean 'prigs'?"

"Prudish ... uh ..." He stared at the ceiling. "Somebody who doesn't know how to have fun and doesn't like to see others having fun. Something like that."

"I understand."

She looked back through the window. The rolling land was brown and arid, covered with sage and black lava basalt, broken occasionally by ravines that were crossed on bridges. Mountains were visible in the distance, their slopes covered with green conifers and peaks topped with snow.

The train stood at the station in Boise. Caleb and Mei Lin looked through the window at the platform.

Steam issued from the engine ahead, billowing, obscuring people on the platform. A woman turned away from the steam and waved her hand before her face. The little girl beside her mother stretched her arms out horizontally on each side and tilted her head back, smiling, eyes closed, inhaling the wondrous mechanical fog.

An elderly woman nearby hugged a young man briefly, turned, and took the young woman beside him in her arms and held her tightly. Tears flowed down the young woman's cheeks. The older woman wiped the tears with a hand and kissed the cheek. She picked up a traveling bag and walked to the coach door. The young woman, hands at her cheeks, leaned on her husband who put an arm around her shoulders.

Others on the platform said their goodbyes, shook hands and hugged and kissed, waved. That ritual done, the travelers walked to the coach doors, luggage and bags in hand. They stood aside for arriving passengers to step down from the train, carrying bags and sacks.

Caleb pulled his watch from a vest pocket and looked at it. He returned the watch to the pocket and turned to Mei Lin.

"Would you like to walk on the platform, stretch your legs?" he said.

She bent to look through the window at the platform. "No. I don't like Boise. You go, if you want. I stay here."

"I understand. Okay, just a couple of minutes." He stood and walked to the door behind their seats.

He started to step down from the coach, then stopped and stepped back for a man who was boarding. The man's head was down, looking at the steps, and did not see Caleb. He looked up, saw Caleb, and pushed the round, steel-rimmed glasses up on his nose. He nodded and boarded.

Caleb nodded in return and stepped down to the platform.

Caleb walked briskly up the platform and stopped beside the engine. He marveled at the intricate structure, gleaming surfaces, and churning steam.

"Booooard!" Two coaches back, the conductor hung from a door, holding a flag. Caleb hurried toward his coach at the rear. Passing the conductor, he raised a hand in salute.

"Don't leave me!" Caleb said, smiling.

The conductor frowned. "Time and this train waits for no one." He smiled.

Caleb quickened his pace, running now. "Goddamned philosopher," he mumbled to himself. "Or a philosophical god. At least, he's god on this train."

Caleb reached his door at the rear of the last coach. He grabbed the bar and swung up the step to the floor, just as the engine chugged into life, and the train began moving.

He stepped into the coach and fell into his seat when the coach lurched ahead. Mei Lin caught him as he fell against her.

"You have nice walk?" she said.

"Yes. Almost got left behind." He turned to her, a mock serious look on his face. "Mei Lin, what would you have done if I had missed the train?"

"I find somebody travel with and buy me nice things." She smiled.

"Oh yeah, and where would you find this person?"

"Maybe him." She motioned with her head up the coach. Caleb looked and saw, across the aisle and five rows ahead, the man with the round, steel-rimmed glasses, sitting in a seat that faced the rear of the coach. He was middle-aged, dressed as a merchant of some sort, certainly not a man who made his living out of doors.

The man stared at Mei Lin. Caleb tried to ignore him, but each time he looked again at the man, he saw the same fixed, empty stare.

"Good luck," Caleb said. He smiled.

They rode in silence, looking through the window at the monotonous landscape flashing by beside the track, the distant mountains appearing to move by more slowly.

"I have never asked you about the Mad Hatter," Caleb said.

She looked still through the window. "There is nothing to say. You know about those places. Like Rat Trap. Same kind people. Same kind life. It make me sad to think about it, talk about it. Don't ask me, please." She turned and looked up at him, took his arm with both hands, leaned on his shoulder.

They rode in silence once more. Caleb closed his eyes, dozed.

Mei Lin stood and looked down at Caleb. She touched his arm. He opened his eyes and looked up.

"I need pee. Where I go?"

"Go up there at the end of this coach." He pointed ahead. "Just at the end, on the left side, there's a door. That's the toilet. If the door won't open, it's locked and somebody is inside. Just wait until they come out."

Mei Lin stood and walked up the aisle, bouncing about and unsteady at first, then easily down the center of the aisle as she found her balance.

Caleb stared through the window. He did not see the middle-aged man wearing the steel-rimmed glasses stand and follow Mei Lin.

Caleb drooped. He stared at his shoes. Each mile the train took them closer to Seattle, the sooner he would have to talk with Mei Lin. He rubbed his face with both hands, then massaged the lower back of his head where the throbbing had been increasing since boarding the train. His stomach churned, and he felt like his insides were being ripped out.

At the head of the coach, Mei Lin tried the toilet door, but it was locked. She looked ahead and saw the open space between the cars. Stepping up to the opening, she looked down at the coupling and below, the rocky roadbed and the rails flashing by. The rhythmic clickety-clack, clickety-clack of the steel wheels on the rails was louder in the opening, and she put her hands over her ears.

She turned when she heard the toilet door open. A woman stepped out, smiled, and held the door open for her. Mei Lin smiled and stepped in. She locked the door.

The man wearing the steel-rimmed glasses had stopped a few steps from the toilet. Now he stepped up and stood in the passageway, facing the toilet door. He leaned against the opposite wall.

The toilet door latch clicked, and he stepped across the aisle to stand before the door. The door opened, and Mei Lin looked wide-eyed in surprise at the man who stood there. He pushed her roughly back into the toilet and closed the door.

The man grabbed her wrist, twisting it. With the other hand, he tore at her dress top, popping two buttons open, and rubbed her breasts roughly. He bent, grabbed the hem of her dress, and jerked it up.

Mei Lin brought up a knee hard into his groin. His head came up, and his glasses went flying. Instinctively, he stooped to catch the glasses. She smashed the back of his head with a fist. He recoiled, released her wrist, and fell against the wall. She pushed him aside and opened the door in one motion, rushed outside, and the door closed with the swaying motion of the coach.

She walked quickly, ran a few steps, colliding against seat-backs on each side of the aisle. Passengers whose seats were bumped looked up and glared at her.

Caleb saw her disheveled hair and unbuttoned top. She collapsed on the seat beside him.

"Man, toilet, he feel me," she said, gasping.

Caleb stood and strode up the aisle, gripping seats on both sides, steadying himself. Reaching the end of the coach, he grabbed the toilet door handle and twisted.

The door opened. The man was on his knees, searching for the lens of his glasses. He looked up at Caleb, eyes wide open and un-focusing.

Caleb grabbed the man's coat, one hand gripping the folds of his sleeve and another his collar, lifted him, and pulled him roughly through the door and toward the opening between the coaches. He held the man's shoulders with both hands and pushed him into the opening and toward the side. The man looked at the flashing rails and roadbed below, jerked his head around to look wild-eyed at Caleb.

Caleb pushed him through the opening. Arms and legs flailing, he fell to the ground at the side of the track where he bounced and rolled down the slope and was lost to view.

Caleb braced himself on the coach doorway with a hand, breathing heavily, gasping, staring at the tracks flashing below. He wiped his mouth with a hand, flexed his neck, took a long breath and exhaled slowly, turned, and looked back down the coach aisle.

Nothing was amiss. No one saw. The man would not be missed until someone at his destination still stood on the platform after the train had arrived and departed. Caleb hoped the man did not have children.

He walked slowly down the aisle. Reaching his seat, he

sat down heavily beside Mei Lin. He did not look at her.

"I saw him. He dead?"

"No. I don't think so. The train had slowed on the curve. He'll have a few bruises to remind him, but he'll live. He'll have a long walk." Caleb put his arm around Mei Lin's shoulders.

"Are you okay?" he said. She nodded.

Maybe he'll live. Maybe I hope he'll live. He's probably a decent sort who just lost his senses for a moment. I knew a long time ago that Mei Lin would be a magnet for trouble. Not her fault. She's pretty, she's exotic, she seems so . . . so . . . out of this world. Out of her world.

14 THIS ROOM HAVE NO COOK STOVE

Mei Lin stood behind Caleb at the check-in desk of the Panama Hotel, watching him signing the register. She held her bag in front of her with both hands and looked around the small lobby. Everything appeared new and gleaming.

The Japanese clerk, middle-aged, well groomed, and nattily dressed, looked around Caleb and smiled at Mei Lin. "I hope you both enjoy our new hotel. It opened just last summer. We are very proud of it, and we hope you enjoy your stay."

"I'm sure we will," said Caleb. "The key, please." The clerk tendered the key to Caleb, who nodded and accepted the key.

Caleb took Mei Lin's arm, and they walked down the hall toward their room. Each carried their bag. The clerk bent forward over the counter and watched them.

They stopped in front of their door. Caleb checked the key to verify that it matched the door number. He unlocked the door, pushed it open, and they went inside.

Mei Lin stopped in the center of the room and looked

around. She still held her bag. "This nice, honee, but it have no cook stove, no sink. We stay here all winter?"

"No, uh, we're staying here only a few days. We'll go someplace else for the winter. You heard the clerk. We'll just enjoy ourselves here for a few days." He took her bag and put it beside his against the wall.

"It fine. I not be bore . . . bored! I . . . will . . . not . . . be . . . bored." She smiled, satisfied with herself.

Caleb took her cheeks in both hands. "Mei Lin. It's okay. Chinklish is okay."

"No. It is not okay. I want speak proper English so other people understand and so you be proud me. Proud . . . of . . . me!" She smiled.

He kissed her on the forehead and looked into her eyes a long moment. He walked to the front and looked down from the second-story window to the street below. She looked at his back, waiting. *Next he is going to say let's get coffee.*

"Let's go walk," he said, "get some coffee."

Caleb and Mei Lin strolled on the walkways along the waterfront. They passed ships that were tied to the docks, American ships and ships from other nations. Crewmen lounged about the docks, smoking, laughing, speaking a multitude of languages.

They walked in Chinatown where all signs were in Chinese, and shops featured Chinese foods and goods. Mei Lin spoke to shopkeepers in Chinese, but she spoke hesitantly and said only what was necessary. On one occasion, she spoke English to a Chinese shopkeeper. The man frowned but nevertheless answered in English.

Caleb was surprised, but he understood. *This China-town holds too many memories for her, unpleasant memories that she would rather forget. Mei Lin, what is to become of you? And me?*

Walking in the middle of a narrow uphill street that was closed to all but local traffic, Mei Lin stopped. She held Caleb's arm and pulled him to a stop. He saw a puzzled look on her face.

"Honee," she said, "they are all men."

Caleb looked around. Sure enough, of the three dozen people in sight, on the street and in shops, only one was a woman. He had not noticed.

"Let's have tea," he said. "Do you see a teashop?"

She looked up the street. "There's one." She pointed to a shop about halfway to the top of the ascending street. They walked in that direction.

"You know about the prejudice against Chinese in Idaho," Caleb said. "It's like that all over the country. It's been that way a long time. Chinese came to this country because they heard that they could get rich. They planned to go home with buckets of gold, so they left their families in China."

Caleb and Mei Lin sat at a round table at the window of the small teashop. They sipped from small porcelain cups, looking occasionally through the windows, watching passersby. Hawkers, suited businessmen, the shop owner across the street arranging fruit in bins, a young woman with a little girl grasping her mother's sleeve, skipping and trying to keep up. They were all Chinese.

"But they didn't find buckets of gold," Caleb said. "When times got hard and Americans fell on hard times, they blamed the Chinese since they were willing to work hard for less pay. The same bad things that happened to Chinese in Idaho happened all over the west coast."

Mei Lin held her cup on the table with both hands and stared out the window.

"Then the American government thought they would solve the problem of hard times by saying that no more Chinese could come to the United States. The Chinese men who lived here couldn't afford to go home, and they couldn't bring their wives to this country, even if they could afford it."

Mei Lin looked at Caleb. "That very sad, honee."

"That's why there are Chinatowns in so many American cities. Chinese like to live among their own people, but they are also prevented from living anyplace else. They have to live in Chinatowns."

Mei Lin stared into her cup, her eyes glistening. "That very sad." She looked up at him. "But we don't have to live in Chinatown, do we? We can live anywhere we want to live. That good." She smiled.

He sipped from his cup and looked out the window to watch three old men in traditional Chinese dress walking slowly down the middle of the street, chatting and gesturing.

The light from the lamppost cast a soft glow through the street windows into their room, describing two rectangles of light, one on the floor at the foot of the bed and the other on the bed at their feet.

They lay side by side, looking at the ceiling, breathing deeply, Mei Lin smiling in the darkness, Caleb grim.

"That so good, honee." She turned on her side and snuggled on his chest. "Caleb," she said.

He turned over to face her. "Caleb?" he said.

"I practice, Caleb, honee."

He pulled her to him and held her tightly.

"Easy, Caleb, honey. Too tight."

He loosened his hold, with his arms still around her. He laid his cheek on her head, moved his hand down her back, her belly, and gently pressed her breast. He sighed heavily.

"Okay, honee?"

He was silent, then answered. "Okay." He squeezed her, then released her and turned over, facing the wall. He stared into the darkness.

The second-floor waterfront cafe overlooked the boardwalk and wharf. Ships were tied with long lines to wharf bollards, some loading, some unloading, others still and waiting. Pedestrians walked on the boardwalk, some in a hurry, knowing where they were going, others strolling, on a morning off or on a holiday.

Caleb and Mei Lin sat at a small table that overlooked the boardwalk and the bay. Their bags were pushed against the wall near their table. The entire wall where they sat was a series of windows from ceiling to tabletops. They looked at the bay where small steamer ferries and oceangoing ships sailed slowly by.

Mei Lin's plate was empty. Caleb had hardly touched his breakfast. He pushed the eggs and potatoes about his plate with his fork. Since they had sat down, he had hardly looked at Mei Lin, instead focusing on his plate and the bay.

"What is it, honee? You must tell me."

He hesitated, glanced briefly at her, then looked through the window at nothing. After a long moment, he turned back to her. He inhaled deeply.

"Mei Lin, you know that there are good people, and there are bad people. Many Americans like Chinese, but many do not. You know that in Idaho, there have been problems when Americans, mostly miners, have forced Chinese to leave their homes. Some Chinese have been killed. You know about all this."

Mei Lin's face fell, and she tensed.

"No, Caleb, honee."

"You know all this," he said. "It's not going to get any better. It's too dangerous for you in Idaho."

"No, Caleb, honee, please."

"I want only what's best for you, Mei Lin. I'm afraid for you. There's no life for you in Idaho, in this country."

"Please, Caleb, honee. I not afraid. I love you. If you want best for me, you let me stay with you. I love you. I do anything for you! I be servant, I work for you! I do anything for you!" Tears filled her eyes, blurring her vision. "I love you."

"Mei Lin, I feel like I'm dying inside, but there is no life for you here. You should be in China, among your own people, your parents and your family, your friends."

"I have no life in China. My mother father think I am dead. My life is here. With you."

Caleb stared blankly through the window, then back at her, then back to the window. *What am I doing? God, what am I doing?*

"There is your ship." He nodded toward the window. An oceanliner was tied to the dock below. She did not look. She slumped in her chair.

"I thought you love me," she said softly. Tears rolled down her cheeks.

"Mei Lin, I'm giving you enough money to buy a business. You are smart, you are a hard worker, and you will be a success in whatever you do. I know you will. You will be safe."

"You don't want me," she said softly. "You say you want best for me. Honee, China not my home. It is not."

He pursed his lips, said nothing. He stared through the window at the ship.

Someday she will acknowledge that this was best. I will

be a shadow in her past, Idaho will be forgotten. As painful as this is now for her, and for me, she will heal and know that everything I did was for her.

She straightened. "You no love me. You throw me away." She wiped her face with both hands. "Okay."

She pushed her chair back, stood, and walked to her bag. Caleb jumped up and hurried to pick up the bag. She brushed his hand away, picked up the bag, and walked toward the door. He picked up his bag and followed.

They walked on the wharf alongside the large liner he had pointed out from the cafe. Aboard the ship, dozens of people, mostly Asian, leaned on the rail, looking down at the wharf, waving to those who had come to send them on their way. Some laughed and gestured, chatting happily with companions, off on a holiday. Others wore long faces, tearful, saying goodbye.

As they walked, Mei Lin stared at the wharf at her feet. Caleb watched her anxiously, wanting to talk, afraid to talk.

What can I say? What hasn't been said? What needs to be said? He walked beside her, watched her, wanting to speak, unable to speak.

They arrived at the foot of the gangway and stopped there. She looked up at him briefly, tear tracks marking her face, looked down at her bag. They stepped aside to let a couple, chatting and laughing, board. Mei Lin looked blankly at the ship.

Caleb held out a small purse. "Here is your ticket and money. Keep it with you at all times. Don't let it out of your sight. It is your future."

She took the purse, glanced at it blankly. She looked down at the tide that flowed slowly at the ship's waterline.

Caleb's face was distorted, in torment. "Mei Lin . . ." He

reached for her, but she jerked her arm away. She looked up at him, and tears flowed.

She grabbed her bag, ran up the gangway, stumbling, her bag bumping into the side of the canvas-covered rail of the gangway. Caleb started to run after her, to help her, but she reached the top of the gangway and disappeared behind the line of passengers at the rail.

She was gone. Caleb stepped quickly to the right, trying to catch sight of her, and back again to the left, trying to find her among the passengers at the rail.

But she was gone.

At that moment, a dockworker at the base of the gangway released a clamp that held the ramp to the dock. A deckhand at the top of the gangway released a clamp, and the cable attached to the gangway tightened. The ramp lifted a few inches from the ship's deck.

"Mei Lin! Mei Lin!" Caleb ran back and forth, bumping and pushing aside others on the dock, trying to find her among the passengers lining the ship's rail. The people on the dock glared at Caleb, frowning at this rude fellow.

"Mei Lin!" Passengers aboard the ship looked down at the crazed man on the dock, shouting and waving his arms.

"Mei Lin! Come back! Mei Lin!"

Mei Lin's face appeared suddenly in the line of people at the rail. She pushed passengers aside to reach the rail.

"Come back!" he said.

She ran toward the gangway, then stopped, turned around, and disappeared into the crowd of passengers.

"My god! She's gone! She's gone!" he said.

She reappeared at once, holding up the purse. She ran to the gangway, stopped. The gangway had lifted a foot above the deck and pulled a couple of feet away from the ship's side.

Mei Lin leaped from the deck to the ramp, but she didn't make it. She landed on her stomach on the ramp, her legs dangling over the end. She slid slowly from the ramp, falling, her legs flailing.

Spectators on the wharf and at the ship's rail gasped. A woman at the rail screamed. Another shouted. "Help her!"

Mei Lin grabbed a metal rod at the end of the ramp with one hand and dangled. The ramp was now four feet above the level of the deck and was still moving away from the ship. She hung above water. Spectators gasped again as one. She hung by one hand, swinging, holding the purse in her other hand.

She threw the purse onto the gangway and grabbed the rod with both hands. She pulled up, straining, until her chest was on the ramp.

Then she slipped and slid off the ramp again, hanging with both hands gripping the ramp bar. Passengers and those on the dock gasped, screamed, called out for someone to help.

Crewmen had begun the slow process of lowering the gangway when they first saw Mei Lin leap for the lifting ramp. Now three crewmen at the opening in the rail where the gangway had been secured leaned out, trying to reach Mei Lin, but she was too far away.

Mei Lin pulled herself up inch by inch until she could grab the vertical poles of the side of the gangway.

Then Caleb was there. He had run up the ramp, bouncing on the sides, falling once, when he first saw her leap for the gangway. He kneeled and grasped her under her arms and pulled her gently to the bed of the ramp. She rose to her knees and picked up the purse.

Caleb helped her stand and supported her as they

walked unsteadily down the lowering gangway, bouncing side to side against the railing.

When they reached the bottom, a crewman helped them step down off the swinging ramp onto the wharf. A loud cheer rose from the people on the wharf and lining the ship's rail. People nearby patted Caleb on the back and touched Mei Lin gently. Not a few people had tears streaming down their cheeks.

Caleb and Mei Lin held each other tightly. He whispered into her ear. "Mei Lin. I love you. I'll never let you go. Never. Whatever happens. I'll never let you go." She gripped his coat lapels with both hands and pulled him close, burying her face in the folds of the coat.

"Ready to go home?" he said.

"No."

He pulled back, frowning. "No?"

"I need to shop. I have no clothes. There, my clothes." She pointed at the ship. The gangway was up, lines had been lifted from the wharf bollards and dropped into the water, and the ship was moving slowly away from the dock.

He smiled. "Little lady, we will go shopping. Anything you want." He picked up his bag with one hand and took her arm with the other, moving her down the pier. People stepped aside, smiling, patting them on the back, wishing them good fortune.

They walked briskly, as if they had someplace to go. He looked up at the sky, then at her. "Mei Lin. Mei Lin. What was I thinking?" He stopped and enveloped her, pressing her head to his chest.

They walked again. "First, we need to get a place to winter," he said. "That will be home for a while. Then we'll shop."

She pulled away from his grasp and looked severely at him. "Okay, boss, whatever you say!" She laughed and grabbed his arm, ran down the boardwalk, pulling him along.

Caleb had not planned to spend the winter in Seattle, so he had made no arrangements beyond putting Mei Lin on the ship. He realized only now that his present and his future, in his mind, had reached an end with her leaving.

My god, what would I have done if she had left? What would have become of me if she had left? He shook his head. He didn't know. He had no idea. He had planned her departure, and he would stand on the dock and watch her ship leave. He felt a great sadness enveloping him.

"Honey, are you okay?" she said. She reached across the table and touched his hand. They sat at the same table at the window of the same small cafe overlooking the wharf where they had sat when he told her of his decision.

His head came up. "What a pair we are! Always having to ask each other if we are okay. Are we always so troubled?" He put his hand on hers. "Yes, I am okay, better than I deserve to be. Mei Lin, I have been so incredibly stupid, so wrong on so many counts. I am so sorry I did not listen, to you and to my own heart. I hope someday you will be able to forgive me."

She took his hand in both of hers. Tears rolled down her cheeks. "Honey, I want go our room, and I want you to take off my clothes, and I will take off your clothes, and we will get into bed, and you will tell me how sorry you are, and I will say that it okay, and we will cry, and we will make love, and it will all be okay."

They stood, and he wiped her face with his hands. They kissed and walked toward the cafe door, with eyes only for each other, as if they were invisible, unseen by the dozen people sitting at tables, watching them, smiling and whispering to each other.

Outside, a cold wind blew the soft rain into their faces. They walked briskly up the hill, she put both arms around his waist and squeezed, and he leaned down to kiss her upturned face.

15 I WANT
TO GO HOME

With the help of the clerk at the Panama Hotel, the only person they knew in Seattle, Caleb found an apartment two blocks from the hotel. It was above a store owned by the clerk's aunt, in the center of Nihonmachi, Japantown. The apartment had a bedroom, a kitchen, and a small sitting room that looked out two front windows to the street. There were a toilet and sink, but no bathtub.

When Caleb questioned the clerk about bathing, he had shown them the metal tub that hung in the utility closet. But, he beamed, there is a wonderful alternative.

They walked to the Panama Hotel where the clerk showed them the sento in the basement.

The sento, a public bathhouse, had two gleaming marble basins, one for women and the other for men, filled with steaming hot water. He explained that patrons undressed and hung their clothes in numbered wooden lockers that lined the wall. The doors of the lockers were decorated with hand-painted signs that advertised local businesses.

Caleb asked the clerk where they undressed. The clerk was confused. Well, here, he said, as they stood before the lockers. What if there are others here? Caleb said. The clerk clearly did not understand the question, but he tried to explain. Patrons undressed before others, but they did not look at each other. They were to be invisible to each other. Oh, Caleb had said.

The clerk gave each of them a small towel to use as a body cover, if they wished. Enough for Caleb, but not large enough to cover Mei Lin. The clerk showed them the faucets at the wall where they were to wash their bodies and rinse before entering the basin of hot water.

"Please remember," he had said, "never go into the bath with soap on your body."

The first time they went to the sento, it was afternoon, well before workers crowded the bath to soak their tired bodies, and it was almost empty. Only two older Japanese women were immersed up to their necks. The women had been talking and laughing softly when Caleb and Mei Lin came in, but now they were quiet and stared unashamedly at them.

Caleb opened a locker at the corner. Mei Lin faced the corner, her nose almost touching the wall, and began to remove her clothes. She handed each article to him without moving from her corner. She glanced over her shoulder toward the women, then turned back to her corner.

You poor woman. Every inch of your body has been seen by evil men, and every orifice of your body has been violated. And still you can blush. My poor sweet girl.

Caleb stood behind her, facing her, his back to the two women. When he reached into the locker to hang up his shirt, he glanced toward the women. They faced the opposite wall, but both heads were turned to look at them. The women made instant eye contact, but snapped their heads around and resumed chatting. Caleb smiled to himself.

"Honey," Mei Lin whispered, without taking her eyes from her corner. He bent forward to listen. "I glad there are no men. I don't like see men's bodies. They are ugly."

He smiled to himself. "Oh?"

She turned her head quickly to him. "I don't mean you, honey. You okay. Just other men. You know."

"Yes, I know." He kissed her cheek. She turned back to the corner, removed her underpants, and handed them to him.

When they were completely naked, they sat on stools before the wall faucets and soaped their bodies.

"You want me to wash you?" Caleb said.

"No, women see. You can feel me in bath."

"Actually, I can't. I'll be in the men's bath, and you will be in the women's bath. With the two women." He looked at the women who faced away from them, chatting softly.

"Oh. Maybe you dry me after bath."

"I could do that, but I would have to face the corner." She laughed softly. He reached over and lightly touched the nipple of her small breast.

"No!" she whispered. "No do that!"

He smiled and took two wooden bowls from a shelf above the faucets, handing a bowl to her. They filled the bowls from the faucet and rinsed their bodies, then stood unsteadily on the wet floor. They replaced the bowls on the shelf and glanced toward the two women. They still faced the opposite wall.

Mei Lin and Caleb walked toward their respective baths. Caleb held his small towel over his crotch and watched Mei Lin. She held her towel at her waist in front, but her backside was completely exposed.

Caleb realized that he had never seen her naked body in daylight. Her exquisite naked body. He watched until she entered the basin. She nodded to the women, who smiled at her. She sank in the water to her chin and looked up at Caleb.

Caleb removed his towel and held it aside.

Mei Lin's eyes opened wide. She ducked underwater. Caleb smiled and stepped into the men's bath.

The weeks that followed were a cold, wet idyll. It rained most days, usually a gentle rain that was cold, but not unpleasant or restricting. They visited Chinatown where Mei Lin delighted in speaking to shopkeepers and vendors in Chinese. She bubbled and laughed, talking to anyone who would listen, all in Chinese. She held Caleb close, and they appeared as one as they walked down the center of the narrow pedestrian lane.

Passersby stopped and watched them. Mei Lin smiled and spoke to them. Sometimes she stopped and initiated conversation with other pedestrians. Caleb was content to stand aside and watch.

She had a particularly intent conversation with an elderly shopkeeper who stood in front of his herb shop, polishing a small urn as they talked. At one point, his jaw dropped, he looked abruptly at Caleb, back to Mei Lin, and he laughed until tears streamed down his cheeks. He looked at Caleb again, bowed sharply to him, and stepped into his shop, still polishing the jug, still laughing. Mei Lin walked over to Caleb.

"All right, what were you talking about?" Caleb said.

"You," she said. "They all very curious about you. This man, he asked if you own me. I tell him no, I own him!" She ducked her head, smiled.

Caleb looked at her a long moment. Then he bent down slowly, settled on both knees before her in the middle of the pedestrian street, and bowed his head.

Pedestrians stopped in their tracks, dumbstruck. They saw this American, kneeling before this young Chinese woman. They looked at each other, frowning.

Mei Lin bent over him. "Caleb!" she said softly. "What you do? Get up! You crazy!" She grasped the folds of his coat lapels and tried to pull him up.

He looked up at her, smiled. He jumped up, grabbed her around the waist, and lifted her off the ground. The circle of onlookers gasped, exclaimed, stepped toward Caleb and Mei Lin.

Caleb slowly lowered Mei Lin to the ground, took her cheeks in both hands, and kissed her softly, hugged her tightly. She leaned back and kissed him.

The onlookers cheered, smiled, went on their way, chatting, looking back at the strange spectacle of an American man and a Chinese woman, deliriously and unashamedly in love.

They walked often along the waterfront, stopping at cafes for coffee and tea. Pike Place market was a favorite stop where they bought vegetables and fish for their kitchen.

On one occasion, they lingered over morning coffee in a small cafe, chatting softly, laughing. There were three other couples. Sitting at a window table, a Chinese girl held the hand of her white boyfriend across the table. They leaned toward each other so close that their noses almost touched. They talked softly, closely, closer, and it appeared that they would kiss at any moment.

Caleb motioned with his head toward the couple. Mei Lin turned and saw them. She smiled. It was not the first mixed couple they had seen in Seattle, but they always noticed. Quite a contrast to Idaho where they had seen no other mixed couple. What was unknown there was, if not commonplace, at least was not rare here.

They stood and pulled on coats. Caleb struggled with a twisted sleeve, and Mei Lin helped him straighten it. They looked again at the couple at the window. His hand was at her cheek. The girl laughed.

Caleb held the door for Mei Lin, and they walked outside, shivered in the sudden cold, pulling up collars and tightening scarves. They walked along the boardwalk, Mei Lin holding Caleb's arm with both hands, clutching him tightly against the cold breeze.

They stopped at a railing and looked out to the bay. Caleb pulled his hands from pockets and leaned on the rail. A ferry sailed northward, two small sailboats alongside, bobbing gently in the ferry's wake. Black smoke rose in a thick column from the ferry's single stack, swirled and scattered in the breeze. Passengers stood at the railing, looking down at the sailboats. A crewman on a sailboat waved.

Mei Lin looked up at Caleb. "You are quiet," she said.

He watched the ferry a long moment before speaking. "I thought I would never be happy again. I thought I would never be able to let the past go and live in the present. I'll always love her, Mei Lin, the memory of her. And Bobby and Sissie."

Mei Lin still held his arm tightly. "Honey, I never wanted you to forget. I can love them with you. I just want you to save a little place for me."

He turned to her and encircled her shoulders with his arms. "My sweet girl. You saved my life." He raised her chin and kissed her. "I've got a big place saved for you."

Mei Lin and Caleb, bareheaded and coats unbuttoned, walked in a small Japantown park. They strolled, going nowhere, their usual morning activity. Mei Lin's hands were pushed into coat pockets, head down.

Grass on the narrow park lawns was anemic and trampled. Planter beds were bare save for husks and dry stalks, some rose bushes that had not been pruned. Leafless tree branches reached out and up like bony skeletons.

The park gradually brightened as the cloud cover thinned and lifted. Mei Lin looked up at the sun through the dark, bare branches of a Japanese cherry tree. On the branches, she watched tiny droplets that had collected from the morning mist sparkle, drop, collect, and sparkle again. She stepped off the walk and stared intently at a low branch. Tiny, fat buds were just beginning to show a hint of pink. One bud, only one, had opened into a cluster of pink petals. She turned to Caleb who stood on the path, watching her.

"I want to go home," she said.

He stood a moment, then walked to her. "I do too, sweetheart. But it may be too early. There might still be snow. There's the pass at Galena."

"Could we get through?"

He pondered. "I could send a telegram to Ketchum."

"I have better idea. Let's take a train to Ketchum now and ask about pass there? If too much snow, we stay in Ketchum until the pass is open. How 'bout that?"

He frowned, pondered. "Hmm. That sounds like a good idea. Let's go to the station right now and ask when we can get tickets. Good idea, peanut! Let's go!" He took her arm and pulled and pushed her down the path toward the main street.

"Okay," she said. "Let's go!" They marched in step down the path. She stopped. "What do you mean, 'peanut'?"

"Nothing. Peanut, sweetie, sweetheart, love of my life, all the same."

She started walking, almost skipping. "Okay. I like 'sweetheart' best."

"Good," he said. They walked with long strides down the path, bouncing playfully against each other. He leaned toward her. "Peanut," he said.

She pulled away, hit him on the arm, and ran down the path, laughing.

16 WELCOME HOME

Caleb stood on the wooden platform at the Ketchum station, talking with the railway agent, the same agent Caleb had worked with on his dredge hardware delivery. Bright sunshine contrasted with the piles of dirty snow along the roadways and perimeter of the station compound. Mei Lin sat on a bench at the end of the platform, her coat buttoned to the top and hands deep in pockets, her eyes closed and face turned up to the warming sun. Their two bags lay at her feet.

"The last wagons over the pass was four days ago," the agent said. "They had a time of it, still lots of snow at the top. Must not have been too bad, though. They turned around two days later and went back. Hadn't heard anything since then. I expect, I hope, they made it across okay."

"Hmm. I'm in no hurry," said Caleb. "We'll sit tight until another party comes over and gives us a report. Do you know where we can put up a few days?"

"You don't have much choice this time of year. Your best bet is the Idaho Hotel, just on the left side down the street here." He pointed. "Summers, some of the townspeople take in travelers, but not winter."

"Much obliged. You'll let me know if someone comes in from Stanley?"

"I'll do that," said the agent.

Caleb raised a hand in salute and walked to Mei Lin. He sat beside her. "Looks like we'll have to enjoy the delights of Ketchum for a few days. Soon as somebody comes over the hill from Stanley to tell us about the conditions at the pass."

"How we go Stanley?" she said.

He stared at the empty tracks across the compound. "If we can find a wagon going over the hill that will take us, we'll do that. If not, we'll have to rent horses. I'd rather not do that since we'd have to pay for their keep until we can send 'em back."

"C'mon, let's get a hotel room," he said, "and then some coffee." He stood and reached to help her up. She batted his hand away and picked up her bag.

"Whatever you say, boss!"

He smiled, picked up his bag, wrapped his other arm around her neck and squeezed, and they stepped off the platform to the street.

The wagon rolled down the road above the cabin. Snow still blanketed much of the meadow, but there were dry patches that showed a hint of green. The sky was clear, but for a line of white, fleecy clouds. The snow-covered Sawtooth range was etched against a light blue background.

The pond was fringed with ice, but at this distance, most of the surface appeared to be open, sparkling, reflecting the drifting clouds. The dredge was tied to the shore where he had left it. Intact, from all appearances.

Caleb inhaled deeply, exhaled. He reached around Mei Lin's shoulders and pulled her close. She looked up at him, smiled.

"Look," Mei Lin said. She pointed toward the meadow. Buck and Chica stood like statues in the meadow just beyond the corral, ears erect, looking at the approaching wagon.

"Chica!" Mei Lin shouted. The horse lurched and galloped toward the wagon. Buck followed close behind. The two horses came up to the wagon and walked alongside.

"Chica, my sweet girl. I missed you." Chica bobbed her head, mane flying and tail swishing.

"God almighty, Mei Lin. I never saw anybody who could hold a conversation with a dumb animal like you can," said Abel.

"Well," said Mei Lin, "that's because she's not dumb. She is smarter than a lot of people I know."

Abel laughed. "I won't argue with that."

Caleb had been relieved in Ketchum when the railroad agent had sent word to the Idaho Hotel that a wagon had arrived from Stanley. He was delighted that the teamsters were Abel Custer, the Stanley friend who operated the feed store, and his son Wally who had occasionally picked up funds at the Ketchum Western Union office for Caleb.

The return journey was faster than usual. The road was clear, the wagon was lightly loaded, and Wally was in a hurry to see his girlfriend. Abel refused his repeated request to drive because, he said, the young 'un tended to exercise the mules too much. He had dropped the boy in Stanley before driving to Caleb's place.

Abel pulled up in front of the cabin and looped the lines around the brake handle. He climbed down slowly, hopping in a circle beside the wagon to exercise stiff joints. Caleb jumped down and extended a hand to Mei Lin. She took his hand and climbed down. Both stretched. Caleb stamped the ground to revive cramped legs.

"Abel, you're a saint," Caleb said. "Thanks for the delivery. I owe you. I'm going to fire up the stove and make coffee. Can you stop a bit?"

"Thank 'ee, Caleb, but I'd best be on my way. Want to get back to Stanley before dark."

Caleb reached into the wagon bed for their bags and dropped them on the ground. They watched as Abel set the mules in motion and turned back up the road. Abel waved over his shoulder.

Caleb and Mei Lin walked around to the side of the cabin. They were quiet, looking toward the pond and dredge.

Caleb cupped his hands around his mouth. "Halloo, the dredge!" he shouted. "Anybody there!"

Immediately two heads appeared from the door of the steam engine housing. Andrew and Cal stepped out onto the deck. They waved.

"Hey, Caleb!" Andrew shouted. "Hey, Mei Lin!"

Caleb waved. "I'll be down later!" The men waved, watched as Caleb and Mei Lin disappeared around the cabin.

Caleb stepped up the stoop to the cabin door. Mei Lin stood behind him. He lifted the latch and slowly pushed the door open. Caleb had warned Mei Lin that they would have a thorough cleaning to do before the place would be habitable. Spider webs and mouse droppings, an inch of dust and an assortment of bugs.

He saw instead a clean cabin, short lengths of wood stacked beside the stove, and clean windowpanes with an open curtain that admitted the bright sunshine.

Caleb turned to Mei Lin. "Welcome home, sweetheart."

The land was emerging from fire and ice. Tiny green shoots of new grass colored the meadow, still covered in a gray ash. Above the meadow, in the forest of black skeletons, some few trees that had somehow survived the fire showed leaf buds on the blackened limbs. On the forest floor, saplings pushed up through the mat of ash. Patches of dirty snow lingered in shady spots along the forest edge.

The dredge was back in full operation. Caleb and Mei Lin, Andrew and Cal, and Tindoor and two other Sheepeaters had worked dawn to dusk this past week to get it ready for the new season.

Everything appeared to be back to normal. Normal, meaning that they were taking little gold. Caleb hadn't sold any gold since putting the dredge back in operation these past two weeks, but he knew that they were not making expenses.

Nor had they ever made expenses from the dredge operation. He had always supplemented the gold income from his Virginia account, but he knew that this could not go on forever.

The first thing he had done on their arrival in Ketchum was to cable his agent. The agent's reply arrived just before their departure. The message confirmed that Caleb's account would be depleted by midsummer if he continued to withdraw at the rate of the previous year.

Caleb's back was against the wall. He had hoped to preserve for emergencies the purse that he had given Mei Lin, but he had begun dipping into that reserve to help meet costs.

And now this new problem.

A man stood in the cabin yard with Caleb, holding the reins of his horse, as Caleb read the sheet that the man had given him. The paper was a legal document issued by the County Clerk in Challis. The document declared that Caleb had not proven up on his claim. It gave him thirty days to respond and prove that his claim was showing a profit. If he could not do so, he must surrender his claim.

"I'm really sorry, Mr. Willis, the man said. "People in Stanley have told me that you're a good man and have worked real hard on your claim."

"I don't understand," said Caleb, "no one has talked with me about this. No one, so far as I know, has any idea about how much gold I'm taking. How did this begin? Where did this come from?"

The agent cleared his throat. He looked aside, then back at Caleb. "Um, well, Mr. Willis, I'm just a clerk, but I hear things. My boss, the county clerk, gave me this paper the day after Mr. Bennett visited him last week. Now, I can't say for sure that there is any connection between Mr. Bennett's visit and this paper, but it's pretty well known hereabouts that Mr. Bennett does not look kindly on any dredging operation in the basin other than his own."

"Yes, I'm aware of that," said Caleb.

"Please don't say I said anything. I would lose my job, for sure. I just don't like to see a good man bamboozled."

"I appreciate it. Nobody will hear anything from me. I promise you that."

"Thank you, Mr. Willis," the agent said. "Good luck." He touched his hat, mounted, and galloped up the road.

"What will you do now, honey?"

Caleb turned to see Mei Lin standing in the doorway. "I don't know. I don't know how all this works. This is something new to me."

Caleb looked at the document, held it at arm's length. "Damn," he said. "Can I never have peace?" He walked to the door and sat down on the stoop. She sat down beside him. They looked outside, each in their own world, silent.

She turned to him. "I have a plan," she said. "I will go to dredge. I say to Bennett I want to work for him. Wash clothes, cook, clean. I get him into bed, and I cut his throat."

Caleb laughed.

"You think I can't do this? I Chink whore, 'member?" She smiled.

"Yes, I think you can do this. And I think you would do it. But I won't let you." He grabbed her around her shoulders and squeezed. She struggled, laughing and pushing him away. He tickled her and pulled her to him and held her tightly until she stopped struggling, and they faced each other, nose to nose.

"Why won't you let me?" she said softly. He held her face in his hands and kissed her lightly. He pulled back and looked into her eyes, brushed a strand of her hair with a hand.

"Because you're *my* Chink whore." He kissed her again. He stood and walked toward the corral, studying the document.

Mei Lin sat on the doorsill, her chin on her crossed arms over her knees, looking into the woods across the road.

17 HOME IS WHERE YOU DE-CIDE IT IS

Caleb's wagon rolled down Stanley's main street. Mei Lin held the lines, and Caleb sat beside her. She pulled up in front of the general store and coiled the lines around the brake handle. Caleb jumped down while Mei Lin climbed down the other side.

They stepped up onto the boardwalk. Caleb spoke to Mei Lin and entered the store. Mei Lin looked into the dark interior of the store a moment, then turned back to the street.

It was a lovely spring day. Two old men sat on a bench in front of the feed store, adjacent to the general store, chatting, laughing, and occasionally leaning forward to spit to the street. Or toward the street since they usually didn't have the range, and their tobacco juice fell on the boardwalk.

Two women wearing ankle-length work dresses and bonnets stood on the walk on the opposite side of the road. They appeared to be talking, but Mei Lin could not hear them.

Mei Lin closed her eyes, smiling, contented, and raised her face to the warming sun. She opened her eyes and saw her.

In the middle of the street in front of her stood a Chinese woman, looking directly at her. The woman appeared to be in her sixties. Her lined face suggested a hard life, but it was a soft, open face. She was short, wearing a long black dress that would have been stylish ten years ago, with lacey white ruffles at the sleeve ends and a high collar, buttoned at the neck. Mei Lin glanced down at her own blue denim trousers and wrinkled calico shirt.

"Mei Lin." The woman said.

Mei Lin was startled. It was not a question, but a statement.

"Yes. I am Mei Lin."

"Nĭ bū rènshī wŏ, Mei Lin, dàn sī wŏ zhīdao nĭ." You don't know me, Mei Lin, but I know about you. The woman walked to the boardwalk and stepped up beside Mei Lin.

"You are better known around here than you might think," the woman said. "People who are bored for conversation will talk about anything or anybody out of the ordinary. We are alike, you and I. We are curiosities. Wŏ mēn lĭang xīng yùn zhăo daò lē haŏ năn rēn, haē dē yăng gúi zī." Both of us were fortunate to find good men, good foreign devils. The woman smiled.

Mei Lin brightened. "Wŏ zhĭ daò. Nĭ sō Polly Bemis! Wŏ tīng shūo guò nĭ." I know. You are Polly Bemis! I have heard about you.

"Sī dē," yes, said Polly. "Mei Lin, wŏ mēn xīan zaì yīng gāi shūo yīng wĕn. Yăng gúi zī mēn bù xĭ huán wŏ mēn shūo zhōng wĕn yín wèi tā mēn bù dŏng. Tā mēn yĭ wéi wŏ mēn zaì shūo tā mēn." Mei Lin, we should speak English now. The foreign devils don't like us to speak in Chinese because they can't understand us. They think we are talking about them. She smiled.

"If what I heard is true," Polly said, "our stories are very similar. I also was sold by my parents and was brought to this country as a slave. I was taken to San Francisco and then to Warrens. The Chinese man who bought me operated the saloon there and expected me to entertain. It was a bad time for me. But the American who owned the saloon watched out for me. He liked me. Now he is my husband. I heard that the man who owns you is a good man."

"O, Polly, wǒ xǐ huān gēn nǐ shūo zhōng wěn." Oh, Polly, I love to talk with you in Chinese. Mei Lin took Polly's hand.

"Wǒ zaì Stanley kuāi lǐang nǐan le cóng lǎi měi yoú gēn rèn hē rèn shūo gūo zhōng wěn. Kě sī haǒ dē, yīng wěn. Wǒ dǒng." I have been in Stanley almost two years and have never talked with anyone in Chinese here.

"But, okay, English. I understand." Mei Lin wiped a tear from her cheek with the back of her hand. "Polly, Caleb doesn't own me. He said that I am free and can go as I please. But I will not go away. I want to stay with him."

"Did you ever think of going home, back to China?" said Polly.

"No! Never! Caleb wanted to send me back, for my own good, he said, but I did not want to go. I refused. I said I would not go. I was very unhappy when he tried to send me back. My home is here. I think he wants me here now. He said he loves me. Did you ever want to go back?"

"At first. When I was so unhappy at Warrens. But when Charlie became my protector, and my lover, I knew my home was here. He also became my owner. He won me in a card game from my Chinese owner. But he said I was free and could leave if I wanted. I didn't want to leave. I wanted to stay with him. You see how alike we are."

Mei Lin motioned toward the bench in front of the

general store, and they sat. They were quiet a moment, then Polly turned to Mei Lin.

"Mei Lin, home is where you decide it is, where you are happy, where you are with someone you want to spend your life with. We have been lucky, you and I. Most Chinese women who come to this country alone come to no good."

Polly withdrew her hand, and they sat in silence, looking at the street, looking into their shared, troubled pasts.

"I think I know how you got your name," said Mei Lin. "When I came to Rat Trap, men called me 'Polly.' But I would not reply. They asked me for my name, but I would not tell them. So they just called me 'whore' or 'Chink' or something like that."

"Men call any woman who works in a saloon 'Polly.' I don't know why... You live on Stanley Creek? Your man operates a gold dredge?"

"Yes. But—nǐ bǐ něng gēn rèn hē rěn shūo—wǒ mēn měi zǎo daù duō saǒ jīn zī." You must not tell anyone—we are not getting much gold. "I don't know what is going to happen. He talks about farming or ranching or dredging some other place. I am worried."

"Mei Lin, you will find a place. This is good country. We left Warrens when the people there made all the Chinese leave. There were deaths. That was a sad time. Now we live on the Salmon, downstream from Stanley. We have a little farm, and we have good neighbors. Times are changing, Mei Lin. Americans around here are not so angry with Chinese as they have been."

Polly stood. "Now I must go. There is my husband." She waved to a man across the street who had just come out of the hardware store. Polly took Mei Lin's hand.

"We must be strong, Mei Lin," she said softly. "Baǒ zhōng nǔ zǔ jǔ hē nǐ dē haǒ yǎng gúi zī zhàng fū." Take care of yourself and your good foreign devil husband. Polly smiled, stepped down to the road, and walked across to her waiting husband.

Dawn, a clear blue sky. Tindoor and Caleb stood on the pond bank near the dredge. Tindoor and two other Sheepeaters had just arrived on foot, ready to work. Tindoor's companions had already boarded the dredge.

The dredge was in operation, and the noise was deafening. Caleb watched the bucketline chewing into the bank. At the other end of the dredge, a steady hail of stones clattered on top of the huge pile of tailings.

"Boss, I tell you something," Tindoor said loudly. "I said I would not say, but I must."

Caleb turned toward Tindoor and leaned forward. "What's that? I can't . . ." He started walking down the bank and beckoned Tindoor to follow. About thirty yards along the bank, he stopped.

"Now," Caleb said.

"Two hunters my village find two Americans in valley other side of village, a man and a woman. He hurt, shot. We bring to village. They say no tell anybody. I say okay, but he worse. Can you come?"

"Wait." Caleb strode back to the dredge, walked up the catwalk, and disappeared inside. A moment later, he retraced his steps to the bank and waved to Tindoor, pointing to the house.

Caleb, Mei Lin and Tindoor, riding one of Caleb's mules, rode into the Sheepeater village. They dismounted and handed the reins to a boy who led them away.

"They here," Tindoor said and walked toward his cabin. Caleb and Mei Lin followed. Tindoor opened the door and held it for them.

On the bed opposite the door, a man lay on his side. His

upper body was bare but for a bandage wrapped around his chest. He was in his mid-twenties, drawn and pale.

He struggled to rise on an elbow, surprised. The woman who was seated in a chair beside the bed looked around. She was a few years younger, but the lines in her face revealed years of suffering.

"Tindoor," the man said, "you said—"

Mei Lin's hands went to her face. "Chica!" Mei Lin said. The woman looked up at her.

"Mei Lin?"

"Chica!" Mei Lin rushed to her, and Chica stood. They reached for each other and hugged tightly. "Chica! I thought I never see you again! Chica!" They separated, looked at each other, and hugged again.

"So this is Chica," Caleb said.

"Chica, this is Caleb. He took me from Rat Trap, same as you." She looked at the wounded man. "I remember you. You are . . . Ray!" He smiled.

"Yes. I think I know you too. Chica talks about you all the time. Mei Lin this, Mei Lin that. I'm glad to finally meet you." He extended an arm toward Caleb. "Caleb—" He grimaced in pain and withdrew the outstretched arm.

"Glad to meet you, Ray, and you, Chica. Now, let Mei Lin look at that wound. She's a regular healer, she is. She has doctored me, and she'll do the same for you."

Chica jumped up and held the back of the chair. "Here, Mei Lin, sit here." Mei Lin sat. She looked at the bandage, lifted it to see the edge of the wound.

"Chica, Tindoor, can you get me a piece of clean cloth and warm water?" The two went into the kitchen while Mei Lin began unwrapping the bloody bandage from Ray's chest.

"Who did this to you?" Caleb said.

"Polly's men. Two of them. Chica recognized one of them from the Rat Trap. We was working on the Wentworth ranch south of here, on the Boise road, and these two rode in one afternoon, saw me and Chica working on a fence, and started shooting. Just started shooting. Some of the other hands heard the shooting and chased 'em off, but they got me, and I didn't even know it till I fell on the ground. Good thing Chica was with me. But if they'd hurt her, I'd uh tore 'em apart, gut shot or no."

"I know what you mean," Caleb said.

"Why would Polly do that?" Mei Lin said. "She must know she's not going to get Chica back. Or me."

Mei Lin still worked on removing the bandage. She stopped when the bandage stuck to the wound. "We'll wait for the warm water, Ray."

"Just meanness," said Chica. She and Tindoor had walked into the room from the kitchen. She gave Mei Lin a handful of cloth pieces.

"Water is warming on stove," said Tindoor. "Ready few minutes."

"Polly is crazy," Chica said. "She just wants to hurt anybody who goes against her. She's crazy. I don't think we will ever be safe, you and me, Mei Lin, until she is dead or gone."

Caleb frowned. "I think you may be right. How did you get here with the Sheepeaters?"

"I didn't want to cause problems for the ranch. They had only four cowboys other than the owner. I was afraid Polly's men would come back. Chica's right. Polly's just plain crazy. She just wants revenge."

Ray shifted on the bed, wincing in pain. "We left. I wasn't hurtin' too bad and thought we could make it to Boise without any trouble. But I was wrong. I was in pretty bad shape when Tindoor found us."

"We were hunting," Tindoor said. "Good elk country where we found them."

Ray lay in Caleb's bed, his chest wrapped in a clean bandage. Chica sat on the bed beside him. Caleb and Mei Lin sat at the table, holding mugs.

"I don't feel real good about this," said Ray.

"Just don't get too comfortable," said Caleb. "Soon as you're up to it, you're off to the bunkhouse. Mei Lin has already hung a quilt at one end, so you'll have your own apartment. Course, it won't prevent you hearing all the night noises from the boys at the other end."

"Or the night noises from our end," said Chica. "Sometimes Ray gets pretty noisy when we—"

"Okay, Chica," Ray said. "They ain't interested in our private goings on."

"Oh. Yeah." She said. She ducked her head and smiled at Mei Lin.

Caleb and Mei Lin smiled at each other, sipped their tea. "Until then," Caleb said, "we'll be quite comfortable on the skins."

Mei Lin looked at the bed of skins and hides that Caleb had spread out at the end of the room. A warm feeling enveloped her as she remembered her introduction into Caleb's life, sleeping on her bed of skins, the comfortable, warm bed of her new life.

Mei Lin stood by the corral holding her horse's reins. She looked at the two horses in the meadow up the slope. The two mules grazed nearby.

"Chica!" she shouted. All four animals jerked upright, looking at Mei Lin. Mei Lin's horse broke into a full gallop toward her.

Chica walked around the corner of the house, wiping

her hands on a dishcloth. "What?"

Mei Lin turned around and looked at her. "What?"

"Mei Lin. You called me," Chica said, "what do you want?"

"No," Mei Lin said, "I called Chica . . . my . . . mare."

Chica frowned. "You named your horse . . . 'Chica'?"

"Oh. Yes," Mei Lin said.

Chica frowned. "Why?"

"Because I love her," said Mei Lin.

Chica opened her mouth to speak, but she could not. She closed her mouth, and tears streamed down her cheeks. She ran to Mei Lin, put her arms around her, and held her tightly.

Caleb stood under the pine where Mei Lin and he had taken their lunch so often. He looked at the jagged line of the Sawtooth range and the broad valley that lay at its foot. This country and this woman had saved his life. Now what was he going to do about it?

He lowered his head, studied the detritus at his feet, raised his head to look again at the mountains, and began to walk. Down the path through the lower meadow, away from the house, his head full.

18 WHO DO
I WORK FOR?

Caleb and three men were ranged around the cold stove at the back of the general store. They were in a spirited discussion, punctuated by an occasional friendly shout, a poke in the ribs, and laughter, then a stern face and furrowed brow.

The sheriff sat with Caleb on the bench in front of the general store. Caleb had made arrangements for the meeting to coincide with one of the sheriffs occasional rounds from his office in Challis. Caleb did most of the talking, the sheriff nodding often, pointing in Caleb's face once to make a point.

The deep green leaves of the arbor vines at Stow shaded the table and chairs where Caleb talked with four Chinese elders. The five sipped tea from delicate porcelain cups, the Chinese speaking softly, nodding often, listening more than talking.

Mrs. Ferncastle and Caleb sat in the parlor of the widow's house at the edge of Stanley. Her husband had died two years before, and her three grown children had scattered, one to Boise, a second to Salt Lake City, and the youngest to San Francisco.

She had served Caleb coffee and sugar cookies and now sat in a wicker chair across from Caleb's couch. As he talked, she frowned, then cocked her head, brightened and smiled, shook his hand with a firm grip when he got up to leave, nodded tight-lipped, hands on hips.

The small meeting hall contained five rows of benches on each side of a central aisle. All thirty seats were filled, and a few men stood in the aisles around the walls. The building was the largest gathering place in Stanley, except perhaps for the Rat Trap, and that was an interesting coincidence, for the Rat Trap was the subject of the gathering.

The building served as a schoolhouse for the valley's eighteen elementary school children, all that could find a means to attend since many lived a distance outside Stanley. It also served occasionally as a church house of whatever denomination that had a layman or itinerant minister who conducted services here. And it served as a gathering place for citizens who needed to discuss issues of interest to the populace. Like the Rat Trap.

Those in attendance included merchants, ranchers, farmers, and miners of all stripes. And four women whom most of those in attendance had rarely seen, the sporting ladies who entertained Rat Trap customers.

The four women sat quietly, huddled together on the last bench at the back, eyes darting about like small timid animals. Two of the women were well past their prime years in the servicing trade, which meant that they approached forty. The other two were newcomers, in their late teens or early twenties, already old hands in a profession that had a short apprenticeship.

Caleb stood at the front, facing the assembly. He looked down at Mei Lin, Ray, and Chica who sat on the front bench. Mei Lin, dressed in her Seattle finery, smiled at him and nodded. Andrew sat on the bench behind them.

"Thanks for coming, folks," said Caleb. He waited for the buzz of conversation to end. "I'm sorry that I wasn't more forthcoming about the subject of our gathering, but I had not finished with arrangements when I called the meeting. All I could say was that we would talk about the future and the part the Rat Trap will play in that future.

"Many, maybe most, of us have come to grief in some way by the Rat Trap. This saloon has been a festering sore as long as I have been in Stanley Basin. I'm sure many of you know that it has been a plague on the area far longer than that." A general buzz of agreement followed.

"This is going to change. The Rat Trap is going to disappear." People looked at their neighbors, and the buzz of conversation rose. Caleb held up his hand. "I have talked with a number of people who have agreed to take part in this transformation.

"Stanley doesn't need an abusive saloon. What it does need is a lodging house and a good cafe." The buzz erupted, including scattered laughter.

"A lodging house?" said a burly, suspendered oldster. "Who would stay there? Drifters and grizzly b'ars?" General laughter.

Caleb laughed, waited for the din to subside. "Folks, last fall, in Boise, I saw the future. I saw a motorcar. You've heard of them. I've seen one. They're coming to Idaho. It won't be many years before the roads between Boise and Stanley and from Ketchum to Stanley will be improved, and motorcars will carry people who want to visit the prettiest piece of country on God's green earth. They'll need someplace to stay." A few laughs, but most people were quiet, leaning forward, intrigued now.

"And they'll need someplace to eat. The main room

of the Rat Trap will be converted into a cafe. It will be operated by two Chinese cooks who had a fine restaurant in Stow before the mill closed. They're sitting right back there. Lin Qingshan and Zhang Xinhu. Stand up, please." The two men, sitting in the back row, stood, smiled, and bowed. Scattered, restrained applause.

Caleb looked at Mei Lin, who nodded and smiled. His pronunciation would do for a novice.

"The rooms upstairs will be fixed up as guest rooms. So travelers will have a place to stay as well as a place to eat." Nervous laughter and snickers.

A big man in the third row stood, squared his shoulders, and hitched up his trousers. "Who's gonna pay for all this? I hope you ain't thinking of passing the hat. It all sounds good to me, but I ain't prepared or able to pay for it." General murmuring.

"Good question. And I have a good answer. I've been in touch with my friend and agent in Virginia, and he's talked with a group who call themselves the National Union for Women's Rights. The group is concerned about anything that prevents women from enjoying political and economic equality with men. They want to help the women who are caught up in the Rat Trap web.

"They're right back there," he said, pointing to the back row. "Stand up, please, ladies," Caleb said.

The four women stood slowly, looking about timidly, appearing ready to bolt at the slightest provocation. The audience turned to look at them. Some of the townspeople smiled, but most were unsure how to react. A few people sitting in the front rows clapped politely.

"The Virginia group has agreed to finance the transformation of the Rat Trap from a hellhole to a community resource." Everyone turned sharply to the front. Loud, racous applause.

"One more thing," Caleb said. "Mrs. Ferncastle, would you stand?" Mrs. Ferncastle stood from her bench in the middle of the room. She smiled broadly, turning to greet the audience, front and back, enjoying the notoriety. Polite applause from the others who did not know why they were applauding. She looked at Caleb who smiled and nodded. She sat.

"You know that Mrs. Ferncastle lives at the edge of town on the Boise road. She is going to convert her house into a guesthouse for travelers and renters. The four ladies from Rat Trap are going to live in two of her bedrooms. And they are going to work at the new lodge.

"Mrs. Ferncastle's other two rooms will be let to travelers. She says she'll also serve breakfast to the travelers. She's going to call her place 'Sawtooths Bed & Breakfast.' Has a nice ring to it." General applause and laughter, a little back-slapping.

"What's gonna happen to Polly?" said a bewhiskered man at the back. "I don't suppose she thinks much of your plan, Caleb." General laughter and raucous comment.

"Yeah. Polly," said Caleb. "The sheriff gave her a choice. She can stay and fight. And get arrested for slavery, kidnapping, and attempted murder. Or she can take the cash that she has stashed somewhere, she's not dumb, and leave the state. And if she ever returns to Idaho, she'll be arrested." General applause.

"What option did she take?" said a man. Laughter and snickers.

"Anyone seen Polly lately?" Caleb said. "She left on a freight wagon three days ago for Ketchum where I understand she will take a train for parts unknown." Cheers all around.

"We're not sure who's going to run the place, but for now, Andrew, my foreman, has agreed to work with Matt, you know Matt, the bartender, he's staying on, to get things moving. Andrew may have to ride to Boise occasionally to talk with people who know about these things. There's Andrew," said Caleb, pointing to Andrew who raised his hand.

"By the way, Matt is keeping the bar open, but that's all the services offered in the Rat Trap at the moment. So let's adjourn to the bar and come up with a new name for the community lodge." Raucous cheers and back-slapping.

The people poured from the meetinghouse in a festive mood. The men headed straight for the Rat Trap, across the road and down half a dozen doors. Some of the women moved off to do neglected chores. Others tarried in front of the meetinghouse, chatting.

Mei Lin and Chica wanted nothing to do with the saloon, and they walked arm in arm toward the general store. When they were resident at the Rat Trap, they had rarely ventured outside. Now they were simply townspeople. This was the first time Chica had returned to Stanley since Ray had spirited her away.

Inside the saloon, Matt was singularly happy about the change in his employment. He busied himself, pouring from bottles whose ownership was uncertain, but this did not prevent him from filling glasses and ignoring the proffered coins from the men leaning on the bar.

One of the men at the bar turned toward his pard, spoke to him confidentially, but loud enough for half the population of Stanley to hear. "Davey, is this really Matt here, or is this somebody who looks a little like Matt? This ain't the Matt who's been pouring drinks here fer the two years I've been comin' to th' Trap."

Bennie nodded, leaned in, replying in like play-acting volume. "Yep, this is Matt. Born again." The two laughed and took generous swallows from their glasses. Loud guffaws from all who heard the exchange, including Matt.

"Everybody good?" Matt shouted over the din. A general chorus of approval followed. Matt took another glass and poured himself a shot. He banged hard on the bar top with his open hand. Everyone jumped as if shot and glared at Matt.

"I've got a toast to make," Matt said. "First one I ever did in th' Trap." It was the longest oration most had ever heard from him.

Matt raised his glass. "To Caleb! A damned fine fellow!"

The men raised their glasses and shouted: "To Caleb!"

"Hey, Caleb," said Matt, "who do I work for?"

"Everybody in this room," Caleb said. "But that's a good question." He turned to the room. "Before you boys get too drunk to think clearly, you need to elect a group of, say, five people, including Matt and at least one woman who knows this place better than anybody else in the town, to act for the owners."

"Caleb for president!" said a merchant who had consumed more than one glass of free whiskey and held his almost empty glass in the air. General chorus of approval.

"Thanks, boys, but not me," Caleb said. "I'm . . . too far out of town. Andrew can spend a night occasionally at the widow Ferncastle's establishment when he needs to do town business. But not me." He emptied his glass, waved to the room, and walked to the door.

Caleb and Ray sat on the bench in front of the bunkhouse. It was a cool, crisp morning and a clear blue sky that outlined the dark crags of the Sawtooths, and the warming sun felt good on their faces.

The dredge was quiet. The only sounds were birdsong and the rhythmic whomp up the hill of an ax striking dead wood.

"Getting along okay with the boys in the bunkhouse?" Caleb said.

"Yeah, everything's fine. They're good men, real easy to get on with."

"You're looking good," Caleb said. "How do you feel?"

"Good," Ray said. "Dying to get to work. I'm much obliged for the help and grub, Caleb, but this hanging around is gittin' to me. I need to get back to work."

"Where to?"

"I 'spect the ranch'll take me back. Soon's I can tell 'em that nobody's looking for us. Least, I think they will."

"I'd like to offer you work here, but . . . things are a bit uncertain."

"Thanks all the same, Caleb, but I'm a cowboy. Gold never held no attraction for me."

"Glad to hear it. Maybe we'll keep in touch," said Caleb. "See how it goes."

"I'd like that. Chica needs a woman friend. They're two of a kind."

"Same goes for Mei Lin. We'll keep in touch. Maybe . . . well, we'll see."

The lamp on the table cast shadows about the darkened cabin. Mei Lin sat at the end of the table in her chair while Caleb poured coffee into their cups. He returned the pot to the stove and sat on his keg.

They sat in silence, each sipping from their cup, staring at the lamp flame that flickered and danced.

"We need to get another chair," said Mei Lin.

"Mmm."

They sipped their coffee in silence. He stared at the flame, then at the wall, back to the flame.

"Okay, say it," she said.

He looked at her and smiled. "Now you're getting inside my head, peanut." She smiled. He leaned back on his barrel. "We're not making expenses, and prospects don't look good. My Virginia money is not going to take us through summer. We're mostly living on the purse that I gave you. We've got some decisions to make."

"I knew you were worried. But, honey, anything you decide to do is okay with me. As long as I am with you, it is okay."

"No, whatever we do from this point on, it's our decision, not mine."

She smiled, sipped her coffee.

"Then I can blame you if it doesn't work out," he said.

She reached over and hit him on his arm and gave him a soft slap.

"I'll still make some decisions," he said, "and I have decided that we need to go to bed. Right now."

She stood, leaned over, and kissed him. "Whatever you say, boss."

19 A NEW COUNTRY AND A NEW LIFE

Caleb and Mei Lin held the reins of their horses. They stood in a copse on a hillside that overlooked the Pilgrim Fork. They could see the dredge, a quarter mile upstream.

Except no stream was visible. If there were a stream, it lay somewhere underneath the piles of stone tailings, fifty yards wide, that stretched like a huge bony diseased serpent from the barge pond down the valley where it disappeared around a bend.

"Honey, you be careful. I don't like this Bennett." When he did not reply, she wondered whether he had heard. "Honey—"

"Mei Lin, you were right." He stared at the tailings. "I haven't paid any attention to tailings before. They will always be here. The land will never recover. This must have been a pretty little valley once. Never again. It will always look just like this."

Mei Lin waited. She had never seen him so sad, so unsure.

"Mei Lin, what are we going to do? You should have gone to China when you had the chance. I have nothing to offer you. I have failed at everything I have ever done."

His face clouded.

Mei Lin grasped his shoulders with both hands and pulled him around to face her. "I tell you what you are going to do, Caleb honey Willis. You are going to do what we came here to do. You are going to go tell Bennett that he needs to buy your dredge. We take the money and go away, start over. You failed everything? No. You took me from the Rat Trap, and you saved my life."

He smiled. "Yeah." He put his arms around her shoulders and held her. "Yeah, I did do something right." He released her and walked to his horse.

"Okay, let's get this thing done." He stood beside Buck, staring at the saddle, pondering.

"You want me go with you?" she said.

"No, you stay. I don't think there will be a problem. Maybe I'll tell him that you are with the Sheepeaters, and you are all watching the dredge. Stay right here. I don't expect this will take long." He kissed her.

"I worry already," she said.

He mounted. "Don't worry. It's going to go fine. I'm coming back with a sack of cash." He wished he were as confident as his words suggested.

Caleb stood at the catwalk, staring at the dredge. It was deathly quiet. He reasoned that either somebody had died, or they were shut down for maintenance or gold recovery.

A worker inside the housing walked by the open doorway and saw him. The man stuck his head through the doorway to the outside to get a better look. He withdrew and disappeared inside.

Caleb waited.

Bennett stepped from the housing doorway onto the deck. He stared at Caleb a long, silent moment.

"Can we talk, Mr. Bennett?" Caleb said.

Bennett glared, hesitated. He stepped aside, leaving the doorway unobstructed.

Caleb walked down the catwalk. At the bottom, he hesitated, nodded to Bennett, and walked inside. Bennett looked up at the hillside, scanned the woods, and saw no one. He stepped inside the doorway.

Caleb and Bennett stood on the landing, overlooking the separating cylinder, now stationary, and the sluices below. All was still and quiet. The muffled conversation of two unseen workers below was punctuated by occasional laughter.

"What's on your mind, Willis?" Caleb turned back to Bennett. He had been looking below, listening to the separated, identifiable sounds in the absence of clanking and banging normal to dredge operation.

"I'll get straight to the point," Caleb said. "It's common knowledge that you don't look kindly on any dredging operation in the Stanley Basin. I've tried to understand why since I'm not in competition with you, but I'll let that pass."

Caleb paused, but Bennett remained close-mouthed.

"So I've got a proposition. I'll sell you my dredge and claim and promise that I will not begin another dredge operation anywhere in the Stanley Basin. Ever."

"Now why would I want to buy your dredge?" Bennett said. "You're not very talkative. Nobody's heard whether you're making any gold or not. I suspect you're not."

"Well, I can tell you this. I—"

"He's making gold, Mr. Bennett." Caleb and Bennett turned to see the man who stood at the top of the stairway that led down to the lower deck.

Caleb started. "You!" It was Cal. Bennett smiled, turned back to face Caleb.

"He's making gold," Cal said, "and he's found a rich vein since opening up this spring. It's got good prospects."

"If that's so, Willis," said Bennett, "why do you want to sell?"

Caleb glared at Cal, then turned to Bennett. "It's not to my liking. I'm a farmer and a cattleman. I figure that now that the operation is making money and has good prospects, I'll sell and make a fresh start someplace."

Bennett turned to Cal. "You prepared to run it for me?"

"Sure, I can do that. I know it pretty well." He grinned.

"Cal, you're a goddamned scoundrel!" Caleb said. Cal smiled.

Bennett was enjoying the exchange enormously. He puffed up, smiling.

"Okay, Willis. You're willing to sell, and I'm willing to buy. At my price. I don't expect you're getting pestered by buyers."

"I haven't announced I'm selling. It's a going operation with good prospects. I'm not giving it away. And I'll need cash. I'm packing up and leaving the basin. You want to see my back, and you'll see it."

Caleb and Mei Lin rode on the well-traveled road alongside the tailings of Pilgrim Fork. They turned off the trail and rode into a dense stand of white pine. They ducked under low-hanging branches and through narrow passages between the trees.

Ahead they saw their wagon, the pair of mules in harness, standing quietly. A canvas tarp covered a heavy load, all they could wedge into the bed.

Cal sat his horse beside the wagon. He nodded to Caleb as he and Mei Lin pulled up beside him.

"I owe you, Cal," said Caleb, "and I won't forget it."

"No, you don't, boss." He grinned. "Most fun I've had in years." He sobered, looked down, looked up at Caleb. "I done you bad, boss, and I'm sorry. I didn't have my head on straight."

"It's all past and done with," said Caleb. "We were ready to move on, and I couldn't have pulled it off without your help."

All three dismounted. Caleb took the reins of Buck and Chica, walked them to the back of the wagon, and tied the reins to the tailgate.

"Where you bound?" said Caleb. "I don't suppose you're calling on the phantom brother in Bozeman."

Cal smiled, ducked his head, looked up. "Naw, that was Mr. Bennett's idea. Sounded kinda silly to me. Naw, I'm headed back to California. I got an honest-to-goodness big brother who has a nice spread near Grass Valley. He'll be glad to see me. I was a pretty good cowboy before the gold bug bit me. And nobody in Grass Valley will know Roderick Bennett."

"How're you fixed for a stake?" Caleb said.

"I'm okay. Payday was yesterday." He grinned. "Have to admit that I also dipped into the petty cash, going out the door." He laughed out loud.

He sobered. "How 'bout you? Where to?"

Caleb looked aside, up to the treetops, reluctant to take this last step, even verbally, this final break with a familiar past.

"Heading over to Wyoming. I hear there's some good cattle country in Jackson Hole for them that's not afraid of a little weather and a lot of hard work. Heard that the mountains look a lot like the Sawtooths. I like that."

"Sounds good," said Cal. He gathered his reins. "Well, I'd best make tracks." He looked aside, removed his hat, turned back to Caleb and Mei Lin.

"Good luck to the both of you. Boss, Miss Mei Lin. You're good folks." He stood beside his horse a moment, staring down at the stirrups, then turned back to Caleb and Mei Lin. "You saved my life out there on Stanley Creek, you know." He replaced his hat, mounted slowly, and walked his horse into the dark copse.

Caleb and Mei Lin watched him 'till he disappeared into the pines. Caleb turned to Mei Lin and took her in his arms. He pulled her to him and rested his cheek on her head.

"Ready, sweetheart? Now it's just you and me. A new country and a new life."

She leaned back, took Caleb's face in both hands, and kissed him. "A new country and a new life," she said. "We're ready, honey, both of us."

She took his hand and pressed it to her belly.

AFTERWORD

It is the careless novelist who thinks he can get away with making it all up. Being creative is one thing; doing violence with what is known is something else. I acknowledge my gratitude to a number of people who helped me get it right. If I failed, it is my fault, not theirs.

Thanks to Gary Gadwa, president of the Board of the Sawtooth Interpretive and Historical Association, which manages the Stanley Museum and Redfish Center. Gary was particularly helpful with answers to my questions about gold dredging in Stanley Basin. But he also instructed me on such minutia as native grasses and other plants of the basin, how locals made log cabins airtight and the chinking material used, the sort of stove they used and the type of steam engine employed on local gold dredges. He is the guru of all things Stanley Basin.

Allan Young, a mining engineer at the Bureau of Land Management office in Boise, advised me on the law concerning dredging claims in 1910.

I am grateful to Sherry Monahan who helped me put the right foods on the plates of my characters, and to Chris Enss who told me what they might be wearing.

Thanks to John Horst for many things, especially helping me find the right guns and accouterments for Caleb. More to the point, I thank him for his inspiration and his veiled admonitions to quit whining and write. Anne Burke and Sue Eoff advised me on the appearance, performance, and care of horses, particularly advising Caleb as he showed Mei Lin how to take care of her mare.

I am grateful to the Pacific critique group for their careful reading of the manuscript and their useful suggestions.

Thanks to Sylvia Rambach and Charles Hwang for Chinese translation and names. The obscenities were my own concoction.

Finally, my thanks to Henry Willis for his courage in the opening years of the twentieth century to leave a promising engineering profession in the East to take up gold dredging in Idaho. I am grateful that he brought his family that included his youngest, Marion, who enjoyed her childhood divided between cultured Boise and the rough happy life in the cabin at the dredge site on Stanley Creek. I am particularly indebted to Henry for his decision later to settle in California's Bay Area where I met Marion's youngest daughter, my sweet wife, Carol.

HOME TO WYOMING

Love is composed of a single soul inhabiting two bodies.
Aristotle

Love is a serious mental illness.
Plato

1

"I was happy there. I never said that before about a place."

Mei Lin leaned into him, grasped the folds of his shirt and pressed her face against his chest. She sobbed. Caleb put his arms around her shoulders and held her, resting his cheek on her head. She drew back, wiped her eyes with the back of a hand.

They stood at the pass, looking at the broad Stanley Basin below that stretched for miles to the distant beloved Sawtooths. The small town of Stanley was a dark shadow on the gray green valley floor, the roads dim lines etched on the plain, the Salmon River a sparkling cobalt blue in the drab landscape.

Beyond the town, Stanley Creek meandered down the hillside and flowed lazily into the pond where the gold dredge had been tied to the shore of the small pond. It was only a short walk from the pond up the hill to the cabin. But they couldn't see all these for the forest and distance.

"I know," said Caleb. They stood beside the wagon, loaded with everything they could carry away from the cabin on Stanley Creek where they had lived, together but apart, sorting out their separate troubled pasts, and finally discovered that they could not live without each other.

"1 know we had to leave," she said, "but it's hard. I never had a home before. Not a real home."

"I know. But home is not a place, sweetheart. Our home is wherever we are. Right now, home is that wagon over there." He gestured with a nod of his head.

"We don't need a bunch of logs and boards to call home," he said. "C'mon." He held her elbow, and they walked toward the wagon. "But we're going to have a log and board home soon enough that we'll love. You'll see."

She took his arm with both hands and leaned her head against his shoulder. "Okay, if you say so, boss."

That was the usual response of his dredge employees, their good friends, to his instructions, and she had picked it up. Caleb always smiled when she said it, for he knew that she said it in jest. She had long since demonstrated that she was his equal. Or *his* boss.

He boosted her up to the wagon seat, walked to the back of the wagon where the two horses were tied.

"Okay, Buck? Chica? Everything all right? Ready for something new?" The buckskin shook his head vigorously, nudged Caleb's shoulder. He stroked the horse's neck and patted his side. He rubbed Chica's muzzle. "Okay, little girl, we'll get you to some good grass in a couple of hours."

Walking to the front of the wagon, he pulled up to the seat beside Mei Lin. He uncoiled the lines from the brake handle and shook them. "Gee-yup, mules!" The two mules leaned into the traces, and he pulled them from the verge back on the road.

"I would feel better about this downhill if we had a brake log tied on at the back," Caleb said, "but we can't do that because of the horses. I'll just have to be extra careful.

It's not a heavy load we're carrying. Nothing like when we hauled the dredge machinery from the Ketchum railhead over the pass."

He looked over to her. "Remember that? We had to triple up to reach the top. Even with twelve mules, it was a tough pull. Then we dragged a big tree trunk to brake us on the other side."

"I remember," she said. "I also remember that you said some words I had never heard before."

He smiled. "The mules had heard those words, and they knew what they meant. If you'll recall, we arrived on Stanley Creek with no trouble and on time. And we had the dredge boiler fired up in less than a week."

He closed his eyes and looked up, smiling, remembering. He opened his eyes, shook his head. He looked over at Mei Lin, saw that she had been watching him. He had seen that fixed stare before, and he had often wondered what was going on inside that pretty head.

"Can you get this out today?" Caleb stood at the counter of the Western Union office in Ketchum.

The clerk studied the message under his billed cap. "Richmond, Virginia. Don't believe I ever sent a telegram to Richmond, Virginia. That's a long way off. Yeah, a long way off."

Caleb frowned, shuffled his feet. "Can you do this? Today?"

The clerk looked up. "Sure can. But you ain't gittin' no reply today. That's fer sure."

"I'll be at the National Hotel until the reply comes in. I'm going to be checking back in here, but you'll let me know if you don't see me in or about the office?"

"Yep, I can do that."

Caleb nodded and stepped out to the porch. He stopped.

A dismounted rider stood beside the wagon, holding his horse's reins. The smiling young man was looking up and talking with Mei Lin who sat on the wagon seat.

Damn. I leave her for ten minutes, and she attracts a horny male like honey attracts a hungry bear. What is it about this woman?

Wait a minute! "California!" Caleb shouted. The man looked up, smiled. Caleb strode to the wagon. "Cal! What are you doing in Ketchum? I thought you were riding to Boise."

"Yeah. That's what I thought. But I ran into a man on the trail, just about an hour after leaving you at Bennett's dredge. He said that it would make more sense for me to ride through Ketchum to Twin Falls, then on to Winnemucca. I'll probably take the train there and get off at the closest station to Grass Valley. I'd as soon be settin' down in a train coach when crossing the Sierra mountains than riding horseback over another high pass. I won't do it though, unless I can take my horse on the train."

"Sounds good." Caleb looked at Mei Lin, then back to Cal. "Listen, it's late. We have a hotel room that has a couch. Stay the night with us and—"

"Aw, no, boss, I couldn't do that."

"There's a folding screen that we can put in front of the couch," said Caleb. "It'll be like a private room."

"You do that, Cal," said Mei Lin. "Please."

"C'mon," said Caleb. "I'll buy supper, and you'll get a fresh start in the morning. Take care of your horse, and meet us at the National in an hour."

"Okay, if you say so, boss. Thanks. Sounds like a good plan."

Cal and Caleb and Mei Lin sat at a table near the window of the cafe. The waitress refilled coffee cups. Caleb nodded his thanks to her. He sipped from his cup. Empty serving bowls and plates suggested a satisfactory supper.

Cal drank from his cup, set it on the table, laughed out loud. Customers sitting at tables nearby turned to look. Cal sobered and looked around sheepishly.

He leaned over the table and spoke softly. "I cain't get over it, the look on your face when I stepped out from behind the bulkhead on Bennett's dredge, and you saw me. Then when you said: 'Cal, you're a scoundrel!' Hah! You're a good actor, boss! You ought to go on the stage.

"I laugh every time I think about it. Then when I told old Bennett that you were making gold on your dredge. He puffed up like a balloon, and you was fit to be tied."

"He would never have bought the dredge if you hadn't told him we were making gold," said Caleb. "Most productive lie I ever heard. He'll find out soon enough that there's little gold in Stanley Creek. When he asked you if you were ready to operate my dredge for him and you agreed, I had a hard time not busting out laughing."

"I'm glad it turned out okay," said Cal. "I still feel bad about working on your place while I was spying for Bennett. Every time I was with him, he sputtered and railed about you and the other couple of little dredges in the basin. He wanted no competition."

"Well, I don't feel bad at all about selling him a worthless operation. The sumbitch tried to burn me out and run me off. And you know too well that his thugs killed my men. My friends."

"My friends too, boss. I didn't have no friends when I went to work for you, and those boys just took me in like they had always knowed me. I think old Larry was the best friend I ever had, and him a man black as midnight. When Bennett's men came down shooting up the place, old Larry tried to protect me, telling me to git back, and he went after that rider. I yelled that he didn't have to do that, and he just kept saying 'git back,' and they shot him like a dog."

Cal bowed his head and sniffled. He wiped his nose with a sleeve. "I still cain't git over it. Sorry, Miss Mei Lin." She rested her hand on his.

"I thought about going after him and killing him," said Caleb, "but I was thinking even then that I might want him to buy me out so we could move on. I didn't know then that I would do that only with your help.

It was a sorry ending, but it worked out all right in the end," Caleb said. He looked at the street through the large front window. "Did you have any problem getting away?"

"Nah, soon as Bennett give you the cash and you left his dredge, he was off in a big hurry with his two bullies. I think they was going to your place to have a look at their new property. I sure didn't want to be there when they come back. I already had my kit packed, and my horse tied up in the woods. I just looked around and when nobody was about, emptied the petty cash and lit out."

He leaned back in his chair and guffawed, sobered and looked around, ducked his head, made a face at Caleb and Mei Lin.

2

"Won't be long now, sweetheart," Caleb said. "We'll reach Victor tomorrow, then it's across the mountains to Jackson Hole."

The wagon rolled on a well-traveled road. Caleb looked from side to side, twisted around to look behind at the road. He pulled the mules off the road on the left side onto a track that showed faint wheel marks.

They continued on this track for about a mile, Caleb searching the woods on each side. After passing through a copse of scattered maples, Caleb pulled the mules off the track to a small clearing. He looked around and wound the lines around the brake handle.

"This should do." He looked over at Mei Lin. "Last night in Idaho."

"You stopped early."

"Got something to do." They climbed down and set to work making camp. They had fallen into a routine since leaving Stanley and went about their shared chores with little conversation.

Caleb looked at the back trail repeatedly, searching the woods on each side of the trail. Mei Lin noticed.

"You're thinking about Bennett?"

He relaxed. "Yeah. Cal got me a little jumpy. And carrying this load of cash has me a little jumpier. And wondering about that Western Union clerk and the bank teller."

"I knew you were worried," she said. "Why didn't you wait to get the money in Jackson?"

"No Western Union office in Jackson. I asked in the Ketchum office."

Mei Lin looked at his waist. "I haven't seen you wear your gun since the trouble with Polly's men."

"Yeah, I'd wanted to be done with guns. But she forced my hand. Remember when we had the ruckus in the Rat Trap, when I told them you were going with me? Polly threatened me, said I didn't know what I was getting into.

"Later on, when you disappeared from the cabin, I knew who was behind it. Mei Lin, I killed three people at that Boise saloon Polly sold you to before I got you back. They deserved to die, but it still haunts me." He shook his head, trying to clear the cobwebs of a painful memory.

She hugged him, took his cheeks in her hands and kissed him. "That was the second time you saved my life."

"Yeah, well." He pulled her close, held her. He released her and looked around. "All right, let's get this camp set up and make some supper before dark."

Caleb unhitched the mules and untied the reins of the horses. He hobbled the animals in a patch of good grass nearby and built a fire pit of stones while Mei Lin gathered short pieces of down wood for the fire. He arranged the kindling, broke up the dry limbs, laid them on and started a fire.

Caleb went to the wagon and fetched a small canvas bag from underneath the driver's seat.

"Come with me," Caleb said. He walked toward a low hillock nearby, carrying the bag. Mei Lin followed. When they were about fifteen paces from the hillock, he stopped. "Stay here."

He set the bag on the ground and walked to the hillock. Looking around, he picked up two short down limbs, arranged them on the ground before the hillock so that they crossed. He walked back to Mei Lin. Reaching into the bag, he pulled out a small pistol, a top-break .32.

Mei Lin frowned. "Where did you get that?"

"Ketchum. When you were napping that afternoon. This is for you. I hope you never need it, but you'll have it if you do." He offered it to her, grip first. "We're going to do a little target practice."

She stepped backward. "I never shot a gun. I never held one," she said.

"I'd rather you never shoot a gun, nor even hold one. But it's an uncertain world we live in, sweetheart, and we're heading to a place that we don't know. This is just for insurance." He held the gun in his palm and offered it again. She took it.

He showed her how to grip the pistol, how to aim, told her how to squeeze. At his instruction, she squeezed the trigger until the hammer clicked down on an empty chamber. Taking the pistol from her, he showed her how to break it. He took four cartridges from a pocket and pushed them into the cylinder, then snapped the barrel in place.

"Any questions so far?" She shook her head.

"Understand everything I've shown you?" he said. She nodded.

He turned and faced the hillock. "See the two small branches on the ground in front of the little hill that form a sort of X?" She nodded.

"Watch the X," Caleb said. He aimed, fired. The bark on the limb two inches from the X shattered and splintered.

She had jerked backwards at the shot, her hands over her ears.

He turned to her, smiled. You'll get used to it. The little .32 is quieter than most pistols. And there's almost no recoil. "Now, you." He offered her the .32. She reached slowly and took it.

"Aim for the X. Hold steady, squee-e-e-eze slowly until it fires."

"Okay," she said. She raised the pistol, held steady, squeezed, fired. The bark an inch from the X erupted into a shower of splinters.

Caleb jerked around to look at her, frowned, looked back at the target. "Again."

She aimed, squeezed, and fired. The bark splintered dead on the X.

"Be damned," he said. "You're a natural. We'll practice some more when we have more space. We're too near the road to do any more shooting. Some passersby might think we're desperadoes of some kind."

He took the pistol from her and reloaded it from the cartridges in his pocket. "This is a five-shot, but you should never have more than four cartridges in the cylinder. The hammer rests on the empty chamber so if you drop it, it won't fire accidentally." He offered her the pistol.

She looked at the pistol. "I get it now?"

"Yep, right now. It's yours. Put it someplace you can get to it in a hurry, someplace the bad guy would not suspect that you would have a gun stashed. I hope you never have to use this gun, sweetheart, but use it if you know you're in danger. The important thing is this, don't show it to anyone unless you plan to use it. If you do use it, you shoot to kill." She winced.

"Sounds terrible, I know, but in a world where not everyone is as good as you and me, we sometimes must protect ourselves. Sometimes the law is not around, especially in the countryside where we intend to live." He took her arm, and they walked to the wagon. She opened a bag of clothing and pushed the pistol under a jacket.

"No, not there," said Caleb. "Not now. That's a good place to stash it when we're traveling. Put the bag under the wagon seat, where you can reach it from the seat. But tonight, put it under your blanket, at your side. You might have to protect me from somebody who wants to kill me and steal our money." He smiled.

"That's not funny," she said.

He sobered. "No, honey, it's dead serious. And remember," said Caleb. "Always remember. The pistol is loaded and ready to fire. Another thing. This little .32 is for close-up. You're not going to do any damage to somebody a hundred yards away. Ten yards, maybe. Closer than that, you've nailed him."

She pouted. "I don't like this talk."

"Nor do I," he said. "Insurance is something you buy and hope never to have to use. But when you need it, you're sure glad you have it."

"Okay, you say so, boss."

"That's home, sweetheart, somewhere down there."

They stood beside the trail at the pass overlooking Jackson Hole. The wide semiarid valley, running north to south, was bordered by rugged mountain ranges on the eastern and western extremities. On each side of the pass where they stood, high peaks bore caps of snow. In the valley below, a river coiled through woods and sagebrush flats, suggesting its name, the Snake.

Caleb removed his hat, pulled a bandanna from his pocket and wiped his face and neck. He glanced at Mei Lin. She pulled her shawl tighter around her shoulders, her arms crossed in front. She stared at the valley.

"Okay?" Caleb said.

"Okay." She looked at him, took his arm. "I just worry sometimes. Every day is new. It's like starting all over again, every day."

He pulled her to him and kissed the top of her head. "That's not all bad. Forget the mistakes, forget what went wrong, begin again with what we have. Right now what we have is that wagon of goods over there, two mules and two riding horses, and a belt stuffed with cash. And you and me. What else do we need?"

She leaned against him. "Yeah, you always right, big cowboy."

He chuckled. "Don't ever lose the Chinklish, Polly. It reminds me of bad times that turned out good."

She smiled, poked him on his arm. "I not 'Polly,' mister."

"All saloon girls are 'Polly.'" He grinned.

"I never answered to 'Polly,' and I never told anybody my name. So they just called me 'whore' or 'bitch.' I preferred either to 'Polly.'"

"That's all gone. Remember, every day is a new beginning. Now you're just 'sweetheart' to me and 'Miss Mei Lin' to everybody else. And anybody who thinks otherwise is going to have a big problem with me."

• • • • •

"I could wake up to this view every day and never get used to it."

"Me too," said Mei Lin. She held Caleb's arm, pulled him close and rested her head against his shoulder.

They leaned on the loaded wagon, staring at the range of jagged peaks at the western horizon. "See the pass there." He pointed. "That's where we crossed."

The breeze whipped their clothing and their animals' manes and tails. Not another soul was in sight in any direction. The team of mules in harness stood quietly, heads hanging, shifting their weight occasionally, making brushing sounds on the lines. The reins of the two riding horses were tied at the back of the wagon. The buckskin nickered and tossed his head.

The sun had just disappeared behind the saddle between the two highest peaks, and the sky glowed with its memory. They watched the filmy cloud layers change from shades of silver and pink to gray and orange and lavender.

"My, my, this is some pretty country," Caleb said. "Looks a lot like the Sawtooths. I like that."

"Lonesome," said Mei Lin. "Do you know what they are called?"

"Grand Tetons, so I'm told."

"Tetons. I never heard that. Do you know what it means?" she said.

He looked down at her and smiled. "Yeah. Big tits."

"Ooh." She smiled, squeezed his arm.

Caleb pulled his arm from her grasp and encircled her shoulders, hugged her close. They watched as the sun dropped further behind the mountains. The peaks darkened until the range was a silhouette on the deep cobalt blue sky.

He removed his arm from her shoulders. "C'mon, we're not going to make Jackson today. We need to find a camp. One more night, sweetheart. I expect we'll sleep in a bed tomorrow. You need something soft." He patted her swollen belly.

She held his hand there. "Sometimes you can feel something move. Probably a foot or an elbow," she said. He put his arms around her shoulders, rested his cheek on her head, looking still at the dark Tetons.

"Did we decide right?" he said. "Maybe I'm too old to be starting all over again."

She pulled back, frowning. "You? Too old? You still a little kid. You young enough to make a baby, you young enough to make a ranch." Caleb looked younger than his thirty-seven years. Mei Lin was not sure of her age, probably nineteen or twenty.

He smiled. "All right, you help me, we do okay."

She swatted his arm. "Don't try! You no speak Chinklish. It too hard you." She smiled. He pulled her chin up, kissed her.

"Okay. Polly." She hit him hard on his arm.

He braced her as she climbed up to the wagon seat, then walked around to the other side. Pulling up to the seat, he grunted with the effort. He uncoiled the lines from the brake handle and shook them. The team moved off, and Caleb pulled them from the grassy verge and across the hard-packed road.

The wagon rolled on a lightly traveled path into a clearing in a small grove of aspen. Caleb had seen the site earlier and had speculated that this might be a stopping place for travelers. His speculation proved true.

They set up their camp and built a fire in a stone circle left by the last people who had camped here. The grass around the circle was still flattened, suggesting that it had not rained since the travelers had made and left their camp.

There was little conversation as they sat on the ground beside the fire, eating their supper of beans and hard biscuit. On this last night of their flight, there was much to ponder. The drive from Stanley had been without incident, a relief from the turmoil they had endured at the dredge site in Stanley Basin. Their life there had been bittersweet, made bearable only by their discovery that they wished to spend the rest of their lives together.

After stowing dishes in the wagon, Caleb gathered sticks and short pieces of down limbs and tossed them in a pile near the fire. He checked the animals, hobbled nearby in good grass. Mei Lin spread their blankets between the fire and the wagon, and they lay down, side by side.

Mei Lin rolled over, put her hand on his cheek and kissed him.

"Remember what you said on the day that you sold the dredge," Mei Lin said, "and we left Stanley forever? 'A new country and a new life.'"

"I remember. That new life starts tomorrow."

3

"Not much of a town," said Mei Lin. "Smaller than Stanley." The wagon rolled down the dusty main street of Jackson. The only street, as far as they could see.

Three old-timers standing on the board sidewalk in front of a sizable general store stopped their conversation and silently watched the wagon roll by. When the wagon had passed, one of the oldsters leaned in and said something to the others, still watching the moving wagon.

Caleb nodded toward the two-story Jackson Hotel, adjacent to the general store. The front of the hotel was red brick, and the side was half brick and half board.

"First brick I've seen west of the Mississippi," said Caleb. "Looks substantial, almost permanent, though not much else about this town looks permanent. The hotel might do for a few nights. Restaurant next door looks good enough."

Mei Lin frowned. "We'll see."

On the opposite side of the road, Lloyd and Tuttle's saloon and a blacksmith shop next door, both badly in need of a paint job. Next, a vacant lot, then Wort's livery barn and Jimmy Hendricks Feeds. Adjacent, a small general store and a couple of other nondescript shops or offices. Both the feed store and the general store were brick-fronted.

Further down the street were a church and a two story building that could be a school or meetinghouse.

A few houses were scattered behind the shops on each side of the road.

And that was the town of Jackson. Caleb pulled the mules to a stop. He coiled the lines around the brake handle and jumped down. "Let's walk back to the first general store. The old boys that gave us the eye as we passed might be open to a few questions." He walked around the wagon and helped Mei Lin climb down. She supported her belly with the other hand.

They stepped up on the board sidewalk and walked back the way they came. The oldsters that had stood in front of the general store were nowhere to be seen. In fact, the only person in view was a woman across the street walking on the sidewalk. Head down and striding, she wore a long dress that billowed in the wind, intent on getting somewhere in a hurry.

Caleb and Mei Lin stopped in front of the store. "Folie's General Merchandise," the sign over the door proclaimed. On each side of the front door, there was a window that was crowded with merchandise designed to lure the walker into the store. In one window, there was a variety of women's products: creams and jewelry and powders. The other window displayed products to entice the men to come in: boots, knives, ammunition, tobacco, small tools.

Caleb held one of the double doors open, and Mei Lin stepped in. He followed, and they stood at the front, their eyes adjusting to the interior, dark after the brilliant sunshine.

Along the left wall, a long glass case displayed an assortment of merchandise: boots and shoes, bedding and cloth products, hats, folded shirts and pants and dresses. Beyond the case, in the corner, a small alcove had been constructed, signposted "Post Office."

A young woman stood behind the display case and in front of the Post Office. She watched Caleb and Mei Lin, a look of apprehension on her face, appearing ready to bolt if these strangers so much as spoke to her.

The wall above the glass case was lined with shelves and drawers. Stacked on the shelves was a hodgepodge of offerings in no particular order. There were soaps, spices, flour, salt, coffee beans, cartridges, dishes, medicines, cigars and cloth pouches of tobacco, sewing materials, ribbons, whips and small tools. On the counter top were neatly folded overalls, pants and aprons. At the front of the counter, jars of colorful candies were arranged to tempt the children.

Bins and boxes against the facing wall held produce such as beans and nuts, pickles, crackers, potatoes. Baskets displayed fresh fruits and vegetables. A small barrel was full to the brim with nails.

A bulletin board was affixed to the wall above the bins. A note tacked at the top of the board invited anyone to put up a notice. Half the town's population seems to have responded. The board was crowded with notices of church activities, sewing circle meetings, gatherings to discuss problems with elk and wolves.

The board also held personal notes: "Hey, Martha, are you coming to town on Friday?" Another in a child's scrawl: "You see Blackie?" At the bottom of the latter, in a more refined hand: "Found. Thank you."

In the upper right corner of the board, outlined by a white cloth divider, notices told of robberies and horse and cattle rustling. Wanted notices with descriptions of the desperadoes, including some with pictures, were also tacked here.

On the right side of the door, some small farm implements and tools and bits of furniture were displayed on the floor. Hanging from the ceiling, requiring the tallest customers to duck and weave, were lanterns, larger tools, harness. Shelves on this wall were loaded with canned goods whose colorful labels pictured the contents.

Beyond these, near the far wall, half a dozen chairs and two spittoons encircled a pot-bellied wood stove. Three of these chairs were occupied by the old men who had watched Caleb and Mei Lin drive down the street. They now watched the two strangers with studied interest.

Near the stove, a short counter supported a cash register, a scale, wrapping paper and a roll of string for tying up purchases. A coffee grinder beside the cash register had a note affixed to it, which suggested that the prospective user ask the clerk for assistance.

The man behind the counter smiled. "Can I help you with something?"

Caleb walked over to the counter. Mei Lin turned aside to look at a display of kitchen utensils.

"You sure can. We're looking for information about where we can spend a few nights."

"Passing through?" said the proprietor. The three old men leaned forward, listening.

"Depends."

"Hmm. Well, there's the Jackson Hotel next door. But if I was you, since you're planning to stop a few days, I'd look into the Barton place just west of town. It's a boarding house that takes in travelers. They're clean and handy, and they serve good meals.

Some people who I've sent there have been real pleased."

"Sounds worth a look. Much obliged. I'm Caleb Willis. I hope I can drop in again and ask you some questions."

"Happy to help. I'm Andrew Folie." He extended his hand, and Caleb grasped it and shook. "That's my daughter, Priscilla, over there." He motioned toward the young woman standing behind the counter. "She's also the postmistress." She smiled and blushed and waved a quick hand as if brushing a flying insect.

Caleb picked up a Sears catalog from the counter. "You advertising your competition?"

The proprietor shook his head. "Well, not advertising, but my customers asked me to get the catalog. Got the Montgomery Ward catalog too." He reached under the counter and retrieved the Ward's catalog. "I give my customers a hand ordering and let them ship to me. It gets them in the store, and they promise me they won't order anything that I stock. It's a toss up."

Folie thumbed through the pages of the Wards catalog. "These things can be town killers, but I try to change with the times. At least, they don't sell eggs and milk."

Caleb and Mei Lin stood on the porch of the severe two-story house. The house and picket fence that surrounded it must have been painted at the same time since they both peeled uniformly.

Caleb knocked.

The door flew open. A grizzled old-timer with a three-day scraggly beard and a wild head of gray hair stood there in the entrance hall, bent forward, almost a crouch, frowning. Still holding the doorknob, he looked hard at Mei Lin, then at Caleb, back to Mei Lin.

He softened, smiled, reached for Mei Lin.

"Come in, little lady." He took her by the hand, pulled

her inside and made to close the door. Mei Lin looked at Caleb, perplexed.

The old man stopped. He looked quizzically at Mei Lin. "You want him to come in, too?"

A woman appeared from the hallway and elbowed the old man aside. "Git away, you old geezer." She turned to Caleb and Mei Lin. "Come in, come in. Don't mind him. He thinks he's the funniest thing on two wheels." The old man grinned, poked the woman lightly in the ribs. She swatted him on the shoulder.

The woman led her guests into the parlor, followed by the oldster. Caleb and Mei Lin looked around, glanced at each other and smiled. Here was a house that bespoke home. During their journey from Stanley, they had talked about the home they wanted, and both saw hints of that place on walking into the parlor.

The wooden floor was almost covered wall to wall with a colorful rag rug. A cushioned window seat was built-in below the three tall windows. Pretty printed curtains hung on each side of the windows. The stone fireplace was cold at the moment, but a bucket filled with a half dozen short lengths of firewood was ready for cool evenings.

Small photographs in frames were arrayed on the fireplace mantle, and pictures and prints hung on the walls. The frames of a couch and two chairs were constructed of nicely-finished lengths of tree limbs. Round and square cushions were tied to the seats and backs. Caleb ran his hand over the polished surface of the couch frame.

"The old man made these pieces back when he still had an eye and ambition," the woman said. "Have a seat." She pointed to the couch. They sat, and the woman sat in a chair facing them. The man stood beside her, resting his hand on her shoulder.

She brushed the hand away and looked up at him. "Bennie, go make us some coffee. You think you can do that without burning the house down?"

"I can do that, my love." He kissed her on the ear. She swatted him. He turned to Caleb and Mei Lin. "Now don't talk about nothing important, or you'll have to say it again when I come back." He walked through the door to the kitchen. Immediately, there came the sound of pots clanking and falling to the floor. Caleb and Mei Lin jumped, looked at each other, then at the woman.

The woman chuckled. "We do have fun, Bennie and me. We laugh a lot. Now, what can I do for you?" She leaned back and yelled at the kitchen. "And bring a dish of them cookies I made this morning!"

"I can do that!" Bennie yelled from the kitchen.

She laughed again, looked back at her visitors. "Okay. That's Bennie. I'm Berta. People call us the 'Busy B's.'" She leaned forward. "Now. What can I do for you?"

"Hello, Berta," said Caleb. "We're Caleb and Mei Lin. We wanted to ask about staying with you for a few days while we look around."

A pan in the kitchen bounced and rolled. Bennie's head appeared in the doorway. "As in looking around or as in looking for someplace to buy?"

"Shut up, Bennie, that's none of our business. Get back to your coffee."

"Yes, m'love." He remained where he was, leaning against the doorjamb.

Caleb smiled. "Right now, just looking. Maybe looking at prospects. We'll be asking lots of questions. To you as well, if you don't mind."

"Hold it right there!" Bennie said. He withdrew into the kitchen. More clattering as another pan bounced on the floor. Then quiet as the three in the parlor listened. Then a continuous clatter and clanging as Bennie walked through the debris.

He stepped through the door into the parlor, carrying a tray with four cups of coffee, a plate of cookies, a small pitcher of sweet milk, a bowl of sugar and two spoons. Setting the tray on a small table in front of Berta's chair, he leaned over, and Berta pecked him on the cheek. He went back to the kitchen, initiating another round of clanking debris as he waded through it, fetched a chair and pulled it to the parlor beside Berta and sat down.

"Help yourself. We don't stand on formalities here," said Berta. Bennie poured milk into a cup, spooned in two scoops of sugar, and gave it to Berta. He took a cup for himself. Mei Lin gave a cup to Caleb and took one for herself.

"I hope you're thinking of settling," Berta said. "We need some new faces around here. And 1 see that you have one in the oven, little lady. When's it due."

"December, I think," said Mei Lin.

"That long, eh," said Berta. "You're gonna be big as a house before then."

Caleb cleared his throat and shuffled his feet. "You folks been in Jackson long?"

Bennie leaned forward. "Hell, yeah, we—"

"Bennie," Berta said softly, without looking at him.

"Oh, yeah. Sony. Yeah, we been here a long time. Even before there was a Jackson. We farmed right here in the '90s. Yeah! When folks started moving in who wanted to open businesses instead of farming, we sold bits and pieces of our homestead for town lots. The town wasn't even laid out till '97. We knew everybody, and everybody knew us.

"There was so many newcomers that needed to look

around, like you, we decided that we would open this boarding house. We had lots of rooms. We built this house to hold a big family, but.. ." He looked at Berta, who looked aside. "But that never happened," he said softly, looking at his feet.

He looked up, smiled, a sad smile. "Anyway, we took in people who had dreams in their heads and motes in their eyes. Some of 'em made it, and some of 'em didn't."

Caleb cut a glance at Mei Lin, then back to Bennie. "I'm wondering whether you know about anybody who might be thinking of selling some property that would carry cows?"

"I do know that," Bennie said.

Caleb and Mei Lin arranged clothing and personal gear in their room on the second floor of the boarding house. When they first stepped into the room, they both stopped in the doorway. The view through the two tall windows was a striking panorama of the Teton range.

"I will never close the curtains," said Mei Lin.

The room was not large, but they agreed that it would do. It was a pretty room, wallpapered with a flower print. A small chifferobe of lightly stained wood that appeared to be another creation of Bennie's stood in the corner. The bed was high-backed and covered with a multi-colored quilt. Both tested the mattress and smiled at the prospect of actually sleeping under sheets and blankets on a real bed. They had not slept in a bed since leaving Ketchum.

As they unpacked some of their things, Caleb commented that he could get used to having people do things for them. Before he had even asked, Bennie had taken charge of the wagon and animals. He said he would put the animals in the corral where he would feed them and rub them down. He would store the tack with the wagon in the barn. Lots of room in the barn, he said, since he hadn't stored hay since giving up farming years ago.

When Caleb protested that Bennie didn't have to do all that, he replied: "What the hell else will I do? Nope, part of the service. You and the missis get yourselves settled. We'll call you when supper's ready."

Caleb and Mei Lin decided that the Busy B's were going to be good friends.

Caleb and Mei Lin sat at the round dining table with Bennie and Berta. The setting sun shone through the two tall windows, describing quadrangles of light on the table and opposite wall.

Caleb had hardly settled in his chair when he turned to watch the golden orb settle in the saddle between two peaks, and the lacy cloud layers begin to turn twenty pastel shades of red and orange and yellow.

"Yeah," said Bennie, "I still watch it and wonder whether it's Mother Nature doing it all by herself, like some folks say, or whether God is out there with His paint brush."

Caleb turned back to the table, smiled. "Whatever the case, it sure is pretty. We used to watch sunsets behind the Sawtooths and felt pretty much the same as you do." He took Mei Lin's hand under the table. She looked at him. What he really wanted to do was kiss her and hustle her upstairs.

"Well," Berta broke the spell. "We have just one more boarder right now, but he won't be here for supper this evening. Said he had some business to attend to. You'll meet him at breakfast. Now tuck in."

Caleb and Mei Lin were quick to oblige. They tucked in to the first meal for many days that they had not prepared together over a campfire. Not that they complained about the meals or the journey. They knew they would remember that trek from Stanley Basin with mixed emotions the rest of their days. They had left a bittersweet experience, an idyll and a trial, that had brought them together. He had saved her life and she his.

And what a supper it was. There was elk roast, boiled potatoes, pinto beans, cornbread and freshly churned butter. For dessert, berry cobbler washed down with coffee and sweet milk.

During the course of the meal, Bennie gave Caleb names and information on some local farmers who might be interested in selling. Most of the settlers in the Hole, he said, had been known to grumble from time to time about water problems, cold winters, hungry elk that got into the haystacks, the short growing season, persistent wind. Loneliness.

But these four farmers that Bennie told Caleb about had talked more than the others about the hardships, even suggesting that they might think about giving it up and pulling out.

"Most homesteaders," said Bennie, "arrive in summer and think they can build a farm just like they left behind. They can't. Jackson Hole ain't like no place where any of these folks lived. It's different. The Hole ain't going to change. The people got to change. It's these folk who couldn't make the change that might want to sell. You got the names." Caleb had taken notes on a pad.

After two helpings of every dish on the table and a large bowl of cobbler, Caleb declared over coffee that they just might decide to stay full time with Berta and Bennie instead of buying property and moving out.

Berta smiled. "No, you won't. You need your own place, and you'll have it. I can tell just from your talk that you are two hard-working folk, and you'll make it. Not like some of these newcomers here who never saw a hard winter. You've seen some of those in Idaho. We've had people stay with us who know the Sawtooth country and said that it can get a mite chilly."

After a hearty breakfast next morning, Caleb saddled Buck for the short ride to town. He had thought about walking after Berta's substantial repast, more breakfast than he was accustomed to, but decided that he should do some scouting around the countryside before returning to the Busy B's place. When he mentioned this possibility at the breakfast table, Bennie volunteered to go along. Caleb said that he didn't want to impose, to which Bennie replied with his usual what-the-hell-else-am-I-going-to-do?

Bennie collected a bridle from the barn, stepped back outside and whistled. Caleb was surprised to see a mule trot from behind the barn and stop in front of him. Bennie looked at Caleb.

"Yeah, I know. 'Why you riding a mule instead of a horse?' Did you notice that Imogene—that's her name—didn't ask me where we're going or why we're going? She just trotted right over here and prepares to do my bidding. Mules are smarter'n horses and a lot of people."

"Guess I can't argue with that," Caleb said, smiling.

When Bennie was finished saddling Imogene, they mounted and set out at a walk. "I can't figure your other guest, Russell Overgaard, I think you called him," said Caleb. "He didn't say a word at breakfast, just grunted two or three times. Does he ever talk?"

"First day he come, that was three days ago, he was nothing but talk. He asked questions about everything. Land, what people are growing, who are the bigwigs in the Hole, what about the Mormons, who owns the stores in town, everything. Since that day, he clammed up. You saw him. I cain't figure him either."

They rode in silence most of the ride. That suited Caleb. His brain was racing as he pondered what lay ahead. He was constantly beset by nagging questions.

What have I gotten us into? Why did we leave Stanley just when things were settling down? I've done a little cowboying, but I don't know the first thing about running a ranch. Just when Mei Lin is expecting a baby, when she needs peace and quiet, I'm taking us into an unknown place.

They pulled up in front of the general store, dismounted and tied their reins to the hitching post.

During the ride, Bennie had suggested that they stop at the store to talk with the gossip circle. The old boys that gathered regularly at Folie's had long since retired from any productive work and had nothing better to do than soak up every bit of news and non-news about anything going on in the Hole. Bennie thought they might be able to add something to what he had told Caleb about land prospects.

Caleb followed Bennie through the front door. Caleb waved to Andrew who looked up from behind the front counter. He saw Priscilla and touched his hat to her. She made her short, brushing-a-fly wave, blushed and ducked through the post office door.

Caleb and Bennie walked toward the store's focus and principal edifice: the stove.

The wood stove was cold on this late summer day, but the idlers were drawn to it from habit. Two oldsters sat behind the stove, and two sat beside it, bent over a checkerboard on a low table between them. All four looked up and waved at Bennie and Caleb. The two at checkers pushed the table aside. Here was something potentially new and interesting.

"Pull up some chairs, Bennie," said Philo. After the newcomers sat down, the usual contingent of the wood stove gathering was complete. Any who congregated here beyond six had to pull up a small nail barrel or wooden box to sit on. The four looked expectantly at Bennie.

"Boys, I'd like to introduce you to Caleb Willis. Caleb's staying with us for a time, and I thought he should get to know the chief source of misinformation in the county."

"Misinformation!" said Philo. "This coming from the biggest bullshitter in western Wyoming."

Bennie grinned. "Caleb, the speaker there is Philo." He pointed. "And that there's Alastair, and John and Pumpkin. Don't ask him why he's called 'Pumpkin.'" Everybody grinned except Pumpkin. He glared at Bennie.

"Okay," said Philo, sitting up straight in his chair, "let's get down to business. Are you contributing or withdrawing today?" The gossip circle always got right to the point. They wanted to establish early on whether newcomers had something to say that the members didn't already know, which they deemed highly unlikely, or whether they were here for information that the oldsters might dispense. The members were delighted with the former, but they were also gratified when they could tell something that the newcomer did not know.

"Well, we might be contributing," said Bennie, "seeing as how you birds don't know everything, but we're mostly here for withdrawing. Caleb here thinks he might want to buy some land hereabouts, and he thought you might be able to give him some information on what's available and who might be interested in selling. I doubt you'll tell him anything more than what I done already told him, but I agreed to let you give it a shot." Bennie grinned broadly.

"Bennie," said Philo, "you're the biggest blow-hard in

five counties. You need to spend more time around the stove. You're wasting your talents up there at the boarding house." All laughed and slapped backs and knees.

"Caleb," Alastair said, pushing the checkerboard table behind his chair, "you come to the right place. We was talking just yesterday. . ." He stopped, rubbed his chin, looked at the ceiling, "or was it Friday ... naw, it was Saturday—"

"Say it, dammit," said Bennie, "it don't matter when it was. I don't even know what you was talking about."

"Right," said Alastair. "We was just saying that there seems to be so many farmers that are talking about pulling up stakes that there might not be enough people to buy stuff to keep this store open. Then what would we do?"

"Lemme translate that for you boys," said Philo. "There are sure enough some farmers who are making leaving noises. Not as many as Alastair suggests, but sure enough some. They talk about the hard winters and short growing seasons, not like back home, wherever that was. Some farmers never did dig wells and are still hauling water. That wears on you."

"I'll tell you something, Caleb," said John. Everyone turned to look at him. John rarely spoke at the wood stove gatherings. Mostly he leaned back in his chair, legs crossed, pulling on his pipe. But everyone knew that when he spoke, he had something to say. So he immediately had the attention of the group.

"I got the property for you," John said. All of the geezers leaned in. Here was something solid coming, something to hang on to. "There's three farmers I know that are talking of calling it quits. Each of them still has his 160-acre claim, and one of them a couple of years ago bought a claim that adjoins his land.

"Purely by chance, or Divine Providence in your case, the three properties abut each other. With one exception. There's a homestead right in the middle of these three that might come available. The poor guy has been trying to prove up on it, but there's a rumor that he's planning to give up on it and file a relinquishment. If he does that, you could pick up that piece from the land office for a buck and a quarter an acre."

John leaned back in his chair. "If you could pull this off, you would have one of the biggest spreads in the Hole."

Everyone looked at Caleb who had listened without comment or question. He slouched in his chair, legs extended and crossed, staring at the stove, frowning.

"Are we done here, Caleb?" said Bennie. "I doubt these yahoos has anything more to tell us. I think we drained anything useful outta them for now." A general good-natured protest rose from the geezers.

Caleb pulled his legs under him and stood. "Yep. Thanks so much, boys. You have given me a lot of good information to chew on. I appreciate it."

Bennie stood, and amidst waves and goodbyes, Caleb and Bennie walked outside to the sidewalk.

"There's just one more stop we should make as long as we're here," said Bennie. "Is that okay?"

"Sure. What's that?"

"You need to meet the sheriff. If he's in."

Bennie led the way across the street and up to a door labeled simply, "Sheriff, Lincoln County." The "Lincoln County" was freshly painted over a background of white paint.

Bennie knocked and opened the door. He stuck his head inside. "Can we come in, Scott?" he said to the room.

"Come on in, Bennie," from inside.

Bennie opened the door and went in. Caleb followed. They saw a gray-haired man with square shoulders, a creased face wearing a stubble of whiskers. He slouched in his chair behind the desk, chewing on a cold cigar. He pushed his chair back slowly and stood.

"Caleb, I want to introduce you to the protector of the poor, the defender of widows, the sheriff who bad men fear, the—"

"Shut up, Bennie," said the sheriff. He took the cigar butt from his mouth, dropped it in the trash basket beside the desk and thrust his hand out to Caleb. "I'm Scott Canlis. Sit down. You, too, Bennie, if you can control that mouth of yours for a while." Bennie grinned. All three sat.

"Heard about you, Caleb," said the sheriff. "Anybody new in the Hole who appears to have money and plans gits talked about real fast. I hope you're finding what you're looking for, whatever that is."

"I am indeed, Sheriff. Bennie has been helpful, also the fellows at the stove at Folie's."

"You're in good hands. Anything I can do for you, you let me know."

"There's something I want to know," said Bennie. The sheriff leaned back. "Why is the Lincoln County sign new on your door?"

"Because Lincoln County is new," said the Sheriff.

"That's something I wondered about when I first learned that Jackson had a sheriff," said Caleb. "Seems a little town to have a sheriff. How does Jackson warrant a sheriff? It's not the county seat, is it?"

"Nope. You're just lucky." The sheriff smiled. "I'll tell you something that most people here don't even know. Bennie will tell the Folie's geezers, so everbody in western Wyoming will know by tomorrow morning. I ain't a sheriff. I'm a deputy sheriff.

"You see, when the population of the Hole started grow-ing in recent years, the county, Uinta County, decided that the sheriff at the county seat in Evanston was too far from the Hole to do any good up there, so they put a deputy sheriff in Jackson. I took over from the first deputy, and I been here since '07.

"Then when they pulled land from Uinta County and set up Lincoln County, that was just last year, the county seat of Lincoln County at Kemmerer was still too far, so they left me here. I don't doubt that as population in the Hole grows, we'll have our own county. Then I'll get my promotion. If I'm still here. I might be sitting with the geezers at Folie's by then."

Caleb stood. "We won't take up any more of your time, sheriff. I'm mighty happy to meet you. I sure hope I won't need your services."

4

Caleb and Bennie rode at a walk on a dusty road in a countryside colored with scattered wildflowers, meadows of wild hay and sagebrush flats. Scattered stands of aspen and ash broke the plain.

Caleb rode with his head down, staring at Buck's mane. Eight hundred acres. If they were all willing to sell. He hadn't dreamed of a ranch this size. John at the geezer gathering said that it would be one of the largest holdings in the Hole. Could he manage a ranch this large? He had worked on ranches, but he had no experience running one. He would need a lot of help.

Could he afford it? Not just the land, but also the stock and equipment to make it profitable. He had the sale price of the dredge. And there were the funds from his Richmond account, the proceeds from selling his engineering business when he lost his family and fled to the West. He had used most of that amount on the dredge investment, but there remained a respectable balance, which he had picked up at the Ketchum Western Union office.

The launch of the ranch would consume the bulk of both sources. He would be on thin ice from that point. No margin for error. He would have to make a profit every year for the foreseeable future. Breaking even would not be acceptable.

"What do you think?" said Bennie.

Caleb pondered a moment longer, looking at Buck's ears. He turned to look at Bennie. "What do *you* think?"

"Don't matter what I think. It's all on you. But I'll tell you this, son. If I was a young man with prospects, I would grab this bronc with both hands and hang on. There'd be bucking and twisting and crow-hoppin' and maybe some hungry times."

He sobered, spoke softly, passionately. "But damn, it sure would be fun." He straightened, shook his head, looked over at Caleb. "But I'm a worn-out old coot. Easy for me to talk. No risk in me talking. It's all on you."

Using the information from Bennie and the Folie's oldsters, Caleb had come up with descriptions of the parcels and something about each of the owners. Bennie had arranged with three of the homesteaders for visits on this day. Caleb had asked the gossip circle and Bennie for their advice on prices he should offer for the farms and had settled on figures that he and they thought reasonable.

Caleb wasn't looking forward to this. He had always disliked talking about money. He particularly hated what he had to do today, offering money in exchange for a vanished dream. He knew too much about vanished dreams.

As they rode toward the first homestead, Caleb pictured in his mind how each parcel would fit into a whole, the ranch that he was building in his head. The closer they came to the first place, the more he was alternately thrilled and terrified.

They pulled up in front of the farmhouse, dismounted and tied their reins to a post in the yard. The farmer and his wife stood in the doorway, waiting. Caleb and Bennie walked to them. Bennie introduced Caleb, and there were handshakes all around. The wife invited them to come into the house.

Inside, they stood in the kitchen. Caleb explained his offer as husband and wife listened without comment. Caleb mentioned his price and said he would pay in cash. If they accepted and didn't want to take all the furniture and furnishings with them, he would buy them.

The farmer's countenance did not change during Caleb's explanation, but the wife's face softened, and her eyes opened wider as Caleb continued.

"There's one more thing, Mr. Calder," said Caleb, "instead of leaving, you could stay on the place and work for me. Your house and outbuildings would be ranch property, and you would stay in them for as long as you worked for me."

Mrs. Calder's face turned to stone as she listened to Caleb's last offering. She looked hard at her husband. "Rob?"

"You can stop right there, Mr. Willis. Bessie and I have been talking about all this since Bennie first told us that you was about to make us an offer. We already decided. We'll sell. As for staying on, no sir-ree. We've had enough hardship here. We had enough hauling water, enough crop failures and freezing winters.

"We've already decided. It's home to Texas for us. I've got a brother who farms near Fort Worth. Him and his wife complain about winters in the twenties, sometimes pretty near zero, but hell, that's nowhere near the minus forties and colder that we put up with here. Nope, thanks for the offer, but we're for Texas."

Calder reached over and put his arm around his wife's shoulder. "We'll miss our girls. They both married fine young men who had the good sense to move on. One married a cowboy who works on a ranch near Rawlins. The other married a merchant, and they moved to Oregon." He looked down at his wife, back to Caleb. "We'll try to get them to come to Texas, but I don't hold much hope on that."

From the Calder place, Caleb and Bennie rode to the second homestead. Bennie introduced Caleb to Jimmy Holmes and his wife, Virginia, who invited them into the house. They walked into the kitchen where she pulled out chairs at the table for the visitors. There were four cups on the table and a plate of cookies in the center.

"Sit down, and have coffee, you two," Virginia said. "We knew you were coming." She fetched the pot from the stove and poured coffee into the cups. The three men sat, and she stood at the stove, holding her cup.

"Thank you for the coffee, Mrs. Holmes," said Caleb. "It's most welcome."

"You're welcome, Mr. Willis. I'm real interested in what you come to say." Her look belied her hospitality. She was not smiling.

Caleb repeated the offer and conditions he had made at the Calder farm. Jimmy, his face as rigid as a stone carving, his arms crossed on his chest, listened without comment. He had not touched his cup. Virginia, standing at the counter, on the other hand, listened with mouth agape and wide-open eyes, growing wider the more she heard from Caleb. Her eyes glistened. She set her cup on the counter,

"I don't know," said Jimmy. "I'm okay with selling. Now about staying on ..." He glanced at this wife.

She glared at her husband, wiped her eyes with the back of a hand. "If we don't go back to Kentucky—now—I will divorce you!" She was not smiling.

The farmer softened. "Sorry, honey. Bad joke." He turned to Caleb. "Thankee for the offer. We'll sell to you and be off for home and kinfolk."

Virginia popped her husband on the top of his head and reached for Caleb. He pushed his chair back and stood in time to be enveloped by her arms.

"Thank you," she said softly, tears rolling down her cheeks. She turned on her husband. "And I'll take the wagon and all the animals and—" She ducked her head and sobbed.

Jimmy stood and put his arms around her shoulders, held her close. "There, now, honey," he said softly. "It's okay. We're going home."

The third homesteader, Will Blevins, a young man in his thirties, said he would sell and stay.

"I love this country so much; it still brings tears to my eyes to look on the Tetons. But it's no place for a farmer. I'm real happy that you'll do the worrying now. And I'm right glad you're building a ranch. I was a pretty good cowboy back in Nebraska before the land bug bit me."

They stood in the small sitting room of the house. Will's wife stood behind him as he spoke, trying to be invisible. He reached back and put his arm around her and pulled her up beside him.

"My wife's a local, she's Shoshone. She's real happy I want to stay. This is her homeland. Her name is Kimana. It means Butterfly." He squeezed her shoulders. She ducked her head, smiled.

"You tell me what you want of me, Mr. Willis, and I'm your man."

"Good," said Caleb. "Stay in your house. It's ranch property now and yours to use as long as you are working on the spread. I'm glad you're staying on. My wife is going to be real happy to meet your wife. And my name's Caleb, not Mr. Willis."

The final property that Caleb had pondered was that of the bachelor that had failed to prove up on his claim. Now that he had successfully negotiated the purchase of the other three homesteads, Caleb figured that this final parcel was critical. It lay precisely in the center of the projected 800-acre ranch. Without it, the acreage would not be contiguous.

Also, there was the question of water. Some piddling streams ran through the other homesteads, but the word was that these were reduced to a trickle or dried up during the summer. There was a fine spring on this final parcel that flowed year round, if the gossip circle was to be believed.

Caleb and Bennie rode into the yard before the frame house. The homesteader stood in the doorway. The riders dismounted, tied their reins to a leaning fence post and walked over to the house. Bennie introduced Caleb to Jedediah.

"Jed," said the farmer. He did not invite his visitors into the house.

A quick glance at Jed and the property was enough to tell Caleb why the homesteader had failed. The house looked sturdy enough, as if it had been built when its owner had faith in his future, but it had been neglected too long. The barn also appeared a substantial structure, but it had deteriorated. Doors hung loose on their hinges, and the siding was warped and hanging. The farm animals were reflections of their owner. The two mules in the corral were bony, and their coats were caked with mud.

A large garden beside the barn was more weeds than vegetables. The size of the garden suggested that either it had been more substantial at one time, or the owner had been a better planner than cultivator. From the look of it, most of the space had never been planted.

Jed was as unkempt as his property and animals. His greasy hair flew in all directions, and his clothes were soiled and worn. He had made no attempt to shave or manage a beard.

Caleb explained his offer while Bennie looked on, frowning. Jed listened with head down or glancing aside. He had a hard time making eye contact.

Caleb waited.

"What do you think, Jed?" said Bennie.

Jed glanced at Bennie, then studied the ground at his feet. He looked up at Caleb. "Well, I got no problem with callin' it quits. I don't know where that puts you and me, though. I filed a relinquishment."

"Yeah, I heard about that," said Caleb.

Jed looked at the sky over Caleb's shoulder. "Maybe I was a little too quick."

"Why is that?" Bennie said.

"Well, you're the second person this week to ask about the place."

"Really. The other guy have a name?"

"Uh, over something. Overboard? Overhead?"

"Overgaard?" said Bennie.

"Yeah, that's it. Overgaard."

"Hmm. Did you tell him you had filed the relinquishment?" said Caleb.

"Nah, he didn't much welcome conversation. Weird guy. Didn't have much to say, mostly nods and grunts. But he was interested in the place. That's for sure."

"Jed, I want to buy your place," said Caleb. "I'll be going to the land office to see what's involved. I'll let you know what happens." Caleb waited but Jed only stared at him.

"What are your plans?" said Caleb.

"Don't have no plans. Hadn't thought about it. I got no kin to speak of. Well, 'cept some cousins back in Georgia that I hadn't seen since I was a boy. Don't rightly care to see 'em now." He looked at Caleb, expectantly, it seemed. "Would it be okay if I stayed on here 'till I decide what I'm gonna do next? I'll work."

Caleb had expected this and pondered his response as Jed spoke. He had decided right off that he didn't see Jed as a long-term ranch employee.

"Yeah. Okay," said Caleb. "Stay in your place for now, and I'll be in touch with you about work. There's not going to be much money in this for anybody works for me until we get the place up and running."

"I ain't worried about that. 'Preciate anything you can pay me. I'll work."

"I see you have a garden out back," said Caleb. "You might want to fence it since I'll be running cows on the place pretty soon."

"I'll do that. I'm pretty good at fencing. Uh, you got wire and posts for me?"

"You can start taking down the fence between your place and Will's and use the posts and wire for your garden. I'll tell Will. He'll help unless I put him on something else."

Jed frowned. "Will. I don't git on too well with him. He's a snooty little prick. Thinks he's something fine."

Caleb pondered. He glanced sideways at Bennie. Bennie looked at him, cocked his head.

"I could git on with his wife, though." Jed snickered. "She's a pretty little squaw."

Bennie glared at Jed, took a step toward him. "Jedediah, you—"

Caleb held up a hand to quiet Bennie. "Jed, you want to stay on the place, you keep your nose clean and your head on straight. Any problem, and you're on the road. Understood?"

Jed blinked. "Sure, boss. Everything's fine." He grinned.

Caleb turned to go, and Bennie followed. Jed leaned on the doorframe and watched them as they untied their reins from the post.

"That fellow has a screw loose," said Bennie. "That's the first time I seen the man talk so much. I seen him in town and heard him talk only a couple of times, and he never did make sense."

"Yeah, he sounds like trouble. Almost makes me hope Overgaard beats me to the land office. Except that I need this place bad. It's the final piece of this ranch puzzle." Caleb scratched his head vigorously with both hands, brushed his long hair back with a hand. "I wonder what Overgaard is up to."

"I got no idea. I'll talk with the gossip circle. Maybe they know something I don't. That'll make 'em real happy."

Caleb pushed his plate an inch from the table edge. "Berta, that breakfast will last me till supper. Tomorrow. I don't know why your house isn't filled all the time."

Bennie stood and began collecting the dishes and utensils, clattering the dishes as he stacked them in his arms.

Berta leaned back and turned around to glare at him. "Have a care, old man! You'll have us eating from the dog dishes!"

Bennie smiled, leaned over and bit her ear. "We don't have a dog, dear one," he said.

She brushed him away. "Well, we still have her dishes." She turned to Mei Lin. "Poor thing got run off by the wolves last spring. I hope she got away. She never came back."

Mei Lin put her hand on Berta's. Berta smiled, a sad smile.

"I'm sorry." Mei Lin brightened. "Berta, I want to watch you make that egg dish some time. So good," said Mei Lin.

Berta smiled, patted Mei Lin's arm. "It's an omelet. Easy peasy. I'll tell you ahead when I plan to make it again. I would enjoy company in the kitchen, even a little help now and then," with emphasis on this last, glancing at Bennie. He grinned.

"And the cobbler," said Mei Lin. "I've never had cobbler before. Caleb told me it was the best he ever ate. So I want to learn."

"Thank you, honey," Berta said. "I'll be happy to show you. Easy peasy." She turned to Caleb. "As for customers, not too many travelers at the moment. You never know. Comes and goes."

"What happened to your other guest, Overgaard?" said Caleb. "I know he's not staying away because he doesn't like your cooking."

"He checked out this morning. He was waiting in the kitchen when I come in. Paid up, didn't say a word of thanks. He volunteered that he was going hunting, as if I was interested in where he was going. Whether he planned to hunt animals or people, he didn't say."

"Well, it's not likely he's hunting for meat," said Caleb. "Is sport hunting popular hereabouts? I've noticed a number of people carrying rifles in their saddle cases. There don't seem to be a great quantity of desperados about, so I guessed they were going hunting."

Bennie returned from the kitchen, carrying a coffee

pot. "It's really taking off. Elk hunting mostly. Some hunters are coming here now to get the big trophy before restrictions are put on the hunting. You see ..." Bennie paused to fill coffee cups all around. He set the pot on the table, sat beside Berta, and drank from his cup.

"You see, big herds of elk used to migrate through the Hole on a regular basis, from the high country south to Green River valley. But when the Hole began to be settled up, and some fences were built, this migration pretty much ended. That meant that there were thousands of elk wintering in the Hole. This pleased the hunters, but not the farmers.

"There wasn't enough forage for the elk in the wild places in the Hole, so they started to feed on crops and haystacks. You can imagine that the farmers ain't too receptive to any of that. Anyway, the past few years, there's been a real die-off. Lots of elk are starving. You see carcasses all around."

"That's very sad," said Mei Lin.

"Yeah," Bennie said. "Some people have taken to feeding the elk in the winter, and there's talk about trying to get some sort of help from government." Bennie sipped his coffee, looked toward the window. "There's other people who see the concentration of elk in a different light. Some hunters, outsiders, are coming in to the Hole to get the biggest trophy before they're all gone. Easy to see where that's going.

"It's sick," said Bennie. "The outfitters and hunters find out where the locals are feeding elk. They wait for the people to leave, then they move in and take their pick. It's really sick. Like shooting cows." Bennie stared into his coffee cup. Berta patted him on his back.

Bennie looked at Caleb. "That's probably where Overgaard is right now. He looks like that sort."

"I saw a dozen elk near the woods when we were out near Will's place," said Caleb. "They were looking right at us."

"Yeah, I saw 'em," Bennie said. "That's where Will feeds 'em, right out at the edge of his place. He has a double gate in his fence right there. He leaves it open most of the time so the fence won't prevent their moving about.

"There's talk about setting aside a piece of property where the elk will be fed," said Bennie, "and there'll be no hunting there. Most of the homesteaders are for it. It'll save the elk, and it'll save their crops.

"The hunters and outfitters sure don't like the prospect of a some place that's off limits to hunting. Some of 'em are hopping mad, especially the outfitters. So far, they've just grumbled, but I think some of 'em could cause some trouble.

"The state tried to help the elk a few years ago when they set up a game preserve that runs from Yellowstone to the Hole," said Bennie. "No hunting in the preserve, they said. It didn't work. There was no enforcement, and people kept hunting all over."

"That's mighty interesting, Bennie," Caleb said. "I suppose I'm going to be right in the middle of all this. We'll talk more. Right now, I need to solve a more pressing problem, for me, at least. I wouldn't tell anyone else, but I don't mind telling the Busy B's that I'm carrying a goodly sum of money on my person, and I'm uneasy about that. Where's the nearest bank?"

Bennie grinned. "You're looking at it."

Caleb frowned. "What do you mean?"

Bennie stood. "C'mon." He went through the doorway and motioned for Caleb to come. Caleb and Mei Lin followed him from the dining room.

They walked across the entry hall to a room that was both a sitting room and office. A couch and easy chair faced the fireplace. On the opposite wall were a desk, stacked with papers and books, and beside it, a huge, black, man-high steel safe.

"What th'—where in hell did you get this monster?" said Caleb.

Bennie beamed. "This was supposed to be at the first bank in Jackson. The guy brought it over the pass from Idaho two years ago in a six-mule team wagon. He spent the winter getting his place set up and then went bust before he got his first deposit. He told me to hell with Jackson and to hell with Wyoming winter, and he sold it to me for enough cash to take him to California. There's still no bank in Jackson."

"Did you need a safe?" said Caleb.

"Hell, no. But I never owned a safe, and now I got one, and it works."

Caleb looked at Mei Lin. She nodded. He tugged the shirt from his trousers and unbuckled the bulging canvas money belt. He pulled the belt from around his waist and handed it to Bennie.

Bennie took the belt, grinned. "You are my first depositor." He twirled the knob a few times back and forth, then pulled the rod down and opened the massive door. Caleb looked inside. It was empty but for a few papers and a small metal box on the floor. Bennie laid the belt on a shelf at the top. He swung the door closed, pushed the handle down, twirled the knob, smiled when the reassuring click announced that the door was locked.

"There you are," said Bennie. "The bank is open twenty fours a day, ever' day." He clapped Caleb on the back.

Caleb knew his deposit in Bennie's safe wouldn't be there long. He needed to pay for the land he had bought. He needed cash to buy cows, equipment, wire, tools. They needed to choose which of the purchased homesteads would be their home and headquarters, and the house and buildings they choose would need to be upgraded. They would need to buy groceries until they had a working garden.

Need, need, need. Am I ever going to generate enough income to pay for everything I need?

The money in Bennie's safe was the proceeds from the sale of his Stanley gold dredge and the Richmond funds. He figured that the stash would pay for the 800 acres with enough left over for one year's operations. This meant that there was no margin for error during that first year. He would have to end the year solvent.

He had promised the three farmers that he would pay them in cash for their homesteads. When one of them said that that was a lot of cash, he told him not to worry. They took him at his word.

Caleb was a little surprised at their trust. They couldn't spend his word. It was cash they needed. Then there was the cost of the relinquishment, a bargain at $1.25 an acre. Every time he made a purchase or an obligation of any kind, he mentally reduced the fund in Bennie's safe.

After an early breakfast arranged with Berta, Caleb hitched the mules to the wagon. Mei Lin and Berta walked from the house, and Caleb helped Mei Lin climb up to the seat. They both wore fleece jackets. He walked around the wagon, climbed up on the seat and took the lines as Berta placed a packed lunch in the bed.

"I've put in a heavy blanket with the lunch," Berta said. "The weather is going to turn one of these days soon. You got to be ready for it."

"We'll be okay," said Mei Lin. "Thanks. We'll be back for dinner."

Caleb shook the lines, and the mules leaned into the traces. They rode silently, watching the team, studying the land on each side of the road, the mountains beyond.

She turned to Caleb. "Why did you choose the Texas people's place for us?" said Mei Lin.

"I didn't choose it, sweetheart. The choice is yours, but I won't say I won't try to influence you." He looked sideways at her, smiled. "We're going to visit both places, and I think you'll understand why I favor it."

After a pleasant drive on a road bordered by lush stands of wild hay, Caleb turned the mules off the road and up a short track to the front of the house. Caleb jumped off the wagon and walked around to help Mei Lin down.

"Only two hours from Busy B's," said Mei Lin. "That's good." She looked at the house. It looked sturdy, and she knew it would be adequate. Our new house, she thought to herself, our new home.

"I like this place, honey," she said. "But you know no house will ever be as good as our cabin above the dredge pond. That will always be home to me, wherever we go and whatever fine house we live in." She was suddenly overcome, and tears rolled down her cheeks.

Caleb took her in his arms, rested his head on hers. "I know, sweetheart. The memory of that place and what we had there will always be in my heart too. You saved my life in that little cabin. But we can't go back. It was a place. What we had there, we have here, and we will have it wherever we are." He leaned back, raised her chin, kissed her lips softly.

"Okay?" he said. She smiled, nodded.

"Let's have a look," he said. Caleb took her hand, and they walked to the porch. The covered porch extended across most of the front of the house. There were two rocking chairs and a small round table beside the door.

He turned around. The view from the porch extended across the flat valley floor to the Teton range. The light blue sky was perfectly cloudless. It was so clear that Caleb could make out craggy features on the slopes.

"My, my, what a sight to wake up to each morning," he said. She looked at him, cocked her head. "Well, if we choose this house, I mean." She smiled.

He stepped off the porch to the yard. A slight breeze brushed his face. It was cool, a hint of autumn? He recalled the comments of old timers and newcomers alike about winter in Jackson Hole. If there was anything that locals talked about most, it was winters in the Hole. *Can it be that bad?*

He walked back to the porch and followed Mei Lin inside the house. They stopped in the hall. A row of pegs lined the wall on the right side for hanging coats and hats. They walked through a doorway on the left to a small sitting room. The fireplace was clean, logs and kindling laid on the irons, ready for lighting. Two tall windows faced west with a view of the valley and Tetons.

Calder had said that they hardly ever used the room. There was a small settee and two straight back chairs, a round table in front of the settee. The Calders had taken few of their possessions. Both buyers and sellers were pleased to agree that the furniture went with the house. They took only personal possessions that they could load in the wagon, things that would remind them of their sojourn in Jackson Hole and make them wonder whether they had made the right decision to leave.

Caleb and Mei Lin stepped from the sitting room to the hall and into the adjacent room. The room was small and cold. There was no stove or fireplace, and the two windows looked like they had not been opened in years. Caleb suspected that they weren't tight and admitted the north wind. Calder had told Caleb that they rarely went into the room and used it only for storage.

Caleb figured that this room could be cleaned up and weather proofed and made into a nice nursery. He looked at Mei Lin and said nothing.

The next room was a long utility room. Brooms and mops hung on pegs. There were pans and tubs for washing, cleaning supplies on shelves. A single window illuminated the space.

Across the hall from the utility room, Caleb and Mei Lin stepped into the bedroom. It was clean, the bed was made and covered with a multi-hued patchwork quilt that Mrs. Calder said she had made. She hated to leave it, she said, but they had to make choices. The wood stove was clean, resting on a metal plate. The four windows of the corner room were bright and clear. If they left the curtains open, they would be awakened by the morning sun.

This will do for us.

Caleb looked at Mei Lin to try to judge her response to the tour of the house, but her face was a mask.

They walked from the bedroom through the hall into the kitchen. With windows on the south and west, it would be the brightest room in the house from noon to sunset. A counter with cupboards ran the length of the room on the south side, ending in a cooler. The back of the cooler was lined with closely fitted slats to prevent birds and small critters from sampling the meats and vegetables inside.

Mei Lin opened cupboards, picked up a pan, then a

bowl, to see what lay underneath. She took out a percolator and placed it on the stove. The sheepherder stove was clean and worn with use. Caleb figured that it was adequate both for cooking and heating. He went to the counter and looked through the windows that gave a good view of the Jackson road that ran in front of the house.

"What about water?" said Mei Lin.

Caleb leaned his back on the counter. "There's a well out back, but the pump is cranky, and Mr. Calder said the water wasn't really drinkable. He said they hauled water. We would have to do that until we have the well upgraded. There's a small, fast-running stream just about a half mile west that Calder said was good water for the house. He said it was year-round and rarely froze."

Caleb looked at the table in the center of the room. "If we take this place, this is where I expect we'll spend a lot of time." Four chairs were pushed up to the table. Caleb wondered whether the Calders had guests often. Perhaps the chairs had not been filled since their two daughters married and moved away.

While Mei Lin continued to rummage through the cupboards, Caleb walked back into the hall and out the back door. He looked over the yard. Ample space for a garden just behind the house. Beyond were fields of wild hay and sagebrush flats. Farther still, across an extensive hay field, stands of willows and aspen suggested a stream.

On the left across an open yard were the outbuildings. He had already walked through the barn on a previous visit. It was sturdy, surprisingly spacious, with a tack room and a few horse stalls. There was a sizable corral adjacent to the barn.

He walked back through the hall to the kitchen where Mei Lin sat in a chair at the table. She looked up.

"What do you think?" he said.

"What if I said 'no?'"

He winced. "Well, I—"

"You silly man. I do what you say." She smiled.

"I'll take that as an okay. Even in Chinklish."

"What about the other place, the Holmes place?" she said.

"The other place. I've seen it. It's not as large as this place, only one bedroom, smaller barn, no tack room. There is no well, and it's farther from the stream where we would get water. We can still look at it, if you like."

She shook her head. Caleb exhaled, smiled.

"Okay," he said. "The Holmes place will be the bunkhouse. It should hold as many as eight hands. Right now, I expect it houses only spiders and mice. The Holmeses left in a bit of a hurry once they had a look at the Ketchum train schedule. We're going to have this place up and running before you know it, and we'll fill that bunkhouse."

"Okay, boss, whatever you say." She stood and walked to the stove. "Look what I found." She showed him the percolator and jar of coffee on the counter. "How about some coffee in our new house?"

"I wouldn't say no to that."

5

Bennie and Berta helped Mei Lin and Caleb settle in at the new place. The Calders' furniture and kitchen utensils and linens were useful, but they would always be the Calders' things. The Busy B's helped them find other bits and pieces that would make the house a home.

Caleb was pleased with the look of Will's place. It was neat and well cared for. He figured that Will and Kimana would be a big help in Caleb and Mei Lin's adjustment to life in the Hole.

Jedediah would stay in his place and undoubtedly make no improvements nor would Caleb offer any encouragement. Caleb was a little ashamed of himself that he wished Jed would decide to move on soon. He had always believed that every man was entitled to a chance to make it, but he figured that Jed had already had a multitude of chances and had made nothing of them.

Bennie was proving invaluable in identifying people Caleb needed to know. He introduced Caleb to Amos Dickens who regularly trailed stock between Idaho and Jackson Hole. Caleb arranged for him to buy fifty cows and three bulls in Idaho and drive them to Caleb's ranch.

Dickens agreed to the terms, which said that if Caleb were not satisfied with any animal, it would be returned to the seller. Dickens was to require the seller to accept these terms in advance of the sale.

At the same time, Caleb and Bennie scouted around the Hole to buy cows that farmers were willing to sell. Some of the farmers had no cows at all, but most had a milk cow or two and a few mother cows. If a farmer decided that he had accumulated more cows than he needed or could feed, he was happy to sell.

For those that were serious about owning cattle, the average local herd was twenty to thirty cows, about all that could be supported on a claim, leaving land for crops and hay. Excess animals were either sold or slaughtered. Caleb was able to pick up a number of breeders from the locals to add to his herd.

Caleb turned to repairing and upgrading. He was determined to have the ranch in good order before winter set in. Bennie and Will filled his head with stories of what had happened to landowners in the hard winter and with what could happen. He wanted to be ready, but the work that had to be done before winter set in was enormous. He needed help and soon. He talked to Bennie.

Bennie delivered again. He rode into Jackson one morning and talked with a couple of young drifters at Lloyd and Tuttle's saloon. He decided that they might fill the bill. The drifters were agreeable and rode back to the ranch with Bennie.

After handshakes all around, Caleb explained that he was building a new ranch, and there was plenty of hard work ahead. The young men listened, nodded.

They might have been mistaken for brothers. Both wore faded, well-used jeans and dark-colored loose woolen shirts. Their broad-brimmed hats were stained identically, their boots were scuffed and heels almost worn down.

It became obvious quickly that Andy was the speaker for the two. Paul held back, head slightly bowed, and deferred to him.

"We ain't afraid of hard work," said Andy.

"Why did you leave your last place?" Caleb said.

"It wasn't no trouble on our part," Andy said. "We left because we wanted to. We wasn't chased off. In fact, the boss said he would raise our pay and let each of us pick out another horse from his herd if we'd stay"

"Sounds like a pretty good offer," said Bennie. "Why'd you leave?"

"Well, we hadn't found our place yet. We want to see the country before we settle down, before we know where we want to settle down. We're still lookin'. We seen some real pretty country since we left home," Andy said, looking at Paul, "what, almost a year ago?" Paul nodded. "Hadn't found our place yet. But I tell ya', I sure do like the looks of this valley. And those mountains!" He pointed at the Teton range. "Whew."

"Where's home?" said Caleb.

"St. Louis for me and Pine Bluff for Paul. Actually, all this was his idea. I ran into him at a saloon in St. Louis. He told me he was heading west, and I thought that was a pretty good idea. Paul said he wanted to be a cowboy, and I thought that was a good idea too." Andy laughed. "We didn't know spit about cows, but I think we can ride with the best of 'em now. Ain't that right, Paul?" Paul almost managed a smile.

Caleb figured that they might be a fit for his ranch and offered them work. He added that he was mighty glad they had not found their place yet.

Caleb had already decided to convert the Holmes place into the bunkhouse. The house and outbuildings there were not as extensive as his place, but the structures were tight and well built and should do for them. He told them to make any improvements they wished, and he would supply boards and tools, whatever they needed. Caleb expected that the place would require little modification to turn it into a bunkhouse, accommodating Andy and Paul and the other full-time or part-time hands that Caleb expected would be needed.

"I hope you boys like the country and the ranch well enough to stay through the winter," Caleb said.

That would be the test. For them and for him. He had decided that he had found his place, his and Mei Lin's. He was used to cold winters during his western wandering and on the gold dredge on Stanley Creek, but if all of the locals were to be believed, nobody has seen a hard winter until they have lived through a Jackson Hole winter.

When he raised the issue of the approaching winter with Mei Lin, she had just pursed her lips and cocked her head, as if to say, So? He had grabbed her and squeezed until she told him to ease up. She patted her belly and smiled. He had taken her cheeks in his hands, stared into the pools of her dark eyes and wondered whether it was possible to love a woman more than he loved Mei Lin. She had touched his cheek and said, Okay? Okay, he had replied.

Caleb and Will and the two cowboys worked long days repairing fences, taking down fences between some homesteads, and putting up new fences to enclose pastures. Will enlarged his hay planting, and Caleb added an extension to his barn for the crop. Jed agreed to put in a hay crop, but Caleb figured he couldn't count on anything from him but talk.

Caleb planned to put up buck-rail fencing around his house and outbuildings. The style had pretty much gone out with the introduction of barbed wire, but it was the standard fencing in Stanley Basin, and he liked the looks of it. It reminded him of good times and bad, but mostly good on balance. It was reasonably easy to build since it sat on top of the ground without the necessity of digging postholes.

He put up barbed wire on most of the 800 acres, and Will taught him some new fencing techniques that were becoming more widely used in the region. This was fencing that was more wildlife-friendly, he said, especially where fences intersected wildlife migration routes. These fences used smooth wire, sometimes with the bottom wire raised and the top wire lowered so wildlife could squeeze under or jump over without being impaled.

Caleb wondered whether ranching was becoming too complicated.

Caleb had been intrigued by what Bennie had told him about the Jackson Hole elk. So he was interested one afternoon when he was in the general store and heard the gossip circle talking about the hard times for the elk in the Hole. He walked over and was welcomed and sat in the proffered chair.

It seems that the elks' forage and migration patterns increasingly were disappearing due to the expansion of ranching and farming in the region. In the past few years, the hungry animals were becoming more aggressive, invading homesteads to feed on farmers' haystacks and growing crops. Some locals wanted to exterminate the elk, but there was a growing awareness that the elk were a resource, both for hunting and tourism, and both were good for the local economy.

There was also a growing sentiment that collided with

the belief that the elk were simply a valuable economic resource. This was the belief that the elk were beautiful animals that were the original inhabitants of the valley and had as much right to be here as the newcomers, perhaps a greater right. This was a belief that if the elk vanished, everybody, all of the inhabitants of the Hole, lost.

Caleb didn't rightly know how he felt about the elk issue. Elk have rights? He had never thought about nature beyond the economic argument that man exploited nature for his own benefit.

On the other hand, he remembered that he had sat often in the shade of an aspen near his cabin on Stanley Creek, staring at the magnificent Sawtooth range, almost in tears. He had never thought about how that view could be converted into economic gain. Maybe the elk did have rights.

The talk in Jackson about the elk was so pervasive that he knew someday he would have to take a position. Damn, why can't he just raise cows without having to think about the local wildlife? Wildlife in the past had been simply animals that ought to be killed as pests or shot for meat. Now this.

As the cool breezes of late summer foretold the approach of autumn, Caleb increased his preparations, and preparations meant spending money. His stash in Bennie's safe was declining at an alarming rate, much faster than he had anticipated, but what could he do? He was careful with his expenditures, but he had had no experience with building and operating a ranch. He winced every time he had to spend money on something he had not even anticipated.

He had paid the Texas and Kentucky bound homesteaders on their departure. Will insisted that he could wait on his payment, but Caleb paid him off as well. He wanted to get the land purchases behind him.

A sizable chunk of the fund also was expended on the stock that he had bought from Idaho and from local farmers. He calculated the quantity of hay that would be needed over the winter and realized that Will's crop and the little grown on the other two claims were insufficient. In addition, he had told Will that he could run his fifteen cows with his herd. They simply would not have enough hay for the combined herd.

Caleb and Will began scouting the neighborhood for farmers who had hay that they would be willing to sell. Will volunteered that if anyone would have hay to sell, it would be the Mormons.

The resourceful Mormons, who lived north of Jackson in a cluster of homesteads called Mormon Row, grew crops and hay with irrigation and were known to sell their annual excess. During their visit to the homesteads along the Row, Caleb was impressed with the Mormons' sturdy houses and barns and crops and the irrigation works. He was pleased to make arrangements to buy a sizable quantity of hay from half a dozen farmers.

• • • • •

Mei Lin and Caleb sat at the table in their kitchen. Dinner dishes were stacked in the sink. They sipped from coffee cups.

"I wish I had gone with you to visit the Mormons," Mei Lin said. "I have heard lots about them. They sound like good people."

"That's my impression too. Hard working people who are devoted to family and community. That is, the Mormon community."

"Is it true that Mormon men can have more than one

wife?" she said.

"I asked the same question of Will. He seems to know about the Mormons. That used to be common among Mormons, but it's against the law now. There is a rumor that some people who claim to be Mormons still practice polygamy, maybe even here in the Hole. Will says they would never own up to it. They would be kicked out of the church."

"This was common in China," Mei Lin said. "Rich men had more than one wife, also some concubines, and they visited whores. I sometimes wonder. I was, I think, sixteen or seventeen when my parents sold me. What if they had sold me to a rich man for a wife or concubine? What would my life have been?"

"No different," said Caleb. "I would have come to China, killed your husband or owner, or whatever he was. I would have stolen you and brought you to Stanley to warm my bed and come with me to Jackson Hole."

Mei Lin stared into her coffee mug. She looked up at Caleb. "I have thought of this before. If that had happened to me, I would be dead by now. Worn out, thrown away, dead." She erupted into tears and covered her face with both hands.

Caleb pulled his chair around to sit beside her. He took her in his arms. "Mei Lin, it's a bad dream. It didn't happen. What happened brought you to me. We must be glad that you were sold to Fuhua who got bitten by the gold bug and brought you to Idaho. You are with me, and nothing else matters."

He pulled her head around to face him, kissed her softly. "Nothing else matters. We are together. There is no past. No Fuhua, no Stanley Rat Trap, no Boise Mad Hatter, only you and me."

Mei Lin stood at the post office cubicle, talking with Priscilla. Mei Lin wore a bright blue, ankle-length dress that she had ordered from the Sears Roebuck catalog a few weeks ago. Mei Lin had picked up the dress only last week, and she wore it for the first time on this trip to town. Not that a trip into Jackson was anything special.

The ordering process for the dress had presented a challenge. Mei Lin wanted a ready-made dress for expectant mothers. Priscilla said that she had never seen such a thing in either the Sears or Wards catalogs. The two women searched in three Sears catalogs and three Wards catalogs. They found nothing. Plenty of styles and colors for women, but nothing for expectant mothers.

Mei Lin and Priscilla wondered why not. There were plenty of expectant mothers who would be delighted to buy a dress designed especially for them. Priscilla observed that a ready-made maternity dress could have a stitch feature that would permit letting out the girth of the dress as the woman's girth increased. They decided that Sears and Wards were missing a large market.

Priscilla suggested that Mei Lin construct her own such dress. With Priscilla's help, Mei Lin chose a dress in the Sears catalog that was three sizes too large. When the dress arrived, Priscilla helped Mei Lin take it in at a number of points. At the waist, a series of stitches were added which pulled the waist in. These stitches could be snipped one-by-one as her belly grew. Priscilla and Mei Lin became fast friends.

Mei Lin came to town with Caleb today to pick up her latest Sears purchase. She had needed some new work clothes and ordered them from the Sears catalog. The purchase was a pair of jeans and a corduroy shirt. Boys' clothes.

She had rarely worn dresses in the past year. When Caleb stole her from the Rat Trap brothel in Stanley, she was wearing a thin cotton dress. She wore the same dress on Caleb's dredge claim for days until she asked him if he had some old clothes that she could wear.

Caleb had taken no notice of her clothing until she asked, and he felt bad about that. He bought her some boys' clothes at the general store the next time he was in Stanley. She had worn boy's pants and shirts ever since.

Visitors to the Jackson Hole ranch, if they didn't know her, often mistook her for a hired hand. Understandable since, completing the illusion, she usually tucked her long black hair under her hat, left her shirt trailing to hide her belly, and worked hard. She was amused, and just a bit flattered, that she was mistaken for a hand.

Priscilla retrieved a package from under the counter and unwrapped it on the countertop. Mei Lin held up the shirt to check the arm measurement. She nodded, pleased with the result.

Three oldsters sat in chairs around the stove, smoking and leaning toward each other, intent on telling or hearing the latest gossip. Or trying to top the latest lies. They had seen Caleb when he first came through the front door and waved. Caleb returned the wave.

"They're an interesting lot, aren't they?" said Andrew. He had walked from the storeroom with an armful of folded shirts. He stopped beside Caleb and set the stack on the counter.

"They are indeed," said Caleb. "They try to appear simple bumpkins, but it's all a facade. My impression is that they are more complex than that. But who would know? They seem to know something about every subject that is brought up and are anxious to talk about it. And quick to talk about anybody and everybody, people they know personally and people they don't know at all, but I have not heard any one of them talk about himself."

"You've hit the nail on the head," said Andrew. "They're very private people. I don't know why, but they want anybody who will listen to them to believe that they are very shallow and uncomplicated. But that's not at all true. I've learned a little about them from comments here and there, but not from anybody in the circle.

"Philo is the chief geezer and the spokesman of the group. Not that he necessarily has earned that distinction, just that he is more assertive than the others. He was in some sort of sales business before moving to the Hole. Alastair was a lawyer, would you believe it, before he started sort of drifting in the head. His sister and her husband brought him with them from Kentucky when they homesteaded. John is the brains of the group. You've probably noticed that he is mostly a listener. But when he does speak, everybody takes notice. They know that he will have something to say worth listening to."

"Pumpkin?" said Caleb.

"Ah. Pumpkin is another case. He used to be called by his name, Frank—that was a few years ago, when he first began coming in. But then everybody started calling him 'Pumpkin.' He didn't like it at first and was embarrassed, but he got used to it. The hearsay is that a whore over in Evanston, the first whore he ever visited, called him her 'sweet little Pumpkin.' So the story goes. Nobody has ever asked him to confirm the story."

"Interesting," said Caleb. "They seem to be a bunch of good fellows. Too often, I think, we don't look beyond a face to get to know the person."

"Yeah, and they care about each other. If any one

of them doesn't show up two or three days running, you wouldn't believe the tension. Where's so-and-so? What's wrong? Is he mad at us? Is he sick? I tell ya', Caleb, if we lose any of these old boys, the Creator's gonna have hell to pay."

"We'll have to hope that it won't come to that any time soon," said Caleb. He strolled over to a counter that featured new products. Picking up a new-fangled can opener, he turned it over and over, frowning.

"Did I see you come in with th' Chink?"

Caleb slowly returned the can opener to the tray. He stared at the tray a moment, contemplating, then turned to see a man behind him, staring at Mei Lin. The young cowboy wore a faded denim jacket that was sprinkled with bits of hay. His sweat-stained hat was tilted to the side of his head. He smelled faintly of dung.

"Do you mean the lady over there in the blue dress?" Caleb said slowly.

"Lady!" He snorted. "The only chinks I ever saw was either a washer woman or a whore, and— ummph!"

The cowboy doubled over from Caleb's blow to his midsection. His eyes bulged, and his jaw hung open. He gasped for breath and stumbled backward.

Caleb gripped his arms gently, guided him back a step to lean against the display counter. Still bent over and gasping, the cowboy looked up at Caleb. By this time, the three old men sitting around the stove were silently watching, delighted, and anxious to see how this interesting episode was going to unfold.

Andrew, wearing a long spotless apron, strolled over and stood behind Caleb, a smile flitting about his mouth.

"On any other day," said Caleb to the cowboy, "I might have just explained the error in your ways, but you caught me on a good day that you've just about ruined." Caleb helped the cowboy to straighten up. The man shook his head, took a deep breath and glowered at Caleb.

"Good," Caleb said. "Now you might want to go over and apologize to the lady."

"Th' hell—" Caleb grabbed the cowboy by the throat and almost lifted him from the floor.

Andrew stepped over, laid a hand lightly on Caleb's arm. "Freddie, you might want to do what the man says. I don't want no blood soiling this floor that I cleaned just this morning. What do you say?"

Caleb released his hold on Freddie's throat.

The cowboy coughed, stood up straight, tucked his shirt in his trousers, grasped the tops of his pants at the waist and shifted the pants rapidly side to side. He looked at Caleb, then at Andrew. He walked slowly across the room to where Mei Lin stood with Priscilla. He removed his hat, almost bowed, and said something to Mei Lin.

Mei Lin and Priscilla had watched the ruckus with mixed emotions. Priscilla had stared, wide-eyed, fearful, her hand over her mouth. Mei Lin had watched with a hint of a smile playing about her lips. She knew by now that the only thing that got Caleb riled was something somehow related to herself.

Mei Lin looked over Freddie's shoulder at Caleb. She cocked her head, her lips pursed in a fashion that Caleb knew meant that she was trying very hard not to smile. Or laugh out loud.

She said something to Freddie. He bow-nodded again, put on his hat, turned on his heel and walked out the door, chin high, almost strutting.

Mei Lin looked across the room at Caleb, her look saying: "What's going on?"

Caleb and Andrew watched Freddie until he was gone. "He's not a bad sort, Freddie," said Andrew. "Just not the sharpest knife in the drawer. I suspect that the next time he sees you, he will tell you how sorry he is. He's all right." Caleb nodded and touched his hat brim.

Caleb walked to Mei Lin. Priscilla smiled at Caleb, gave him a quick brushing-a-fly wave and withdrew, walking into the post office cubicle.

"Mei Lin," said Caleb, "why is it you attract trouble like flowers attract bees?"

"Because you dress me in pretty clothes and say nice things to me. I begin to believe the nice things you say." She took his arm, and they walked toward the door. Caleb waved to Andrew over his shoulder.

6

Caleb had never been comfortable mixing socially with people. It wasn't until just days before leaving Stanley that he began to get to know his neighbors. And that was only because there had been a real shakeup in the valley that he had set in motion.

He was instrumental in shutting down the notorious Rat Trap saloon and brothel and running the owner out of the state. This was the same madam who had bought Mei Lin from the men who had killed Fuhua, the same madam from whom Caleb had stolen Mei Lin. The same madam who later had her kidnapped and sold her to a Boise brothel, from which Caleb had rescued her again. The grateful townspeople knew all this and were sorry to see Caleb and Mei Lin leave.

Caleb and Mei Lin had exchanged visits with friends on occasion since settling in the Hole, but the first real social occasion they attended was the harvest festival at the Clubhouse on the town square. There were displays of products grown locally, but no one spent much time on them. For the most part, people simply dressed up and came prepared to drink punch and coffee and catch up on the latest gossip.

Since this was their first festival, and since the curiosity about this rancher and his pretty Chinese wife—was she his wife?—had quickly become the talk of Jackson, questions were inevitable. Caleb and Mei Lin expected them and braced themselves.

They had hardly gotten inside the hall and picked up their cups of punch when three smiling women marched over to them at the punch table. The women said their polite hellos, hope you are settled in nicelys, how are you getting alongs. Then they got down to business.

"Where are you from, Mei Lin?" said Mrs. Hendricks. Wife of Jimmy Hendricks, owner of the feed store, Mrs. Hendricks was well known as the chief gossip and rumor-monger in town. "How did you meet Caleb?" She smiled, waited. The two other women with her smiled, looking at Mei Lin expectantly.

"My story is not interesting," said Mei Lin.

"Oh, we are interested!" the three women said, almost in unison. They closed in on Mei Lin.

"Okay. My parents in China couldn't feed me, so they sold me so I would not starve. The man who bought me brought me to Washington to help him look for gold. Then we went to Idaho to look for gold. Some bad men stole his gold and killed him. And Caleb found me. And here we are."

"Oh," Mrs. Hendricks said. Her hand went to her lips. She actually blushed. "Uh, I see. That's . . . an interesting story." Her eyes darted right and left, as she looked around, searching for an escape.

Caleb had watched all this. He had seen it more than once. Friends and strangers seemed compelled to learn how this pretty young Chinese woman had met this refined middle-aged Easterner. The questioners were always embarrassed when they heard her story. They would have been even more embarrassed if she had told them the whole story. Invariably Caleb had to rescue the questioner.

He walked over to the group. "Mei Lin, do you want some more punch?" She nodded, smiled at the ladies, and walked with Caleb to the punch bowl. He took her empty cup, refilled it and handed it back to her.

Mei Lin took the cup, sipped. "The next time someone asks me how I met you," said Mei Lin, looking over the room, "I'm going to tell them that I was a whore and that you liked my company so much, you bought me." Both laughed so loud that in spite of the buzz of conversation half of the room turned toward them. Mei Lin smiled and stared them down until they turned away.

"I'm going to talk to Priscilla," she said. She motioned toward the door where Priscilla stood alone, her hands clasped primly at her waist.

Caleb watched her go. He knew she felt a special affinity for Priscilla because she had been that timid person most of her life. Fearful, insecure, reluctant to risk contact. No more.

Caleb walked to the window and looked outside. The evening sun hung just over the Teton range, just beginning to turn a light purple. It was his favorite time of day.

Caleb had always found a way to deflect questions of any sort about himself. Mei Lin had helped him come to terms with his past, but he was still not ready to talk with strangers about it. He had come to terms with it, but he had not forgotten it, and he still hurt.

He had lost his entire family back in Richmond. His sweet wife, his boy and girl. The sickness took them all. He had sold his business, told his agent to give the money to the poor, but the agent was also a friend who said he wasn't thinking clearly, that he would need the money when he got his head straight.

He wandered westward, looking for anonymity or death. He spent most of his days and nights in saloons where he drank and was beaten to a pulp more than once. Everyone considered a drifter a soft target. In time, he learned to fight and use a six-shooter. He had killed. Two sons of bitches who wouldn't leave him alone. They needed killing.

He bought sex a few times when his brain was so addled with alcohol and loneliness that he wasn't thinking straight. He always cried, and the whores generally didn't like that. One actually kicked him off the bed. Another had stroked his cheek and cried with him.

He eventually reached Idaho and built a gold dredge. He wasn't interested in success, rather occupation. But his life took a turn in Stanley. He met Mei Lin. He beat hell out of a couple of cowboys who were abusing her in the Rat Trap saloon and paid the uncooperative madam for her release.

Their relationship was distant at first. She stayed with him in his cabin on Stanley Creek near the dredge, but they hardly touched. Caleb tried to find a place for her with a nearby Chinese community. He even tried to send her back to China. But Mei Lin knew where her place was. With Caleb. He finally realized that he loved her and welcomed her into his heart.

Caleb had found new meaning in his life with Mei Lin. He sold the dredge, and they left Stanley and their beloved Sawtooths for a new life together in a new place.

Mei Lin leaned against the wagon, a shawl wrapped around her shoulders. She wore a dress of homespun that Berta had made for her. As her girth increased, she now wore women's clothes, as she called them, more often than her usual boy's pants and shirt.

Caleb, Will and Jedediah worked on the first length of buck-rail fence that would eventually surround his house and outbuildings. He showed the others how to make the A-frames and how to prepare the poles for mounting on the A-frames.

"That's the damnedest fence I ever seen," said Jed. "It's just settin' on top of the ground. Damn elk'll just walk right through it."

"Actually, they don't," said Caleb. "A fence is a fence. They pretty much leave it alone."

"I never seen one of these," said Will. "Why don't you just build a regular fence?"

Caleb flexed his back. "Well, I like the looks of the buck-rail, and since there's no buried posts, it's pretty easy to move one way or the other if you decide you've put it in the wrong place."

Jed shook his head. "Okay, you say so." He walked to the back of the wagon where he reached for a couple of poles from the bed. He stopped, leaning into the bed, stared at Mei Lin's profile as she watched Caleb and Will. She seemed to sense his stare, turned and looked at him. He immediately looked down and pulled the poles from the wagon. He lifted the poles to his shoulder and carried them to the fence line.

Jed dumped the poles beside the fence. He glanced abruptly toward Mei Lin, then as quickly back at Caleb. "Just be a minute," he said to Caleb and trotted to a thick stand of sagebrush, disappearing behind it. Caleb and Will positioned a pole on two A-frames

"I don't like that Jed," Mei Lin said. "Creepy."

The wagon rolled along the fence line. Caleb shook

the lines. The breeze picked up, and Mei Lin wrapped her shawl over her head. She also wore Caleb's jacket. When he saw her shivering, he had removed the jacket and given it to her. He said that his heavy shirt was enough until he cooled down.

"Yeah, I know what you mean," said Caleb. "He won't be around much longer. I must contact the land office and get title to that place. They said they had paperwork to get done before they could issue title to me.

"Then I'll set him on his way. Hate to do it since he seems such a lost soul, but he's not a worker, and I could use his place for storage. I'll give him notice."

They rode in silence, glancing at the Teton range where the sun was slowly descending into a saddle, the land darkening, the lacy clouds turning twenty pastel shades of pink and orange and ocher.

"Caleb, honey?"

"Yes, sweetheart."

"I want to get married."

He straightened, looked at her, frowned. He softened, smiled. "Strange. We've never talked about that. Of course, we'll get married, sweetheart. Why hadn't we done it? So much going on. We'll talk on it."

Mei Lin stood in the front doorway and waved to Caleb who had just mounted Buck. He waved and set out at a lope. He was anxious to post a letter that he had written just that morning. Mei Lin and Caleb had talked late the previous evening about plans for their wedding. Not a word had been said about marriage until two days ago, and now they could talk about nothing else.

They agreed that they wanted Ray and Chica here. Not just for the wedding, but permanently. They wanted them to move here. The letter was addressed to Ray Hutton at the ranch outside Stanley.

Chica, a Mexicana, was Mei Lin's only friend at the Rat Trap brothel. Ray had stolen her a few months before Caleb had spirited Mei Lin away. Mei Lin and Chica went their separate ways, and Mei Lin thought she would never see Chica again.

Polly, the Rat Trap owner and madam, was furious at the loss of her properties and vowed to recover them. Two of her thugs had kidnapped Mei Lin when Caleb was away from his cabin and sold her to the brothel at The Mad Hatter in Boise. An enraged Caleb had killed the thugs and The Mad Hatter madam and brought her back to his cabin on Stanley Creek.

Polly never gave up looking for Chica. When her men found Ray and Chica working on a ranch outside Stanley, they tried to take her. Ray fought them, and they shot him before being driven off by ranch cowboys.

Afraid their presence on the ranch could mean trouble for the owner, Ray and Chica fled, bound for Boise. They had hardly set out when Ray took a turn for the worse. A party of Sheepeater hunters found them on the trail and took them to their village. Three Sheepeaters had worked for Caleb on the dredge, and they told him about the couple they had found.

Caleb and Mei Lin went to the Sheepeater village where Mei Lin and Chica were reunited.

In time, Caleb and others in Stanley chased the madam from the valley and turned the Rat Trap into a community property. Now safe, Ray returned to his work at the ranch. About this time, Caleb sold the dredge, and he and Mei Lin set out to start all over again in Jackson Hole. Mei Lin was a willing party to the move, but it meant that she was going to lose Chica again, maybe forever this time.

But that was all changed now. Caleb's letter asked Ray and Chica to come to Jackson Hole. He described the ranch that he had built and his long-term plans. He said that he needed help from people he trusted. He offered Ray the position of ranch foreman.

He would settle them in Jed's place, and he and his hands would help him with improvements. He assumed that Jed would be long gone before their arrival. He told them about his and Mei Lin's plans to marry and said that they would be happy to have their two good friends be part of the ceremony.

Caleb had read the letter to Mei Lin. Her excitement had risen with every paragraph, every word. She could not contain her wild joy at the prospect of having Chica only a short ride away.

Mei Lin still stood in the doorway, staring at the Jackson road where Caleb had disappeared. Wait! What if they would not come? Mei Lin and Caleb had not considered that maybe Ray and Chica were happy with their present condition. Maybe they would not want to pull up stakes where they had a good living and good prospects to move to a region that was still a relative frontier and a situation with uncertain prospects.

She shook her head. Worrying about it would not change anything. She would wait for a reply. Surely they will come. Won't they?

She needed some air. She went into the house, took a jacket from a peg in the front hall and pulled it on. She wore a long cotton dress that she had let out twice. Sitting in a kitchen chair, she removed her house shoes and pulled on riding boots.

She walked along the buck-rail fence to the end, where work had stopped the day before. Two A-frames and a stack of poles lay at the end of the fence. She continued to walk in a meadow of fescue, running her hand through the tall bentgrass, heavy with tiny spikelets.

At the bottom of the meadow, near a line of dense willows, she stopped. Down the line of willows, about fifty yards away, a lone saddled horse stood, head down and reins trailing, apparently grazing. She searched the meadow and saw no one. She stared at the horse, not knowing what to make of it.

She turned back to the willows in front of her. Caleb had told her that the willows bordered a small stream, but she had never seen it. She hadn't hauled water from this stream since the approach was too marshy, according to Caleb.

She walked along the edge of the dense growth, found a narrow opening and walked through, pushing soft branches aside. She saw the stream, about three feet wide, bordered with hardstem bulrush. She stepped toward the stream, pulled back when she felt her boot sink into the spongy grass.

Then he was on her. Hands encircled her waist roughly and pulled her to the ground. Jed fell on her and ripped her bodice, squeezing her breasts. He reached down and grasped the folds of her dress, pulling the dress up, his other hand fumbling with his belt buckle.

"Wha—" He rolled off her and rose up on his knees. He stared at her, holding his belly, blood oozing between his fingers. "Wha—"

Mei Lin rolled on her side to her knees. She held a small knife, blood dripping from the blade. She thrust the knife toward him, and he fell on his back. She scrambled up, pulled up her skirts with a hand, the other hand still holding the knife, and ran toward the cut in the willows.

When Caleb returned in late afternoon, he pulled Buck up at the hitching rail in the front yard, dismounted and tied the reins. He would say hello to Mei Lin and then take care of the horse.

He stepped into the quiet house to see Mei Lin sitting at the kitchen table, staring at the window. He saw her torn bodice, skirts wet and caked with filth, her face marked with streaks of dried mud and hair disheveled. Her bloodied knife lay on the table.

Caleb pulled a chair beside her. She turned her head to him.

"Are you all right?" he said softly, looking into her eyes.

"Yes," she said, "I'm okay. He's not." She looked at the bloodied knife.

"Jed?"

"Yes."

"Is he alive?"

"I think so."

Caleb rose and went to a dresser in the sitting room. He opened a top drawer and took out a six-shooter in its holster. He pulled the pistol out, twirled the cylinder, confirmed that it was loaded. He pushed the six-shooter into the holster, strapped on the belt and walked toward the front door.

"Caleb?" said Mei Lin from the kitchen.

"Lock the doors, Mei Lin."

He slammed the front door, mounted and kicked Buck into a gallop.

The two miles to Jed's place was but a moment, but it seemed an eternity. Caleb pulled Buck to a sliding stop in the yard and jumped down. Dropping the reins over the hitching rail, he reached the door in two steps, kicked the door hard, and it fell off its hinges into the room. He stepped through the doorway.

Jed sat at the table, hunched over. He looked up at Caleb, his face contorted in pain. Caleb grasped his jacket with both hands, jerked him up and smashed his fist into his face. Jed fell backward and collapsed to the floor. He lay still on his back, his bloody hand at his stomach. He stared at the ceiling.

"You cain't hurt me more'n I hurt. She stuck me, boss, she stuck me."

"She shoulda killed you, you son of a bitch. I want you out of this house by tomorrow morning, or I'll finish what she should have done. If I see you tomorrow, you're a dead man."

Jed did not move. His face was crunched in pain, his eyes squeezed shut. He opened his eyes to slits. He looked at Caleb through wet, half open eyes.

"I'm dead already." He winced, his eyes clinched shut, and tears rolled down his temples.

Caleb stood over the prostrate Jed, pondered. He kneeled beside him. He moved Jed's hand where he gripped his bloody shirt. Caleb unbuttoned the shirt and looked at the puncture wound. He stood and went to the cupboard, rummaged in the cloths and towels.

Pulling out a reasonably clean cloth, he ripped it into two pieces, looked around.

"Don't you have any water in this shack?"

"Out back, pump."

"You've got a well?" said Caleb. This was a surprise. He knew that many of the homesteaders, all better off than Jed, still hauled water from the streams.

Jed nodded, winced, his eyes squeezed shut. "Yeah. Thought I was gonna be a fine farmer once on a time. Long time ago." He shuddered, turned his head to the side.

Caleb shook his head, opened the back door and saw the pump. Expecting it to be as reliable as its owner, he pumped it and was surprised to see the stream of pure water. He wet the cloth and went back to kneel beside Jed. He cleaned the wound with the wet cloth, tossed that aside, and wiped the cut dry with the other cloth.

He went back to the cabinet and selected a large piece of sacking and ripped it into strips. Tying the strips into a longer length, he kneeled beside Jed. He folded a cloth into a square and placed it on the puncture. Pushing the long strip under Jed's back, he tied the strip around his waist, pressing the pad over the wound.

"Careful with this. It's probably going to fall off, but maybe it will hold till you can see the doc in town tomorrow. He'll fit you with a proper bandage."

Jed looked at Caleb, eyes barely open. "I'm going to town tomorrow?"

"Yeah, on your way out. I'll send Will over to help you pack your wagon."

Jed raised his head off the floor. "I got no place to go, boss. I got no kin, and I don't know nobody. And winter's coming." Jed choked on a sob.

"Then you better head south."

Jed's head fell back to the floor. He stared at the ceiling. "I'm dead. I'm a dead man." Jed sobbed softly, tears rolling down his cheeks.

Caleb stood, rolled his head back, grimaced. He had come to Jed's shack to kill him. If not that, at least to hurt him and evict him. Now he's feeling sorry for him?

Caleb leaned down, gripped Jed's lapels, pulled him up, and helped him sit in the chair. Jed's head was on his chest. He wiped his face with a dirty sleeve, stared at the floor.

Caleb leaned against the table, stared down at Jed.

"What went wrong?" Caleb said.

Jed looked up at Caleb. He wiped his eyes with the back of a hand. He inhaled deeply, exhaled, looked at his hands in his lap.

"I had hope. Once. I had some money, a little money my daddy left me when he died. Back in Nebraska. I came to the Hole to have my own place. Place where I could bring a wife and live good. I built a good house. I paid for help. Put in a garden, hay, got some cows, paid to put in a well.

"I met a pretty girl who I thought liked me. I had hope. But she married a fella from Idaho. That was the end of it. I stopped trying. And here I am." He stared at the wall, tear tracks marking his face.

Caleb looked through the empty doorway to the yard, saw Buck, a tumbleweed roll past the door, Buck shying. He pulled a small roll of bills from his pocket, peeled off a few notes and laid them on the table. Jed looked at the bills, puzzled, looked up at Caleb.

"Like I said, I want you out of here tomorrow. Will is going to help you load up. Go to Jackson, and see the doc. Tell him I'll pay. Then you look for a place. Talk to Folie at the general store and Hendricks at the feed store. Tell them I sent you. Ask if they have any work for you or if they can suggest something.

"This $20 will help you eat for a time. If you find something in town, I don't want to see you. Ever. Stay out of my sight. You ever see Mei Lin, anywhere, you run. Do you understand all this, Jed?"

Jed nodded.

"You understand this, Jed!"

Jed lowered his head, wiped his eyes with a hand. "Yeah, I understand."

"If you don't find any work in town, you head south."

Jed looked at the bills on the table, looked up at Caleb. "Thanks, boss. I . .. I'm sorry." Jed sobbed, his face contorted, as tears came again. "I don't know why you're doing this after . . . I'm really sorry."

Caleb shook his head, walked through the door. "Damned if I know myself why I'm doing it," he mumbled softly. He mounted Buck and rode away at a lope.

Caleb pulled up at the hitching rail in front of the house. He dismounted and tied the reins. Mei Lin leaned against a porch post. She had changed her clothes, washed her face and combed her hair.

He walked to the porch, touched her cheek.

"Is he okay? Did you kill him?" she said.

"He's better than he deserves to be. I patched him up and told him that this was the last time I want to see him. He'll be gone tomorrow. He won't bother you again."

"I feel sorry for him," she said. "He seems so ... so lost."

Caleb wrapped his arms around her, kissed her softly. "Yeah. He's a lost soul. He told me his story. Sad. I'll tell you some time. I suppose he's like a lot of homesteaders, here and everywhere, who think they're going to put down roots in a new place, and everything's going to be right and wonderful. And they're disappointed when it doesn't turn out that way at all. Things just don't fall into place, and they can't cope, and they give up, and everything falls to pieces. Yeah, I feel sorry for him, too, though if he had fought back, I'm afraid I would have killed him. I was that angry."

Mei Lin hugged him. "I'm glad you didn't hurt him."

Caleb released her. "Let's get some coffee. I need to settle down."

They walked through the front door and into the kitchen. Caleb took two cups from the cupboard while

Mei Lin prepared the coffee in the percolator. He sat in a chair, holding the handle of his cup, idly twisting the cup, watching Mei Lin and staring through the window.

Mei Lin poured coffee from the steaming percolator into the two cups, replaced the percolator on the stove and sat down. They sipped from their mugs in silence. Caleb stared at the window.

"Say it," she said.

He smiled. "Now you're getting inside my head, peanut... You should have had the .32 with you when you were out walking. I got that for your protection. You never know when you'll need it. Like today."

"I know. I forgot it. I won't do that again. But the way things turned out, I'm glad I didn't have it. I might have killed him. I don't think I could have lived with that. He's not a bad man."

"You can say that because you stopped him. What if you hadn't stopped him? You would have found out how really bad he could be."

She stared into her coffee cup.

"I'm glad you had the knife. I'd forgotten about the knife."

"I always have it. Always. Ever since I arrived with Fuhua in Washington. He gave it to me and told me the same thing you told me about the gun. He said it was for protection. He said that he hoped I never had to use it, but if ever I was in danger, I should use it. He showed me how."

"Did you ever use it? Before today? I never asked you."

She looked up at him, looked down at the table, stared into her cup. She stood and walked to the counter, refilled the cup. She stood at the counter a moment longer, looking out the window above the sink. She came back to the table, sat down, looked into her cup.

"I killed a man."

He recoiled. "You ... killed a man?" he said.

"He wanted me to do something I didn't want to do. I told him I wouldn't do it. He tried to make me do it. He was drunk. I tried to get away from him. He hit me with his fist and tried to force me to do it. I stuck him. When he didn't stop, I stuck him two more times. He fell on the bed.

"I was scared, terrified. I ran downstairs, crying. Polly caught me at the bottom of the stairs and asked me what was wrong. I told her. She called me a slut and slapped me hard. She was very angry. She asked me the man's name. I told her I didn't know, and she sent one of her men to look.

"He came back down and said it was Eddy. Polly calmed down a little. She went over to the bar with him, and they talked. She came back to me, took my arm and led me to a table in the back. She said listen to me. Eddy's body is going to be discovered on the road ten miles out of town. Eddy was never here today; he hasn't been her in a month; you haven't seen him in over a month. Do you understand?

"I told her I understood. I was still upset and crying, wiping my tears. She said Eddy was a troublemaker. He had hurt her girls more than once. She said don't worry about it. I was surprised. It was the only time Polly ever said anything kind to me. She never did again.

"I still wake up at night, going over all this. Over and over and over."

Mei Lin slumped, laid her head on her arms on the table. She was drained. Caleb reached across the table, touched her head.

"What you did was the right thing to do," he said. "That man, Eddy, was nothing more than a running sore, a poisonous snake that had to be killed. You did the right thing. You don't need to be bothered by this anymore. It's done.

By telling me, you are finished with all this." He raised her head till they were eye to eye. "Okay?"

She smiled. "Okay, Dr. Willis. Or are you a shaman, chasing away my evil spirits?"

"Whatever works," he said.

Caleb shook the lines, and the mules quickened their pace. Mei Lin and Caleb, wearing jackets and hats, sat on the wagon seat. The wagon bed was loaded with fence wire and boards. They were bound for the bunkhouse, the farthest property from their own place.

In case they decided to spend the night, they had brought bedrolls and a supply of meat and vegetables that Andy and Paul would be happy to share. The two cowboys had already complained good-naturedly about each other's cooking. Andy had asked Caleb to require that his next hire be a good cook as well as a good cowboy. He had smiled when he said it, but Caleb suspected that he was dead serious.

The wagon rolled through a countryside that was showing unmistakable signs of the onset of autumn. Aspens on the mountain slopes and flats had turned from dull green to yellow to burnt gold. The papery white bark of the aspens contrasted with the colorful leaves. Cottonwoods along streams and marshy places displayed brilliant yellows.

"Stop!" Mei Lin said. Caleb pulled hard on the lines.

"What?"

"Didn't you hear? Listen." They sat motionless, listening.

Then they heard it. A primitive sound, half mule's bellow, half pig squeal, sounded from an aspen grove. A male elk's bugling announced his urgent search for a mate. A moment later, another elk appeared from a more distant thicket into the meadow and bugled.

Then it was still and quiet again. They looked around, listened.

"That's all the music for now," Caleb said. "We need to get to the bunkhouse." He looked up. "This sky is looking a bit threatening. Don't really expect snow, but the locals tell me not to try to second-guess the weather. There's a hint of what's coming." He motioned toward the Tetons. The peaks wore a solid white mantle, and the slopes below were lightly dusted with snow.

Caleb shook the lines, and the mules moved off. He loved the autumn season, his favorite time of year, but he had heard so much about the hard Jackson Hole winters that he worried.

He was determined to be ready. He had already begun buying hay from the Mormons, and he and Mei Lin had become friends with the Barkers and the Budges, long-time Mormon residents who had lived through winters in the Hole.

Caleb had asked the Mormons what they did about the lack of game in the winter. Caleb routinely shot elk and deer for meat, but he had been concerned when locals told him that game could be as scarce in winter as it was sometimes in summer. That's when he learned about the Mormon practice of canning and curing elk and pig meat.

The Mormons said they would be glad to sell some preserved meat if they had a surplus. When he told Mei Lin, she said that she wanted to go with him on his next visit with the Mormons. She wanted to learn about canning and curing. And Mormons.

Dusk approached as the wagon rolled on the road to the bunkhouse. They had not planned a long day, but there were some unexpected distractions on the way.

They had hardly set out when the overcast darkened and lowered. Then the cloud cover over the Teton range lifted, revealing a well-defined band of bright sky above the peaks. Caleb stopped the wagon, and they stared at the range, as the band of light changed color from aqua to blue to salmon. Then the cloud lowered, and the band was gone.

"Wow," said Mei Lin.

Caleb shook the lines, and they pulled ahead. After only a few minutes, he pulled up again. He got down from the wagon and walked to a bunch of a half dozen cows beside the road. They walked slowly away from him, and he followed. He looked closely at one cow in particular.

Later, back on the road, Mei Lin grabbed Caleb's sleeve and pointed. He pulled up. They watched a coyote and four pups tearing into what appeared to be the remains of a fawn. The coyotes were only a short stone's throw from the road, but they ignored the intruders into their domain.

The cloud gathered and darkened. The breeze quickened, and Mei Lin raised her collar. Caleb shook the lines.

Caleb pulled up in front of the bunkhouse just as snowflakes began to swirl about the wagon. Mei Lin looked up, smiled, and stretched out her arms.

"Glad to see you folks, but you coulda left the snow at home." Andy strode from the barn toward the wagon.

"Oh, Andy, I love snow!" said Mei Lin.

"Yeah, well, I do, too, as long as I'm just lookin' at it and not trying to work in it. Now, come on in the house, and I'll have a fire going in a jiffy." He extended a hand to help Mei Lin down.

"If this weather gets serious, you might better spend the night," said Andy.

"We considered that and brought bedrolls and a couple of buffalo robes just in case," Caleb said. "We also brought an elk roast, potatoes and beans and a pan of cornbread. Just need warming up. That is, unless you'd rather fix up something special for supper."

Andy grinned. "Not likely. Let's get your truck in the house, and I'll take care of the mules."

After the wagon was unloaded, Andy built a fire in the stove and went out to tend to the mules. While Mei Lin worked on supper, Caleb went outside and stood under the porch that Andy and Paul had built to shelter the stack of firewood. They had already cut and stacked a good supply. He looked at the western horizon. The band of deep blue sky between the heavy overcast and the dark outline of the Teton range was sufficient to see the sun ball slip behind the mountains. The snow now fell in large flakes and had covered the yard.

"Beautiful, isn't it?" said Andy. He walked under the porch cover, dusting the flakes off his coat. He stood quietly beside Caleb, watching the mountain absorb the light and darken.

"I stand here most days about this time, looking at just what we're looking at. I don't mind sayin' that sometimes it almost brings tears to my eyes. You 'member when Paul and me first got here, and I said we hadn't found our place yet? Well, I don't know about Paul, but I thank I've found my place. I can't imagine now being any place I can't see just what we're seein' right now."

"I understand," said Caleb. "I begin to feel the same way. By the way, where is Paul?"

"That boy, he don't have enough sense to quit work 'till he cain't see to work. He'll be along any minute now. He was out looking at a bunch up north of here."

"When you get a chance," said Caleb, "have a look at a bunch just about a mile south. They were on the west side of the road, about a half dozen when we saw them. There might be a case of pinkeye. Could be just weed litter in her eye, but it could be pinkeye."

"We'll check on it tomorrow," Andy said. They looked aside at the sound of hooves. "Well, here he is, now that you can't see your hand in front of your face." They watched Paul ride toward the corral.

Andy yelled. "Hurry up! We've got a real supper tonight, and I'm fixing to eat your share!" Paul waved and led his horse into the corral.

7

"Damn, Caleb, I wish you had written to us a long time ago. We woulda come anytime."

Caleb and Mei Lin sat with Ray and Chica at the kitchen table, sipping hot coffee. Ray grinned. He said that Chica had almost squeezed the life out of him when he read Caleb's letter to her. He had sat down and wrote a reply that very day.

Ray said that he and Chica weren't unhappy at the ranch outside Stanley, but they had missed their friends and jumped at the chance to join them in Jackson Hole. They settled their affairs, packed and set out in a week. They had been surprised by a substantial snowfall in the Tetons and counted themselves lucky to get through at all.

"That Teton Pass is something," Ray said. "They told me at Victor that it's open all winter, but I don't believe it. We had a pretty good snow on the uphill, and we was lucky to have a herd of cows ahead of us beating down the snow. We was also lucky to have a family traveling right behind us 'cause we had to double-team on the uphill.

"The uphill and the pass was bad enough, but it was a pretty scary downhill on the packed snow. The log we was pulling for a brake kept sliding on the packed snow and ice and bumping into the wagon. All told, if things had been just a little different, you might not have seen our bones till spring."

"We're real happy you made it over safely," said Caleb. "Some of the old timers hereabouts have told me that we're in for an early winter this year. Guess you were pretty lucky.

"We'll put the wagon in the barn for the night," said Caleb. "Bring some bedding in the house, and we'll put you up in the spare room. I've moved stuff around so you have some space.

"We'll take you to your place tomorrow. The boys have done some repairs and have begun to get it in shape for winter. You're still likely to get some whistling through the walls until you can tighten it up. There's hay in the barn and enough groceries to do for you till you can get into town."

"Chica!" said Mei Lin, gripping her friend's arm. "You're going to be just two miles away. We can visit every day!"

"I don't know about that," said Caleb. "You're not going to be riding much with that belly cargo, even in the wagon." Mei Lin frowned at him, smiled.

"I know!" said Chica. "Mei Lin, you're getting so big! I'll come see you, and we'll talk so much. Remember how we used to talk? Every time we weren't... we weren't. ... Remember, we would find a place and talk about things we wanted to eat, things we wanted to do, we talked about the outside, clothes we wanted to wear—"

Mei Lin put her hand on Chica's. "We can remember that talk because talking about good things was the only way we survived. But we will never talk about Rat Trap.

That year was a bad dream. But we survived."

"We have all lived through bad times, but it's only good times ahead!" said Caleb. "It's going to be cold good times. Ray, let's get your wagon stowed and your stuff in the house while the ladies work on a welcome dinner for our good friends." Caleb stood and clapped Ray on the back. Ray jumped up, and they went out.

Mei Lin and Chica sipped from their cups. "I have a new horse," said Chica.

"I saw her tied to your wagon," said Mei Lin. "She's pretty."

"Do you know what I named her?"

"What?"

"Mei Lin."

Mei Lin frowned. "You named your horse 'Mei Lin?' Why?"

"Mei Lin." Chica laughed. "I asked you the same question when you told me you named your horse, 'Chica'. Remember? Remember what you said?"

Mei Lin smiled. Her eyes glistened. She replied softly. "Yes, I remember. Because I love her." She reached over and hugged Chica. She leaned back, wiped her eyes with a sleeve. "Our mares are going to be confused. Maybe us too."

"Not me," said Chica. I call my horse 'Mei' and you 'Mei Lin.' Why don't you call your horse something else? How about. . . 'Chiquita!'"

"Chiquita? What does it mean?"

"Little one, little Chica."

"Okay, that will do. Unless I forget and call you 'chiquita.'"

Caleb and Ray sat their horses in the yard at Jed's house. Caleb watched Ray as he looked over the house, the barn and corral.

"It doesn't look like much, but there's a good house and a good barn, if you look beyond the loose boards and peeling paint and loose shingles, and—"

"You don't have to sell me, Caleb. You know, this will be the first house Chica and I have lived in together. On the ranch, we had a room that was attached to the bunkhouse. This is a big step up for us."

"It's going to be a lot better. We're going to put this place in tiptop shape. I've already told Andy and Paul that their main job for now is to help with repairs and upgrading this place. They have lots of experience since they did the same to their place when they moved in."

Caleb reached over and clapped Ray on the shoulder. "We're real glad to have you here. You go on and have a look at the barn. I'll catch up. Need to look at something here."

Ray turned his horse and waved over his shoulder, heading for the barn. Caleb dismounted and tied his reins to a post in the yard.

He walked to the porch, noted that the door that he had knocked off its hinges had been repaired. He opened the door and walked into the dark kitchen. He looked around, and everything he saw reminded him of Jed. He was suddenly overcome with a profound sadness. He knew what loneliness and loss and despair could do to a person.

I've killed Jed as surely as if I had shot him dead.

On a snowy November morning, Caleb and Mei Lin were married. Ray was Caleb's best man, and Chica was Mei Lin's bridesmaid. Berta and Bennie completed the wedding party. Caleb had suggested that they include other friends, for they had become rather popular in the Hole, but Mei Lin did not want to make the wedding more awkward than it was. She was eight months pregnant and, as Berta had predicted months ago, as big as a house.

Not a few townspeople had stopped and watched Mei Lin and Caleb get down from the wagon, bundled up against the cold, but obviously dressed in their finest at mid-morning on this day when nothing was going on in the town to warrant dressing in one's finest.

Then they watched Ray and Chica, strangers to most, dressed in their finest, riding behind the wagon, dismount and join Caleb and Mei Lin on the sidewalk.

The four walked to the office of the town's only Justice of the Peace, Dan Leiter, where they met Sheriff Canlis and Berta and Bennie, also dressed in their finest, standing out front. The spectacle of Berta and Bennie all spruced up most perplexed the curious townspeople who now numbered a dozen gawkers.

The ceremony was a simple affair. The JP read from his book, the four members of the wedding party answered as they were instructed, and the groom and bride kissed as custom required. Mei Lin laughed out loud when Caleb didn't know whether to lean over her swollen belly to kiss her or kiss her from her side. Chica hugged Mei Lin, leaning carefully over her belly, her eyes moist. Ray gave Caleb a vigorous handshake and a slap on the back.

It was all over in ten minutes. Bennie and Berta stepped over and congratulated the newlyweds.

"Now there's an old custom in Jackson Hole," said Bennie. "Every man in the audience gets to kiss the bride."

"What!" said Berta. "I never ..."

Bennie grinned at Mei Lin who smiled and leaned toward him. He pecked her on the cheek. Bennie turned to Caleb and the sheriff, beaming.

Berta stood with hands on hips. "Well, by God, that means that I can kiss the groom!" She took Caleb's cheeks with both hands and kissed him lightly on the lips."

She jumped back, eyes opened wide. "Oh, did I just do that?"

"You did," said Caleb. "That must mean that we're all kin of some sort. So let's enjoy a family dinner." He motioned toward the door.

Outside, the spectators, standing on the packed snow in the street, and finally guessing the reason for the gathering and fine clothes, had grown to twenty people. They cheered as the wedding party exited the office.

Caleb waved to the group. He reached back and pulled Mei Lin up beside him. "I would like all you good friends and neighbors to meet Mrs. Willis." Mei Lin smiled, lowered her head. The townspeople erupted in cheers. The wedding party stepped off the sidewalk and the people closed around them, all smiles and congratulations.

"Caleb." The sheriff beckoned. "Come over here just a minute." Caleb stepped back up on the walk where Canlis stood.

"There's something you should know. When I went to see Dan this morning to get your marriage paper, he told me that that a friend of his over at Cheyenne told him there's a lotta talk at the capital about the government passing a law that outlaws marriage between a white man and a Chinese woman."

"What! That's the stupidest thing I ever heard of!"

"Yeah, but you and I both know that there's a lot of stupid people running the government. My friend said that it looks like the law is going to pass. Dan said he didn't know what effect such a law would have on marriages that have already been done, but he thought you oughta play it safe. He suggested that we fiddle with the marriage paper in case some busybody got to nosing around. He even came up with a name to put on the marriage paper:

May Lynn Leach."

Caleb frowned. "Are you two yahoos serious?"

"Up to you."

"No. Scott, I'm going to marry just once, and I want to make it legal and correct."

Canlis grinned. "That's what I told Ben. Here's the paper." He handed the marriage certificate to Caleb. He took the document and read the name of the woman he was marrying: Mei Lin Lee.

Caleb smiled. "Thanks, Scott. You're a good man." Caleb clapped him on the shoulder and stepped off the walk to the crowd on the street. He took Mei Lin's arm and held her tightly as they walked on the slippery ice and packed snow toward the restaurant.

Standing in the shadow two storefronts from the Justice of the Peace's office, two men watched the party crossing the street.

"Well, the little half-breed bastard won't be a bastard after all," said one. The other nodded.

Mei Lin and Caleb wore their heavy jackets and caps. Mei Lin had a shawl wrapped around her neck. Snowflakes whirled about in the light breeze. Caleb shook the lines, and the mules quickened the pace. Jackson was soon left behind.

"That was a fine dinner," said Caleb.

"Yes, it was." Mei Lin coughed.

Caleb looked over. "All right, Mrs. Willis?"

She cleared her throat, smiled. "All right, Mr. Willis."

"Almost there. We'll get you warmed up. I'll make some coffee. And anything else you want."

"Anything I want. Okay." She turned to Caleb. "Am I legal now, honey?"

"Of course, you're legal. Hmm, well... I see what you

mean. I'm not sure. I'll find out. But you must be. You are married to a citizen."

"Am I a citizen? I want to be a citizen."

Caleb looked sharply at Mei Lin. "Well, this is something new. Who have you been talking to?"

"Mrs. Hendricks. She said women in Wyoming can vote. Honey, if I am a citizen and can vote, it will mean so much to me. It will mean that I am not a foreigner. It will mean that I belong."

"I will find out."

"She said that my baby will be a citizen. So my baby will be a citizen, and I am married to a citizen. Doesn't that mean that I am a citizen?"

"Ah, it's all becoming clear, at last." He grinned. "You married me for political reasons. You want to become a citizen so you can vote and hold office and—"

"Don't be a silly man." She was not amused. "You know what I mean."

"I'll investigate. Wyoming has a good reputation for women in politics. I have no doubt whatsoever that you will be the first Chinese female governor."

She hit him hard on his arm, then took the arm with both hands and snuggled close.

• • • • •

Caleb rolled out of bed and pulled off his nightshirt in one motion. He grabbed his pants from the chair and stepped into them. He took the shirt from the chair and pulled it on while walking to the window.

He wiped the moisture from the window with a hand and looked out. The storm that had moved in just after supper last night had silently added a foot of new snow to the yard.

He walked into the kitchen, still buttoning his shirt. The kitchen was dimly illuminated by the four windows. Caleb stopped, his hands still holding the two sides of the shirt. He shivered. The kitchen was usually warm.

He had felt guilty more than once that it was Mei Lin who rose in the dark to light the fires in the house. A few days ago, when he protested that this was something he should do, she had put hands on hips, cocked her head, and replied: "Okay."

It wasn't the response he had expected. "Okay. . . uh, from now on—"

"From now on, nothing. You want to cook breakfast, too?"

He had smiled and kissed her lightly on the lips. "No, ma'am. Let's keep the chores just as they are."

He had expected to find Mei Lin in the kitchen this morning, tardy in her task of lighting the fires. But she was not there. He looked in the sitting room, in the bedroom that was used for storage, the utility room. He opened the back door and looked around the yard. Nothing. He closed the back door and strode down the hall to the front door, looked outside. No Mei Lin, and nothing appeared to be amiss.

He rushed back to the bedroom. There she was, lying in bed with the covers pulled almost over her head. He had been so accustomed to the usual routine that he had not noticed in the dark bedroom that she had not moved.

He pulled the cover from her head. She rolled slightly to look at him through slits, pain on her face. "Honey, I don't feel good." He felt her forehead. It was hot. She pulled the cover to her chin.

"Sweetheart, I'm getting the doctor. Will is coming. I'll send him soon as he gets here. I'll be right back."

"Don't leave me, Caleb!" She reached for him.

"I'm just going to the kitchen, sweetheart. I'll be right back."

He rushed to the kitchen, wet a cloth from the pail on the counter and returned to the bedroom. He bent over, dabbed her forehead, felt the cloth. It was warm.

"It hurts. Honey, it hurts."

"Where does it hurt, sweetheart?

"My belly. My stomach."

Caleb raised his head, eyes closed. *God, what can I do? If anything happens to her, that will do it for me. I'm a dead man.*

He started at the loud knocking. He jumped up and ran to the front door, threw the door open.

"Morning, boss." Will's grin evaporated when he saw Caleb's long face. "What's wrong?"

"Will, ride to town, get the doc, tell him to come right now. I don't care what he's doing. Maybe he won't be drunk this early. Just get him here. Mei Lin's real sick. Go."

"On my way." Will ran to his horse, untied the reins, mounted and kicked his horse into a gallop.

Winston Winslow stood beside the bed, rubbing his whiskered chin, studying Mei Lin over the reading glasses that rested on his nose. Doctor Winslow was nobody's first choice for anything, especially doctoring. He had made no attempt to update his medical knowledge and hadn't read a medical journal in the twenty years since his retirement from the army. But he was the only doctor in the vicinity of Jackson, so he was the doctor everyone called.

Winslow divided his time between his homestead five miles north of Jackson and a town office. Lately, he spent most of his time in the Jackson office since he had pretty much given up on farming, and the office was closer to the saloon.

Winslow bent down and opened his black bag. He extracted a small scalpel. "I shall need a shallow pan and a clean wet cloth," Winslow said.

Caleb stared at the scalpel. "What do you plan to do?"

"We need to balance the bodily humors. I'm going to bleed her."

"Bleed her? I thought bleeding went out years ago."

Winslow turned slowly to face Caleb, lowered his head to see him over the glasses balanced on his nose. "There are still certain conditions that call for renewing the blood flow," said Winslow, "releasing the bad humors." Scalpel in hand, he turned to Caleb. "The pan and wet cloth, please."

Caleb stood motionless a moment, looking at Mei Lin. Her eyes were closed, seemingly sleeping. Beads of perspiration stood out on her forehead and temple. Caleb went out to the kitchen. He returned a moment later with a pan and wet cloth.

Winslow placed the shallow pan on the bed beside Mei Lin. He took her arm and laid it across the pan. Wiping the scalpel with the wet cloth, he rubbed Mei Lin's arm below the elbow with the cloth. He took her hand, pushed his glasses up on his nose, and extended the scalpel toward her. He straightened, cleared his throat and, shifting the scalpel in his grip, dropped it on the bed. His hand shook.

He retrieved the scalpel, cleared his throat and touched the scalpel at a point just below her elbow. He pushed the blade into the flesh, making a smooth cut. Blood trickled from the wound and dripped into the pan.

Caleb winced and turned away.

Winslow watched the blood flow from the cut. He straightened, wiped the blade on the cloth. "There." He turned to Caleb. "In a few minutes, bind the arm with a clean cloth. I will come back in the morning, and we will continue." He dropped the scalpel into his bag and closed it. He picked up the bag and made to go.

"Doctor," said Caleb. Winslow stopped. "What of the baby?"

"Ah, the baby." Winslow frowned, pondered, head down. He looked up. "This has nothing to do with the baby. This has no effect on the baby.

"Till tomorrow," said Winslow. Bag in hand, he took a single step toward the door. He stopped and turned to Caleb. "Um, do you have a drop of elixir? For the ride to town, you understand? Very cold out there today."

"No, don't keep it in the house," said Caleb.

"Um, unfortunate. Unfortunate." He walked into the hall, took his coat from the peg and struggled into it. Caleb opened the door and closed it behind him. He stared at the closed door, head down.

He went to the kitchen, found a clean cloth in the pantry, tore it into two pieces. He wet one of the pieces from the bucket and walked to the bedroom. He felt Mei Lin's forehead. It was warm. He dabbed the wet cloth on the wound, then dried it. He wrapped the gash with the clean cloth, ripped the ends and tied it.

Mei Lin opened her eyes, dark and sunken, to look at him. He stroked her cheek, leaned down and kissed her lips. She tried to smile, coughed and turned on her side. He pulled the cover to her neck.

Doc Winslow came again the next morning and bled her. On the third day, he came again and bled her as Caleb watched, his anxiety growing and his bile rising.

On this third day, when Caleb opened the front door for the doctor on his departure, there stood Kimana on the porch. The doctor, upset that Caleb once again had not furnished the fortifying whiskey, brushed by her as if she were invisible.

"Kimana?" said Caleb.

"May I see her?"

Caleb pushed the door open and stepped aside. Kimana went in and walked directly to the bedroom, removing her coat as she walked. Laying the coat gently on the foot of the bed, Kimana looked at Mei Lin.

She lay in a fetal position, covers grasped tightly around her neck. Her hair was disheveled, her eyes sunken and dark, her complexion dry and pasty. Kimana felt her hot forehead.

Kimana pulled the cover down gently to look at the arm where the cuts had been made. She opened the bandage slowly, gently, and recoiled at what she saw. A redness spread from the wound, darkening at the extremities. She replaced the bandage and pulled the quilt up to cover her shoulders.

Mei Lin opened her eyes to slits. "Kimana?" she said softly. "Help me," just a whisper.

Kimana forced a slight smile, put her hand to Mei Lin's cheek. She took Caleb by the arm and guided him to the kitchen.

"You must send this doctor away. He is killing her. Caleb, I know. He has done it before. Last spring, before you came, a woman was sick after accidentally eating some rat poison. He bled her. We said he should make her vomit right now, but he would not listen. He said bleeding her was the thing to do. We begged her husband to send the doctor away, but he said the doctor knew more than we did. The woman died."

"But what can we do? There is no other doctor."

"Caleb. Listen. My grandfather is a healer. A shaman.

He may be able to help her. Will you let him come? There is no other white doctor, and this doctor will kill her. Will you let my grandfather come?"

Caleb pondered, looked toward the bedroom, back to Kimana. "Yes. Come quickly. I'm afraid, Kimana. She's past eight months now, and I'm .. ."

Kimana nodded, picked up her coat from the bed and ran to the hall, pulling on her coat as she went. She opened the door and ran to her horse. Caleb watched her as she untied the reins, mounted and kicked the horse into a gallop.

Caleb and Kimana stood beside Mei Lin's bed. She lay on her back, covers pulled to her chin, her complexion sallow. Kimana touched her cheek. Mei Lin opened her eyes, blinked, turned on her side, withdrew into her blankets.

Kimana opened a small canvas bag and took out some herbs and a vial of oil. She touched Mei Lin's cheek. Mei Lin's eyes fluttered open, closed. With her other hand, Kimana pulled the covers down slowly to reveal the bandaged arm. She gently removed the bandage, soiled with blood and pus. Handing the bandage to Caleb, she took from him the wet cloth he held. Wiping the wound clean, she applied herbs and oil on and around the cut. She took some small strips of cloth from the bag and tied a bandage loosely around the wound.

Kimana went to the kitchen and brought back a shallow pan and cloth. With the wet cloth, she gently wiped Mei Lin's face and arms. She handed the pan to Caleb, then pulled the quilt to cover Mei Lin's shoulders. Then she pulled the cover from the side of the bed to expose Mei Lin's abdomen. She moved her hand over Mei Lin's huge belly, stopping a moment, moving again, stopped again. She pulled the quilt to the side of the bed to cover her.

She straightened and turned to Caleb. "I can feel the

baby moving. Just a little. Maybe the baby is not affected by this. I hope so." Caleb nodded. He did not trust his voice to speak.

Kimana motioned with her hand for Caleb to follow. She stopped in the hall, handed him the canvas bag. "Here are herbal tea leaves. I will fix it. We must try to get her to drink it, just a sip at a time." He nodded, set the bag on a small table below the coat pegs.

They went out the front door to the porch. They stopped there, protected from the snow flurries that swirled about in the light breeze. A foot of snow lay on the ground.

In front of the porch, a four-foot square had been cleared of snow, and a mat of pine needles lay on the bare ground. A canvas tarpaulin was stretched overhead, the corners tied to the porch and tree limbs.

Kimana's grandfather sat on the bed of pine needles. In front of him, a circle had been cleared of needles. A small fire within the circle had almost burned down to coals, an errant flame rising occasionally.

The grandfather did not look up when they stepped from the doorway. He sprinkled pine needles on the coals. The needles burst into a tiny conflagration that as quickly was gone. The aroma alerted the creator of a need or request. Next he lit a small bundle of sage and crumpled bits over the coals. He waved the smoke inward, over his body. Sage drives out evil, illness, anything negative. This was followed by bits of sweetgrass dropped over the coals while a flat braided length of sweetgrass was lit, and the fragrant smoke anointed his body.

He reached into his tobacco pouch and sprinkled some over the coals. Lighting his pipe with a taper from the fire, he blew smoke first down to honor the earth, then skyward to honor the Great Spirit. Thence to each of the four directions to honor the winds that bring rain, grass, game, and food.

All this Kimana explained, whispering softly to Caleb.

As Grandfather watched the fire, the flames lowered, flickered, and the last ember became ash. The grandfather nodded to Kimana who rushed to him. She helped him stand, picked up a pouch from the ground and handed it to him. She took his elbow and helped him to the porch and through the door. Caleb followed.

In the bedroom, they stopped beside the bed. Mei Lin's cheeks were bright red, and perspiration beaded on her temples. She opened her eyes to slits, unfocusing, looking at nothing. Her eyes closed. Caleb felt that he could not breathe.

Grandfather spoke softly in Shoshone to Kimana. She pulled the covers down and exposed Mei Lin's abdomen. Mei Lin's eyes fluttered opened, closed. Caleb glanced at the wood stove. The fire he had built earlier in the stove radiated heat.

Grandfather took from his bag a deer antler with the sign of the thunderbird drawn on it in a red color. A single bear claw and a single feather dangled from the antler on rawhide cords. He waved the antler over Mei Lin, then laid it on the bed beside her.

In a small wooden bowl, Grandfather prepared a poultice of sweet grass and bear root mixed with tobacco and an oil. He applied the poultice to Mei Lin's abdomen and nodded to Kimana who pulled the covers up to Mei Lin's shoulders. Grandfather turned to Caleb, nodded, and he and Kimana walked from the bedroom.

Caleb stood on the front porch, leaning against a post. He looked across the hay fields and meadows and watched the cold sun rise slowly from behind the mountain range in the east. A heavy overcast projected a gloom that matched his mood.

All signs of the grandfather were long since gone. It had been three days since he had sat at his fire and performed the healing ceremony. Daily snowfalls since then had added almost two feet of new powder in the yard.

Caleb had slept little in the three days as his life seeped away, hour by hour.

"Caleb." He turned and saw Kimana standing in the doorway. "Come."

He followed her to the bedroom. His head throbbed, and every muscle and fiber tensed.

He stopped. Mei Lin's eyes were open. She smiled, a mere hint of a smile, but a smile. He rushed to the bed, bent and smothered her with kisses. Tears rolled down his cheeks.

"Mei Lin, sweetheart, honey." She laid her hand on his cheek. He leaned over, and she kissed him.

Caleb stood and turned to Kimana. "Kimana, you saved her life. And mine. How can I ever repay you?"

Kimana smiled. "There is my payment." She looked at Mei Lin, who smiled, her color good, her fever gone.

"I have made soup and herbal tea and soft vegetables." Kimana said. "I will come again tomorrow. Now I must go and see if I still have a husband." She smiled. Caleb hugged her tightly, much to her surprise and embarrassment.

"Did Kimana's grandfather really heal me?" said Mei Lin. She sat on the bed, her legs under covers and leaning against a pillow at the headboard. Caleb sat in a chair beside the bed. Each held a coffee cup. Empty breakfast dishes were stacked on the floor at the door.

"I have asked myself the same question a thousand times. I don't have the answer. The Christians pray for help from their God. The Indians pray for help from their gods. Or spirits. Who can say which deity hears their prayers and which chooses to respond?

"I would like to think that the old shaman's incantations cured you," he said. "If I can convince myself that he did, we'll surely call on him again. More likely, you were cured by Kimana's herbs and giving old Winslow the boot so he couldn't bleed you anymore.

"The more I think of this whole affair, the more I realize how stupid I was to let Winslow have his way. What a quack! I'm going to talk about this with anyone who will listen. We need a real doctor in Jackson."

8

Due largely to the pushing, pulling and wheedling of Caleb, Doctor Robert Sims opened a practice in Jackson in mid-December. Young Doctor Sims had only recently completed his training in Philadelphia and had planned to partner with a doctor in Cheyenne.

Caleb had heard about Sims at the gossip circle in Folie's store only a few days after Mei Lin's recovery. Fortuitously, the new doctor was the brother of Charles Sims, a homesteader whose farm was just north of Jackson.

Caleb had ridden to Sims's farm that same afternoon and talked about Jackson's urgent need for a doctor. Charles thought it was a dandy idea to have his little brother close at hand. He doubted that little brother would be interested.

For days thereafter, Caleb talked with some of the leading citizens of Jackson who joined with him in their entreaties to Doctor Sims. Sims hesitated at first, wondering whether the population of Jackson and environs was sufficient to support the sort of cutting edge practice that he had in mind.

Caleb and other Jackson locals convinced the doctor that the region was on the cusp of a population surge.

They cited the growing tourism that would attract both tourists and workers to staff the tourist hotels and other service venues. They talked with passion about the town's urgent need for a doctor who was up to date on the latest developments in health care.

Young Sims was persuaded. He had initially welcomed the security that would have come with partnering in the established office in Cheyenne, but he now was wildly enthusiastic about the opportunity to open his own practice in a town that really needed him.

On his arrival in Jackson, Doctor Sims was greeted by his brother and Caleb. They expected young Robert to be exhausted by the long train journey from the East to Victor and the grueling wagon crossing at Teton Pass. They had not counted on his excitement with the country and the prospects. They settled him in at the Busy B's and promised to come for him in the morning.

As promised, Robert was ready and standing on the porch when Caleb and brother Charles arrived the following morning. They had brought a saddle horse for him. Caleb had offered the previous day to pick him up in the wagon, but Robert demurred. If I am to be a proper westerner, he had said, I must learn to ride.

The trio rode at a walk, Robert doing most of the talking, asking questions about the town, the people and the country. They pulled up in front of Andrew Folie's store. Folie waved from the doorway. They dismounted and tied reins to the hitching rail.

Folie joined the others in the street. He pointed to the two windows on the second floor above his store where the doctor's office was being built. He had already disposed of the detritus that had accumulated in the upstairs spaces. The remainder, the stuff that he might need someday, he had transferred to a room in the back of the store. A private stair to the doctor's offices, he said, was already under construction on the side of the store.

Folie quoted the amount of the rental. When both Sims and Caleb registered surprise at the modest figure, Folie grinned. He assured them that the low rent would be augmented by the prestige and new business that the store would enjoy from the proximity of the doctor's office. All shook hands on the agreement.

Caleb said goodbye to all, walked to his horse, mounted and set out for home at a lope. He was pleased with the day's work. He could not know that he would be the source of the doctor's first serious medical challenge.

Like almost everyone else who lived in the Hole, Caleb shot elk for the larder. But he was beginning to wonder about killing them. He knew how Mei Lin felt. During a conversation with her about the elk question, she had repeated Bennie's earlier comment that shooting elk was like shooting cows. They often saw gaunt elk on the unfenced part of their property. Standing quietly, waiting for death. Mei Lin more than once forked hay over the fence to the hungry elk.

The plight of the elk had worsened this year. Caleb's haystacks were protected by fencing, but elk often fed at homesteaders' stacks that were not fenced. Farmers chased them away, but they came back.

Now Caleb and other ranchers and farmers were beginning to wonder whether the elk could be saved. Their grazing lands and migration routes had been taken over by settlement. They had always been a part of the natural environment of the Hole, and now their numbers were declining. Caleb and others began to talk about the possibility of setting aside land dedicated for the elk, maybe including a plan to feed them regularly in winter.

The prospect of making elk a special case was not universally accepted. Professional hunters and outfitters who made big money hosting eastern and European hunters vigorously opposed it. They wanted no interference in their lucrative trade. And elk were the most popular game.

Hunting as a business proposition was not new in Jackson Hole. It began in the 1890s. The most spectacular hunt was an expedition in 1897 organized specifically to kill elk for trophy heads. A railroad tycoon named W. Seward Webb, a son-in-law of William Vanderbilt, and his large party barreled cross-country in a ten-car luxury train. Arrangements had been made in advance for all trains on the tracks to be shunted off on sidings for Webb's passage.

Jackson Hole continued in the opening years of the twentieth century to be the best place in the country to hunt elk. But even the outfitters knew that the elk population was in trouble. The herds faced serious competition with growing settlement and tourism based on the region's scenery and recreation.

Nevertheless, the outfitters pursued their occupation. Now, they promised the trophy hunter the best rack before the elk were gone.

Caleb was brought face to face with the elk issue one morning when Mei Lin galloped into the yard and pulled Chiquita to a sliding stop at the barn where he was working. She dismounted and ran to him, colliding against him.

"Wait a minute, sweetheart. What's wrong?" he said.

"Caleb, they shot elk at the haystack! I yelled at them, and he told me to get away! He said I might get hurt. He said I might get shot accidentally. He laughed!"

"Who said this?"

"The man from Busy B's. Remember, the first time we

stayed there. Russell something."

"Russell Overgaard." Caleb took Chiquita's reins from her. "I'm borrowing your horse."

"No, Caleb! They'll be gone now. They were packing up when I saw them."

When Caleb pulled Chiquita to a sliding stop at the stack, he saw only the blood-soaked ground. They hadn't even taken the time to field dress the elk. Caleb figured that they probably assumed that somebody would respond to Mei Lin's alarms.

I'll respond all right, Overgaard.

Caleb stood in the Jackson Hotel doorway, looking up and down the street. He walked to the feed store and went inside. A moment later, he came out. He looked around, then walked to Folie's. He went inside and came out a minute later. Alastair followed.

Caleb looked right and left. And saw him. Overgaard walked in the middle of the street between two companions. He talked animatedly with them, gesturing and swinging his arms, making a point, and did not see Caleb as the trio passed.

Caleb stepped off the sidewalk and walked up behind the three men.

"Overgaard!" Caleb said.

Overgaard stopped, turned around, and Caleb punched him hard in the jaw. Overgaard was thrown backward and fell, spread-eagled.

"What th—" He struggled to his feet, wiped the blood from his mouth with the back of a hand.

"You threatened my wife, you son of a bitch. Nobody threatens my wife."

"Th' Chink whore! You—"

Caleb punched Overgaard hard in the stomach, doubling

him forward, then a blow to his jaw. Overgaard crumpled to the ground and lay still on his back. His companions, open-mouthed, looked down at the prostrate figure, then back at Caleb.

"I don't care if he wakes up or not," said Caleb, "but if he does wake up, tell him that if I ever catch him on or near my property, I may need to shoot him. Accidentally." Caleb walked away, rubbing his fist.

Alastair stepped off the boardwalk and clapped Caleb on the back. Caleb stopped.

"You nailed that no-count sumbitch good, Caleb! You nailed him! I heard about the run in Mei Lin had with him and his hunters. He had it coming to him. And did you know that the dirty sumbitch is a tusk hunter?"

Caleb frowned. "Tusk hunter? What's that?"

Alastair straightened, smiled. There was nothing that members of the Folie's general store gossip circle liked better than to know something that somebody else did not know.

"Some dirty sumbitches kill elk for their two big teeth, incisors, they're called. Pure ivory, they are. People make expensive jewelry out of 'em. The tusk hunters will kill elk, knock the tusks out and leave the dead elk for the wolves. What people need to do is kill the tusk hunters and knock out their front teeth! That's what I think!"

Caleb patted Alastair on the back and walked on, head down, rubbing his fist. Funny how the Jackson's Hole elk were always popping up in conversation.

Mei Lin leaned on a corral post, watching Caleb brushing his horse.

"Would you really shoot him?" she said.

"What do you think?"

"Well, since you have already shot people who did bad

things to me, I think you would shoot him. But, Caleb, this is not Stanley, and you're not close with the sheriff here like you were in Stanley. Mrs. Hendricks heard about what you did, and she even said that Overgaard could have you arrested for assault or something like that."

"Yeah, he probably could, but I don't think he will. He and his kind, the professional hunters and outfitters, are not too popular in Jackson and the Hole at the moment. I don't think he would want to draw any attention to himself and what he does for a living."

She leaned on the top pole of the corral, her chin resting on an arm. She stared across the corral and the meadow. He watched her as he brushed. He could sense her moods.

"What are you thinking about?" he said.

She looked at him, pondered. "I can't stop thinking about Stanley. I wonder sometimes whether we did right to leave. Now that Rat Trap is closed down, and Polly is gone, would our life in our little cabin on Stanley Creek be more peaceful than here? I loved that little cabin."

"I did too, but have you forgotten that we weren't making a living with the gold dredge? Have you forgotten the problems we had with Bennett who wanted to force us out or burn us out?

"No, we did the right thing. Here, we have prospects. We have friends. We have Chica and Ray. And, sweetheart, we have a baby coming, and we have a real doctor in town." He reached through the corral poles and patted her belly.

"Okay, we do have prospects. And 1 have a husband who says he loves me and will shoot anybody who calls me a Chink whore. But, Caleb, I was a Chink whore." She smiled.

He leaned over and kissed her. "Yeah, but you're my Chink whore."

Chica pulled up at the hitching rail in Caleb's front yard. She dismounted as Caleb walked over to her from the barn. He took the mare's reins and tied them to the rail.

"What a nice surprise, Chica. Mei Lin's going to be real happy to see you. She's been a bit low lately."

"What's wrong?" Chica said.

"Don't know. Maybe nothing. Maybe it's just what comes with having a baby. We haven't had any experience with that."

They stepped up on the porch. Caleb opened the door, stepped aside, and Chica went in.

"Mei Lin, where are you?" Caleb said. "Chica is here!"

They walked into the kitchen. Mei Lin sat at the kitchen table, a coffee cup on the table before her.

She leaned back in her chair, eyes closed, rubbing her swollen belly. She opened her eyes and looked up at them.

"Hi, Mei Lin," said Chica. Chica glanced aside at Caleb.

Caleb bent over and kissed her upturned face. He frowned. "You don't look comfortable, sweetheart."

"That's because I'm not comfortable." She grimaced. "This bundle gets heavier every day. My back hurts. Now I've got a pain in my stomach." She rubbed her abdomen. "And my head hurts bad. What's happening, honey? I never have headaches. I'll be glad when this is finished. I haven't felt this bad since the other trouble, but that's a long time ago."

"I'm sorry, sweetheart. I'm not surprised that your back hurts. You've put on a bunch of pounds lately. This baby's going to be big enough to do some chores right off. Why don't you lie down? You look real tired."

Mei Lin stood slowly, weaved and stepped backward awkwardly. Caleb caught her. "Let's get you to bed," he said. He held her at the waist and walked her into the bedroom. Beside the bed, she stopped, leaned on him.

Mei Lin looked at Chica. "Sorry, honey," Mei Lin said. She lowered her head. "Dizzy," she said, weaving. With Caleb's help, she sat on the side of the bed. He lifted her legs onto the bed, then with an arm at her shoulders lowered her to the pillow.

She sat up abruptly. "Pan!" She pointed at the pan on the table beside the bed. Caleb grabbed the pan and thrust it into her lap, barely in time to catch her vomit. He handed the pan to Chica and helped Mei Lin lie back on the pillow.

"Try to rest, sweetheart," said Caleb. He walked from the room, gesturing to Chica to follow. When they were in the hall, he stopped.

"Chica, I need to ask a favor. Would you stay with Mei Lin while I ride to town? I'm getting the doctor."

"Of course," she said, "you go." He ran for the door, grabbing his coat from the hall peg as he passed.

Doctor Sims and Caleb stood beside the bed. Mei Lin, grasping the covers at her chin, looked up at them through sunken eyes outlined by dark circles. Beads of perspiration stood out on her forehead and temples. Standing on the opposite side of the bed, Chica dabbed at Mei Lin's forehead with a wet cloth.

Sims opened his bag and took out a device with an inflatable sleeve and an attached bulb. He pushed the sleeve up Mei Lin's arm above the elbow, tightened it and squeezed the bulb. He watched the reading on the gauge.

"That's for blood pressure?" said Caleb.

"Sphygmomanometer. Blood cuff. Yes, for blood pressure." He looked at the reading on the gauge.

"How is it?" said Caleb.

"High," Sims said. "When did she first complain about the bad headache?" He removed the blood cuff and dropped it into his bag.

"Just yesterday," said Caleb. "That was a surprise. She never has headaches."

"Any pain, abdominal pain or back pain?"

"Yeah, she said her belly hurt. And her back. I assumed that was because of the weight she's carrying."

"Dizziness?"

"This morning. She almost fell before I caught her."

"What about shortness of breath?" Sims said.

"Not that I know of. Except she did gasp a couple of times after the dizzy spell."

"Has she been nauseous?" Sims said.

"Yes, seems she's going to vomit her insides out. We keep a pan on the table there." He pointed.

"Mmm." Sims pondered. "Has she been urinating regularly?"

"She keeps telling me that she needs to pee, and she wants to pee, but she hasn't gone for two days. She hurts."

Doctor Sims leaned over the bed and moved his hand back and forth before Mei Lin's eyes. Her eyes were open, but the pupils did not follow the hand movement. She seemed to stare at the opposite wall. Sims stood, frowned.

"What is it?" said Caleb.

Sims looked aside at Caleb, turned and walked to the hall. Caleb followed.

The doctor stopped in the hall, turned to Caleb. "Mr. Willis, Caleb. Your wife displays the symptoms of a condition that we call preeclampsia. I'm sorry to tell you this, but this is not good. There is no treatment, really, and it can only get worse."

The blood drained from Caleb's face. "Can nothing be done?"

"Your wife displays all of the symptoms, Caleb. All of

them. Her life is in danger. There is one thing that could save Mei Lin's life. Birth of the baby. If you agree, we will induce labor. Now. Right now. She is almost full term, so this would not be a premature birth."

Caleb tensed, frowned. "Is inducing dangerous for the baby?"

"Preeclampsia is not good for the baby. But it can be fatal for your wife. Inducing will not change anything except that it may save your wife's life."

Caleb turned away, rubbed his head vigorously with both hands.

"You need to decide, Caleb."

Caleb turned back to face Sims. "Yes, go ahead. Tell me what we can do."

The morning sun sent shafts of light through the window that described shapes on the floor and side of the bed. Caleb sat in a chair alongside, holding Mei Lin's hand, watching her steady breathing, the rise and fall of her chest. Her eyes were closed. Her forehead was cool to the touch, and her color was better, only a little lighter than usual. He raised her hand and kissed it.

Dr. Sims and Chica stood in the hall, heads down, waiting, listening.

Mei Lin's eyes opened. She saw Caleb, his head down. "Honey," she said softly. He looked up. She tried to smile.

"Sweetheart!" He leaned over and kissed her lightly on the lips. She smiled faintly again. "How do you feel?" he said.

"Good," she said. "Good." Then she saw his long face, his eyes puffy and clenched. Her face fell. In that instant she knew.

"Tell me," she said.

"Sweetheart... I'm sorry, I must tell you." Tears welled

up in his eyes. "Dr. Sims saved your life, but he could not save the baby."

"Noooo," she cried out, tears streaming down her cheeks. "Oh, Caleb, no, no. I wanted this baby. I wanted this baby." She burst out sobbing. He pulled her up and took her in his arms. She rocked back and forth, sobbing, gasping, coughing.

"I'm so sorry, sweetheart," he said.

She scooted back and leaned against the headboard, wiped her eyes with a hand. "Was it a girl?"

"Yes, a beautiful little girl."

"I want to see her."

"Honey, I don't think that would be a good idea. Dr. Sims said you would be able to get pregnant again and—"

"I want to see her. Bring her to me."

"Sweetheart—"

"Bring her to me!" She coughed, wiped her eyes with the back of a hand.

Caleb stood and went to the hall. Chica handed him the little body enclosed in the small blanket that Mei Lin had bought to wrap her baby in. He walked to the bedside, stood there a moment, as if trying to decide what to do.

Mei Lin reached out for the little burden. Caleb handed the body to her. Mei Lin cradled the baby in her arms, pulled the blanket from the face. She stared at the little face, serene in death. She gently touched the cold cheek.

"I was going to call her 'Annie,'" she said, studying the pretty little face. "I was going to ask you if it was okay." She looked up. "Would it be okay?"

"Yes, sweetheart," he said softly, almost choking, unsure of his voice. "It's a beautiful name." He reached for the bundle.

"Not yet," she said, still studying her baby's face with

its perfectly formed features.

"Sweetheart."

"I want you to bury her in the back of the house inside the fence, at the edge of the garden."

"Honey, that may not be—"

"Caleb, this is what I want. Please."

He touched her cheek. "Yes, sweetheart. If that's what you want."

The days passed, as if on a schedule that had been decreed from the beginning. Caleb bought hay from the Mormons and other farmers for it had been a good year for hay. He fed his cattle, and he fed the hungry elk that gathered across the fence from his haystack.

Wrapped up in their heavy coats and scarves, Caleb and his men repaired fence that was damaged by heavy snowdrifts. A few cows were lost to the severe cold and snow, but most had survived in the shelters they had built, anticipating the hard winter that the gossip circle predicted.

The winter was not as hard as forecast, and the thaw began early. Wildflowers peeked up where only a white mantle had been yesterday. The first blades of green grass pushed up in the yard through the slush and detritus of decaying leaves. The pale winter sun gave way to warming sunshine, and the sweet song of the mountain bluebird announced the arrival of spring, that all was in order and all was right in the world.

Mei Lin had not shared in the universal relief at the end of winter and arrival of spring. She had not noticed. She sat most days in a rocker on the small back porch, rocking slowly, staring across the yard at the mound and cross that marked Annie's grave and the meadow and mountains beyond. Rocking slowly back and forth.

Caleb stayed at home on most days, leaving the running

of the ranch to Ray. He had tried to coax Mei Lin into the house without success. Only with difficulty was he able to persuade her to dress warmly and accept the coffee or tea that he offered her as she sat in her chair. Rocking, rocking, staring blankly, staring at the grave and the outbuildings and meadows. She abandoned her post only at sundown when she could no longer see the grave.

Inside, she did her chores, washing dishes, cleaning and dusting. She accepted Caleb's offer to help with the cooking. She did not smile or offer conversation with Caleb or Chica. When either hugged her, she laid her head on a shoulder, but her arms were limp. In bed, she lay near the edge, facing the wall, avoiding his touch.

Caleb worried that he had lost her.

He was working in the barn one sunny morning when he heard Mei Lin talking. He walked outside to see her at the corral saddling her mare, speaking softly to her. She looked up, saw him, tightened the girth. She swung up into the saddle, pointed the horse to the road and set out at a gallop. He watched her until she disappeared behind an aspen grove.

It was evening when she returned. Standing on the porch, Caleb watched her ride to the barn where she unsaddled Chiquita and brushed her. Then she turned her loose to run and roll in the meadow as she watched.

Mei Lin walked to the house. She stepped up on the porch, reached up and kissed Caleb lightly. She hugged him around the waist as he encircled her shoulders. She leaned back, her arms still around his waist.

"Doctor Sims said I could get pregnant again?"

"He did."

"Then why are we standing here?"

They sat beside each other at the kitchen table, holding

steaming mugs of tea, looking through the front windows at the sun ball hovering over the crest of the Tetons. Mei Lin wore a light robe, wrapped tightly. She was barefoot. He was fully dressed in pants, shirt and boots. She smiled.

"Okay?" she said.

"Okay," he said, smiling. He reached over, slowly pulled the robe aside until a breast was exposed. He lightly touched the nipple. He addressed the breast: "Where have you been these two months?"

She laughed out loud and tightened the robe. "We've been here," she said. She sobered, looked at the window. "Well, not really here. I thought I would never be happy again. I thought my life had ended with... with . . . losing her." She looked back at him. "But we're still here. We have each other."

"We do, and we'll never be apart again, whatever happens to us. Right?"

"Right." She frowned, smiled.

"What's wrong?"

"Caleb, honey, can we go back to the bed?"

"Now?"

"Right now." He pushed his chair back so abruptly that it tumbled over. She jumped up, and they scurried to the bedroom together, shedding clothes in the hall.

9

Spring was the time for repair, renewal and growth. Caleb instructed Will to expand his hay acreage. Under Ray's supervision, Andy and Paul rode and repaired fences. They also began work on an extension of a fence at the northern extremity of the ranch.

Caleb decided that conditions warranted an expansion of his herd. He contracted again with Amos Dickens to buy cattle in Idaho and trail them to the Hole. The hundred Dickens bought raised Caleb's herd to four hundred. He was now not only one of the largest landholders in the region; he also owned one of the largest herds.

Caleb took some pride in this fact, but he would also admit to being on edge. His cash position was such that he must make a profit this year and every year in the fore-seeable future. Unless he could sustain a good measure of success, he could lose it all. He would share his concern with Mei Lin if she asked, but he hoped that she would not.

With the expansion of the herd and the opening of new hay fields, the water problem loomed larger than ever. They had upgraded the well at the ranch house, but it barely satisfied the needs of the house. Mei Lin had been hauling water in the wagon from a small stream every few days since they arrived in the valley.

Caleb had decided just last week that that she would haul no more water. He still chuckled and had to control his urge to laugh out loud when he remembered what led to this decision.

The small stream where Mei Lin got the water was only a half hour's drive from the house. She always enjoyed the solitary trip to the stream, and she didn't mind the hard work of filling the barrels with her pail. She had rarely seen anyone at the stream, only occasionally others who were also hauling water. But last week was different.

She was almost finished filling the barrels when a bewhiskered stranger—she had never seen him before, guessed that he was a drifter passing through— pulled up nearby, dismounted and led his horse to the stream. Since he first saw her, he had not taken his eyes off Mei Lin. He dropped his reins and walked slowly toward her.

"My, ain't you a purty little piece. What do you say we have a little fun since there's nobody here but the two of us?"

Mei Lin rolled her eyes and set the full pail on the ground. She reached into the bag under the driver's seat and pulled out the little top-break .32. She pointed the pistol at the cowboy's head.

"Get on your horse, asshole, and ride off, or I'm going to put a small hole in your face."

The stranger, wide-eyed, open-mouthed and jaw sagging, stepped backward, stumbled off balance, tried to find a footing, stumbled again, tripped and fell on his back in the shallows. He rolled over, scrambled up and ran after his horse that had bolted. Water sloshed from his boots at every step.

Mei Lin laughed out loud, bent over, her hands on her knees, still holding the pistol. She looked into the meadow and along the brush-covered streamside for the frustrated Romeo, but he had disappeared.

Reaching into the wagon bed, she replaced the .32 in the bag. She hefted the brimming bucket and poured it into a barrel. Dropping the empty pail in the wagon bed, she climbed up to the wagon seat, uncoiled the lines and shook them. She smiled, then laughed again.

It was the last time she hauled water. When Caleb told Ray the story, Ray grinned and insisted that he do the hauling for the ranch house until Caleb could get a new well for the house.

At dinner that evening, Caleb told Mei Lin how proud he was of her, that she was able to take care of herself.

She smiled. "Thank you."

Caleb forked a chunk of boiled elk into his mouth, studied his plate. "Did you call him an 'asshole'?"

She blinked. "How did you know that?"

"You always call bad guys, 'assholes'. It's okay. It's a good Chinese expletive."

She jabbed the handle of her fork on the table, causing him to jump. "I've told you that 'asshole' is not Chinese!" She glared.

"Well, you've used it so often that I assumed it was Chinese." He grinned.

"It is not Chinese, and it's not a nice word. I don't say it anymore. Well, not unless somebody upsets me. Like today."

"Don't upset me. Honey." She smiled.

Mei Lin and Chica cleared the dishes from the table and stacked them in the sink. As they washed the dishes, they talked about the ranch, Caleb's plans for improvements, their own chores, their plans, their disappointments and hopes.

When they were finished, Mei Lin made coffee and took cups out front to Caleb and Ray who sat on the porch stoop, talking and watching the sun drop behind the Tetons.

Mei Lin returned to the kitchen and poured coffee for Chica and herself. Chica sat at the table while Mei Lin fetched a candle from the counter, lit it with a match, and set it on the table. She sat, and they sipped from their cups.

They sat silent, sipping their coffee, savoring the quiet. The only sound was the indistinct conversation and soft laughter of Caleb and Ray on the porch. The candle barely illuminated the table in a bubble of light.

"What did you think about at Rat Trap, after the day was over, and you were alone?" said Chica.

Mei Lin sipped, looked up into the darkness, sipped again. "I thought, every night, how I would kill myself. I did, every night. If Caleb had not taken me, I would be dead now. I would have killed myself, or a job would have killed me. I fought every job. Some of them liked that. It aroused them. Then it was like rape to them, and they liked that. Some didn't like it, and they were the ones that hurt me.

"There was only one man I didn't fight. Do you remember the preacher who came in one night, almost closing time?"

"Yes," Chica said. "He was a strange man."

"He stood at the bar, waving a Bible and trying to preach to the room. Some people laughed; most just ignored him. Polly told him to stop. She said she was going to have him thrown out unless he bought a drink. He put the Bible in his bag and ordered a whiskey.

"I was sitting at a table near the stair by myself. He kept

looking at me. He finished his drink and ordered another one. When he was half finished, he sort of weaved and came over and sat by me. He started talking about heaven and hell. He said the good people went to heaven, and the bad people went to hell.

"I had never heard about heaven and hell, and I listened. He said that everybody in Rat Trap was going to hell if they kept doing the things they were doing. He said hell was a terrible place where all kind of bad things happen, and there is no happiness, and everybody there is evil.

"I told him I don't need to go there. I said I was already in hell. He put his hand on mine and started crying. He said I was a poor girl, and he wished he could do something for me. He touched my breast and left his hand there.

"Polly must have seen, and she came over to the table. She told him that he had to either take me upstairs or leave. He looked at her, then drooped. He was drunk on less than two whiskies. Polly said what's it going to be, upstairs or out?

"He stood, and I don't think he knew what he was going to do. Polly handed him his glass and said to finish it. He drank it down. She took his arm and walked him toward the stairs. She told me to follow. We walked up the stairs like that. At my door, she made him pay and pushed him inside. Polly stood there until I followed. She closed the door.

"I was confused, Chica. I felt sorry for him and just knew that I would rather be with him than somebody who was going to hurt me. He didn't know what to do. I had to help him. He cried all the way through. He didn't even finish."

Mei Lin slumped. "Why am I talking about this? I said I would never talk about Rat Trap." She wiped a tear with a hand.

Chica laid her hand on Mei Lin's. "We can't erase what happened, honey. We can remember and be glad that life is finished. We're still here. We aren't those two girls at Rat Trap. We're somebody else."

Mei Lin's attempt at a smile ended in a frown. She put her hand on Chica's. "Yeah, we're somebody else. But sometimes I still wonder who I am."

Caleb had often visited Mormon friends to study their irrigation works. Now he was ready to introduce irrigation on his own ranch. He was convinced that his production of hay would be enhanced and that the gardens at each of the houses also would benefit.

The Mormon farmers said they would be happy to help. Caleb, Ray and Will toured Mormon irrigation works and listened to the instructions offered by the farmers. When Caleb was ready to begin, Hiram Barker came to Caleb's ranch to supervise the construction of feeder canals and water gates. Caleb, Ray and Will and Andy and Paul worked on the canals and asked lots of questions.

Mei Lin's garden was an early beneficiary of the irrigation works. She had put in a vegetable patch in the backyard just inside the picket fence, beside Annie's grave. She had been inspired by a visit to Will and Kimana's place. When she saw Kimana's flourishing garden, Mei Lin had decided that she wanted one of her own.

Kimana had been quick to offer help. She often rode down to the ranch, working beside Mei Lin in the garden. Sometimes they worked so late that Kimana spent the night on a pallet in the storage room.

In the past, Mei Lin had appropriated some of the household water that she had hauled in barrels from the stream for her garden. Now Caleb had a small feeder canal constructed to deliver water to the garden and the barn.

The domestic well also was updated. Caleb contracted with a couple of enterprising fellows in town to push the well deeper and install a new hand pump. They told him about a new electric pump they had read about, but Jackson Hole had seen nothing of that wonder.

Following a winter that was one of the mildest in recent years, the fresh days of spring gave way to an early summer.

Days were pleasantly warm. Nights were still cold, though not the numbing temperatures of winter or freezing temperatures of early spring. Workdays were long, hardly interrupted by the short refreshing rain showers.

Things were looking up for Caleb. He lost no more than half a dozen head during the winter, and those were the weakest cows. A few score spring calves augmented his herd, and he began working on plans to market the steers. He had heard so much about the onerous task of driving cattle to the nearest railroad that he was determined to try to find local buyers. He pondered investigating the possibility of serving local hotels and restaurants that catered to the growing tourist trade.

Caleb and Ray rode to Yellowstone to inquire about servicing the large hotels in the park. They had gone with the single-minded purpose of talking about selling cattle, and they learned enough to warrant further investigation.

But they also saw the park's natural wonders and were dumbfounded. Each vowed to play the tourist and come back with his wife simply to see the attractions that were drawing crowds to the park.

Caleb and Mei Lin walked into Folie's general store on a sunny late spring day and were immediately welcomed by a chorus of greetings and waves from Andrew and

Priscilla and four old boys sitting at the cold stove. Mei Lin walked to the housewares counter. Priscilla joined her there. Caleb walked to the gossip circle at the stove and sat down. Philo clapped him on the back.

"Well, what lies are making the rounds this morning?" Caleb said.

"Lies? Do you refer to the eternal truths we have been discussing?" said Alastair. Caleb smiled.

"We're speculating on who's going to enter the horse races at the fair and who's going to win the final race," said Philo.

"What fair is that?" Caleb said.

Philo leaned back, smiled smugly. "You don't know about the fair. Well, let me inform you." He looked around at the circle of geezers, puffed up, smiling, ready to pontificate. Ready to tell something that somebody, Caleb in this case, didn't know.

"Well, it's not much of a fair," Philo said, "but it's fun. It's always been a casual conglomeration of races, bucking horse contests and general socializing.

Difference this year is that it's going to be organized." Philo snorted. "Damn if 1 don't hate to see fun things get organized." There was a general murmuring of agreement from the others.

"Anyway," Philo said, "this year it's going to be organized. They even have a grand name for it. Frontier Days. They say there's going to be chariot races, bucking bulls and steers, the usual bucking horses. All kinda stuff to eat. All that's fine and good, but the best part of the fair is the horse races.

"All the cowboys who think they got a fast horse and all the breeders from the Hole and beyond come together for a run. Indians from all over think they have the fastest horses, and they always show up. It's a chance to see some fine horseflesh, and it's fun to watch. And the betting's great fun and high stakes."

Mei Lin had turned and listened at the first mention of the race. She walked over and stood behind Caleb.

"Do you mean anybody can enter?" said Mei Lin.

"Sure," Rick said. "You want to enter, missy?" The four men laughed. Caleb did not laugh. He looked sober-faced at Mei Lin. She smiled at him.

Caleb stood. "Keep good notes on any world problems you boys solve today. I'll want to know what I don't have to worry about anymore." Smiles and waves, and Caleb and Mei Lin walked outside.

They strolled on the sidewalk toward their horses. She held his arm, pulled him close and squeezed his arm. Caleb stopped, turned to Mei Lin who had stopped beside him.

"All right, what is it?" he said.

"I want to race."

● ● ● ● ●

The Frontier Days fair was in its third and final day, and riders and wagons from every direction still converged on the fair site south of Jackson. A community of tents and wagons and concessions was arrayed around the racetrack and extended in all directions. The conglomeration was larger even than the town of Jackson.

Hundreds of people wandered around the grounds, munching on exotic treats, chatting, gawking. On the perimeter, visitors who had come a distance, too far away to return home at night, had set up tents. Beyond the tents, temporary corrals had been constructed to tend the mules and horses of these visitors.

Early arrivals had seen the Roman races, which featured

riders standing on the backs of two horses, a five-mile relay race and a mix of bucking horses and bulls. All great fun, but the main event and most widely anticipated event was scheduled for the third day. The final of the horse races.

There were so many entries for the horse races that elimination heats had been run the first and second days. The final scheduled for the third day featured the best horses in the trials.

Caleb and Mei Lin had just received the information that was provided to each of the fifteen contestants that had survived the trials. Mei Lin won both of her races on day one and two by more than three lengths. Caleb was surprised at how calm and confident Mei Lin appeared.

"Easy peasy," she said. Caleb raised his eyebrows. "I got that from Berta." They looked at the paper that told about the arrangements for the final race that afternoon.

"I'm going to water Chiquita," said Mei Lin. She led the horse away. Caleb continued to read the race instruction sheet.

Three men standing nearby had watched all this and talked among themselves. After Mei Lin left, one man detached himself from the group and walked over to Caleb. The man was dressed in a fine woolen suit and black tie. He touched his hat.

"Could I talk with you for a minute?"

Caleb looked up, lowered the sheet. "Sure," he said, "what can I do for you?"

"Well, it's more about what I can do for you. I'm Wilbur Reasoner. No reason why you should know me. Our paths have never crossed. I deal in horses and mules. I been racing horses at this fair as long as there's been a fair. I also race at Cheyenne, Laramie and most other places in Wyoming and Colorado where there's races. I customarily win.

"Now, this here Jackson race is small potatoes as far as racing goes, but local people enjoy it and bet big on it. The winner makes a bundle from the betting. Point of all this is, we don't get too serious about our racing. We just like to have fun. We do get serious about our betting.

"Now, I said I customarily win the races and the bets. But I'm not greedy. I want others to share in the winnings. So here's the way it works. I identify the five best horses and talk with the owners. The owners can win betting money in two ways. My horse wins the race. You can win money betting on my horse, or you can bet on your own horse to place or show. Either way, you get a share of my winnings.

"My man has watched your horse on Day 1 and Day 2, and she's pretty fast, but she's never raced before, so far as I've been able to learn. So you would get five percent of my winnings. Then when—"

"Hold on, Mr. Reasoner," said Caleb. "If you have the fastest horse and always win, why are we talking?"

Reasoner smiled. "I leave nothing to chance. I like a sure thing."

"Then what you've left out of all this bullshit is that you want us to throw the race."

Reasoner smiled again. "Well, let's just say that we're going to put on a good show, and we know how it's going to end."

Caleb saw Mei Lin coming, leading the mare. "Hey, Mei Lin, come over here." He waited till she arrived. "Mr. Reasoner here wants us to throw the race so his horse can win. What do you think about that?"

"What does this mean, 'throw the race'?" she said.

"It means that you will agree to lose the race on purpose so his horse can win," said Caleb," and he will win big money by betting on a sure thing. He promises us a share of the winnings."

Mei Lin frowned, looked hard at Caleb, back to Reasoner. "Is that true, Mr. Reasoner?" said Mei Lin.

"It sure is," Reasoner said, smiling.

"You asshole, I would never agree to that!" Reasoner recoiled as if he had been struck. He turned to Caleb who was having a hard time not laughing out loud.

"Willis?" Reasoner said.

"It's her horse and her race."

Reasoner fumed. "I know about you two. I'll be dammed if I'll let a dumb cowboy and a Chink wh—"

In an instant, Caleb was in Reasoner's face. "Hold it, Reasoner, before you say something you'll wish you hadn't said. The first person who called my wife a Chink whore had his face seriously rearranged. The second is dead. The third, who lives right here in Jackson, had the good sense to take off his hat and apologize. Now, what is it you wanted to say?"

Reasoner glared at Caleb, then turned on his heel and strode to his two cronies who had watched the exchange. The three walked toward the large tent beside the racetrack.

Caleb put his arm around Mei Lin's shoulders as they walked in the other direction, Mei Lin leading Chiquita. Caleb guffawed. Mei Lin punched him hard on his arm.

Fifteen horses were lined up behind the start point. Each rider wore a number pinned to their shirt. Mei Lin was the only woman competing. Riders held their jittery mounts in check while trying to jockey as close to the start line as possible as they stared at the official who held a red bandanna high over his head.

Mei Lin glanced at the horse and rider beside her. Caleb had pointed them out to her earlier. It was Reasoner's horse, Bedo. The horse was almost two hands taller than Chiquita. The rider looked down at Mei Lin. He smiled.

Mei Lin did not smile. She turned back to the front. The official holding the flag began the countdown, and a horse three places over from Mei Lin burst across the line. The official shouted, and the rider pulled the horse back into line.

The countdown was started again, and the same horse again burst across the line. The official shouted that if it happened a third time, the horse would be disqualified. The rider nodded and pulled his mount a good five feet behind the line of horses. The official began the countdown again.

The flag dropped, and the horses lunged ahead, hooves pounding and the crowd waving and cheering loudly, urging their favorites on.

Chiquita and Bedo ran neck and neck at the front of the pack. They rounded the first turn and were lost to the view of the crowd by a cluster of aspen in the middle of the track.

Bedo's jockey reined his mount toward Chiquita until they ran stirrup to stirrup. He pulled sharply left and bumped the mare hard. Mei Lin almost lost her seat. The jockey again pulled Bedo leftward to bump Chiquita, trying to force her off the track.

Mei Lin whipped out her quirt and leaned across to strike the jockey's face. Again and again she struck his face, opening bloody gashes on his cheek and forehead. The rider jerked side to side, back and forth to escape the lashing, and Bedo answered the movement of the reins, swerving side to side.

The jockey pulled away from Chiquita to escape the

lashing.

Mei Lin had fallen behind slightly during the lashing, but she now had full control and drummed the mare with her heels and whipped her with the quirt. She pulled ahead around the last turn and crossed the finish line a length ahead of Bedo. The crowd went wild, cheering and throwing papers and hats in the air.

Mei Lin rode slowly to the winner's circle, beaming at Caleb who arrived there as she rode up. She dismounted, and Caleb hugged her. The official who had started the race also waited there. He did not look happy. Nor did Reasoner, who stood in the packed mass of spectators near Caleb. He alternately glared at Caleb and Mei Lin and the official.

At that moment, another official, identified by the sash he wore, rode up and hastily dismounted. He whispered to the presiding official who had leaned over to listen, nodding. He smiled.

The presiding official turned back to the front and spoke loudly to the crowd. "The horse named Chiquita ridden by Mei Lin Willis is disqualified." The presiding official pointed at the official who had just spoken to him. "This race official observed the rider, Mei Lin Willis, striking the rider of a horse beside her with a quirt, forcing that rider to fall back. Therefore, Chiquita does not win this race, and Chiquita and Mei Lin Willis are barred from ever racing again at the Frontier Days celebration."

Mei Lin and Caleb were aghast. She shouted at the presiding official. "He was trying to force me off the track! His horse bumped me, more than once! It was on purpose!"

The presiding official looked at the official who had brought the report of the quirting. "I did not see that," the second official said.

The presiding official turned back to the crowd. "With the disqualification of Chiquita, I declare that Bedo, which crossed the finish line behind Chiquita, is the winner." The official glanced furtively at Reasoner, who smirked. Reasoner looked at Caleb and caught his eye. He raised his chin slightly, as if to remind Caleb: this is the way this thing is done.

"This is not fair," Mei Lin said, tears welling up in her eyes. Caleb stood beside her, unsure how to react. He put an arm around her shoulders.

The presiding official ignored Mei Lin and turned to the crowd. "Mr. Reasoner, if you would just step over here and—"

"Hold on there." The voice came from somewhere in the crowd. Everyone looked around for the speaker. A man pushed to the front. He wore a cloth with a number pinned to his shirt.

"I was riding just behind the two horses in the lead. The little lady is correct. What she says is exactly what happened. Bedo's jockey bumped her at least three times. He was clearly trying to force her off the track. She was protecting herself when she quirted him." The crowd murmured.

"And did a damn fine job of it too," the rider said. "Did you see his face?" The crowd laughed and cheered.

The presiding official cleared his throat, looked around, as if for support. "Well, it's your word against a race official."

"Bailey doesn't lie!" shouted a man in the crowd.

"If Bailey says he saw it, he saw it!" said another.

"The track official and I don't disagree at all," said Bailey. "He says he didn't see it. I *did* see it."

The crowd roared its approval and surged toward the

podium where the official stood.

The presiding official winced. He stepped backward and looked around, seemingly looking for an escape route from the angry crowd. He looked pointedly at Reasoner who stared at him, grim.

The official looked away from Reasoner and spoke to the air. "I declare Chiquita the winner." The crowd roared again. Reasoner glared at Caleb who could not suppress the slightest hint of a smile.

"And, Mr. official, what of Bedo?" yelled a voice, followed by angry shouts from the crowd.

"Yeah, what about the cheating Bedo?" shouted another. The crowd roared, laughed, and voices shouted at the official to do his duty. The crowd surged toward the official.

The official took another step backward, looked around nervously. "Uh, um, I declare that Bedo is disqualified," the official said softly. He promptly plowed into the crowd and disappeared. The people roared and laughed, slapping each other on the back.

Mei Lin and Caleb embraced. She pulled back and whispered into his ear. "Did you bet?"

He smiled. "Oh, yes, I did. We won a bundle." They walked away from the winner's circle, Mei Lin leading Chiquita. Caleb put an arm around her shoulders and squeezed. "Well done, sweetheart."

As they walked through the dispersing crowd, some congratulated Mei Lin, clapped Caleb on the back, told Mei Lin what a fine horse she had.

They saw the man called Bailey ahead, standing beside a wagon. The reins of the horse he had ridden in the race were tied to the back of the wagon. He was in the process of removing the saddle. Mei Lin and Caleb walked over to him. He looked up and smiled.

"Thank you for speaking up for me," said Mei Lin.

"Least I could do. I enjoy racing and horseflesh too much to see cheats getting the top hand." He extended his hand to Mei Lin. "I'm John Bailey." She shook his hand.

"I'm Mei Lin Willis. This is my husband, Caleb." Caleb and Bailey shook.

"That's a fine little quarter horse you have there," Bailey said.

Caleb frowned. "Quarter horse?"

"Yeah, short and stocky, muscular, deep, broad chest, wide head."

"Why 'quarter horse?' " said Caleb.

"They're known for their speed over short distances. Did you notice how long today's track was?"

"It looked pretty short, now that you mention it," said Caleb. "Somebody said it was a quarter of a mile."

"There you are. The guy you had the run-in with, the one that was disqualified, was racing a thoroughbred. Bedo would have beat all of us on a longer track, even without the shenanigans, but a good quarter horse will beat him for the first quarter mile."

"You know your horses," said Caleb. "Are you local? Haven't seen you in town."

"I've got a place about five miles south. Run some cows, but I have mostly horses. It was mostly cows before the tourist business took off. Now I supply mounts for the hotels and tourist outfitters. You?"

"I run cows, two miles northwest. I'm intrigued about the tourist business. I haven't really pinned down a market yet. Do you think they might be interested in buying beef?"

"Why not? If they haven't committed elsewhere. Worth asking. Let me give you some names." He reached into the wagon bed, rummaged around in a bag and pulled out a pad and pencil. He scribbled names and contact information, tore the sheet off the pad and handed it to Caleb. "Good luck."

"Many thanks," said Caleb. "Sounds most interesting."

"Before you get away," Bailey said, "let me show you something." He beckoned for them to follow him. Caleb walked beside Bailey, and Mei Lin followed, leading Chiquita. They walked past a storage building and around a small barn and stopped in their tracks.

"There's the future," said Bailey.

There sat four automobiles parked side by side. A crowd of men and women stared at the autos, hands on mouths or cheeks, desperately wanting to touch, but warned off by the practiced smiles and bulk of the four men dressed in suit and tie who stood before and behind the vehicles.

The gawkers whispered, almost in reverence, as they walked around the strange apparitions. The smiling guards were happy to answer questions. They proudly identified the white-tired Whiting Runabout, a spacious Patterson Touring, a gleaming cream-colored Firestone-Columbus Roadster, and a bright red Berg Touring. The names meant nothing to the people for these were the first automobiles they had seen.

"People who come to the valley now," Bailey said, "the hunters and sightseers, the tourists, they come by train and wagon and horseback. That's going to change so fast, it's going to make your head spin.

"I'm told three of these autos came down from Yellowstone, and one came over Teton pass from Victor. I sure wouldn't have wanted to be in the one that came over the pass. That's no road for autos. In fact, a wagon did follow, in case of problems.

"The thing is, they all got here. And this is just the beginning. Roads are going to be improved.

They're going to be graded and topped with materials that will make travel in all weather possible. Everybody seems to want to visit Jackson Hole. They're going to come by automobile, and they are going to come from all over.

"And they're going to need someplace to stay," said Bailey, "and good horses to ride, and good steaks to eat." Bailey smiled. "Nice to meet you folks. I expect we'll talk again." He walked toward his wagon, waving over his shoulder.

Caleb and Mei Lin looked at each other, each wondering what meaning all this had for them.

Three men standing under a stretched awning near the autos had silently watched this exchange between Bailey and Caleb and Mei Lin. The men wore heavy gray coats, loose and long, cloth peaked caps and motoring goggles pushed up on the forehead.

When Caleb and Mei Lin and Bailey had said their goodbyes and walked their separate ways, the three men huddled, two deferring to the third who spoke angrily, pounding his fist in a palm.

10

Mei Lin sat in the porch swing, moving slowly, back and forth, pushing gently with a foot on each swing backwards. The swing had been installed only the previous week. It was made of wooden slats and suspended from the porch ceiling with thin chains.

A carpenter in Jackson had built the swing to Caleb's specifications and had since sold ten more, identical to Caleb's, to Jackson residents. Caleb had had a swing like this at his Richmond home and had drawn the plan from memory.

He leaned against a porch post, watching Mei Lin and smiling, remembering. His wife, Beth, swinging slowly, little Bobby beside her, gripping the chain with one hand and Beth's sleeve with the other, fearful. Two-year-old Sissie sitting in her mother's lap, arms outstretched, laughing with each dip on the backward motion. He had told Mei Lin all this when he first mentioned that he wanted a porch swing.

Caleb turned to look at the distant range, darkening as the golden sun ball lowered slowly into a saddle. Mei Lin saw the single tear roll down his temple before he turned away and wiped it with the back of a hand.

"Honey," she said, "it's okay. I told you before. I don't want you to forget her. It's okay to remember her. I want to love her with you. There's room in my heart for her, and your kids."

She stopped the swing, stood and came to him. She leaned against him and put her arms around his waist. He hugged her and rested his head on hers. "Yeah, I know," he said. "You're an angel. You must be the only human being with that capacity, and I love you for it. Even if I forget to tell you how much I love you." He kissed the top of her head.

Caleb and Mei Lin rode along a fence line toward the western extremity of the ranch. This ride had become a common outing for them lately. It was part work, checking fence, but it was mostly an opportunity to be together, to talk, an interval between their separate chores that kept them apart.

He had marveled more than once how this woman of his saw so much more in the land than he did. He was not immune to beauty and diversity, but for the most part on this ride he saw a field of good fescue, fat cattle scattered about, turning grass into beef. He liked what he saw.

On this ride, she saw a pair of Black-capped Chickadees sitting on the top strand of fence wire, which he had missed. She pointed at a Black-billed Magpie flying overhead he had not seen.

She held out a hand to stop him. He reined in. When he started to ask why they were stopping, she shushed him with a finger to her lips. She looked around anxiously, then smiled ear-to-ear when a dark bird flushed from the grass. She said she had heard the catlike meow and knew there was a Gray Catbird around.

Mei Lin had been spending time recently with two women in Jackson who shared her love of birds. They walked around the town and in the adjacent fields, looking for birds. Birdwatching, they called it. She had said that it was catching on.

Reaching a fence corner, the extremity of the ranch, they turned toward a haystack. When they drew alongside the stack, two men stepped out from behind the hay. Each held a pistol leveled on them.

Caleb and Mei Lin pulled up. Caleb looked behind, and another man who had rounded the stack stepped out, pistol aimed at them. He faced front again.

"Mr. Bennett," said Caleb.

"I've been looking for you, Willis," said Bennett, "a long time. Never thought I'd find you purely by chance."

"Now why would you want to find me?"

"Nobody makes a fool of me, Willis. Not you and not your lackey, Cal."

"You'll never find Cal."

"Oh? Heard from anybody at Grass Valley, California lately? Oh, he's found. He was a talker."

"You son of a bitch. You won't get away with anything around here. There's law and order in Jackson Hole."

"We'll see about what can be done around here. Get down."

Caleb and Mei Lin dismounted. The third man who had come up behind them took Mei Lin's arm and leveled his gun on her.

"Now here's what we're gonna do, Willis. You knew damn well your dredge wasn't making money. You sold me a piece of junk. So you're gonna fetch the money that you stole from me, and I'm gonna tell you where to bring it. The Chink stays with us to be sure you don't get any smart ideas."

Bennett leaned toward the man beside him, his eyes still on Caleb. "Take her horse, and put it with ours." The man pushed his pistol in his belt and took Chiquita's reins. He led the horse toward the haystack.

Caleb glanced at Mei Lin. She looked hard at him, opened her eyes wide and blinked twice rapidly.

Mei Lin reached for her coat lapels, as if to tighten them. She slipped a hand inside the jacket, pulled the .32 from a pocket. Turning her head, she looked at the man who held her arm, the slightest hint of a smile on her lips. He frowned.

Mei Lin fired through the sleeve at him.

Bennett jerked around toward Mei Lin to see his man falling. He whipped back in time to see Caleb's pistol aimed at his chest and fire. Caleb swung the six-shooter on the haystack and dropped the third man when he charged from behind the stack with gun drawn.

Caleb bent over Bennett and looked for signs of breathing and saw none. He stepped to Bennett's crony and confirmed that he was dead. He walked over to Mei Lin who stood over her fallen captor, pistol in hand. Caleb nudged him with his foot.

"Well, I did say that little .32 was effective at short range, didn't I? Can't get much shorter than six inches." He touched her cheek. "You okay?"

She took a deep breath, exhaled. She shuddered. "I'm okay."

He looked around at the three bodies. "We got a bit of a mess here. We'll leave 'em where they lie. Let's go home, and I'll ride in for a visit with the sheriff. If he's in, he'll want to come out straight away.

"I'll have to figure out how to tell about what started

this. That's going to be a very long story that will require a large pot of coffee. Think you could make up some cobbler while I'm away? Bennie told me that if I ever need to get on the sheriffs good side to feed him cobbler."

"Miss Mei Lin, that is a fine cobbler." Sheriff Canlis scraped the plate with his fork, put it into his mouth. "You wouldn't have another bite or two, would you?"

Mei Lin retrieved the pan from the counter and spooned out a full serving on Canlis's plate.

"Ah, thank ya', ma'am. That's the best cobbler I've had in ages. Best since my dear wife passed on to her reward these five years ago. She made a fine pie, and I must say, Miss Mei Lin, this reminds me what a good cobbler tastes like." Then he ignored Caleb and Mei Lin while he devoured the bowl of pie as if he had not already eaten a full serving.

When his plate was again empty, Canlis pushed the plate a couple of inches away, and reached for his coffee cup. Mei Lin poured refills for him and Caleb. She returned the pot to the stove and sat in the chair beside Caleb.

The sheriff leaned forward, elbows on table. "Okay, down to business. We got us three dead bodies out there in the wagon. Caleb, your story is the most entertaining tale I've heard in a long time. And I believe you. Whether anybody else who don't know what a fine fellow you are will believe you is something else. You got anybody else who can back you up on the story?"

"We did. Cal, who I told you about. But I suspect that Bennett found him in California. And killed him."

"I'll follow up on that," said Canlis. "Grass Valley, you said. I'll also contact the sheriff at Stanley and see what he can tell me. Where'd you say he's located, Challis, was it?" Caleb nodded.

The sheriff chuckled. "The best part of this story is Mei Lin's knocking off that yahoo with the .32. If I ever need to put up a posse, young lady, I want you to join us and ride beside me." He chuckled again. Caleb and Mei Lin smiled.

"Now I have a nice coat with a hole under the arm," she said.

"Caleb," said Canlis, "you must've been able to read her mind to be ready for Bennett so fast."

"When she opened her eyes wide and blinked like that, something she's never done before, I knew something was coming."

"Well, so far, so good." Canlis pushed back in his chair, stood. He took his hat from the back of the chair. "I don't want to say nothin' out of order here, but I can't see this being any problem for you, Caleb. You'll probably be called on to make a statement, but everbody around here knows you, and I can't see this going anywhere. Sure wish we had somebody who could back you up on your story, though."

Canlis put his hat on, pulled it down, looked at Mei Lin and touched the brim. "Nice to see you, Miss Mei Lin. Thanks for that cobbler. My, that was good." He turned and walked through the door, muttering under his breath, but loud enough for Mei Lin to hear, that that cobbler was worth a ride out this way any day.

As summer temperatures gave way to cooler days and colder nights, the lower slopes of the Teton range blazed yellow and orange, with scattered flashes of red. Cottonwoods that lined the banks of the Snake and other watercourses showed brilliant yellows and subdued orange hues. Aspens on the hillsides and willows and other shrubs in moist areas and shady canyons displayed shades of yellow and red.

Wildlife also changed with the seasons. The eerie bugling of male elk sounded from the woods and meadows, often attracting an interested female or another male who challenged the bugling elk to a sparring match. A slow faceoff, interspersed with furious head butting was often the result. Male moose that were vying for female attention acted in similar fashion.

Bears, seldom sighted in other seasons, became more active and more visible, devouring quantities of berries and other foods to build up fat for the approaching hibernation. Wolves seemed to be less shy as the temperatures dropped.

Caleb anticipated the approach of their second winter in the Hole with some satisfaction. With help from Andy and Paul, he improved the house's insulation. He had an extension added on the north side of the house with access through the utility room. The new space housed a toilet and bathtub. And, wonder of wonders, water inside the house to the kitchen and the bathroom. A new windmill was erected at the well in the back yard.

Caleb came into the kitchen after inspecting the windmill. Two cups were on the table. He hung his hat on the back of a chair, sat down and watched Mei Lin at the stove.

"That windmill is going to keep us in all the water we need. No more hauling water." He twisted his coffee cup on the table. "Coffee 'bout ready?"

Instead of the percolator, she brought a teapot to the table.

"Tea!" said Caleb. "Where did you find it? I thought we'd used up all we brought from Idaho. I've tried a dozen times to get somebody in town to stock it, and they just ignore me. They just frown and tell me that nobody in the Hole drinks tea except the eastern dudes."

She poured tea in their cups. "That may be right. I told Marjorie how much you liked tea in Idaho, and she got it for me when she went up to the dude ranch to visit friends."

Caleb picked up his cup, smelled the fragrance and smiled. He sipped the tea. "My, that's good."

She went back to the counter and picked up a tray holding a plate of freshly baked corn muffins, a bowl of butter, and a knife. She put the tray on the table.

Caleb sliced a muffin and spread butter on the steaming pieces. He finished the muffin in four bites and took another.

Mei Lin sipped her tea, smiled. "I never thought we would have water in the house. Everything is so new, honey. Everything is getting easier and better."

Caleb leaned back in his chair. "Yep, that sure is true. But all that improvement is nothing compared to one more important change."

She frowned. "What do you mean?"

"You, Mei Lin Willis. Last year, you couldn't cook, you couldn't shoot, you didn't know how to use a percolator, you didn't know how to bake corn muffins, you couldn't put a saddle on a horse. You couldn't even speak English."

She frowned. "Hey! I speak English last year. You know what I say!"

"Well, my little eastern exotic oriental sweetheart, you spoke Chinklish that I could understand most of the time."

She sniffed, frowned. "Hey mister, I not oriental! I Chinese!"

"Yeah, I know." He smiled. "Look at you now. Nobody would take you for native-born, but you speak better English than most of the locals around here."

"Well, my big old educated eastern handsome cowboy, I just imitate you."

She stood, walked around the table, leaned down and kissed his ear. He pushed his chair back and pulled her onto his lap. She kissed him on his lips and his cheeks. He caressed a breast through her shirt. She took his face in both palms, kissed the tip of his nose.

Nose to nose, he looked into her eyes for a long moment. He removed her hands from his face, frowned. "What do you want?"

"I want a telephone."

He laughed. "What! A telephone! We don't need a telephone."

She pursed her lips, pouted, stood and walked back to her chair, sat and sipped her tea.

"Do we want everybody in the Hole to have access, even voice access, to our house?" Caleb said.

"We could telephone the sheriff or the doctor instead of having to send somebody to fetch him."

"Hmm. There is that," said Caleb. "I'll think on it."

He didn't think on it very long. The following morning, Mei Lin told him at breakfast that she had decided that they were going to get a telephone.

"I will take care of it," she said. Before he had a chance to respond, she was talking about groceries they needed to buy and a mule that needed doctoring and the corral gate that needed bracing, and what did he want for supper, and ...

All he could do was smile. When she finally paused for breath, he said, "Okay."

Caleb approached winter with a lean, basic herd. Only in recent months, he had solved a problem that had vexed him from the time he had arrived in Jackson Hole. He had worried about marketing his beef. He had initially figured that his options were to drive steers to the nearest railhead or trail them to Idaho to population centers there.

Instead, using the contacts given him by John Bailey, he had discovered local markets. He now sold to a contractor who butchered and supplied dude ranches and hotels and restaurants throughout Jackson Hole, including the town of Jackson.

He had also contracted to drive cows north to an agent who supplied beef to tourist hotels and spas in Yellowstone Park. At the same time, he had earned a reputation as a good source of mother cows for farmers and small ranchers in the region. Prospects were looking up.

Mei Lin rode Chiquita at a steady lope. Caleb had been reluctant at first to agree to her going to Jackson alone, but it was an easy, short ride, and she said that she wouldn't be long. She wanted to visit the telephone exchange and learn what one must do to get a telephone in a home. She was excited at the prospect. Caleb was still unsure about the contraption, but she was sure she could convince him.

In town, Mei Lin tied up in front of Folie's and went inside to visit with Priscilla. Priscilla had already told Mei Lin about the convenience of the telephone that Andrew had installed at the store. She had shown the instrument to her and explained how to use it. From that moment, Mei Lin was hooked.

Mei Lin waved to Andrew as she headed for the front door. Outside, she walked to the telephone exchange three doors down and went inside. She did not notice the man across the street who stood in shadow in an alleyway between the saloon and feed store. Watching her.

After a half hour, she came out carrying a few papers. She walked on the sidewalk to the hitching rail where her mare was tied, stuffed the papers into a saddlebag and mounted. She set out at a lope.

The figure watching her withdrew into the shadow.

Freddie rode off the main trail in tall, wild hay and sagebrush. He kept Mei Lin in view while trying to avoid any appearance that he was following her. She never looked back.

Freddie had avoided contact with Caleb or Mei Lin since that day in Folie's when he had insulted Mei Lin, and Caleb had been prepared to reduce him to trash. When he saw either of them on the Jackson streets, Freddie had run for an alley.

After but a short time trailing Mei Lin in this fashion, Freddie watched her pull her horse off the trail and walk her to a small stream. He pulled up when she dismounted and stood beside the mare as she drank.

Freddie rode into a willow copse and dismounted. He tied his horse to a branch and pulled a rifle from its case. He watched. There was no other person in sight. Only Mei Lin.

It was quiet, still. Freddie looked up. A Golden Eagle soared high overhead, rising and falling easily in the light breeze.

He looked back toward Mei Lin. She stood beside her horse, reins in hand, preparing to mount. Freddie straightened and brought the rifle up sharply. He aimed, lowered the rifle, leaned forward as if to look more closely.

He raised the rifle slowly, aimed, hesitated. His head lowered, he sighted, fired.

Mei Lin jerked around at the shot and looked for the shooter. At the same time, she stepped back against Chiquita, still searching the back trail, and withdrew the .32 from its holster tied to the saddle.

She saw the man fall from behind a large Cottonwood on the back trail, not fifty yards away. She whipped around, right and left, pistol extended, unsure what happened. Then she saw Freddie.

She pointed the .32 at Freddie, then toward the fallen man, back to Freddie.

Freddie rode his horse at a walk toward her. He held the rifle loosely at his side. She lowered the .32.

"Was that your shot? Freddie?" she said. "Did you shoot him?"

He pulled up, dismounted and held his reins. "Yes, ma'am." He removed his hat. "Sorry if I scared you, Miss Mei Lin. I saw this fellow watching you in town. He looked like he was up to no good. When I saw him ridin' out behind you, I knew he was up to no good, so I followed him. When I saw you stop and then him stop and dismount and draw his rifle, I knew what I had to do. He was sure 'nuff aimin' at you. I hope it was all right."

"All right? Freddie, you saved my life." She tugged his sleeve, and they walked to the prostrate man.

They looked down at the body that lay face up. One hand still gripped the rifle stock that lay across his chest.

"He sure looks dead, all right," Freddie said. "You know him?"

"No. Why should he want to kill me?"

Freddie stared at the body. He shook his head.

Caleb and Andy worked on a new fence a couple of hundred yards behind the house. The posts were in, and the bottom strand was in place and taut. They worked now on the top strand. Andy stretched the wire as Caleb drove staples into a post.

Andy straightened, looking across the pasture over Caleb's shoulder. He let the tension out of the strand.

"Boss." Caleb looked up. Andy motioned with his head. Caleb turned around and saw Mei Lin and another rider approaching. The rider led a third horse that carried a burden that looked an awful lot like a body tied across the saddle. Caleb and Andy watched them come.

Mei Lin and Freddie pulled up. Caleb walked to the

led horse, looked at the body. He bent down, looked at the body's face.

He straightened, still looking at the body. "What's going on?"

"Freddie saved my life," said Mei Lin. "He killed this man who followed me from town. That man was going to shoot me. Freddie got him first. Why would anyone want to kill me? Do you know him?"

"I don't know him, but I know who he is."

Caleb walked on the Jackson sidewalk and stopped when he saw the sign that read: Wilbur Reasoner, Cattle and Horse Sales. Caleb pushed the door open and went inside.

Reasoner sat at a roll top desk, glared at Caleb. He leaned back in his chair. His companion, dressed nattily in a wool suit and tie much like Reasoner's, was bent over the desk where he had been studying a document. Still leaning over the desk, he looked at Caleb. He straightened, looked from Caleb to Reasoner. He was obviously confused.

"I have no business with you, Willis," Reasoner said.

"That may be so, Mr. Reasoner, but I have business with you. You might be interested in what I have in back of your place." Caleb stepped toward the door, looked back at Reasoner.

Reasoner frowned, unsure how to respond. He stood and followed Caleb. They walked outside, down the sidewalk and turned into a narrow walk space between the two buildings.

In back, Reasoner recoiled when he saw the two horses tied to the hitching post. One was Caleb's. The other had a body strapped across the saddle.

"What the hell's going on?" Reasoner snapped.

"I believe this belongs to you," Caleb said. "I saw him with you at the fair. You know what's going on, so I won't bother you with details. What you don't know is that he wasn't very smart and got himself killed.

"Now we got us a dead body here. It's yours now. Question is what do you want to do with it? If you want to report this to the sheriff and tell him what this is all about, you do that, and I'll have to tell him my story. By the way, we have a witness that your man was trying to kill my wife."

Caleb walked to his horse, untied the reins, turned back. "Reasoner, I'm at the end of my patience with you. If anything like this happens again, I'm not going to need to talk with you about it because you're not going to be able to hear me." Caleb mounted and kicked Buck into a gallop.

Caleb wondered whether he had made the right decision to handle this affair directly with Reasoner. Caleb was of the old school where men settle disputes between themselves. But that was the old days. Jackson had a good sheriff now who would not be happy if he learned that Caleb had been hauling around a dead man who tried to murder his wife and failed to report the affair to him.

Caleb was still on edge on how the Bennett affair was going to settle. He didn't want to add to that problem this new problem. More to the point, he didn't want Freddie to get charged when he was just trying to protect Mei Lin. No, he'll let this one simmer. Maybe it will just simmer and settle.

Mei Lin answered the knock at the front door. She opened it, and there stood the sheriff, hat in hand. He smiled.

"Miss Mei Lin."

"Come in, Sheriff. I'll get Caleb." She stepped out to the porch. "Caleb!" she yelled. A moment later, he stepped from the darkness at the barn door. He waved.

Mei Lin went back into the house, ushered Canlis into the kitchen. On the table were three bowls and three coffee cups.

"Sit down, Sheriff. Caleb will be right in. I'll pour coffee." She went to the stove, opened the door and reached in with a thick cloth. She brought out a large dish of cobbler, still steaming.

"Oh, my," said the sheriff, "now this is my lucky day, visiting just when you were baking." They both laughed.

Caleb came into the kitchen. "Scott."

"Caleb."

Caleb went to the sink, washed his hands, came to the table and sat. "Your messenger said you said you wanted to talk. I could have come in to the office."

"Nah, I wanted to ride out. Don't get out of town enough to suit me. Anyway, you know damn well why I wanted to talk to you here instead of the office."

He grinned at Mei Lin as she was loading his dish with warm cobbler. She spooned servings in Caleb's bowl and her own. Then she fetched the percolator and filled the three cups.

Canlis took a large bite of pie, closed his eyes as he chewed. He opened his eyes and took another bite. "I sure wish you folks would get on the telephone. It can be a nuisance when you get calls from people you don't really want to talk to, but it can be a handy tool."

Mei Lin looked at Caleb. "See," she said. She replaced the percolator on the stove.

"Actually, Scott, we are on the telephone," said Caleb. "Got it just two days ago. Sorry I didn't tell you. Mei Lin fought it tooth and nail, but I convinced her that we needed to move in to the modern age."

Caleb smiled and flinched, raising his arms to protect himself when Mei Lin swung at him and punched him on the arm.

"I get the impression that things aren't exactly as you describe them, Caleb," said Canlis, smiling.

The sheriff returned to the cobbler, finished it and scraped the plate. He sipped his coffee, then leaned back. "Okay, to business."

Caleb and Mei Lin exchanged an anxious glance.

"I got news from Challis."

Caleb exhaled.

"The sheriff has talked with the workers at Bennett's dredge," Canlis said. "He told them about what happened to their boss down here. Their reaction was not exactly what he expected. They cheered. Damn right, they cheered. That's what he said. It seems that nobody liked the boss.

"There's more. Bennett had never talked about kin, and the sheriff couldn't find any. The two men with Bennett at the haystack were his top cronies. The point is that there is nobody has a claim on the dredge. So the sheriff helped the twelve workers to form a partnership that will operate the dredge for the benefit of the partners. What do you think about that!"

"That's a surprising turn," said Caleb.

"And that's not all!" Canlis was enjoying this. "When I told the workers what had happened to Bennett and his two sidekicks, they said they would testify that they had heard Bennett say many times that he was going to get even with you and Cal. The sheriff took statements and sent them to me. Signed statements that I'll use if anything comes of this. I don't expect ever to have to use 'em."

"I'm glad to see this put to rest," Caleb said. "I'm sorry, actually, what happened to Bennett and his men, but he forced it on me."

"Hell, Caleb, you and Mei Lin are heroes!" That evening, Canlis told the Folie's gossip circle about the Bennett affair, knowing full well that the entire population of Jackson Hole would soon know the story, and that was okay.

The days grew shorter, the nights colder. Deciduous trees, which only a few short weeks ago had exploded in a riot of color, now were bare and their black branches reached up like bony fingers toward the gray overcast. Scattered tiny snowflakes that swirled in the light breeze gave way to large flakes that fell from dark, heavy clouds.

Snow fell every day, making movement outside and work of any sort difficult for man or beast. Caleb had persuaded two of his hands that lived in town to stay on in the bunkhouse with Andy and Paul since they might find it impossible to ride in some days. Both said their wives were delighted with the arrangement.

One of the cowboys asked Caleb what he expected them to do in these conditions. Caleb had only said that they should be ready to ride when needed and to keep their warmest clothing dry.

Caleb had taken the wagon to town a couple of weeks ago in a light snowfall. He didn't know that it would be the last time he would make the drive for over three months. He had visited the gossip circle at Folie's store. All waved to Caleb when he entered, and John pulled a chair near the stove for him.

The geezers were uncharacteristically subdued. They huddled around the stove, alternately warming hands and feet, standing occasionally to warm their backsides. They glanced at Caleb and each other, seemingly waiting for someone else to offer.

"So what's in the offing, boys?" said Caleb.

They looked at each other. "Gonna be a bad one," John said. "Worse than we thought. I feel it in my bones. I've seen bad winters, I tell ya, and this is going to be a real bad one." He looked over at Philo.

"Lay in all you can," Philo said. "Stuff is going to be in short supply before spring thaw. Unless we're all wrong, and that ain't likely, won't be long before you'll find nothing edible to buy at any store in town. Even if you could get to town, and that's not likely either."

Caleb said his goodbyes to the group and expressed his hope that for the first time in living memory, they were wrong. Nobody laughed.

Then he proceeded to do what he had come to town to do. He drove the wagon to the two grocery stores and bought all the provisions the wagon would hold. He noticed that store shelves, customarily replenished promptly from storerooms, were largely empty. The owner at the till in one store confirmed that his storeroom was almost empty as well. He hoped for one more good delivery from his suppliers before snow blocked railway tracks and wagon roads, but he was not optimistic.

Caleb came through the front door, stomped on the mat to remove the snow from his boots. He hung his hat on a wall peg, shook off his coat and hung it on another peg. He walked to the kitchen and stopped.

Mei Lin stood at the window, looking at the yard that was covered with a blanket of snow. She sighed, and her hands went to her face. She sobbed. Caleb went to her and took her cheeks in his hands, kissed her. She took his hands, held them on her chest.

"Why can't I get pregnant? The doctor said I could get pregnant." Her eyes filled, and tears rolled down her cheeks.

Caleb had seen her often lately, standing at the back window, looking at Annie's grave. She had tended the grave, keeping it free of weeds, watering the flowers she had planted there until the blossoms were gone and the leaves withered and fell. When snow began to fall, she had brushed it from the grave until the storm had driven her inside and covered the grave and the garden and yard with a heavy blanket of snow that deepened with each storm.

"I'm sorry, sweetheart. You will get pregnant. I promise. It will take time. You will get pregnant." She turned around in his arms and grasped the folds of his shirt, pulling him close, pressing her head to his chest.

She leaned back, wiped her eyes with a hand. "Okay, you say so," she said. "Let's get supper, and you can tell me what's going on."

11

The winter was everything the oldsters in the gossip circle had predicted. Worse since they had never seen a winter like this. Successive snowstorms dumped their burden until fences disappeared under drifts, snow piled almost to rooflines of barns and houses, and most outside work was at a standstill.

Cows crowded under sheds that Caleb and the hands had built all over the pastures. The ground around the sheds was kept open only by the movement of the cattle. Hay was hauled to them on sleds pulled by teams that plodded on roads of packed snow, made passable by repeated use and constant shoveling by the exhausted hands.

Caleb had known that there were not enough sheds to shelter the entire herd. Some cows found scant shelter in the scattered woodlands; some stood motionless in the open or drifted before the constant wind.

These last haunted Caleb and Mei Lin and the hands.

Evenings, when the wind howled, and the storm threw thick flurries clattering against windows, Caleb and Mei Lin sat at the kitchen table, sipping coffee from mugs, talking about anything but the weather in the soft lantern light in the kitchen, knowing what was happening in the pastures and along the fence lines.

On a rare day when the storm abated, Caleb rode out under a pale sun and gray sky. He rode through an ethereal landscape, like a place he had never seen, a new country. Familiar landforms, undulations, risings and gullies, all gone. Now there was only a uniform, white landscape, almost flat, without form or distinctive feature.

He pulled up at Will's place. The snow reached half way up the side of the house. A walkway had been shoveled free of snow. Kimana answered his knock.

"Caleb. I... wait, I'll get Will." She brushed past him, stepped off the porch and walked to the side of the house. She shouted toward the barn. "Will! Caleb is here!"

Caleb frowned. This was a Kimana he had never seen before. She was gaunt, unsmiling, not the happy young woman he knew. He was surprised that she was wearing a heavy coat when she came out of the house.

Will came striding around the corner of the house. "Caleb. Good to see you. Come inside. Come in." He led the way into the house. It was little warmer in the house than it was outside. Caleb looked around the dark interior and at the cold fireplace.

Will and Kimana were somber, unsmiling. They seemed withdrawn, even embarrassed. They still wore their heavy jackets, buttoned from top to bottom.

"Let's sit in the kitchen. Sorry I can't offer coffee," Will said. Caleb waved him off. In the kitchen, brighter than the dark sitting room, Will sat down heavily in a chair, and Caleb sat opposite. Kimana stood in the doorway, leaning against the jamb, her hands pushed into coat pockets.

Will, head lowered, studied the tabletop. Caleb glanced at Kimana. She looked at him blankly. He turned back to

Will. And waited.

"Right," said Will. He pushed his chair back and turned toward Caleb. He explained that they had run out of firewood some time ago. Since then, they had been heating only one room in the house, the sitting room, by burning hay, bits of fences, corral posts and almost an entire side of the barn. On days when the weather was mild, like today, they had no fire at all.

They had long since emptied their pantry and were subsisting largely on wheat ground in a small coffee grinder. Kimana made bread loaves from the ground wheat.

Caleb was shocked. He had never been exposed to real deprivation, and he found it hard to comprehend.

"Will, you should have come to me. We have stocks that we would have shared."

"I didn't want to bother you. I figured you must be having the same troubles we have. I guess I wasn't too careful about putting up stores. We never had a winter like this."

Will looked up at Kimana, then back to Caleb. "Boss, I had to kill a steer. It had wandered into the yard. All by itself. Not another beast in sight. Stiff-legged and stumbling, never saw anything like it, just wobbling. It was on its last legs, and we needed meat something terrible. I'll make good on it."

"By god, never mind about the damn cow. Somebody or something must be looking out for you." Will nodded.

"Will, you and Kimana come to our place right now. Come in the wagon."

"Aw, no, boss. That's too much. We'll—"

"Will, goddammit, you and Kimana are friends. And you work for me. We've got lots of hard work to do once winter's finished, and we need to be ready.

All of us. Besides, Mei Lin needs company. She's getting tired of my face being the only other human in sight. She's going to be so happy to see you, Kimana."

"Aw, Caleb," said Will, "it's late, and—"

"Good. You'll have to spend the night. Now go get the mules hitched up. Kimana, I want you to hit him up aside the head with the fireplace tongs if he balks on this. Will you do that?"

Kimana smiled. "Whatever you say, boss." She stepped over to Caleb and put her arms around his neck and hugged. Caleb's eyes opened wide. He glanced sideways at Will and smiled as he hugged her. She pulled back, looked quickly at Will. He smiled. She ducked her head and grasped Will's arm with both hands.

"I've got to go over to the bunkhouse to see how the boys are doing." Caleb said. "You'll get to my place before me. My, Mei Lin's going to be so happy to see you!"

Caleb and Will walked through the outside door together, turning up coat collars. Will extended his hand to Caleb. "You're a good man, Caleb Willis, 'bout the best I ever knew." Caleb took his hand, and they shook. Will turned and strode toward the barn.

It troubled Caleb to see Will and Kimana in such a condition. He was ashamed that he had not visited them sooner, not so much to check on them, but just to see them. He didn't have many good friends in the Hole, and they were good friends. He wished Mei Lin had come along today. She wanted to come, but he had been afraid the weather might play some tricks.

He was glad he had ridden to Ray and Chica's the week before. They were in fine shape. They had prepared for the winter better than Will and Kimana, the old hands in the Hole. He vowed to make plans with Mei Lin for a visit with their old friends. As soon as the weather breaks.

Leaving Will's place, Caleb rode to the bunkhouse, an easy ride of little more than a half-hour. He found Andy and two of the other hands shoveling snow between the house and the barn. They were not at all unhappy to put down their shovels for the prospect of coffee.

Walking toward the house, Andy explained that Paul and the other two hands were taking advantage of the break in the weather by hauling hay on the sled to the shelters. They had loaded hay from the stack nearest the house, which was just about depleted. Andy pointed to another stack that lay at the far edge of the field in front of the house, near a willow copse.

Caleb stopped, frowned. The field was carpeted by a few feet of snow, but the ground around the stack was beaten down. Dark shapes encircled the stack. Caleb looked at Andy.

"Yeah, elk. They been working on that stack all winter. They'll likely finish it before we can get to it."

"How are we fixed for hay?" said Caleb.

"All things considered, we're doing all right. I thought we had put up enough hay to sell some in late winter, but I think we better hang on to it. We don't know how long this confounded weather is going to last. I gotta admit too that we've been burning some hay when we can't get to the woods. We still got a good supply of cut wood, but we're being cautious and trying to make that last by gathering down stuff and burning some bits of hay now and then. Hope that's all right."

"You do what you must."

"The elk?" said Andy.

"Let them have the stack."

"Thanks. Hoped you'd say that." It was well known that Andy had a soft spot for the starving elk and had spoken up in town gatherings that were convened to discuss the elk question. He was among a growing number of locals who advocated a preserve where elk would not be hunted and would be fed when conditions warranted.

Caleb pulled up at his corral just as the sun dropped behind the Tetons. He dismounted and stood quietly, reins in hand, watching the day end. Overhead, the sky was a heavy gray mass, but a thin line of clear sky showed above the peaks. He watched the line change a dozen pastel shades of gold until the gray mass lowered, and the light was gone.

After tending to his horse, he strode to the house as a light snow began to fall. He stamped on the porch, opened the door and stepped inside. He stopped at the kitchen door. The kitchen was light and warm and was most inviting after the cold ride. Caleb saw the table, already set for supper. Will and Kimana, sitting at the table, coffee cups in hand, smiled at him. Mei Lin scowled at him.

"Hurry up! Sit down!" she said. "If you hadn't sent Kimana and Will for a visit, I would be mad at you. Supper's been ready. Sit down!" She reached for him and hugged him, then patted his cheek, ending with a light slap. She smiled and kissed him.

Caleb sat down as Mei Lin brought bowls of boiled elk, roast potatoes, green beans, and hot biscuits to the table. She refilled coffee mugs and sat down.

The bowls made the rounds as each spooned out servings. Will took a bit of meat, then a forkful of potatoes. He smiled as he chewed. "Mei Lin, this is as good a supper as I ever had, and my Kimana is a pretty good cook."

"Thank you. I'm so glad you came today. It has been too long." Mei Lin touched Kimana's hand. "Kimana, we need to visit. We'll meet with Chica soon."

"Don't make any big plans until this weather breaks," said Caleb. "Shouldn't be too long now."

Caleb and Will stood on the front porch, buttoning coats and turning up collars. They looked at the road where Mei Lin and Kimana stood talking.

"That breakfast is going to keep me going for days," said Will. "We won't forget what you and Mei Lin did for us. We was in bad shape." Caleb smiled, nodded.

"Okay, let's get some stores on that wagon," said Caleb. "You get the mules while I load the goods. Looks like you're going to have a clear day for the ride home."

Caleb and Will walked on the pathway that was bordered by three feet of snow in the yard. They stopped on the road, which was beaten down and packed from the passage of men and animals.

"Look." Mei Lin pointed down at her feet. A six-inch strip of the icy crust in the middle of the road had melted to the roadbed, and a thin trickle of water cut a tiny shallow crevice in the muddy surface.

Mei Lin looked up at Caleb. "Is it over?"

"It's looks like it's the beginning of the thaw sure enough," he said. "We'll give it two or three more days. Will, if we don't get any more weather, tell Ray to meet us at your house on Thursday. Caleb rubbed his stubble. "I'm not looking forward to this."

Caleb's fears proved prophetic. A series of warm days and a steady south wind had hastened the thaw, and the snow pack steadily lowered. Caleb, Ray and Will rode out to the pastures and along the fence lines.

They knew what to expect, but they were still shocked at the carnage. Enough snow had melted to reveal the carcasses of cows that had drifted with the storms and piled up at the fences. Wolves and other predators had been at work on the dead animals. The thawing carcasses were just beginning to smell.

The animals that had huddled under shelters had fared better, but their ribs protruded against their slack skin. The ground around shelters was beaten down where cows had moved out in search of grass. Haystacks near shelters were just about finished.

Caleb lost almost a hundred cows. The economic impact was devastating, but the worse part, for him, was the knowledge that the animals had suffered terribly before dying in the bitter cold.

Spring came late that year, and it arrived rather abruptly when the meadows and woodlands fairly burst into color over the gray slush. Paintbrush arrived in abundance, appearing as reddish flames at the base of the dull sagebrush scrub. The Oregon Grape with its dainty yellow flowers added splashes of color. Here and there in the meadow, the Silky Phacelia bore thick stalks of exquisite purple flowers.

Caleb had little time to enjoy the delights of spring. Tallying up his winter losses and assessing his prospects, Caleb made a decision that six months ago he would not have given a second thought.

A Laramie banker had been pestering him for almost a year to sell him a piece of property on the northern edge of the ranch. The banker was planning to retire and wanted a new challenge. He wanted to open a dude ranch.

Caleb was of two minds about dude ranches. They took good land out of production, and they caricatured the whole idea of ranching. He didn't much like the idea of pretend ranching. On the other hand, he loved the outdoors and horses and fresh air, and did he have any right to deny city folk an occasional opportunity to enjoy the land as he enjoyed it every day?

If he had to sell a piece of the ranch, the acreage the banker wanted was the right piece for both of them. The parcel was probably the least productive section of the ranch, with a thin soil, less wild hay and more sagebrush. But it abutted against the boundary of the national forest, and it had the best views of the mountains and the valley.

Caleb hated to give up any part of the ranch, but he had no choice. He needed cash for operating expenses till he got his herd built up again. He contacted the banker and said that he was ready to talk.

Caleb came to an amicable sale agreement that satisfied both Bartholomew Anderson and himself. They agreed that the transaction would be beneficial to both in the long run. Anderson said that he hoped he could call on Caleb for advice on Jackson Hole affairs and guidance on the intricacies of setting up a "play ranch," as Caleb called it, even to Anderson's face.

Anderson didn't mind. It was precisely what he was doing, building an outdoor playroom where guests with deep pockets would play at cowboying. Caleb and Anderson understood each other and became friendly, if not exactly friends.

With the proceeds of the sale to Anderson, Caleb dispatched Amos Dickens to Idaho once more to buy stock. He put his hands to work repairing fences that were damaged by the storms. To compensate for land lost in the sale to the dude rancher, Caleb applied for and received permits to graze stock in the national forest.

Caleb closely followed Anderson's progress setting up the dude ranch. He was still a bit edgy about the whole affair. What would all this mean for him and his ranching operation? If Anderson were successful, there would be a bunch of strangers in the valley, literally next door.

Following Caleb's recommendation, Anderson bought horses from John Bailey and introduced Caleb to Jude Patrick who would operate the principal feature of the dude ranch: teaching the guests to ride and leading them on trail rides, mostly in the national forest.

Jude was a handsome young man in his mid-twenties who had ten years experience as a cowboy on a ranch in eastern Wyoming. Anderson had met him when vacationing on the ranch of a bank client. He had been impressed with Jude's way with horses and later, when he had decided to plunge into dude ranching, offered him a job.

At Anderson's invitation, and sometimes without invitation, Caleb visited the fledgling dude ranch. He was alternately intrigued and appalled with the progress. It was a ranch, and it wasn't a ranch. He talked with Jude about horses and the national forest where the dudes would ride and where Caleb grazed his cows.

Occasionally, Mei Lin accompanied Caleb on visits to the dude ranch. Jude was largely mute when Mei Lin was part of the group. But he could not take his eyes off her and was brought into the conversation only with some difficulty. Caleb noticed, but thought nothing of it, a passing fancy. He had seen too often how men were drawn to her. Mei Lin did not notice.

Caleb felt comfortable on the dude ranch. Maybe it would work out. He was impressed with Anderson's business skills and Jude's handling of the stock. He liked both of them. They were fine fellows.

On one visit, while Anderson showed Caleb a new corral, Jude and Mei Lin, standing by the nearby barn, had a particularly intense discussion about riding in which Mei Lin displayed her knowledge of form and technique. Jude asked whether she would consider coming to the ranch occasionally to instruct the female dudes on riding skills, perhaps lead some trail rides. He said he would clear it with the boss. Mei Lin was profoundly flattered and said she would talk with Caleb.

Anderson had listened to Caleb with one ear while trying to eavesdrop on Jude and Mei Lin. He caught snippets of the conversation and wished he had heard more. When Caleb said that he and Mei Lin needed to go and walked toward the ranch house to fetch their horses, Anderson said he would catch up.

Anderson watched Jude touch his hat to Mei Lin and walk into the barn. She walked toward Anderson, smiled.

"Mei Lin, a moment," said Anderson. She stopped.

"I need to go. Caleb is waiting."

"Just a moment. If I heard right, Jude asked you to come up and lead trail rides with him."

"Yeah, something like that. He said I would lead women riders."

"Mei Lin, I really hope you will consider doing this. I've never seen Jude so, so animated. He's really capable at what he does, but he's a moody fella, doesn't talk much. He hardly speaks with anyone on the ranch, never smiles. He hasn't seemed happy here, and I thought I was going to lose him. I've never seen him like he was just now. He has talked with you more than all the rest of us put together, even smiling. He has really opened up to you. Please do this. I think he likes you."

Mei Lin smiled. "I like him too. He's nice, and really good with horses."

"Mei Lin!" She and Anderson looked up to see Caleb waving, holding their horses' reins.

"Goodbye," she said. "I'll think on it."

Caleb and Mei Lin sat at the kitchen table, holding

coffee cups. Caleb was reluctant at first to consider the arrangement. But Mei Lin was so enthusiastic, he gave his approval. She needed something to do besides cooking and ranch work. She had been lonely during the winter. Caleb had persuaded her to ride occasionally with him, but for the most part, she had stayed in and around the house, alone. He knew she needed to be around people.

She also needed something that recognized her unique qualities. He knew she was good with horses. Whether she would be good with guests was something else.

With Caleb's blessing, Mei Lin agreed with Jude that she could come up twice each week. It was less than an hour's ride. She would leave after an early breakfast and promised Caleb that she would be home before sundown.

The construction of the dude ranch had begun in March just days after the deal was concluded between Anderson and Caleb. Anderson confessed to Caleb that he was so sure he would prevail that spring in his quest to buy the tract that he had begun planning before the deal was settled. By mid-summer, Anderson welcomed his first guests.

The enterprise was a winner from the opening day. Much of the success was attributable to the riding program. Jude and his hands were masters in handling the horses, and Jude and Mei Lin were excellent instructors. Both led rides on trails that began on ranch property and continued on paths in the national forest.

Mei Lin enjoyed the rides immensely and quickly became a favorite of the guests. She helped them with riding, explained the habits and fine points of their mounts and generally became their mentor. She loved the work and the camaraderie.

Mei Lin initially worked solely with women, but gradually men began joining her groups. Not a few of the middle-aged and older lotharios tried to get close to the pretty, young Celestial, but she fended them off with a smile, without offending them and, in most cases, leaving them relieved that they were not taken seriously.

Mei Lin was so popular with the guests that she agreed to Jude's pleas that she add a third workday to her weekly schedule. Soon, she was leaving home at first light and having breakfast with Jude in the dude ranch dining room. She and he needed more time in the morning to plan the day's activities. That's what she told Caleb at dinner one evening. He accepted her explanation without comment and without looking up from his plate.

At the end of each day, Mei Lin and Jude unsaddled their mounts and rubbed them down, talking all the while about horses, the mountains, the trails and the guests. It was always the best part of the workday for both of them.

Later, Mei Lin said her goodbyes to guests and Jude and set out at a lope for home. Seated at dinner, which she and Caleb had prepared together, they talked about their day. Caleb mostly listened, head down, studying his plate.

On one particular day, it all changed. Mei Lin's group, high on a forest trail, was hit with a sudden storm. Mei Lin herded the party into a gap in an outcropping for shelter where they waited out the storm. At the end, at dusk, they made their way down the mountain, wet and cold.

Jude insisted that she take a room, gratis, have a warm bath, and spend the night. He would telephone Caleb and explain. She hesitated, unsure what to do, but Jude was persuasive, and she relented. He brought some borrowed clothes to her room and went back to the lobby to make the call.

They had dinner together in the dining room and drank a bottle of good white wine. They exchanged stories of their ordeals that day, riding in the storm, taking refuge, laughing at their predicament and assuring the guests that this was just part of the wilderness experience.

Afterward dinner, they stood on the terrace, wine glass in hand, watching the sky darken over the Tetons, the sky changing from blue gray to deep cobalt. They stood close, looked into each other's eyes and soul, kissed. She pulled away, said goodnight, and walked through the door to the lobby.

Later, when he knocked on the door to her room, she opened it, and he came in, closing the door behind him. He put his hand to her cheek, leaned down and kissed her softly. His hand found her breast and caressed it. She sighed and stepped back, and both knew it was over. His face turned ashen, he looked once more at her, eyes brimming, turned and went out, closed the door slowly until it clicked shut.

Early next morning, Mei Lin walked into the lodge lobby. She wore her own clothes and carried the borrowed things. She stopped, rubbed her temple and closed her eyes, willing the throbbing in her head to go away. She opened her eyes, looked around and saw the woman who cleaned rooms. She said something to her and gave her the clothes.

"Mei Lin." She turned toward the voice. It was Anderson. "Have you seen Jude this morning?"

"No."

"Uh, I thought... I saw you last evening on the terrace with him. I thought you might... uh, you haven't seen him this morning?"

"No."

"He's always the first one up around here, already at work before most of us are out of bed." Anderson frowned at Mei Lin. Waiting.

"I haven't seen him. I'm going."

"This is very strange," he said. "It's not like him."

"Maybe he slept in. I'm going." She took a step toward the door.

"Mei Lin." She stopped, turned around.

"I know how he feels about you," Anderson said. "He would tell you if he was thinking something."

"He told me nothing. I'm going." She stepped toward the door, stopped, turned back. "Where does he keep his tack?"

"There." Anderson pointed through the door at a long barn beyond the yard. They walked out and across the yard to the barn. Anderson opened the door, holding it open for Mei Lin.

She took one step into the barn and stopped, gasped, her hand to her mouth. Jude hung by his neck, the rope wrapped around a beam overhead, his body twisting, as if on a wind-up mechanism that coiled in one direction, reversed, twisted the other way.

Anderson stared at the body, his mouth hanging open, as if hypnotized. Finally, softly: "My god, what have you done?"

Anderson shook his head, turned and ran out. Outside, he called: "Ben! Danny! Somebody!" The sound of running feet on the hard ground, and two men rushed inside. They stopped when they saw the hanging body, slowly twisting on the beam.

"What th' hell."

"Do something!" said Anderson. He stood behind the two hands.

One man grabbed a stepladder from the wall, dragged it beneath the body and opened it. He climbed up, pulled a knife from his belt scabbard. The man on the ground gripped Jude's legs, and the other on the ladder cut the rope with a knife. They gently lowered the burden to the ground. The men stepped away and looked down at what had been Jude that morning. His open eyes stared at the rafters that had taken his life.

Mei Lin held her cheeks with both hands. The blood had drained from her face, and her mouth was dry. "Somebody... somebody... close . . . close his eyes." She choked back a sob.

One of the men bent down and pulled the lids down, closing the eyes. Mei Lin put her hands over her eyes. She dropped her hands to her side, turned and walked toward the door.

"Mei Lin?" said Anderson who stood at the door.

"I need to go home. My head .. . Caleb will worry." She walked through the door and was gone.

Mei Lin pulled her horse up in front of the house, dismounted and dropped the reins. She walked into the house, leaving the front door open, and collapsed on the bed fully clothed. She stared at the ceiling, finally closed her eyes and squeezed them, squeezing the tears out until they ran down her temples.

Caleb had been working in the barn when he heard the hoof beats of a galloping horse. He thought it must be one of the hands, giving his horse a good run. When he came out, he saw Chiquita standing at the hitching post, head down and reins trailing on the ground.

Caleb hurried inside the house, looked around frantically, saw Mei Lin on the bed. He leaned over her, touched her cheek, her forehead. She opened her eyes, puffed, red and brimming with tears.

"What's wrong, sweetheart?"

She grabbed his hand with both of hers and pulled him

down. He knelt beside the bed. He waited, looking into her eyes.

"Can I rest a while? I'll rest... and I'll tell you. I'm okay. Just need to rest."

Caleb stroked her cheek. "All right, sweetheart. I'm right here. You rest. It's all right, now. You're here in your bed, and I'm here." She closed her eyes and turned away. He removed her boots and pulled the blanket up to cover her shoulders.

Mei Lin and Caleb sat on opposite sides of the kitchen table. Each held a coffee mug. Mei Lin raised her mug, holding it with both hands, her hands shaking. She sipped, lowered the mug to the table.

"He blamed me. Maybe he's right. Maybe it was my fault." Tears streamed down her cheeks. She wiped the tears with the back of her hand.

"You were not responsible. It wasn't your fault."

"I shouldn't have let him ... I didn't encourage him, but..."

"You don't drink alcohol, sweetheart. You didn't know what you were doing. I'm surprised you were even conscious."

She smiled, a weak, almost smile. "My head was spinning. I stumbled and almost fell on the stair when I was going to my room."

She reached over and took his hand in both of hers. "Can you ever forgive me? I was wrong, and I'm sorry. That's not me, honey. I'm so sorry."

"Sweetheart, don't think about it. It was the evening, the mountains, the sunset, the wine, a handsome boy, a lot younger and better looking than the old man you married."

She squeezed his hand. "No, honey. Well, it was all those things, but mostly the wine." She tried to smile without much success.

"Okay. But you owe me one."

She frowned. "What do you mean?"

"Well."

"Oh no. What I did was wrong, and I'm really sorry, but that doesn't mean you can do the same thing." She was only half playing with him.

"Well."

She wiped her face with the palms of both hands, straightened in her chair. "Caleb. Do you remember back at your place on Stanley Creek when you said you were trying to find a place for me with the Chinese people at Stow? Do you remember what I said I would do if you did that?"

"I remember."

"I said I would kill myself if you put me there. I meant it."

"I know you did."

"And I would have done it. But if you fool around with another woman, I would not kill myself.

I would kill *her*. Then I would have to decide what to do with *you*." She tried to smile and choked on a sob.

"I believe you would do that, too."

"I would. I would."

She burst into tears and sobbed, her hands on her cheeks. He stood and hurried around the table to her. He helped her stand and guided her to the bedroom where he pulled the covers down and supported her as she lay down.

"Now you sleep all day and all night, and tomorrow's a new day, and all will be right with the world. And us." He leaned over and kissed her cheek. She bobbed her head and closed her eyes, curled up on her side and pulled the covers to her chin.

A week later, Caleb rode at a gallop to the dude ranch.

He pulled up in the courtyard, dismounted and tied the reins to the hitching rail. He strode across the yard, stopped a cowboy who was walking toward the corral, leading his horse. Caleb spoke to him, and the cowboy pointed at a barn. Caleb strode toward the open barn doors.

He walked into the barn, saw Anderson standing before a horse stall.

"Anderson, I need to talk to you!" Anderson turned at Caleb's voice. "Caleb." "We've got something to sort out. You don't need to talk unless you have something useful to say. You need to listen. I heard in town that you've been mouthing off about Mei Lin being responsible for Jude's death."

Anderson stepped backward. Caleb's reputation for when he was riled was well known. At the moment, Caleb was riled.

"Well. . . she didn't stop him," Anderson said. "I saw them."

"Hold on. You mean that because she didn't punch him in the eye, she was responsible? Let's get this straight. He came on to her. She left the terrace and went to her room. Alone. He came to her room; she didn't go to his room. Then she backed off and put a stop to it.

"Besides, by the time they left the dinner table, she was drunk. They finished a bottle of wine, the two of them. She doesn't drink. That's more alcohol than the total of what she's had in the two years I've known her. In spite of a spinning head, she was able to fend him off. Yeah, fend him off! He made all the moves. Not her.

"Do we have an understanding on this affair? Enough that you'll keep your goddamned opinions to yourself. This has nothing to do with Jude. Mei Lin liked Jude; I liked Jude. He was a fine fellow, and I'm sorry he's gone.

But let's not try to find a cause for his death outside his troubled head."

Anderson fidgeted, looked past Caleb at the barn wall. Caleb turned and walked through the door.

Riding at a lope toward home, Caleb glanced at the meadow beside the road, saw the patchwork color of wildflowers in the hay field. He reined Buck into a walk, then stopped. Dismounting, he gathered an armful of flowers.

At home, he got down at the hitching rail and walked to the porch. Mei Lin sat in the swing, moving the swing gently with a foot. Caleb handed her the flowers. She thanked him and laid the bouquet on the swing beside her.

"I'll put them in water," Caleb said and reached for the flowers. She picked up the bouquet and handed it to him. She smiled thinly, politely. He stood a moment looking down at her, then walked into the house, carrying the flowers.

He worried about her. Since the affair at the dude ranch, she had not been the same. She was withdrawn, like that other time when a life had gone from her universe. This time it was different, but it was the same. She felt loss, for which she blamed herself. She had listened to Caleb's repeated attempts to convince her that it wasn't her fault, just as he had when she lost Annie, but she could not shake the feelings of guilt in either case.

She stopped the swing, stood and walked down the steps of the porch and around the house to the backyard. There was little but outlines in the yard to indicate that there once was a garden there that had produced vegetables and flowers. Now the plot was covered with weeds and scattered anemic vegetable sprouts that had come up volunteer.

Only Annie's grave was tended. It was free of weeds.

A small vase at the base of the headstone held a fresh assortment of wildflowers. She changed the flowers every three or four days.

As she stood, holding back tears, a western bluebird alighted on the top of a picket behind the grave. She remembered a passage—why should she remember?—from a bird book she had seen at Folie's: "The bluebird carries on his back the blue of heaven." She shook her head. How can anything be so beautiful in a world that was so filled with ugliness and cruelty?

As she walked back around the house, she saw a Western Meadowlark strutting in the front yard, its tail flicking and the black V on its breast emphasized by the brilliant yellow underparts. Mei Lin stopped and watched the bird poking and probing in the yard.

12

Caleb visited Will this sunny morning to see how he was coming with his hay crop. He also wanted to see the new mowing machine. He expected the contraption to revolutionize the production of hay.

When he returned home that afternoon, he was surprised to see a smiling Mei Lin on the front porch. When he pulled up at the hitching rail, a dozen birds exploded into flight from the yard.

"Hey, you!" she shouted at him. He recoiled, surprised, and she smiled again. He dismounted and walked through the gate to the yard. He saw the half dozen pans in the yard that held crumbs and seed.

He frowned. "You're feeding birds?"

She smiled again. "Yes! It's wonderful. I love to watch them. Did you see them? An orange one, and a little yellow one, and a brown one with a gray head, a big long-tailed black bird with a white chest. And there was a brown one with black specks and a red cheek."

"Honey, would you ask your friend in Jackson, the one that made the swing, if he would make some little pans or houses that I could put crumbs and seeds in and hang up on the porch or in a tree? Some birds came to the trees and watched, but wouldn't go to the pans. Maybe they would come to something hanging that had food in it."

He almost laughed out loud at the absurdity of feeding birds, but if it pleased Mei Lin, he would do it. Anything to see her smile again.

"I will go to town as soon as I can, and I will ask Bob to make a dozen feeding stations for you. Where did you get the seed?"

"I watched the birds in the field, where they were feeding, and I gathered seed from those plants."

"You are a wonder, Mei Lin Willis, and I love you." He took her in his arms and kissed her. He pulled back, frowning.

"What?" she said.

"I never thought about it. I don't know your birth last name. I never asked you."

"My last name. My full name was Lee Mei Lin. Lee is a common name, like Smith in this country. Lee. I haven't said that name since I left China with my owner. He never said it, and no one else knew it. I..."

Tears filled her eyes. She grabbed Caleb's lapels and pulled him close, buried her face in the folds of his shirt. He put his arms around her shoulders and held her.

"There, I've done it again. I'm sorry, sweetheart. I didn't mean to bring up anything unpleasant. I'm sorry."

She wiped her eyes with his shirt. "I'm okay. Just a little . . . just a little ... not quite myself."

He pulled back. "Tell you what. Let's go for a ride tomorrow. No work. Just ride because we want to. The weather is nice. I wager we'll see wild birds, maybe a coyote or a beaver. I heard a woodpecker in the woods near the elk haystack a couple of days ago. We'll ride there."

"The elk haystack?"

"Yeah, Will and I decided to let the elk have it. They still haven't recovered from that hard winter, and we have plenty of feed for the stock.

• • • • •

"Who is that?" said Mei Lin. In the distance, a man stood beside the elk haystack. He held the reins of his horse. He appeared to be studying the ground at the base of the stack.

Caleb and Mei Lin rode along the fence line that separated the ranch from the national forest. It was a fortunate situation since Caleb grazed his cattle in the forest under permit. A gate in this fence gave access to the forest. It also was good for the elk since Caleb could open the gate, and the elk could move directly from government land to the haystack that Caleb had allotted to them.

As they neared the haystack, they saw what the figure was studying. Four elk carcasses lay at the base of the stack. The man looked up, and Caleb recognized him.

"Hello, Randy," Caleb called. They pulled up and dismounted. "Mei Lin, meet Randy Allen, the fiercest forest ranger in the West."

Randy smiled, touched his hat to Mei Lin. "Caleb, Miss Mei Lin." They looked at the carcasses. "Nasty business. Tuskers."

"I've heard of tuskers," said Mei Lin. "Why do they do it?"

"Poachers kill elk just for the eye teeth. Some people think the teeth make good jewelry. Elks Club members like to mount them on watch fobs as a badge of sorts. This ever happen before, Caleb?"

"Yeah, couple of times."

Randy stared at the carcasses. "Tusking used to be a

bigger problem than it is today. Got so bad about five years ago that a bunch of ranchers and farmers who wanted to help the elk formed a vigilante committee and threatened to hang tuskers. The vigilantes cooled down, but they still warned tuskers to clear out or face the consequences. Tusking was even made a felony by the state. But we still have the problem. Any time somebody can make a lot of money without working too hard, there's people who will take any sort of risk.

"Caleb, I'd like to stake out a couple of my boys here soon as we can get a lead on the men that I suspect. I'd like to catch them in the act rather than take them on suspicion. I'll let you know." He moved to his horse, put a foot in a stirrup, pulled it back.

"Something else you might help me with. The sheriff has been asking around about some drifters that don't seem to be going anywhere or doing anything in particular. Yet they hang around. They been seen in the saloons mostly and riding about the countryside. Looking. Thing is, one of my men, recently hired from Nevada, recognized one of the drifters who was suspected in Nevada of rustling cattle. Saw his picture in the post office."

"Rustling? And they're looking around in the Hole? Rustling cattle in the Hole? That must be some sort of challenge. There's so many fences and such small ranches. They couldn't move stolen cattle down the roads."

"What about the national forest?" said Mei Lin. Caleb and Randy looked at Mei Lin. "There are trails everywhere," she said.

"Trails are pretty narrow, hard to move cattle on them," said Randy.

"Most of them are narrow," said Mei Lin. "But there's a wide trail that runs north and south, just about a mile from the national forest boundary. I led groups from the dude ranch on this trail many times.

It's a popular trail, wide enough for three or four people to ride side by side."

"Hmm. Possibility," said Randy. "Let me think on it."

"If you're going after the rustlers," Mei Lin said, "I'll go with you and show you the trail. If you don't know that country, you'll waste time looking for the trail. You'll thrash around so much, the rustlers might hear you." She looked at Caleb, then back at Randy. "I need to go with you."

Caleb smiled. "No, you don't need to go, and you're not going. You need to give Randy and me a good description of the country and tell us how to find the trail." She smiled. It was the reaction she expected.

Caleb turned back to the ranger. "There is this one thing," Caleb said. "My ranch sets smack on the old elk migration route. My fence that borders the national forest interrupts that route. I knew that when I built the fence, so I put in a gate. I open the gate during the elk migration season so they can pass through. There's another gate in the other fence where the old migration route left my property. That's a lot of gates the rustlers could open to move stolen animals."

"Yeah, let me think on that as well." Randy swung up on his horse. "I'll be in touch. He kicked his horse into a lope.

Two weeks later, Randy met Caleb at the sheriff's office in Jackson and gave him some news. He had telephoned Caleb the previous evening to set up the meeting. Randy and Caleb sat in chairs before Sheriff Canlis's desk. The sheriff slouched in his chair, chewing on a cold cigar.

Two tuskers had been arrested at Caleb's haystack.

They were working on an elk they had just killed. Randy was delighted that he caught them in the act. He also reported that the Wyoming Elks Club had notified the local office of the Forest Service that they would do what they could to end the practice of members using elk teeth for ceremonial or jewelry purposes.

And there was more. Randy reported that his superiors told him that the creation of a refuge for elk was virtually a certainty. It would be located on federal land northeast of Jackson. Elk would be protected from hunting, and they would be fed when necessary.

"Glad to hear that," Canlis said.

"That's good news indeed," said Caleb. "Now the beasts should be willing to give me back my haystack." They laughed.

"Now, on that other problem—" said Randy.

"Randy—sorry to interrupt—you got the tuskers booked?" said Caleb.

"Yeah. Sheriff has them, waiting for the judge."

"Was one of them named Overgaard, by chance?"

"Yeah," said Randy. "Strange name. How'd you know?"

"Gut feeling," Caleb said. "I've had run-ins with him before. He's a bad one. Glad you got him."

"You won't have any more run-ins with him any time soon," said Canlis." Now that tusking's a felony, he'll spend some time at Rawlins."

"Rawlins?"

"State Pen."

"That's good news," Caleb said. "Now, sorry I interrupted. What's the other problem?"

"What I talked with you before. Rustling," said Randy. "Good news on that problem as well. One of my men, who is a pretty good tracker, has confirmed what we suspected.

A rancher down south of Jackson reported to the sheriff that he had lost two cows. My man tracked the cows and two horses from this ranch into the national forest to a little box canyon where they're collecting the cows.

"Well, he didn't actually see the cows, but he heard them. You might see a scattering of cows grazing in a national forest, but you don't normally hear a bunch of cows raising hell in one place in a national forest. This little box canyon is only a couple of miles from the boundary. Almost due west of your place, in fact, Caleb."

"That might explain why I'm missing three cows since last week," said Caleb, "give or take one or two. I don't know whether my cowboys' arithmetic can be relied on."

"Figures," Randy said. "You're the third rancher who has lost a few head just in the past week. It seems they are taking only a few cows from each place, I suppose figuring that the owner will not notice. God, who's not to notice? These yahoos are not too bright."

Canlis removed the cold cigar stub from his mouth and tossed it into the wastebasket. "Bad guys as a rule ain't too bright. The point is, we're putting a posse together, Caleb, and we hope we can count on you."

"Sure, I'm in. Just tell me when. I ... I would rather not be armed."

The sheriff leaned forward in his chair. "Well, you wouldn't be much good to us, then, would you? These fellows might have something to say about us riding into their camp and arresting them for cattle rustling. You got a problem with protecting yourself and doing your part to get your cows back? Or are you content to let others do it for you?" Canlis wasn't smiling.

Caleb looked aside, then back at the sheriff. "You see, Scott, I've killed people." Randy and Canlis looked hard at Caleb. "The sonsabitches needed killing, but I still don't feel good about it. It still bothers me. But your point is well taken. I'll be armed."

"Good. We're gonna do this thing soon. Next day or two. I'll get in touch. You both have telephones, I think." They nodded. "I'll telephone you." The sheriff stood, signaling that the gathering was finished.

First light. Caleb and Mei Lin stood in the kitchen, their empty breakfast plates and coffee cups still on the table. He rotated the chamber of the six-shooter to verify that it was loaded. He slid the pistol into its holster and strapped it on. Mei Lin watched.

"I thought I would never have to wear it again," Caleb said. "I thought we were finished with guns."

"I'm sorry, honey. But as long as there are bad people with guns, good people will need guns. But I wish you weren't going. I will worry."

"I'll be fine. There will be a dozen people in the posse. There'll be a few ranchers who never shot a gun in anger in their lives, but I wager most of the members will be young cowboys who wish they had been born thirty years ago when wearing a gun was as normal as wearing a shirt. I'll worry more about these kids than the rustlers."

They looked up at the sound of hooves in front of the house. Mei Lin followed Caleb from the kitchen to the front door. He opened it to see a dozen mounted men in the road in front of the house. He took a jacket from the peg and pulled it on.

"You be careful," she said.

He leaned down and kissed her, a hand at her cheek, and walked out.

She had watched him go like this before, and she was already worried. She closed the door as the posse kicked their horses into a gallop up the road toward the national forest.

"There's four of 'em," the ranger said softly. He stood before the mounted posse. "It's about a hundred yards up this incline, then about fifty yards on a game trail down this narrow gulley to the head of this little box canyon. Couldn't tell for sure, but it looks like about fifty head in there."

"Okay, get mounted and lead on." A rider handed him the reins of his horse. The ranger mounted and set out at a walk.

Canlis turned in his saddle to face his posse. "Now, you men, keep in mind that these fellas up ahead are just trying to make a living. They may be bad guys, and they may be good guys who're hungry. We mean to convince them that they have been caught and are under arrest. We should be able to do that without any gunplay. Understood?"

The riders nodded.

"No talking now," said Canlis. "The next talking will be me telling the rustlers about the error of their ways." He led off at a slow walk. Caleb rode beside him, and the others bunched up behind them.

As Caleb had suspected, the majority of the posse's members were young cowboys with pistols strapped to their waists who had talked excitedly for most of the ride. Now as they neared the rustlers' camp, their excitement and nervousness mounted.

The ranger led the posse off the main trail down the game path that ran alongside a narrow tumbling stream at the base of the gulley. When the trail leveled off, they rounded a heavy stand of chokecherry shrubs.

And there they were. The four rustlers lounged around a campfire. Two sat cross-legged, and two were stretched out. The four were shocked at the sudden appearance of the posse and jumped up, wide-eyed, staring as if at specters.

"Easy, boys, don't do nothing foolish that you're gonna regret," said Canlis. "It's just a few cows. Nobody needs to get hurt over a few cows. Now if any of you has a gun, you need to toss it this way on the ground."

"Hell, you say!" A young man with a wild head of hair and wearing a heavily stained jacket pulled a pistol from his belt. He leveled on nobody in particular and fired.

The rider next to Caleb shouted a muffled "Ah!" and fell from his horse.

The shooter made to swing his gun toward the sheriff, but before he could complete the swing, his head jerked back. Blood spurted from his forehead, and he fell backward to the ground.

Posse members whipped around and stared openmouthed at Caleb who was pushing his six-shooter into its holster.

"Whoa," said one of the young cowboys softly.

Canlis turned back to the rustlers who had arms stretched high over their heads. "Are we done? You fellows all peaceful now?" The men nodded. "Any of you have any weapons, drop them on the ground. You can lower your arms."

One young man stuffed his hands into his pockets, looked around blankly as if searching for a place to hide. Another stared blankly at the sheriff, waiting. The two seemed to withdraw into themselves.

"Nobody has a gun," said the third man, who appeared to be the leader of the group. He looked down at the body stretched out beside the fire circle, the gun still held in a death grip. "Only this young fella who just wanted a little excitement. First time he ever wore a gun, he said. Thought it was really something to wear a gun." He shook his head slowly. "What am I gonna tell his Mama?"

He looked up at the sheriff. "Sorry about your man. I hope he's not hurt bad."

Canlis turned to look at the posse members behind him. Two men had dismounted and lowered the injured rider to the ground where they were applying a bandage to his shoulder wound.

One of them looked up at the sheriff. "He's not hit bad. He'll be okay, I think." Canlis nodded. He looked up and saw Caleb riding slowly up the game path toward the forest trail above.

Caleb stood on the porch, leaning against a post. He stared at the floor. Mei Lin sat motionless in the swing. Both held coffee mugs.

"He was just a boy," said Caleb. "Probably never held a pistol in his hand before. Probably didn't expect to use it. Just wanted to strut a little and pretend he was a tough customer, like in the good old days. No doubt he'd heard lots of stories about those days. I should have winged him and hogtied him. I coulda told him something about the bad good old days." He sipped from his cup.

"No. What you did was right. If you had winged him... what does that mean?"

"It means hit him somewhere besides between the eyes. Arm, leg, anywhere that wouldn't kill him."

"I understand. But if you had just winged him, he might have been able to shoot again. He might have killed you. You did right."

Caleb turned and looked up at the sky, almost clear but for a few wispy clouds on the horizon. "Yeah, I expect you're right, Lee Mei Lin Willis. You usually are."

She smiled, sipped her coffee, pushed on the floor with

a foot to swing backwards.

"Reminds me of something," said Caleb.

"What?" she said, but he was already striding toward the barn.

Caleb and Mei Lin walked on the boardwalk toward the end of town. Caleb stopped and took Mei Lin's arm.

"We need to stop here a minute," said Caleb.

Mei Lin looked at the door. "The sheriff's office?"

"Yeah." Caleb opened the door and held it for her. She looked at him, and he motioned with a nod to go inside. She walked into the office. He stepped in and closed the door.

Sheriff Canlis sat behind his desk. He grinned and stood. He threw the cold cigar stub in the waste-basket and stepped around the desk.

"Caleb. Miss Mei Lin. I'm glad to see you this fine day," said the sheriff.

"Morning, Scott," said Caleb. He turned to Mei Lin. "Mei Lin, the sheriff is going to do the honors."

"Honors? What honors?" Mei Lin frowned at Caleb.

Canlis extended his hand. Mei Lin smiled, took the hand and shook briefly. She frowned again, puzzled. Canlis sat on the edge of the desk.

"Miss Mei Lin," said Canlis, "Caleb here tells me you want to become a citizen."

"Yes. I do."

"Okay, here's what we'll do. I have some questions that I'll ask you, and you reply. Sound okay?"

"Yes, sir. Thank you." She was nervous, looked anxiously at Caleb.

"Okay. First thing is, don't call me 'sir.' You'll make me think I need to give a sermon or pronounce an edict or something."

"Okay," Mei Lin said, smiling.

"Okay. Are you married to this handsome gentleman standing beside you?"

She frowned, looked at Caleb, back at Canlis. "Yes."

"Is he a citizen?"

Mei Lin looked again at Caleb, perplexed "Yes, he is."

"Then I declare you a citizen of the United States of America and the state of Wyoming, Mrs. Caleb Willis. Now that didn't hurt, did it?"

"That's it?" said Caleb. "Can you do that?"

"Hell, it's done already," said Canlis. "I done a little investigating. Miss Mei Lin, you became a citizen on the day you two married. Since 1907, I'm told, marriage in this country determines a woman's nationality. You marry a United States citizen, you're a United States citizen. What do you think of that?"

Mei Lin stared, open-mouthed. She looked at Caleb, then at Canlis, back to Caleb. "I'm a citizen! I belong!" She looked back at the sheriff. "I can vote?"

"Yes, you can vote. Well, you can vote for anything in Wyoming, but not for anything about the United States. Women nowhere can vote in national elections. There's a bunch of hothead women back East agitating for the national vote, but they're not going anywhere with that.

"Say, Miss Mei Lin, why don't you run for town government? There's talk about some local women wanting to set up a town government, even though we're not officially a town." He grinned.

Canlis turned to Caleb. "How about that, Caleb. All the old boys who think they're having problems with the old lady at home, what's gonna happen if they get control of the town's affairs?" The sheriff guffawed. Mei Lin glared at him. She was not smiling. He noticed and sobered.

"Not much chance of that," said Caleb. "We'll be on our way, Scott. Thanks for officiating at Mei Lin's citizenship inauguration. I suppose we'll get a document attesting to the citizenship?"

"Yep, soon's I can get the judge's ear."

Caleb and Mei Lin shook Canlis's hand and left the office. Outside, Caleb put his hat on and made to walk off. Mei Lin did not move.

"Why do you think women will not be elected to town offices? And why does the sheriff think women will not get the national vote? I have heard something of that. I think they will get the vote."

Caleb looked at her, frowned.

She stamped her foot. "Maybe I will run for a city office! Or a county office!"

"If you run, you will win. I'm sure of it, and I will support you." He smiled, and she fumed. She knew this smile, the smile that signified that he did not mean a word he said, the smile that said he was toying with her.

13

Mei Lin, Chica and Kimana sat at Mei Lin's kitchen table. Coffee mugs were on the table and what was left of a batch of cookies that Kimana had brought. Only two remained, and Mei Lin took one.

"Um, so good," Mei Lin said. "What is the sweet taste?"

"Chokecherries. They are everywhere. Easy to pick. You must go with me."

"I will," said Mei Lin. She picked up her mug.

They sat silent, sipping their coffee, waiting.

"Mei Lin, you said you wanted to talk to us about something," said Chica.

"Yes," Mei Lin said. She set her mug on the table, looked up. "Have you ever voted?"

Chica frowned. "Voted? No, I don't vote. I don't think I can vote. I leave that to Ray. But I don't think he has ever voted either."

Kimana shook her head. "Why would I want to vote? I know Will has voted. Women can't vote, can they?"

Mei Lin leaned over the table. "Yes, they can vote! If they are citizens."

Chica and Kimana looked at each other. "Are we

citizens?" said Chica.

"No. I don't think so," Kimana said.

"Yes, you are! Both of you. It doesn't matter that you are Mexican and Indian. You are married to an American citizen, so you are a citizen. And you can vote. Women have been voting in Wyoming since 1869. Mrs. Hendricks told me. They can't vote in national elections, but that might change before long. Women all over are trying to win the right to vote."

"But, Mei Lin," said Chica, "women voting? How do the men feel about that?"

"There will always be some men on their high horse, but most of the men around here seem to be okay with it. And let me tell you this! There's some talk about women running for offices in Jackson and the county. In the election coming up this fall!" Mei Lin smiled and leaned back in her chair.

Chica and Kimana were speechless. Whether from lack of interest or from the enormity of the implications suggested by Mei Lin was unclear.

Mei Lin and Caleb sat in chairs before Sheriff Canlis' desk. He slouched in his chair, chewing on a cold cigar. He removed the stub and tossed it in the waste-basket.

"I'd rather be talking with you at your house, and you know why." He looked over at Mei Lin and smiled. "But you said you were coming in today. I 'preciate you dropping by."

"You said on the telephone that you wanted to talk with us about something," said Caleb.

"Yeah. I'm right glad you're on the telephone, by the way. Makes things a lot easier. I wish more of the people hereabouts would get on it."

Mei Lin looked at Caleb, smiled.

"I know you're good friends with some of the Mormon Row people and visit occasionally," Canlis said, "and I'm wondering. Have you heard any talk up there about anybody's got more than one wife? I got some anonymous tips that somebody up there's breaking the law with more than one wife."

Caleb frowned. "No, I've not heard anything."

"You, Miss Mei Lin?" said Canlis.

"No."

"Good," said Canlis. "I hope it's just somebody spreading a rumor to try to cause somebody trouble. You'll let me know if you hear anything beyond the rumor." He stood. "I won't keep you. I know you have business in town."

Mei Lin and Caleb stood. Caleb shook hands with Canlis. They walked out to the sidewalk, closed the door. They looked at each other, puzzled.

"I wonder what that's all about," Caleb said. Mei Lin shrugged. He took her arm, and they walked across the street toward Folie's. "Let's find out."

Inside Folie's, they stopped at the door, waved to Philo, Alastair, John and Pumpkin sitting at the stove. Caleb and Mei Lin walked over, and Caleb pumped handshakes with the four.

"Welcome to the fount of all knowledge," said Philo. "Are you going to imbibe today? Contribute? Withdraw?"

"I have a question that I would like to pose," said Caleb.

"Now that sounds promising indeed. Sit down, sit down," said Alastair. He pulled up a chair for Caleb, and he sat. Mei Lin stood behind Caleb's chair.

"You can sit, too, Missy," said Alastair. "Just don't tell any of your lady friends that we broke a cardinal rule of the circle." He motioned her to the chair beside Caleb.

She smiled and sat down. "Thank you. I am really

honored." The four men guffawed.

"What is it you want to ask, Caleb? If it's simple, we'll solve the problem before lunch. If it's difficult, we may have to adjourn to Lloyd and Tuttle's for refreshment to stimulate our brains."

"It's an easy question. Is there a rumor going about that somebody in the Hole has two wives?"

The woodstove philosophers looked at each other and leaned back in their chairs.

"I think what you mean to ask," John said, "is whether there is a Mormon hereabouts that is practicing polygamy."

"That's about it," said Caleb.

"There is such a rumor," said Pumpkin, "but we cain't pin it down. Nobody wants to talk about it. The Mormons sure don't want to talk about it, and they would know, wouldn't they?"

"Where did you hear this, Caleb?" said Philo.

"I don't think it's a secret," said Caleb. "From the sheriff."

"There's something else that's not a secret, but not a lot of people know it," said Philo. "And it probably has nothing to do with the rumor at hand. Scott Canlis is a Mormon. Well, he's a Jack Mormon."

Mei Lin frowned. "What's that?"

"Somebody who was a practicing Mormon, but became inactive or maybe stopped believing, but still has good feelings about the people in the Mormon church. Does that make sense?"

"Yes, I understand," said Mei Lin.

"So if Scott has heard a rumor about somebody in the Hole that has two wives," Philo said, "as sheriff, he is bound to try to find that person because he has broken the law. But I'll bet he hopes he can't find that person."

Alastair and Pumpkin nodded.

"There's another rumor, and I hadn't been able to pin this one down either. Anyway, there's a rumor that Canlis has a brother down in Utah who is in the lockup. This is what happens to a man who has more than one wife, and he's caught. He is put in jail, and the wives are left to fend for themselves. That's not good."

"Hmm," Caleb pondered, looking at his outstretched legs. "Have you ever talked with Scott about the polygamy rumor in the Hole?"

"He come over a week or so ago and asked us right here. We said we had heard the rumor," John said, "but knew nothing for sure. He said, 'fine,' and seemed satisfied with our answer. Like Philo said, I don't think he wants to find this person."

Caleb stood, and Mei Lin rose. "Much obliged, fellows," said Caleb. "Interesting. Most interesting." He waved, and the oldsters raised hands in acknowledgement or goodbye.

"Any time, Caleb," said Philo. "Come back when you need any more information about anything or any problems you need solved. World problems welcomed." Pumpkin laughed.

Caleb waved over his shoulder as he walked to the door, followed by Mei Lin.

Outside, Caleb and Mei Lin walked on the sidewalk toward their horses. Mei Lin caught Caleb's arm and stopped him.

"Honey, I just remembered something. Do you 'member when we visited the Barkers two weeks or so ago when you had questions about those irrigation canals?"

"Yes, I remember."

"Remember after we talked a while Naomi said that she was going to get more coffee and went into the kitchen, and a while after that, another woman brought the coffee. I had never seen her before."

"I remember that. I'd never seen her either, and I've visited the Barkers more than you."

"Do you remember that Hiram introduced her as Miriam, Naomi's little sister?"

"Yeah."

"When we were finished with our coffee," Mei Lin said, "and you and Naomi were talking about something, Hiram got up to help Miriam take the dishes to the kitchen. When they were going through the kitchen door, I heard him say real soft, 'thanks, honey.' Then he jerked his head around and looked right at me."

"Hmm. I guess it's okay to call your sister-in-law 'honey.'"

"I don't think so," said Mei Lin.

Mei Lin, Kimana and Chica huddled around a choke-cherry bush, large as a small tree, in a roadside patch. The slender branches, laden with the black fruit, bent almost to the ground. The women plucked the berries and dropped them into their baskets. Some of the berries did not reach the baskets. Almost as many went into mouths as baskets.

"I'll never get a full basket," said Chica, "I'm eating so many. They are so good!"

"Sometimes the berries are not good to eat right off the bush," said Kimana, "but these are sweet."

"Look at your hands!" said Mei Lin, pointing. "Your fingers are purple."

Chica looked at her fingers, put them in her mouth and sucked on them. "It doesn't come off."

"Don't worry," said Kimana. "Most will wash off, but you'll be colored for days."

Mei Lin straightened, flexed her back, and saw two riders approaching at a walk on the road. She glanced at Chica and Kimana who watched the riders.

The two cowboys pulled up alongside the women. They grinned. "What have we here," one said. "Three purty wimmen all by theirselves picking berries."

Chica smiled. Mei Lin and Kimana did not. They stared at the men.

"My, my," said the other rider, "I never saw such a bunch of purty little pussies in one place all by theirselves in a long, long time."

Mei Lin rolled her eyes back. She put a hand in her jacket pocket, glanced at Kimana, then looked back at the cowboys to see the near one starting to dismount.

The cowboy froze, his leg still in the air above his horse's back, when he saw the .32 that Mei Lin pointed at his face. He looked at Kimana to see the skinning knife that she held at her side.

"I whistle real loud," said Chica. "If I whistle, our husbands will ride out of that bunch of trees over there," she pointed, "and be here in a jiffy. Our husbands are real mean when they're riled up."

The cowboy threw his leg back over the saddle and settled down. He looked at his pard. They looked around nervously.

"Uh, is this the road to Jackson?" the cowboy said.

"It is," said Mei Lin. "Just keep riding the way you're headed. You'll like Jackson." She kept the pistol leveled on him.

The cowboy touched his hat. "Thank you, ma'am. We're on our way." They kicked their horses into a gallop.

Mei Lin returned the pistol to her pocket. Kimana pushed the knife into the scabbard in her boot. The three women watched the riders until they disappeared around a copse. They looked at each other, smiled and burst into laughter.

"Our husbands are in that bunch of trees?" said Mei Lin. "Where did you get that?" She laughed. "Does Ray even know where you are?"

"I told him I was going to your place to visit," said Chica.

"That's what I told Will!" Kimana said. They laughed again.

"I didn't know you had the knife, Kimana," said Mei Lin.

"I always carry it. Grandfather gave it to me. It was Grandmother's skinning knife. I have used it to skin elk and deer, but I have never skinned a cowboy." Mei Lin and Chica chuckled.

"I guess we better get back to my house," said Mei Lin. "They might make up a posse to come looking for us. And our husbands are real mean when they're all riled up." They doubled over laughing.

Caleb and Mei Lin tied the reins of their horses at the rail outside the feed store. They stepped up on the sidewalk. Caleb opened the door to the store.

"I'm going to see Priscilla," said Mei Lin. Caleb waved over his shoulder and went inside. Mei Lin continued down the walk toward Folie's, stopped when she saw two women walking on the sidewalk across the street. She stood a moment, watching, then crossed the street and hurried to catch up with the women.

Caleb came out of the feed store, slammed the door shut and strode across the street to the sheriff's office. He knocked on the door and pushed it open without waiting for an answer. Canlis looked up from a folder of papers. He laid the pen down.

"Scott, I'm glad to find you here. Can I have a minute?"

Canlis nodded.

"What's this about a body that was found south of town?"

"Yes, we did find a body south of town."

"Somebody said it could be Jedediah Adams," said Caleb.

"Sit down, Caleb." Canlis gestured to a chair, and Caleb sat. "It was Jedediah Adams. He was a homesteader you bought out, wasn't he?"

"Yeah. Well, I bought his relinquishment at the land office. Where'd they find him?"

"There's a shallow cut down there, about two miles south, well off the road. The cut's hidden by a bunch of sagebrush. That's why the body wasn't found for a while. Already starting to decompose when a couple of boys found it when they was looking for a loose horse.

"I went out when they told me about it. It was a miserable sort of camp. Little hut made out of canvas and boards he had scavenged from a wagon behind the camp. One dirty old blanket in the hut was the only evidence of a bed. There was no mules or horses around. Guess he sold 'em or ate 'em, though I didn't find any animal bones around. Bits and pieces of all sorts of junk was all around the camp."

"How did he die?" said Caleb.

"Like I said, the body had begun to decompose and stunk something awful. The doc said it looked like he had starved to death."

Caleb recoiled as if he had been struck in the face.

"Seems he had done some odd jobs around town for a while," said Canlis, "but never lasted more'n a few days. He was seen from time to time scrounging in garbage cans and begging from people. Don't see much of that in Jackson. Some people was angry, but some felt guilty somehow, like they should've been doing something for him."

Caleb stared through the window.

"I killed him, Mei Lin. I killed him just as sure as if I put a gun to his head and pulled the trigger."

"No, you didn't. You could have killed him at his house, but you didn't. You told him he had to leave because of what he had done to me. You fixed his wound, and you gave him money. Whatever happened to him after that was because of who he was, not what you had done to him."

"What a sorry way to die," Caleb said. "The poor man needed help. He didn't need to starve. I didn't even know he was there. I told him he better stay out of my way. I told him that I didn't ever want to see him again. I wonder how many times he saw me in Jackson and ran. God, Mei Lin." He slumped, shook his head.

She put an arm around his shoulders and laid her head on his back. "It's not your fault, honey. It just happened. Bad things happen. We don't like it when bad things happen. Sometimes we can do something about it. Sometimes we can't."

Caleb and Ray rode their horses slowly through a scattering of grazing cattle.

"We're in good shape," said Ray, "best we've been since I got here. Grass is good, and they're putting on pounds. Last bunch I run up to the agent brought the best price yet. He was real pleased."

"If he was pleased, I'm pleased. You've done a fine job with the place, Ray. Don't know what I would have done without you. And Mei Lin! I don't what she would have done without Chica. She's had some bad times since we've been here. Chica has been a tonic.

"Did she tell you about the berry-picking set-to?" Caleb said.

Ray laughed. "Oh, yeah. I laugh every time I think

about those two poor cowboys, coming up against them three women. And you know what? Now, Chica wants a gun. Just like Mei Lin's."

"Maybe you should get her one. Mei Lin's little .32 has been pretty useful for her."

"Yeah, so I hear. But what if she had killed somebody with it? Would that give you and her something to think about?" said Ray.

"If she had shot somebody, he would have had it coming."

"Even so, would it still bother you and her?"

"When I think about what could have happened if she hadn't had it on the couple of occasions, she used it, that would bother me a lot more."

"Yeah, you're probably right." Ray paused. "Hell, Caleb, I don't own a pistol myself, only the Winchester I use for hunting. I don't know whether I could even use that on a man. Unless he was going to hurt Chica."

"That's what I'm talking about," said Caleb. "We do what we have to do."

Ray looked at the Tetons, back to Caleb. "Yeah, I guess there are still some sonsabitches around that we could do without." He looked back at the mountains. "I remember back when the new century opened, they said that everything was going to change, everything was going to get better. Horses would give way to automobiles, yelling would give way to the telephone, and guns would give way to, I don't know, reason?"

Caleb frowned, looked hard at Ray, smiled. "By god, Ray, you're a philosopher. I don't know about things getting better in the new century. Sometimes things seem to change, but then if you look closely, they turn out to be the same."

Riding toward the house, Caleb saw his two mules in the pasture behind the barn. The more vocal of the two greeted him as usual with a whinny that became a bray and ended in what sounded like a rolling belly laugh. Then he saw two mules inside the corral.

He pulled up and stared at the two strange mules. He looked at the barn. The double doors of the barn were closed. Normally they were tied open, day and night.

What's going on here?

He looked around. Nothing else seemed to be amiss, but he wished he had his six-shooter. Dismounting slowly, he looked over the yard again and beyond to the meadow. He tied Buck's reins to a corral pole and walked slowly to the house.

He opened the front door and shouted. "Mei Lin?"

He heard the sound of a chair sliding on the floor, and she walked from the kitchen to the hall.

"Everything okay?" he said.

"Yes, come in here." She led the way to the kitchen. Caleb stopped. There sat Hiram, Naomi and Miriam.

"Hiram!" said Caleb. "Good to see you. Naomi. Miriam." They smiled. Caleb did not.

"Sit down, honey," said Mei Lin. "We will explain."

14

Caleb pulled a chair from the parlor to the kitchen table beside Mei Lin's chair. Hiram, Naomi and Miriam sat opposite. Mei Lin poured a cup of coffee for Caleb, re-filled the cups of the others and sat down. Caleb sipped his coffee, set it down and waited.

"When we heard the rumor about somebody in the Hole practicing plural marriage, we knew our secret was out," said Hiram. "Some of our friends knew about us, and they wouldn't give us away. But some others, Mormons, mind you, don't agree with the practice and might tell.

"You see, United States law has outlawed plural mar-riage, and church leaders have given in to the pressure and abandoned it. But some of us don't agree with the church leaders. We believe the practice is God's will, and we wish to continue. That's no longer possible here, in the Hole.

"Sheriff Canlis is a friend and a good man, and he would not wish to harm us. I think he has known about us a long time, but now with so many people hearing the rumor, he has to take an interest. He will have no choice if we are found out. He will have to come after us."

"Caleb, I talked with Naomi and Miriam in Jackson,"

said Mei Lin, "and I said I would help. I didn't know they had decided to leave until they arrived in their wagon this morning when you were away. The wagon is in the barn. It's loaded with as much as they could pack in."

"We don't want to cause you any trouble," said Naomi. "Mei Lin was so understanding, we hoped you could see us on our way. We thought about asking help from neighbors, Mormon neighbors, but the brethren are not talking much now about plural marriage. There's so much controversy, they are fearful, and we don't know for sure how each of our neighbors feels about it. We don't know who we can trust."

"What about your house and your things?" Mei Lin said.

"Some of my brother's family will live in our house," said Hiram. "They will tell anyone who asks that we are visiting relatives in Utah. When everything has quieted down, they will sell the house and the furniture for us."

"Where will you go?" said Caleb.

"We thought of going to Canada," Hiram said. "The brethren are not bothered there. But we would not know anyone. We decided to move somewhere else. There are still some small towns where we are going where plural families live in peace. The local authorities know about them, but choose not to take notice. They seem to be safe as long as nobody outside the community talks about them. We have kin-folk who will help us get settled. I won't tell you where we're going so you won't have to lie in case someone questions you."

"Do you have enough food to take you where you are going?" said Mei Lin.

"We have a good supply, and we will buy anything we need on the way," Hiram said.

"Well, I wish you good fortune, wherever you go," said Caleb. "Have you had supper?"

"We had a good meal before coming here. Now, we will go to the pallet that your good wife has made for us. We'll leave tomorrow before first light. We expect to pass Jackson in darkness and be well on our way before sunrise."

All stood, and Hiram, Naomi and Miriam walked toward the spare bedroom. Naomi and Miriam each smiled, took Mei Lin's hand and gently squeezed it. When they had entered the bedroom, the door closed.

Mei Lin turned to Caleb. "Did I do right?" she said. "They are breaking the law."

Caleb took her cheeks in his hands, kissed her. "You are a good woman, Lee Mei Lin Willis. We'll let them go in peace. They're hurting no one. Except maybe themselves."

The sheriff sat at the kitchen table opposite Caleb. Mei Lin refilled the coffee cups, replaced the percolator on the stove and sat in the chair beside Caleb.

Canlis spooned the last bite of cobbler in his mouth, closed his eyes and smiled, still holding the spoon. He laid the spoon in the bowl and pushed the bowl away a few inches.

"Thanks for telephoning, Scott," said Caleb. "Gave me time to finish up in the barn and wash up."

"Sorry I couldn't get here before noon, but I was busy with ... well, something. Thing is, Buddy, the farrier from the livery, you may know him, he was riding down from the Row yesterday, and he said he rode for some time behind the Barkers who turned off the road in the direction of your place. Now, why did he tell me this? Because I asked him if he saw a loaded wagon leaving the Row yesterday."

Mei Lin and Caleb looked blankly at him.

"Did you happen to see the Barkers yesterday?" Canlis said.

"They did stop by," said Mei Lin. "We invited them in for coffee. We like them. They are good people, good friends. I understand they are friends of yours too."

Canlis wrinkled his forehead, twisted his cup on the table. "Yes, they are." Canlis looked at Caleb, then back to Mei Lin. "Did they have anything to say?"

"Why, yes," Mei Lin said, "Hiram asked if our irrigation canals were working okay. He helped Caleb build the canals."

Canlis waited for more, but Mei Lin just smiled and sipped her coffee. "I don't suppose they said where they were going," he said.

"No, they didn't," said Mei Lin. "Sorry."

"Hmm." Canlis pushed his chair back and stood. "Well, I'd best be on my way. Lots to do at the office. Caleb." He extended his hand, and they shook. "Miss Mei Lin. Thanks for the conversation, and thanks for the cobbler. My, that's some cobbler."

Canlis walked into the hall, retrieved his hat from the peg and went outside. Caleb and Mei Lin followed him to the porch. Canlis turned around.

"Thank you for all the information. The matter at hand is closed."

The slightest hint of a smile played about his lips. He put on his hat, pulled it down, walked to his horse. He mounted, waved, and set out at a lope toward town.

Caleb and Ray sat their horses in a pasture of scattered grazing cattle.

"He didn't give me an exact number," said Ray, "but I figure he'll take twenty-five head. I'll get the boys to put 'em together this afternoon. We'll get on the road first thing tomorrow."

Since reaching an agreement with the buyer up near

Kelly, Caleb had had no trouble marketing his steers. The buyer was happy to find a reliable beef supply for his business with the dude ranches and hotels in the valley and in Yellowstone.

Caleb stared at the horizon where the sun had just cleared the range that formed the eastern edge of the valley. "Sounds good," he said, without looking at Ray. "I'll leave you to it."

Ray turned in his saddle and followed his gaze.

"I'll never get used to it," said Caleb. "Not if I live here a hundred years. It's some pretty country. If there's a God that made it, this is where he lives."

Ray waited. He shifted in his saddle.

After another long minute, Caleb shook his head. "C'mon to the house. We're finished here. We'll get Mei Lin to make us some coffee." They kicked their horses into a lope.

Caleb and Ray tied their horses' reins to the rail in front of the house. They walked toward the porch. They stopped and looked at each other. Shouts and laughter were coming from somewhere in the house.

"One of 'em's Chica," said Ray. "Funny. I left her at the house."

"Mei Lin's in there, for sure," Caleb said. "Sounds like more than two though. More like a half dozen."

They walked up on the porch and into the house. Hanging jackets on wall pegs, they glanced at each other as the buzz of excited conversation increased in the kitchen.

"I don't think they even heard us come in," said Caleb.

"That you, honey?" said Mei Lin. Caleb and Ray walked into the kitchen. There sat Mei Lin, Chica and Kimana. They were all smiles, holding coffee cups on the table.

"Coffee?" said Caleb. "I suspected you were drinking

whiskey. What are you three up to?"

They looked at each other, giggled.

"You still have any coffee in that pot?" Caleb said.

"Sit down," said Mei Lin, "I'll get it." Caleb went to the sitting room and brought a chair to the kitchen. Mei Lin took two cups from the cupboard and filled them from the percolator. She set the cups before Ray and Caleb, then pulled her chair around and sat between Kimana and Chica.

Ray and Caleb sipped the hot coffee. "Now. What's going on?" said Caleb. "Something's going on besides coffee."

Kimana and Chica looked at Mei Lin. "I have been talking with Mrs. Hendricks," Mei Lin said. "She said that even though Jackson is not an official town, not incorporated, it should get ready for when it is a town. She said the rumor is that it will be incorporated soon, probably in a year or two. She said that some people in Jackson think that a town government should be set up now so it will be going when the town is official. She thinks this should be done as part of the election this year."

"Sounds reasonable," Caleb said. "I've heard the rumor too. Word is that we might be incorporated next year, certainly by 1914. What's with this new interest in town government?"

The three women smiled. "We are going to register to vote!" said Mei Lin. She lifted her chin. "And ... we're going to look into running for the town council. That's what Mrs. Hendricks called it."

Ray and Caleb laughed, then sobered quickly when they saw the reaction from the women. They were not smiling. Chica and Kimana looked at each other, embarrassed. Mei Lin glared at Caleb.

"You think that's funny?" said Mei Lin.

"No, sweetheart," said Caleb, "it's not funny ... actually. Voting is one thing, but... women running for political office?"

"Mrs. Hendricks said that women vote all over the state, and women have been holding office all over. She said that less than 250 people in Jackson can vote, and most of them are women. She said that most women don't usually vote, but if a woman was running for office, maybe they would."

"Got a point there, Caleb," Ray said.

Caleb leaned back in his chair. "If you were to run for office, Lee Mei Lin Willis, what is your platform?"

"My what?"

"What would you want to do if you were elected to the town council? What would you do for the town and its citizens?"

"Don't make fun of me, Caleb Willis, or you'll get no supper," Mei Lin said.

"I'm not making fun," Caleb said. "I'm serious. You'll have to tell the voters what you would do for the town."

She frowned, looked at her hands on her cup. She looked up at Caleb. "All right. First, I would tell the voters that we need a clinic. Dr. Sims heard Mrs. Hendricks was talking about a town government, and he came to talk to her when we were with her. He said we need a clinic that would provide services that he can't offer by himself. He thinks the hotels and dude ranches would like to tell their guests that Jackson has a clinic that will take care of them if they are sick or injured. And I would tell the voters that we need to improve the school building and pay the teachers more and—"

"I'm for all that, Mei Lin," said Ray. "I'll vote for you."

Caleb laughed. Ray did not. Nor did the three women

who glared at him. Ray grinned.

"Sorry, Mei Lin, I thought all this was in fun," said Caleb. "When we came up, you three were laughing your heads off. I thought it was a lark. But I see you're dead serious. So I will be too. I'll vote for you and work for you to get you elected. If that's what you decide to do. You would do a good job. We have too many deadbeats in political office." He smiled at her. She nodded, smiled.

"There's just one question I have," he said.

"What's that?"

"If you get elected, will you still fix supper?"

"Yes, honey, I'll still fix supper, and breakfast and lunch." She stood, kissed him on the cheek, turned to Chica and Kimana. "Let's go out on the porch and let these two voters have their coffee."

Mei Lin, Chica and Kimana, accompanied by their husbands and Mrs. Hendricks, appeared before the circuit Judge in Sheriff Canlis's office one September morning and registered to vote.

When it was finished, the husbands congratulated their wives. Mrs. Hendricks beamed during the signing in and told anyone who would listen that she was responsible for their becoming involved in the political arena.

The three new voters accepted the good wishes of their husbands and suggested that the men go to Folie's or a restaurant or anywhere for an hour or so. The women had business to conduct at Mrs. Hendricks' place.

The four women left the sheriff's office and marched across the street toward the feed store. The husbands watched from the sidewalk. The sheriff chuckled, went back into his office and closed the door. The three husbands decided that they would toast the expansion of the electorate at Lloyd and Tuttle's.

"What went on at the feed store?" said Caleb.

Mei Lin and Caleb had said their goodbyes to their friends at Lloyd and Tuttle's and the feed store and now rode at a walk toward home.

"Honey! At the back of the feed store, there is a gathering place like the stove at Folie's. There's a cushioned bench built in under the two windows. In front of the bench, there's a round table and three chairs at the table.

"It's where friends of Mrs. Hendricks— Marjorie, she told me to call her 'Marjorie,'—it's where she and her friends meet and talk. Two of her friends were sitting there when we came in. When we were seated, she introduced us to them. Then she made tea in the back room.

"While she was making tea, we talked with the two women. One is named Ann. The other is named Polly! I almost laughed. I hope she didn't notice. They're nice. Ann is a schoolteacher. Polly's husband works in the feed store and livery.

"Polly!" Mei Lin giggled. "I wonder whether she knows that most whores and madams are called 'Polly.' I'll never tell her. I bet her husband knows.

"Mrs. Hendricks, Marjorie, came in and poured the tea and sat down. We had a lot of good talk. It was exciting. Here's what we decided. We're going to try to get on the ballot as a team. We'll run for Mayor and three councilmen. Councilwomen? Marjorie will run for Mayor, and for the three council members, Ann and Polly ... and me! Can you imagine? Me! A Chink whore on a town council!"

"Stop it," said Caleb. He smiled, in spite of the admonition. "You're a United States citizen. You're already a better citizen than most Americans who were born in this country."

"Thank you, honey. Chica and Kimana said they would

help in the election, but they said they didn't want to run for any office, so that worked out fine."

"How did you come up with the mayor and three-person council idea?" said Caleb.

"Marjorie talked with Sheriff Canlis about it. He described the city government at Kemmerer, he said that's the county seat, and said it would probably be the same when Jackson is incorporated."

They rode in silence. Mei Lin looked at him. "What do you think?" she said.

He turned to her. "Citizen Lee Mei Lin Willis, you're a wonder. You've come a long way. I'm proud of you. You're a citizen. You're a voter. You're going to run for a political office. And you're going to win. You have everything you have wanted."

She looked down at Chica's mane. "Not yet, honey."

"Mei Lin?"

"I want a baby. Then I'll have everything."

Caleb closed the corral gate, and they walked toward the house. Mei Lin took his arm, held him close. He looked down at her. He saw a single tear roll down her cheek.

He stopped. "What's the matter, sweetheart?"

She wiped the tear with a hand. "I'm just so happy. I didn't tell you what happened at the feed store." She pulled his arm. "Let's get coffee, and I'll tell you."

They walked inside, and Caleb sat at the kitchen table. He leaned back in his chair, exhaled heavily and watched. This was his favorite place and his favorite moment, what he looked forward to more than anything else. Watching Mei Lin make coffee had a strangely calming effect on him. Watching her make coffee, his mind cleared, and he was content.

When she was finished, she poured coffee into two

mugs, brought them to the table and sat down.

She sipped her coffee. "After Marjorie told us about her plans for the election, she showed us the paper she had drawn up that she wanted to show Scott. She said she wanted each of us to read it carefully and then sign at the bottom if we agreed with everything in the paper. Each of the others read it and signed. When it came to me, I looked at it a long time. I looked up, and the others were watching me. I didn't know what to do. I was very nervous, and they knew.

"Ann took my hand. She said, 'you can't read, can you?' I was so . . . so ... what do you say, embarrassed. I cried. She put her arms around me and told me not to worry. She said I was a smart young woman, and she would teach me. She said I would learn very fast. I couldn't stop crying. Why are some people so bad, and some people so good?" The tears came, and she wiped her eyes with both hands.

"I'm not sure I can answer that, but you're such a good person, Lee Mei Lin Willis, that good people will always be attracted to you."

A gathering of thirty or forty people, men and women and a scattering of children holding their parents' hands, stood before a small outdoor podium set up in the square in front of the Clubhouse. Mrs. Hendricks spoke to the assemblage about the approaching incorporation of the town and the need for a government to be in place before that event.

Ann, Polly and Mei Lin stood immediately behind Mrs. Hendricks. Behind them, Kimana and Chica stood, looking around furtively, apparently wishing they were somewhere else than under the gaze of the largest collection of people they had ever seen in one place.

Caleb stood at the back of the spectators. He paid close

attention and was alternately amused and proud. Amused at the speech and affectations of Mrs. Hendricks, proud of Mei Lin, Chica and Kimana.

A man sidled up beside Caleb. Caleb glanced at the man and was repelled by the whiskey stench.

The man leaned toward Caleb. "Would you look at that? Never seen nothing like it. Women running for office. What's the world coming to? And foreigners at that! I've seen the white women in town before, but not the others. Sure never seen the foreigners. What th' hell they doing up there?"

Caleb took a step away from the man. He looked back to the podium. "Actually," Caleb said, "they're not foreigners at all. Everybody on that podium is an American citizen.

"The Indian woman, wearing the brown dress, her ancestors were in this country before yours got off the boat. The Mexican woman in the green shirt, her people were in the country long before your people stepped ashore. The Chinese woman," Caleb turned to the man and leaned into his face, "is my wife."

The man pulled back. "Oh ... uh ... learn something ever day, don't we? Uh, good t' hear. Hmm." He took a couple of steps back, turned and weaved down the middle of the street. Undoubtedly back to Lloyd and Tuttle's, Caleb thought.

Caleb turned his attention back to the rally at hand. Mrs. Hendricks was speaking with fervor about the medical clinic that she wished to see built for the betterment of Jackson residents and visiting tourists.

This sounds familiar. He looked at Mei Lin. She was looking directly at him. She smiled.

15

The all-female ticket was elected. They received 210 of the 235 ballots cast in the 1912 election. That they had no serious opposition undoubtedly contributed to their success. The all-male opposing ticket was put together only days before the deadline for filing, and the candidates spoke at only one public forum. And rumor said that they voted for their opponents.

The four women were delighted that they were elected on the same ballot that sent Woodrow Wilson to the White House.

Mrs. Hendricks was elected mayor, and Mei Lin, Ann and Polly were elected to the council. In response to Mrs. Hendricks's questions, the county had already explained that any deliberations or decisions by the elected officers would be advisory only since they had no real power. Nor would they receive resources to finance their activities.

They would in fact be playing at governing until Jackson was incorporated as a town. This was satisfactory to the elected non-officials. In an unguarded moment, Mrs. Hendricks admitted to being terrified at the prospect of having any real power to make binding decisions.

Caleb and Mei Lin pulled up before Jimmy Hendricks Feeds. Caleb waved to Sheriff Canlis who stood on the sidewalk watching them. Canlis waved, removed the cold cigar from his mouth and tossed it to the street. Caleb and Mei Lin dismounted and tied their reins to the rail.

"Scott," said Caleb. "How are you this fine day?"

"Still vertical," said Canlis. He touched his hat to Mei Lin. "Miss Mei Lin." She smiled.

"I'll be with Marjorie," said Mei Lin to Caleb. "Come get me when you are ready to go."

"Okay." He turned to Canlis. "The ladies have a council meeting." Mei Lin smiled and walked to the door of the feed store.

"What are you up to, sheriff?" Caleb said.

"Jimmy told me you were coming in," Canlis said. "Come over to the office. Want you to meet someone." They walked across the street and down the walk to the sheriff's office. Canlis opened the door and went in. Caleb followed.

A smiling young man, about thirty, sat behind the sheriffs desk, pen poised above paper. He laid the pen down and stood. Caleb saw the star pinned to his shirt. Caleb turned to Scott, frowned.

"Caleb, this is Nathan Eldridge. My replacement. He's taking over here."

"What! Your replacement?" said Caleb, open-mouthed.

Eldridge smiled, extended his hand, and Caleb shook, still frowning.

"Yep. I told the county that I was packing it in, and they sent Nathan up to get checked out. He's staying at the Busy B's for now. I told him not to get used to Berta's cooking or Bennie's rants."

"Nice to meet you, Nathan," said Caleb. He turned to

Scott. "What th' hell—"

Canlis held up a hand, palm outward to Caleb, turned to Eldridge. "Nathan, you are in charge the rest of the day. Is that okay?"

"Sure, Scott. I got it," said Eldridge.

"Thanks for that," said Canlis, "just didn't think I should be leaning on the bar at Lloyd and Tuttle's while I was on duty. I need some refreshment." He beckoned to Caleb. "C'mon, Caleb. I'll buy you one."

They walked toward the door. Canlis stopped, turned back. "Nathan, if the prettiest woman in western Wyoming comes in looking for Caleb, tell her we're in the waterin' hole." Eldridge smiled and raised a hand. Canlis and Caleb walked outside, and Canlis closed the door.

"What's going on, Scott. You hadn't said anything about retiring."

"Let's get a whiskey, and we'll talk."

They strolled down the sidewalk to Lloyd and Tuttle's. Canlis held the door of the saloon open for Caleb. They went in and walked to the bar. The bartender came over, bottle in hand.

"Two whiskeys, Monty," said Canlis. The bartender reached to the counter behind him, fetched a bottle and poured.

The saloon was quiet. It was empty but for two men, dressed as merchants or dudes or Sunday School teachers, who sat at a table in the far corner, talking softly. The sun, low in the sky, sent columns of light through the west-facing windows that described rectangles on the floor.

Canlis sipped his whiskey. Caleb took a swallow. Waited.

Canlis sipped again, set his glass gently on the polished bar top, stared into his glass. "Doc Sims told me I had to change my habits, or I'm going to kick the bucket. He said it was a heart condition. He described it, but it's over my head. Said he could send me to Denver where they might be able to help me, or they might not. Anyway, to hell with that. I don't think I could see the Tetons from Denver.

"I don't mind. Not really. It's time, I suppose." He turned to look at Caleb, smiled. "I'd rather sit with the geezers at Folie's than lay in a hospital bed in Denver." He looked into his whiskey glass, swirled it, took a swallow. "If the old boys will have me."

"So you're not leaving Jackson?"

"Naw, Caleb, this is home. Since I lost Vera these five years ago, I been rattling around in that old farmhouse. I've thought from time to time about moving where I have kinfolk. I have a cousin at Sweetwater in West Texas and another outside Amarillo. Both of 'em have said they would like to have me nearby, but moving back to Texas would be like moving to the moon. Too far away and too strange now."

They sipped their whiskeys, studied the rows of bottles behind the bar, above the bottles the large print of the chubby reclining naked woman with a hand over her most private part, the bartender sitting on his stool at the other end of the bar.

Canlis held up his whiskey, swished the amber liquid. "The other day, I was eating dinner at the hotel, and next to me was a couple of dudes, all dressed up in their new cowboy clothes. The woman says, 'I do so love the Old West. We were born fifty years too late, Arthur.' Or something like that.

"The Old West." He stared into his glass, swirled the whiskey, tipped the glass up and emptied it. "Monty!" he called to the bartender, held the glass up. The bartender shuffled over, refilled Canlis' glass. He offered the bottle to Caleb who shook his head. Monty returned the bottle to the counter and went back to his stool.

Canlis peered into his glass, frowning, as if expecting to see something more than whiskey. He raised the glass and sipped. "The Old West. I seen it all, Caleb."

Canlis turned to Caleb. "Did you know I was from Texas?" Caleb shook his head. "My daddy was a cowboy on a ranch near Fort Worth. He joined the army when the war broke out in '46. I was just one year old. He was killed in Mexico. I never knew him."

Caleb watched him. *Is this what happens when you decide to retire? You look into the deepest recesses of your soul? And you talk. Is this a lament for a wasted life or a celebration of a life well lived? Scott, what is it?* He waited.

"Comanches took my mama at our place near Fort Worth when I was ten. I never saw her again. But I remembered her, and I missed her terribly." He looked at the ceiling, closed his eyes, squeezed them tight, opened his eyes, looked at his glass and sipped his whiskey.

He tipped the glass up and swallowed, set the glass on the counter, gripping it tightly with both hands. "I lived with my mother's sister till I was fifteen when I became a cowboy myself. Outfit I was with caught wild longhorns in north Texas and sold 'em to ranchers to stock their spreads. Them longhorns was somethin'.

"Well, we heard stories about how much a longhorn was worth up north, and we got the bug. I was on one of the first drives from Texas to Montana." He looked sideways at Caleb. "Yeah! Would you believe that?

"That was something I'll never forget. Caleb, I saw stampedes, thunder and rainstorms, paid off some Indians in what's now Oklahoma with a few cows. I almost drowned crossing the Red. I woulda drowned if I hadn't grabbed my horse's tail, and he pulled me across.

"Damn." He emptied his glass, called to Monty for a refill. The bartender sauntered over, refilled the glass. He pointed the bottle at Caleb who held up his hand, palm outward.

Canlis took a good swallow from his glass. "I saw buffalo. Wild buffalo." He shook his head. "Old West. Damn. I saw people die, Caleb. Good boys. Saw one git run over in a stampede. Saw one got hit by lightning when he was trying to keep the herd together one night in a hard rain. I saw my pard get shot by a drunk cowboy from another outfit for nothing more than a joke that the cowboy took the wrong way."

Canlis stared at the wall above the rows of bottles. "I saw lots of pretty country. Plains and mountains and prairies and wildflowers and ..." He lowered his head, squeezed his eyes shut, swallowed a sob.

He took a deep breath, raised his glass and emptied it. "The Old West. It's gone, Caleb. It was hard times, but it was grand, and I seen it all. What we got now is this new West. The new West, it does show some promise." He looked into his empty glass.

"Yeah. I helped build it, the Old West, and it was grand." He looked up a long moment, as if searching for something on the ceiling, but his eyes were closed. He opened his eyes and looked sideways at Caleb. "But, damn, wouldn't it be fun to tear it all down and start all over again?" He smiled, a guarded, sad smile.

The saloon was quiet. The two men who had sat at the table in the corner were gone. Monty sat on his stool, staring at the windows on the wall opposite. The sun had set, and the buildings that could be seen through the windows were in shadow, the mountains a dark mass.

Caleb emptied his glass. "If the new West shows promise, Scott, you had a lot to do with it. I'm sorry to hear about the heart problem, but I'm right glad you're staying on, as long as that's what you want to do. I'm sure the old boys at Folie's will welcome you to the circle. They wouldn't admit it, but they can use some fresh blood to help solve world problems."

Scott looked around the room, called to the bartender. "Monty, where are all your customers? I never saw this place empty this time of day."

"Don't know," said Monty. "People seem to be spending more time in cafes these days. And there's something doing at the Clubhouse. Did you know they're showing movie pictures up there now? Seems people don't have as much use for a saloon as they used to."

"Be damned," Canlis said. "Got a newspaper last year and movie pictures this year. What's next?" He pushed his empty glass across the bar top, stood awkwardly and stretched. He walked toward the door, waved without looking back. Caleb followed him outside and closed the door.

"Caleb, don't pass on nothin' I said in there. I'm drunk and nothin' I said bears repeatin.'"

Caleb laid his hand on Canlis's shoulder. "What you said in there is the most rational talk I've heard in some time, Scott. You're a philosopher and a poet."

Canlis turned to him, his eyes crinkled, smiled, an imitation of a smile.

Caleb looked down the street. Shadows of buildings extended across the street to the sidewalk opposite. "I guess the council is still in session, or Mei Lin would have come looking for me. I'd best rescue her from Mrs. Hendricks." He turned to the sheriff. "Scott, if your duties are going to taper off, come out soon for a social visit. Give us a call ahead so Mei Lin can do some cooking."

"I'll do that for sure," said Canlis. He coughed, thumped his chest lightly with a fist.

"Okay?" said Caleb.

"Okay." Canlis put on his hat. "Say goodbye to the missus for me." He clapped Caleb on the back and walked around the corner of the saloon toward the livery where he kept his horse during the day. He weaved unsteadily, put out a hand to a wall to steady himself.

Caleb watched him go. He wondered whether he should give him a hand. No, Scott wouldn't want that. He smiled. He doubted Scott would even remember this conversation when he had revealed more about himself than he ever would have sober. Caleb was glad it was only a short ride for Scott from the livery to his house just outside town.

He never made it to the house. He was found the next morning by the hired hand that came each day. The sheriff had dismounted at his corral and collapsed at the gate. His horse, reins trailing, was still standing beside the body when the cowboy found him.

Caleb and Mei Lin sat at the table in their kitchen, holding coffee cups on the table. The evening sun cast twin shafts of light on the floor and their legs. On Caleb's ride from town, a few errant snowflakes had fallen from a low cloud and swirled about his head. Since arriving home, the cloud had thinned and lifted.

"Doc Sims said it was a massive heart attack," Caleb said. "He said he had told Scott to cut back on his drinking. Scott tied one on yesterday, and I just watched him."

"You didn't know," said Mei Lin, "and that's the end of it. Why do you always try to blame yourself for something that happens to somebody else? It's not your fault."

"Yeah, I suppose." He looked through the windows at

the mountains, clear now after the earlier overcast. "I think he knew. I think he was saying goodbye. To us, and to his own self, the life he had lived." He leaned back and sighed deeply. "He was a good man."

"What happens now?"

"That's what Doc Sims and the new deputy, Eldridge, and I talked about. Scott had no kin hereabouts, and nobody can find a will. I told him about the Texas kin-folk Scott mentioned, but they weren't able to find any addresses in his things."

That morning, Caleb had put together a group of half a dozen citizens, including Mayor Hendricks and the new deputy to help with the funeral and decide what to do with Canlis' possessions. They decided that if they couldn't locate the Texas kin, the house and furnish-ings would be sold and the proceeds used to finance the work of the town council, particularly to advance the plans for a medical clinic and increasing the salaries of teachers. It was assumed the funds would last until the incorporation of the town.

The sheriff was buried at the small Jackson cemetery. Most of the town's population and many from throughout the Hole were there to witness the interment. A Mormon layman said a few words about Canlis' devotion to doing what was right as decreed by the law and his conscience. Philo and John added that they were grieved to be deprived of his wit and wisdom.

Caleb talked about what the sheriff had said that last evening in the saloon. About his experiences in what he called the Old West, and the promise he saw in a new West. Doc Sims said that the sheriff was perhaps unknowingly passing the torch to a new generation.

Mei Lin and Caleb stood on their front porch, watching

the sun turn from bright golden to molten gold with a red cast as it dropped into a saddle in the Teton range. The field before them wore a light dusting of new snow.

He laid his arm on her shoulders and pulled her close. She put an arm around his waist.

"That was very sad and very touching," said Mei Lin. "I don't like funerals. But I like what everybody said. Especially what you said about a New West. We have the New West right here, don't we? We've got a new ranch, we have all our good friends, and we have a new town coming. And we have a telephone and a new hay baler!" She laughed.

He looked down at her, smiled. "Yeah, we have all those things," he said.

"I also liked what Doctor Sims said about a new generation in this New West." She leaned back and looked up at him. A hint of a smile played about her lips. "Did you like what he said?"

"Yes, that was—" He looked sharply at her. "Are you trying to tell me something?

She grinned, put her other arm around his waist and squeezed with both arms.

"You're pregnant! Are you?"

"Yes! That's what Doctor Sims said. I went to see him after the funeral when you went with the deputy to the sheriff's office. Doctor Sims said I was over three months."

He took her face in both hands, kissed her lightly on her lips. "A New West and a new century and a new baby."

"Now I will have everything," said Mei Lin. "I am home."

AFTERWORD AND ACKNOWLEDGEMENTS

If I were to list all of the people who assisted in the writing of this narrative, the dozens who offered snippets of information, suggestions, musings, advice, criticism and glasses of wine, the list would be very long. So I will simply thank them and hope they find that I have distilled their data satisfactorily.

I thank the Pacific Critique Group for their careful reading of the narrative and for their comments, corrections and inspiration, namely Betsy Keithcart, Judy Pierce, Jennifer Hoffman, Marilyn Erickson, Pamela Pan, Lorraine Ramsey, Leslie Liberty, Mary Ellen Dempsey, Jan Alexander, Jennifer Grainger, and Daniel Hobbs. Thanks particularly to Jennifer Hoffman for her help with content and formatting.

I am grateful to Candy Moulton for answering questions about Jackson Hole, the town of Jackson and early settlers.

It's the fortunate writer who has friends who are authorities on specific topics. Thanks to John Horst for putting the right guns in the hands of my characters. Chris Enss advised on what clothing my women would be wearing and what they would not be wearing. No ready-made dresses for expectant mothers in 1912.

Dave Clark, MD, described certain medical symptoms and conditions so I could afflict my characters accurately. Steve Turner, MD, did likewise and also provided the details of a shaman's healing ceremony.

IF YOU LIKED THIS, YOU MIGHT LIKE: COFFIN JACK: A WESTERN DUO

ONE-EYED COFFIN JACK IS A DEADLY MAN.

Coffin Jack is a dark souled assassin that does not possess much; he lives alone with only feral cats for company in his isolated shack in the mountains and barely ventures down to civilization except when he gets the call.

Joined by his now partner, Lowell Devereux – a naïve reporter who was unceremoniously thrown into the path of Coffin Jack while seeking uplifting stories to inspire the readers back east – the two are out prove all that they are capable of. Their wild journey takes them across country to confront a series of deadly challenges and plunge into an esoteric nightmare that transforms the pair. From there they are taken on a trail through the darker side of the Old West where factions differ and it is a new enemy they must face…

A tongue-in-cheek Western with all the blood and thrills of a regular rough ride, or as Coffin Jack might say, "Ya gotta own a pinch of salt for this one."

Coffin Jack: A Western Duo includes – Deathdealer and Gravedigger.

AVAILABLE NOW

ABOUT THE AUTHOR

Harlan Hague traveled a circuitous road to western literature. A native Texan, he earned business degrees at Baylor University and University of Texas and worked in management for four years before receiving his enlightenment and switching career and field to teaching history. He earned a further two degrees, the last a Ph.D. in history from University of Nevada, Reno. He taught United States history, American West and the environment at San Joaquin Delta College and summers at Cal State Stanislaus and University of Oregon.

While teaching, Hague wrote a few dozen history articles on the American West that published in scholarly journals. He turned to writing books and, in the process, received a number of academic and professional honors and grants, including National Endowment for the Humanities.

Since turning to books, Harlan Hague writes about people searching for redemption and fulfillment in the West, running from their demons, leaning on others. He likes endings that close with a sigh and a question. His books have won several awards in national competitions. His screenplays, mostly based on his books, have earned some notice and are making the rounds.

Made in the USA
Middletown, DE
04 March 2021

34817697R00274